THE GORILLAS
ARE COMING

The Golden Child Saga Book One

Mark Bermingham

Special thanks to Justin Haag for the valuable feedback, editorial advice, enthusiastic support, and friendship. Please check out Justin's own work at:

justindhaag.medium.com.

And my sincerest gratitude to all the storytellers who have inspired me regardless of the medium.

Dedicated to two most important ladies in my life:

To Shirley Bermingham, for easing my fears and nightmares when I was little.

And to Heather Bermingham, for helping me manage the adult terrors that can't be so easily wished away.

PROLOGUE

The gorillas are coming.
Because it is night.
Because it is dark.
Because he is alone.
Because he is scared.

S amuel Redden was alone in his room, under the covers, waiting for the inevitable arrival. He couldn't remember how long the gorillas had terrorized him, but it seemed like forever. Peeking above his comforter, Samuel could see his Han Solo action figure perched on the lowest level of his toy shelf above him on the wall. So much better to focus on the brave space pirate than to glance at the window a few feet away. *Where they would be coming from.* Han was never afraid, never turned away from danger, not even when Darth Vader was waiting in the Cloud City dining hall after Lando betrayed him. *Why can't I be brave?* Samuel felt a chill, his body getting queasy. He was shaking a bit too, and the more he tried to stop, the worse it became. His forehead held a cold sweat and his teeth began to chatter. *Why do they hate me? What did I ever do to them?*

The first several times, Samuel had thought it was just night-mares. *Mom and Dad still believe that.* But the fourth time, when the first temporary bite mark appeared, he knew it was real. If only the marks would stay so his parents could see. Or Patrick. Samuel couldn't lie still any longer. And there was no way he could sleep. His thoughts were out of control. Anger seized his heart when he thought about Lucy, the air-headed babysitter. His parents and Patrick were out tonight – Patrick with his friends, Mom bowling with hers, and Dad at his regular place, the bar. And the teenage girl refused to listen to Samuel's pleas. Why couldn't she put the night light back in like he asked? The rules were there for a reason.

Samuel swept his legs onto the floor, shrugged off his comforter and blankets, and glanced sheepishly around. He could hear the wind push against the old house, feel the scratchy rug under his feet, and smell the aroma of the cinnamon air freshener on his dresser to his right. All normal sensations. He tried to latch onto that as he thought about the rules. They were his rules, formulated by him, but since they kept the gorillas at bay, he also viewed them as the greatest universal truths. When something works, a young boy finds it hard to question.

Rule #1 – The light kept the monsters at bay. Any illumination rendered him safe. They didn't visit during the daytime. And as long as Samuel's night light was on, he was beyond their reach. Unfortunately, Samuel's bedroom had no overhead illumination with a master switch. All he had was the one outlet in the far corner of his room near the door. His dad was a stern man and didn't think his boy should have on the "baby" light. They used to have a bright lamp on top of a small table plugged in, but one night when his dad took away the night light, Samuel managed to escape the killers and switch on the lamp at 2:00 in the morning. This act put Dad into a fury when he saw the glare from under the door. He removed this alternative light as punishment and refused to put it back in, no matter how hard Samuel begged. His word was the law in this house. But Patrick understood the rules' importance and would sneak in the night light when Dad was out or already in bed. Speaking of Patrick:

Rule #2 – His older brother also prevented the horrors. Samuel wasn't sure if it was the aspect of not being alone, but the gorillas hadn't dared to strike when his roommate was present. Or maybe the attackers feared the pre-adult confident alpha male. All that mattered to the boy was that it worked. Regrettably, Patrick was a nineteen-year-old who had a social life, spending many late evenings out, leaving Samuel alone.

Rule #3 – The bedroom was the stalking ground. Even though Dad would accost him for it every time, once Samuel ran out of the room into the hallway, the gorillas could not follow. Once upon a time, Samuel's bedroom was a sanctuary, a place for play, for reading, for talking to Patrick. Not anymore. When night fell, it was a place of hopelessness. But luckily, he had that escape clause. He could always leave his room. But he was almost as afraid of Dad's temper as he was of the evil monsters. So he tried not to do that. He truly believed his sleeping area to be haunted now, but the last time he said that to Mom, she cried. So he didn't say that anymore. Sometimes a kid had to keep things to himself.

Samuel could see his dark reflection in the full-length mirror across the way on the closet door. If it were a clearer image, one would see a brown-haired, green-eyed, eight-year-old whose skin was white as a sheet, even paler than his pasty skin usually was. He wasn't a bad looking kid, although his curly messy hair on top never allowed him to look as smooth as some of his classmates, especially John Jordan, the coolest one in class. Unlike John, Samuel wasn't athletic, and due to a slight case of cerebral palsy, quite clumsy and awkward. He was picked on, called retard and nerd, and sometimes found it easier to be alone. Sure he had some friends, but if he was being honest with himself, his fellow geek/nerd buddy Peter was his only real one. Solitude was often his escape, his refuge. Not now, though. What he wouldn't have given at that moment for some company - even that Becky Tompkins who liked to pick on him mercilessly - so that he could have protection against the demons.

Samuel moved slowly to the middle of the room. *What should I do? Call for Lucy? She already called me an infant for wanting the light. She's too busy talking to her friends to care about my life-threatening situation. I could just run out. But then she would tell Dad.*

BOOM! Samuel's heart wrenched some more and his body suddenly felt hotter. Something was smashing the house outside his room. A rational person would have argued that it was the wind brushing branches against the siding or make the remark, "Old houses just make weird noises." But Samuel knew that sound. It was too loud to be a branch and certainly was not simple creaking. It was a thunderous sound effect, a course gorilla hand rattling the foundation, belonging to those seeking to frighten their favorite victim. This was part of their joy, part of what an adult would call foreplay. It wasn't enough to hurt him, to one day kill him, but the sadistic creatures needed to reduce him to a quivering fool, to humiliate him. Samuel had a theory about this. He viewed them as more than normal gorillas; they were creatures of fear. They were strengthened by his terror. But knowing something and fighting it were two different things. He knew if he could just be brave, he would take some of their power away. But when the gorillas came, they touched something primal inside him, reducing any strength he had into nothingness. **BOOM, BOOM, BOOM!** *Oh God, there's a bunch of them out there. I know it.*

Samuel fought his terror long enough to force his legs to run (more like stumble) across the room to the door that led to the hallway. He pounded his fists against it, crying out, "Lucy! They're here! The gorillas are here! Please help! Please help. Please help." His pleas got more pitiful with each word out of his mouth until it was no more than whispers that only he could hear as he crumpled against the door. *Why can't she hear them? Why can't anyone hear them but me?* Finally, Samuel made up his mind. Discipline from Papa or not, he was getting out of here. He jumped up and grasped at the metal door handle. His palms were so sweaty that he lost his grip. He tried again and again to no avail. He wiped his hands against his undershirt and figured he would, at last, be free. But once again, the handle would not give. *She locked the door. She locked it from the outside.* Samuel knew that was possible, but no one had ever done it before. "That bitch!" Samuel exclaimed. He wasn't one to swear, he was a good boy after all, but it was a desperate moment. He started to cry in a miserable fashion, heaving and moaning like a beaten puppy. Almost in answer, the noises came again. **BOOM! BOOM! BOOM! BOOM! BOOM!** And now the window at the foot of his bed started to rattle, sounding like it would give out at any moment. Samuel added screams to his sobs. *Surely, she would hear my screams at least.* But no one came. Patrick's bed was at this side of the room, and he looked over at it for comfort, but there was none to be had.

Several minutes of this agony continued to the point where Samuel could no longer hear the monsters' attempts through his screams and blubbering. Then the boy started to hyperventilate, gasping for some semblance of breath. He was recently diagnosed with asthma, and he honestly didn't understand what that meant beyond the fact that he had trouble breathing sometimes. But this was at another level. He found himself pushing his lungs desperately for any kind of breath, any sort of relief. At last, he lay down, collapsing his mouth against the rug, chewing on it, looking for a respite from the suffocating feeling he was having. It took several minutes, but he finally breathed and tasted the dirt on the carpet and curled himself in a ball. Another minute passed while he took several more deep breaths in, the weight on his lungs lessening. The shock of the respiratory ordeal passed, and he noticed all was quiet in the room. That included him; his crying had halted at some point. *Wait a minute. It's quiet.* The gorillas had stopped. *Is that possible? They never gave up without the light or Patrick before.* Samuel opened his eyes, and reluctantly looked over to his bed. It looked peaceful, serene, his bedroom as it should be.

I have to check. Despite his heart's warnings and all common sense, Samuel felt the pull to get to his feet and start moving towards the window. *If I can only see that it's clear outside, I will go to sleep and even welcome a regular nightmare.* Not noticing he was still shaking from the fright, Samuel dragged his feet to the window. *You can do this. Come on. Just pull the blinds up and be free from it. Han would do it.* Suddenly he put himself in the cantina facing off against Greedo, his trusty blaster near his leg. Confidence perked within him. *I will do it. But I have to do it fast. It's like when Pat pulled the band-aid off my leg that time after I skinned it playing ball against the steps. Okay.* He reached out quickly, grasping the cord that controlled the old mini blinds, having a much better grip than he did on the doorknob. Despite all he had been through, Samuel allowed himself to hope as he pulled down hard, and the outside was lain bare in the top half of the window above the air conditioner. His family lived in the little country hamlet of East Eden, New York, with not even a street light nearby, but what he saw was as clear as day to him. And that hope he held just a moment prior? Gone, gone in a flash.

Staring back at the child was a grotesque furry face bathed in a sick, green light that illuminated the side of his yard and the foreboding woods behind. The gorilla's head was huge, filling the whole window. Its fur was matted and spotted with dry blood all around the face, especially near the mouth. The mouth: that was the worst part. It was large and opened wide with razor-sharp teeth protruding like scissors, dripping drool and blood to the ground below. The beast stood upright on its legs, much straighter than a real gorilla should have, and he raised his right hand, an appendage that had claws on it, more cat than simian and ridiculously long. Samuel was frozen in place, shock having taken over his whole body. He couldn't feel a thing physically, only terror in his heart. Then a new image filled his view. Behind the gorilla, dark shapes oozed from the woods behind and entered the yard. *There has to be fifty of them! I'm dead.* Just when Samuel thought it couldn't get any worse, the alpha gorilla at the window, which resembled a large black-haired male only with the added elements from hell, let out a howl. This scream was one part primal animal and another part ghostly shriek, and its power threw Samuel back through the air until his body slammed into the far wall.

The pain shooting down Samuel's head and back was rough, but what it did was awaken him from his stupor-like state and allowed him to move. He placed his hand on the back of his cranium and felt blood seeping down his hands. He whimpered as he could hear the house shake again. *What do I do? I can't run. I absolutely can't fight them. Pat, where the hell are you?* Given no options, Samuel regressed. He turned back the clock a few years and became a toddler in his mind. And using the best logic of a toddler, Samuel found his body jumping up and running to his bed. He dove under his comforter and hid. There was no logic in this move, but the covers made him feel safe even with the horrific sound effects beating around him on the wall. *If I can only wait them out until big brother gets here. Yes, I can make it.* Hope again. And as before, hope was quickly dashed as a new noise reached the child's ears. The glass of the window shattered, sending the air conditioner flying, and it crashed in the middle of the floor. It sounded like an explosion in a movie. Samuel could feel the shards of glass crumble on top of the blankets. The gorillas had broken things before, but just like with his injuries, the window would be magically fixed when he was no longer alone. This fact would not help him if he didn't survive. Having these thoughts and reflections was something that comforted him on some level. *At least I'm not a total baby.* Then he smelled them.

The pungent smell of what could only be described as bloody manure entered his nostrils. *They're in the room!* Not only was their unholy stink evident, but he could hear them sniffing with their otherworldly noses, pinpointing his location. There were also growls and rumblings as the creatures fought among themselves, not in anger or excitement but in asserting their dominance. The group leader, who Samuel called Alpha in his head, came to the forefront again. He huffed louder and even hissed at the others so all knew who would feast first. The thought of being eaten alive was obviously Samuel's greatest fear, and its resurgence this October night brought a new effect to his body. His pants felt wet and began to smell. *Oh, man. I am a baby.*

But even his heroic characters from the comics and movies would have a tough time maintaining their composure as the gorillas now approached, led by Alpha. He could tell they were close with how the temperature around him seemed to increase, just like when he and Mom entered that sauna room at the hotel in Toronto. And of course, the beasts' animalistic growls of anticipation grew clearer and clearer until he knew they were standing over his bed. Then all was still again. This was the worst part, the tension of anticipation. He could feel their presence, knew they were raising the claws to strike, opening their mouths to feed. Alpha let out another howl, and Samuel answered this with a scream of his own. His bedsheet was then wrenched from his puddle of a body...

"Sammy, what the fuck! Are you okay?"

I'm not dead. What was that voice? Reluctantly opening his eyes, Samuel was taken aback by the dull illumination coming from the hallway light. He blinked and observed a shape. But it was not furry, bloody, or full of sharp appendages. It was an older teenager with black hair and a worried face, wearing a yellow t-shirt with a pizza stain. *Pat!* Samuel jumped up from his bed and gripped hard onto his savior. He didn't think he'd ever hugged anyone so hard. He didn't want to let go. Tears once again flowed from his eyes, but this time they were tears of joy and relief. After a couple more seconds, Samuel finally felt good enough to speak to his brother. "You said fuck."

Patrick let out a hardy laugh. "Are you going to tell Mom?"

"No."

"Well, good." Patrick gently pulled away from Samuel and looked him up and down in a concerned state. "Are you okay, little chief?"

Samuel smiled back at his worried sibling. "I am now."

Patrick guided his little brother to sit on the edge of the bed with him. "It was the gorillas, wasn't it?"

Samuel nodded his head and said with a timid voice, "I peed myself."

"I know," Patrick said in a voice that was reassuring, much different than he sounded with his friends or girls at college when he tried not to let his guard down. "Don't worry about that. They can't hurt you now that I'm here and the light's on, right? The rules?" There was no sarcasm or meanness to Patrick's approach, just trust.

"Yep. Hey, Pat? Why do you believe me? You've never seen any proof like they say on Mom's law shows. They broke the window tonight and look at it. Nothing! The air conditioner is back in place too. And my scars are always gone. Am I even bleeding? From my head?"

Patrick touched his brother's skull and came away with a dry hand. "No," he said in a dead-serious tone.

"So why do you believe me?"

Patrick sighed and was silent for what seemed like an eternity for Samuel. "Dad's a dick about this kind of thing. And Mom...well, Mom is just a frightful person when it comes to you. You need someone who understands. That's me. I'm intrigued by the supernatural, but it goes beyond that. I take this protector thing seriously. Belief gives these creatures power, and your faith in me fights them. That's what I think." Samuel's eight-year-old brain was not developed enough to understand what Patrick was really saying here. The teen was concerned, though not about the threat of otherworldly gorillas, but of his "little chief's" sanity.

"Thanks!" Samuel exclaimed. "We sure showed them tonight."

Patrick looked away with a sad look on his face. "You got that right, Sammy. Now let's say we go to the bathroom, clean you up, and tell off that stupid-ass babysitter. I can't even go out after the game without worrying about you being left with these terrible sitters."

Feeling vigor returning to his bones, his mind, even his soul, Samuel smiled broadly, adorably, dimples showing in his cheeks. It would have melted the hardest of hearts. "Awesome! Can I call her bitch?"

Patrick laughed again. "Sure, bud." With that cleared up, the older brother put his arm around Samuel's shoulder, led him out the door and down the hall to the bathroom.

Outside the window near Samuel's bed, tall pine trees bent in the slight breeze. And just beyond them, a six-foot dark shape sped off into the woods.

PART ONE – CHILDHOOD TERRORS (1985)

CHAPTER 1

T he next morning dawned. At the kitchen table, Patrick Redden was eating Frankenberry doused in milk and fiddling with his 1927 Yankees APBA cards. But he was doing this absentminded. Any other day, he would be intent on looking closely at either the Babe Ruth retrospective baseball card he'd glued on the back or considering the actual play card and how awe-inspiring the home run possibilities were. Or he'd at least be savoring the sugar rush from his favorite cereal. But he now pushed away the bowl and put the cards aside. Thinking about sports strategy games or even eating took a backseat today. Patrick was too concerned about his baby brother.

Patrick kept trying to still his racing thoughts, but his mind wasn't allowing it. *Sammy is not a normal kid. There's something wrong. If these are nightmares, they're not like any nightmare I've ever had. He sure thinks they're real. And while I humor him, clearly that can't be the case. But they are certainly more than run-of-the-mill night terrors. I just don't get it.*

At that point, Shelley Redden, the matriarch of the family, entered the room. She was forty-eight. Her brown hair was starting to gray, but beyond that, she didn't fit the older mother image that Samuel was sometimes embarrassed about; the kids at school all had younger parents, and it made him feel weird, though he would never tell his mom. Samuel was the surprise, youngest of seven, though the others besides Patrick were gone from the home on their own adventures now. Years had taken the regular wear and tear on Shelley, but she was still attractive, not skinny but not overweight, with sympathetic brown eyes to match her chestnut hair with its streaks of silver. She was a stay-at-home mom and her commitment to her children was of paramount importance to her life. Mrs. Redden was also a most sensitive person, so as soon as she entered the room, she knew her college-attending second youngest was in a reflective, concerned place. She turned left after coming into the kitchen, her destination the sink and counter area that overlooked their front driveway. The coffee maker was on the counter, and she began to empty the old grounds before saying without turning, "Patty? What's wrong?"

Patrick sighed. There was never any hope of hiding things from his mom. He sometimes wondered if she overcompensated in this area since Dad was so closed off emotionally. Possibly. "It's Sammy." Pouring the water into the coffee maker, Shelley's shoulders slumped. When you have your last child ten years after you thought you were done childbearing, a special kind of attachment comes about. He or she becomes the family's focal point, and a level of connection and protection that wasn't hereto experienced before is also born. So when Patrick mentioned Samuel's name, Shelley's heart sank down hard, making her feel a little queasy. She knew what this was about, and it always upset her.

"I don't want to talk about it," she said.

A look of mixed disappointment and slight anger creased Patrick's brow and worked its way down his facial features. "Mom, sit." She finally turned and then made her way to the table, taking the seat across from Patrick. To the left were the windows to the back yard. She glanced for a second, not really looking at anything specific, before focusing on Patrick. The two of them were in opposite states in being ready for the day: Shelley already dressed in her white and blue housedress with Patrick decked out in the same thing he wore to bed the last night, his holey Cincinnati Reds t-shirt and cut off sweats. Shelley made a note of this mentally, as she always had to push Pat to get moving in the morning. "We can't keep ignoring this, Mom," he said. "It happened again."

"Keep your voice down," Shelley said in a correcting whisper. "I don't want Sammy overhearing us talk about him like this."

"Don't worry about that. He's fast asleep now. After the restless night he had, he'd sleep to noon if you let him. Now, please listen. You know Dad's going to keep pushing our worries away." Patrick cast a look behind him before continuing, looking at the clock above the stove and making sure the man he was talking about was already at work. He now put on a lower timbre of voice, imitating Claude Redden, his father. "You need to toughen up, boy. You're weak. That's all this is. Too sensitive." Patrick shook his head while rolling his eyes. "Dad's solution to everything."

Shelley placed her hands on her lap to hide her lightly shaking hands. "Why are you bringing this up, especially first thing in the morning?"

"He had another bad night, and every time it seems worse, and it scares me more," Patrick said. Before he said this next thing, he stared into his mother's face intently for a moment; he figured she would see the frustration in his features, but he hoped the compassion showed through too. "You know Sammy feels like he can't come to you and Dad about this, right? Dad's obvious, no one can talk to him, but with you, the poor kid knows how emotional you get, so he avoids confiding in you. So I'm left to handle it. I love the kid, but it's too much."

These remarks cut Shelley to the core. It wasn't just the idea that her baby felt like he couldn't come to her with his problems because of her emotional weakness. But also how her second youngest was looking at her; no one wants to disappoint their children. She sighed and put her right hand over her face. "I just don't know what to do."

Patrick got up, changed seats to the chair closest to Shelley, reached out, and touched his mother's other hand. "Well, we have to act. Without Dad."

Shelley removed the fingers from her face and gazed long and hard at Patrick. The idea of going around her husband, the short-tempered, unmoving Claude, put fear into her that wasn't easily shaken. He was a big guy, an intimidating man in both stature and the mental power he held over the household. He'd never lain a finger on his wife and indeed loved her in his own way. But he was often cold, standoffish in general, and a bit rough with the children. "Spare the rod..." was his favorite bible verse. It never crossed into the level of child abuse, but he skirted that line. And his temper with his wife was short if even the littlest thing was off in the house or his routine. In short, he was a scary man. *But this is Sammy we're talking about. He needs me. I have to be stronger than this.* She nodded her head, "Okay. What do you think?"

Patrick was a little surprised that 1) she had agreed to do anything and 2) that she was deferring to him. He was now in college but still had his immature side that didn't leave most young men until their mid-twenties. He liked to party and still needed some encouragement to clean his room (attending the nearby community college, he continued to live at home). So being asked by his mom to come up with ideas here not only flattered him but brought a bit of pressure that he wasn't sure he wanted. But like Shelley, he felt he needed to rise to the occasion for his little brother. He didn't want to hesitate too long and make her question the faith she had in him, so he blurted out the first thing he could think. "A psychiatrist?"

"That makes sense," Shelley replied, "but how do we keep that from your father? You know how he controls the money." Claude was certainly a traditionalist; he'd often said he'd be so happy to still live in the days pre women's lib. He actually gave his wife an allowance and never allowed her to even peek at their joint checking and savings accounts.

"I can pay for the first sessions with the savings from my job." Patrick had a work-study job at the school book store. *I really want to keep saving for the car, but this is more important. Sharing a car with mom is a pain, but that's life.* It was as if Shelley had read his mind as she started to shake her head in the negative. But he cut her off. "No, Mom, buying myself a car can wait. This is a family emergency."

Shelley smiled, but it was a sad one, a mix of pride in her son but discouragement in the reality of being a lower-middle-class family. *I wish we could give the kids more.* "Okay, I guess we should start researching shrinks," she said.

"Great. I'll start looking in the phonebook right away. I'll let you know. And for God's sakes, Mom, let's get a lamp in there. If Dad is going to be such an ass about it, I'll move it into the closet when I leave for the day."

Shelley just nodded, agreeing to this too and feeling more wretched by the moment.

Patrick stepped away from the table, dumped his uneaten cereal in the garbage, and rinsed out the bowl. He smiled at his mother before heading out the kitchen, crossing through the spacious dining room and down the hallway to the bedroom he shared with Samuel. Shelley got up slowly from the table, smelling the freshly brewed coffee but not feeling like drinking anything now. Instead, she went to the sink and started the process of washing some dishes while looking out the kitchen window, her eyes staring at the area of the road and the "Dead End" sign. Before long, she dropped the plate she was working on, letting it submerge itself in the sudsy water. Then she started to cry, her head bowed, her body shaking.

CHAPTER 2

A few days later, it was a Thursday morning. Samuel was busy being bored at his school in Eden town proper. His class was fifteen minutes into Ms. Jeffer's third-grade math instruction. He hated math. They were working through the multiplication and division routines, the dreaded times table. It wasn't that Samuel was a stupid child; he was just disinterested. If his teachers and the school administrators had taken a closer look at him, they might have diagnosed him as having ADD. But this was a different era. And to her credit, Ms. Jeffers had broached the subject with Shelley Redden during the first parent-teacher conference this year. Samuel's father did not attend, having no time for those "overpaid sweet talkers from the school." And while Shelley took the words from Samuel's teacher to heart, she knew that exploring this issue would inevitably lead to further discussions about his mental state, and the nightmare situation would suddenly come out in the open. At that point back then, she certainly wouldn't have that. It had been a process over several months to get her to the last few days where she would consider outside help.

So as it often happened in school, Samuel's mind wandered. It went to the inevitable place, the gorillas. While they couldn't attack him in the daytime like this with the rules in place, that didn't mean he was free of their power. The mind is a fragile thing, and young Samuel's had been irrevocably altered. Even a psychologist wouldn't consider it shattered, but it had been broken to an extent. Children are often hardier than the world gives them credit for, but there are strains that most obviously take a toll. It's quite evident in abused kids or those who face an early tragedy, like losing a parent or sibling. And it was most clearly present here, with the mental assault Samuel underwent each and every evening with the gorilla incursions. So the creatures had a hold of his mind. There was no escape from that part.

As Ms. Jeffers droned on, her fingers tracing the number eight columns on the overhead display, Samuel tried to keep his focus. But slowly, he found the teacher and the numbers blurring away. He rubbed his eyeballs, and when he looked again, he saw something completely different. Something impossible. A gorilla manifested itself in his kindly teacher's place, still jabbing at the glowing numerals, but now with a pointy talon. Samuel gasped and glanced around at his classmates, but there was no reaction from them. The enormous, monstrous simian turned away from mathematics and zeroed its attention on the boy. It inched forward, and Samuel could see the other trademark elements of his tormentors: the blood dripping from the mouth, the matted fur, the odd, upright stance. The creature advanced, the porcelain floor creaking under its weight, and the rest of the kids surrounding Samuel disappeared.

The gorilla kicked out, sweeping away the first row of desks, shattering them against the wall to Samuel's left, the window side. This left Samuel open to him, a few feet away. The terrified child started to push back in his seat but found he could not get up. *I'm paralyzed. But this isn't real this time, right? It's daytime. Does it matter, though?* As the gorilla started to huff and growl, almost like a dog, cold sweat developed on Samuel's brow. His eyes darted all around the room, first fixating on the door, but instantly knew that wouldn't work, with it being at the front of the classroom. Running in that direction meant trying to dodge the two columns of desks to the side of him, which wasn't ideal for a clumsy kid. He then glanced towards the just disposed desks, moving his eyeline up to the row of windows. But unlucky for him, it was a slightly chilly fall day, and Ms. Jeffers was always cold, so she had closed and locked them. Even if he climbed over the toppled furniture, there was no way he could get one of the windows opened and climb out before the monster destroyed him. Samuel felt trapped with indecision and began to shudder. But then something took over the boy, an emotion he rarely demonstrated. Anger. He screamed, "Get out of here! I hate you! You smelly bastard!"

Finally, Samuel was able to make the only physical move he could find in his power, and that was to push off with his feet, launching his desk backward. He landed on the floor with a thud, hitting his head painfully. The chair was one of those desk/seat combos and he was pinned underneath, the claustrophobia overwhelming him as he stared at the desk part near his face. Normally, he could have squirmed away but he was in no state now to react quickly. This sent a new jolt of horror inside him, knowing that he was now easy prey for the gorilla. The monster stood over Samuel, its mouth arching in a sinister fang-filled grimace. It leaned towards him. Samuel knew his luck had run out, and he simply stared at his attacker in a stupor, like a deer in the headlights. *Why did the rules fail me?* For a second, his sight got fuzzy again. Then it quickly cleared. And there was no gorilla. What was left was almost worse. A classroom of his peers either staring in disbelief, pointing, or laughing at him. He wished Pete was there to stick up for him, but he was out sick this day. Ms. Jeffers was standing in front of his toppled desk, with a scowling expression that was somehow also caring. "Samuel Redden. What in the world?" she asked.

To his left, Samuel could hear Joey Jones, the class clown and smart-mouth, say, "What smelly bastards? You, Redden?"

Ms. Jeffers shot an angry look at Jones, which quieted him immediately. The teacher ran a tight ship. She was prematurely gray-haired in her mid-fifties, wore wire-rim glasses, and was a little portly. But she had the energy and passion of a twenty-year-old. She didn't spend any more time investigating the situation but let her helper character traits take over as she lifted one side of the desk and asked Samuel to push up. Simultaneously, Sally Nolan, a kind-hearted classmate, grabbed the other side without even needing prompting. Samuel was then sitting upright again, his face red as a beet. Ms. Jeffers now had her sympathetic face on, and that should have been comforting, but Samuel just felt like her earthy-brown eyes were boring into his soul. He looked away. "Don't worry, Samuel, I won't yell," she said, "but what happened there? Are you okay?"

Samuel still wouldn't face her, lowering his head to look down at the dirty old tiles on the floor. He could still hear mild snickering and the other kids shifting in their chairs. "I'm fine. It's nothing, Ms. Jeffers," he finally replied.

"Nothing? Not good enough. What's going on?" Ms. Jeffers looked more intently at Samuel and then said, "Follow me." She turned and started walking to the door leading to the hallway. "And if I hear much more than quiet conversation, expect extra math drills tomorrow, dear ones." She turned back and smiled when she said this, which gave the warning some kindness while still not minimizing the weight behind it. Ms. Jeffers did not make empty threats.

Samuel pulled himself up and trudged behind Ms. Jeffers into the hallway, and she closed the door. The passageway was empty since classes were in session, except for Mr. Trudeau, the janitor, who was mopping up the floor at the other end. Samuel glanced around, still trying to acclimate himself back to reality. There weren't lockers on each side of him like at the junior/senior high since these kids hung their coats in the cubbies inside the rooms, and instead the walls were decorated with colorful student art contributions. There was a glass display case outside the school office halfway down the hall with various plaques of school achievement awards and engraved "Reach High" type inspirational sayings. Ms. Jeffers kneeled down in front of him, touching his arm gently. "Did you have a nightmare?" She knew his background. While it wasn't brought up at the parent-teacher conference, Samuel's mother had called to chat with her about the psychiatrist option two days ago.

Please don't make me talk about this; it hurts to remember them. But Samuel knew he couldn't lie about it to her. He liked his teacher, and now that he was away from the other kids, he felt a little bolder. "Not a dream. More like watching a TV show. It's hard to explain. What was that word you taught us? An allusion?"

Ms. Jeffers grinned. "An illusion. "I-L-L. With an I. What was it? Those gorillas your mom told me about?"

"One of them, yes. Must have been my imagination."

Ms. Jeffers appeared sad, not just in her facial expression but in the way her body lurched a bit, clearly showing the internal reaction she felt about her charge's pain. "That's understandable. You're going to see the psychiatrist at Gates soon?" When Shelley called her, Ms. Jeffers told her it was indeed a good thing to try. They had a school psychiatrist at Eden's Grover L. Preiss Primary School, and this man, Mr. Dolgon, had talked to Samuel that day, but it was somewhat beyond him, or at least in need of more intensive work.

"Tomorrow after school. I'm scared." Samuel was never one to share his emotions with his elders, but he couldn't hold this in now.

Ms. Jeffers' heart wanted to break. She wondered why she couldn't help them all, the unfairness of the world plaguing her. She once again put her hand softly on his arm, something she couldn't get away with the "tougher" kids, and if she were a high school teacher, this approach certainly wouldn't have worked. But she had a good feel for kids like Samuel. "Your therapist is going to be very nice. I know it's hard to talk about things that frighten you, Samuel, but you'll be brave. And then one day, there will be no more gorillas."

"Not even at the zoo?" Samuel asked.

Ms. Jeffers couldn't prevent the laughter from escaping. She loved the innocent ones. "No, those are real gorillas. We just want to get rid of these nightmares, the bad ones. Gorillas are actually very loving, family-oriented animals."

"That would be better than what mine want to do," Samuel said. "Thanks, Ms. Jeffers. I'm sure you're right about the doctor. My mom said she and Patrick are going in with me, so I won't be alone at least." *Like at night. Hopefully, this guy will find a new rule.*

The next day came and went. Samuel was returning home from school, still nervous about meeting the doctor. The bus never dropped him off at his house. He lived at the end of a dead-end road/turnaround, and there weren't any other kids on the primary bus for his street, Siegel, so it just stopped at the corner, and he had to do the half-mile trudge home. Often his mom would pick him up after he was dropped off, but she had a doctor's appointment of her own this day. He made it about halfway down his street when he started to pass Jake Steiner's house. This kid was one of the worst bullies in the middle school. He was three years older than Samuel, but in 5th grade, not 6th, held back a year. He was of the classic "steal your lunch money" mold, except he never made any demands, just knocked people over and kicked them usually. The coast was clear as far as Samuel could tell, and he decided to pick up his pace. But before he could get ten feet, he heard a squeaky yet intimidating voice bellow, "If it isn't little Sammy Redden!" Samuel's heart just about stopped in his chest. His legs became weak, feeling rubbery and useless. Gorillas may have been the most significant threat in his life, but the day-to-day trials of being a kid was nothing to sneeze at. He felt nakedly out in the open and utterly helpless as he turned towards Steiner's house. Lo and behold, there was the brute stomping towards him, coming from behind the building. Jake was a big boy for a fifth-grader but seemed even larger to Samuel's eyes. He had a red crew cut, a square Neanderthal face, and was always sneering.

"I heard from my cousin what you did yesterday in class, punk. What the hell was that? Some kind of seizure. You really are a freak." He reached out and pushed Samuel back a pace with his right arm.

"Can you just leave me alone and let me go home? It's been a tough week, and I have an appointment. My mom is waiting for me." Samuel's voice was quiet and shaky. He knew Mom was probably not back from her haircut, but that's what came out.

"Aww, momma is waiting for her little cub. What appointment, freak? A geek meeting?"

Every time Steiner said the word "freak," Samuel's soul took a little beating. He didn't want to be like this, he didn't want to be different, he wanted to be like the other kids. But he knew he wasn't. None of this was normal. He felt like crying, but he couldn't let this bully see him like that. It would only make matters worse. And he knew he couldn't tell him about the session with the shrink as that would get out at the school, and then he'd be a focus of attention, not just to the taunts of bullies but also to everyday funny looks from most of the kids. He wouldn't have that. He hated school, but the one thing he had going for himself was anonymity. "I can't tell you," he just about whispered.

Jake Steiner was not used to rejection. Usually, he got what he wanted through force and sometimes through the sheer mystique of his reputation. His caveman countenance turned a little rosy, and his unusually large hands for an eleven-year-old squeezed into fists. "What did you say to me, freak?"

"Please stop calling me that, Jake."

This enraged Steiner even further. "Don't talk to me like we're friends, you stupid spazz!" He reached out with his oversized hands and grabbed hard onto each side of the light jacket Samuel's mom made him take this morning, bringing him closer. Samuel could smell peanut butter and jelly on his oppressor's breath. It made him want to cough, but he held that need in check; that certainly wouldn't have helped things. "Now, you tell me where you're going, or you'll get a true beating. None of that pushing around and arm pulls like usual." He began to shake Samuel back and forth. "Tell me!"

"No." Samuel was shocked at his reticence. He understood a big beating was coming up, something he'd never experienced before. He was afraid of the pain, of the blood, of the embarrassment. But the gorillas and anything related to them was not information that other kids at the school could have. And if it started to go around the place that he was seeing a psychiatrist, how long before his nightmares became public knowledge? That would be a nightmare of a whole other sort. So no. The bully would not get this information.

"WHAT DID YOU SAY?" Steiner was beside himself. Not once

in his career as a bully had someone stood up to him like this, rejected his demands. It didn't make any sense to him. The little freakazoid was going to get the thrashing of his life and didn't care. Originally all Jake was going to do for a few minutes was mock the baby mentally and maybe knock him on the ground and empty his book bag. Now he was going to destroy him. It wasn't often that Steiner had actually used his fists on his charges; he even found it less satisfying. But when necessary, he would do it. It was also rare for him to lose his temper when doing his thing. That was happening now. And while his household was consistently an angry place, his life outside of the house was joyful in its cruelty to others. This wasn't fun for him. "YOU'LL TELL ME!" he screamed. He took his right hand and slapped Samuel's left cheek. Hard. An immediate red mark appeared there. Now that made Jake a little happier.

Samuel had never quite felt such a sting. Not even when he stepped on that bumblebee last summer. He whimpered slightly and felt his instincts kick in. He pulled backward and managed to fall on his butt, his shirt ripping. This only enraged his tormentor more. "GET OVER HERE! I'LL KILL YOU!" Samuel now felt a new fear. *Maybe Steiner **will** kill me.* The little monster threatening him was reaching levels of human rage that Samuel had never seen, short of TV shows. *How can I escape this? My house is still a ways away. I'm stuck. Why do I always get stuck? Why can't I just be left alone?* He started to crawl in reverse, pushing on his legs like a crab. His bookbag was lying in front of him, forgotten. His only consideration was survival, and despite his emotional damage and issues, survival was one thing Samuel Redden knew; he did it every night when the rules were broken. Steiner wasn't the fastest kid; he was bulky and strong but not lithe. But even so, Samuel had his asthma and wasn't sure he could outrun Jake; he could already feel a little hitch in his breathing. So he kept backing up, but after several feet, he was stopped by Mr. Bosworth's finely cultivated shrubs bristling into his lower body. He could go no further.

Steiner lumbered forward and towered over him. He smiled cruelly. "I warned you, loser. Now you pay." The pre-pubescent attacker stomped on Samuel's abdomen with his muddy boot, causing a clawing agony and, worse, loss of breath. This happened so fast and was such a surprise that Samuel had no time to even consider moving out of the way. For a moment, he felt panic hit him along with the pain as he struggled to find air from his lungs. It was a good five seconds before he was able to let out a wheezy exhalation. His immediate instinct was to reach for his inhaler, but the bag was too far away now. Tears started to form in his eyelids despite all his best intentions of not showing weakness. He looked up into Jake's eyes, begging for mercy without words, but he was like a gazelle gazing up to a lion. There was no leniency to come.

Steiner kneeled beside Samuel, grabbed him by the t-shirt again, and smashed his face with a hard fist strike. Samuel could feel his lip split and tasted the coppery blood that soaked his tongue. Physical pain and fearfulness mixed together fully now. His body hurt more than it ever had in his life, but there was also the fright at how much more he could take, whether he would have to go to the hospital and most of all, that the agonizing torture would keep going. "Please stop," he managed to say to Steiner, although it was more of a lisp with how his mouth was. "I'll tell you. I'll tell you!"

Steiner let out a boisterous guffaw. And then, as if he had heard Samuel's earlier thought, he said, "Too late, shit stain. You're going to miss that appointment and make a trip to the hospital instead." If Samuel wasn't in such a state of panic, he would have noticed how much his tormentor sounded like a bad pulp novel or crime show. Steiner was making efforts to exude coolness like he was playing to an audience while at the same time inflicting this horrible beatdown. But there were no more words after that last one. Only action. Steiner punched him three more times. Two more in the mouth and once in the eye. Samuel's vision became foggy on that left side, and he knew his eye was probably swelling. And he realized that Steiner was probably right: he would miss meeting the psychiatrist. And that made something click inside the young victim. Something he didn't know to any great extent to that point.

It was anger. Previously, when attacked by the gorillas, anger had not been at the forefront. It was always fear that ruled. Yes, Samuel often asked God why he was targeted, and he definitely experienced indignation at people that didn't believe him, like Dad and the babysitters. But those feelings were always at the background of his emotional spectrum, like images in a car's rearview mirror. Not now. He discovered that he'd never really known a red-hot sensation like this before, and it wasn't simple anger like in the classroom the day before. It was quickly progressing to fury, to hatred. He *needed* to see this brain doctor; he had to get rid of the gorillas. He'd waited a long time for his mother to get involved and for himself to feel any kind of hope. And this thick-headed piece of shit was trying to take that away from him. Samuel wanted to kill him. His asthma had disappeared, along with all pain, lost in this new state of his. Samuel knew his face was probably starting to look puffy and swollen and that normally Steiner would be reveling in these effects of the beating. But when he took a good look at Jake, Samuel noted that the thug clearly wasn't seeing the wounds he inflicted but was transfixed by something in his victim's expression. Jake's father had beaten him since he was five, and he always had that same look, that mask of rage. And Samuel, too, was observing a familiar reaction above him. It was the face of fear. Steiner was scared.

"What the fuck?" Steiner said as he took a step back. It wasn't just the younger kid's newfound inner strength that had riveted the most feared boy in Eden Middle School's 5th grade.

He was staring with comedically bugged out eyes at Samuel's hand, his right hand. It was glowing. The limb was bathed in the color and power of the sun. The aura wrapped around it like a transparent glove. And the rays were starting to bend outwards towards Steiner. "What are you doing, freak?" Jake muttered, all his bravado gone. The air around them was suddenly several degrees warmer, and to Samuel, his insides felt so blissful as if someone had thrown a blanket around his soul.

"Hey, Steiner, get away from him!" a voice shouted from behind the bushes. It was Mr. Bosworth running out from his house, just now noticing Samuel laying in the road with the known hellraiser Steiner standing near him. "Get back to your house, you little ass!" Steiner, still dismayed by the bright glare and suffocating heat that was no doubt going to attack him, and knowing he didn't mess with adults, turned around and ran in his lumbering gait back to his house.

Samuel felt like he was coming out of a dream. He glanced down briefly to the right side of his body and finally saw the glow, but it was now dissipating to dim light. A few seconds passed, and the phenomenon phased out entirely. He blinked a few times, wondering what had just happened. His hand was curled tightly in a fist, and he certainly didn't remember doing that. But all of the moments after the anger came were hazy to him. By the time the illumination was utterly gone, its after-effects like golden waves wafting into the breeze, Mr. Bosworth arrived. That comforting, fuzzy warmth was also gone and replaced by the return of his body's pain. Samuel felt like every part of him was bathed in coals. He groaned.

"Are you all right, son? Should I call the police? Your mom?" George Bosworth looked down at Samuel with a downcast and alarmed face. Samuel's neighbor was around his mother's age. He was a small man, thin, with balding black hair. He always dressed preppily, currently wearing a button-down white shirt and dressy tan pleated pants, befitting his career role as an accountant. He was always so kind to Samuel. George was single, and rumors were that he was gay. But Samuel never cared about that; he just knew that he was such a nice man. Sometimes he wished he was his father. "Samuel? Do you hear me?" Bosworth asked, pressing now.

Samuel began to stand, was a little unsteady on his feet, and George lent an arm. With his muffled speech, Samuel said, "I'm okay, Mr. Bosworth. Can you just give me a ride home? I have an appointment."

George nodded, smiling, hoping to make Samuel feel better, but it came across with its underlying upset. "Of course. But that Steiner punk needs to be put in his place. You shouldn't let this slide."

Samuel felt a return of that spite he had experienced earlier against Jake and also something else he didn't quite recognize. It was alien to him. He thought for a moment. *Is it power? Strength?* "I don't think he'll bother me again," he said.

"Why?" his neighbor asked.

"Why what?" The feeling had passed, and Samuel Redden was again the scared, damaged kid that just wanted to get home, feeling completely out of sorts. "Oh, I don't know. I'm tired. Can we just go?"

CHAPTER 3

Shelley Redden tried her best to hide her distress and upset at her son's condition. George Bosworth was good enough to walk Samuel to the door and explain as much as he could about what happened. She was a wreck but did her best to maintain her propriety while he was in the house. She'd just returned from her hairstyling and had been rushing around, getting ready for Samuel's necessary psychiatric visit. Then this was dropped on her. But while Shelley was generally a nervous person, she also had that motherly instinct that taught her to put her feelings aside as much as she could. So after George left, she quickly got Samuel into the bathroom to check him out. His eye was black and swollen, and there was a split lip to go along with it. Luckily his teeth were intact, and he could still see out of his eye. He had a big ugly bruise on his stomach that frightened her as much as the eye. She cleaned him up with a bath cloth, treated his injuries (with Neosporin, Ben-Gay, and bandages), and was quite ready to take him to the doctor, if not the ER, to get him looked at. But Samuel was fighting her.

"Mom, I have to see that head fixer." If you had asked Samuel why this was so important to him, he couldn't have given a decent answer. He just felt an urgency that wasn't there even a few days ago. He needed to get help now. And a more selfish reason came up too; if he missed it, Steiner got what he wanted. Samuel felt a prideful need to have that win, at least.

"That can wait, kiddo. What if your eye closes up, or you lose your vision?"

"I can see fine. If it closes up, you can bring me in the morning. Plus, this guy is a type of doctor, right? He can tell you if we should go into the hospital right away. It's important to get rid of the gorillas. I can't do this anymore."

Shelley looked at her son with patience and understanding. "I know. And I'm so sorry it took this long for me to do something." That was hard for her to say, and it made her heart ache, but she was glad she finally told him. "But I don't like the way you look."

"I look like a warrior, right?" Samuel flashed a smile, giving her a look that would have made you thought he had no problems more immense than doing his math homework or eating his vegetables.

This caused Shelley to fight back the tears. But it also made her think about how much she loved her amazing boy. "Yeah, I'm scared, tough guy." Samuel giggled, but the action caused his mouth to hurt, and he winced. Shelley shook her head and said, "I'm probably a bad mother for agreeing to this, but we won't cancel. But if Dr. Santiago even hints that you need to go to the ER, we're going. I don't think you need stitches, but I'm no doctor."

"Thanks, Mom." Samuel reached out and put his arm around her from where he was sitting on the closed toilet seat. She kneeled in closer and squeezed him tightly. He wanted to recoil, as his injured stomach hurt despite the wrap his mother had put around it, but this was so nice. He was not yet at that age where he ran from his mother's embrace and attention. And he indeed was a momma's boy. This made him think about his dad. "Mom, who's coming with us to the appointment?"

She slowly pulled away from him and said, "Patrick still plans to be there. He better since it was his idea. He's coming right from his last class." She paused and then grinned, "That will be nice, right? No pressure on you. It will be like our whole family is getting counseling!"

Not our whole family. "I knew about Patrick. But what about Dad?"

Shelley tried to hide a look of disappointment but was sure she failed at it. "I think Dad is working late at the plant tonight." Claude Redden worked at the local GM plant assembling engines, but Shelley was lying. He was going out bowling with his buddies and then to Mcghee's for many beers. And as planned, he was not told about this mental health visit. But she couldn't tell Samuel that; he so wanted his dad's approval and help. A little white lie here to prevent further heartache.

Samuel looked down. "He doesn't know, does he?"

Damn, Shelley thought, no fooling this kid. "No, Sammy, I didn't tell him."

"Why can't he help me, Momma?"

Sadness seemed like the order of the day for Shelley, as this made her so miserable. She wished she knew the answer to this question and realized it went to Claude's core, his upbringing, his character. More comfortable for him to ignore the root of an issue and be hardened than to deal with emotional problems. Samuel wasn't the only one who felt this coldness, and it was often on lonely nights lying beside this man that she wondered how they ever ended up married. But that was *her* problem. She tried to come up with the best way of answering this question without betraying her bitterness. She came up with something, a response that she could present as a truism, without portraying the whole story. "Your dad's job is to stay strong for us. He does that by going to work, putting food on our table, and fixing things around the house." But he can't fix *us*, can he? she thought. "Sometimes that makes him hard to talk to, I know, to make him understand your problems, but he is not heartless. He loves you." That was the best she could do until Samuel was older and maybe understood these things better. She hoped it would be enough.

"He never says he loves me."

"That's what I'm saying. Your dad just doesn't know how to show emotion. But it's important to him to put this roof over our head and take care of us, and that shows love." Shelley didn't want to delve too far into her own emotions, but she realized she was maybe rationalizing things for herself here also, trying to find the good in a cold marriage.

"Will we ever tell him that I'm doing this?"

Good question, Shelley wondered. She had no clue. She figured it best to be honest now. "I don't know, Sammy." She thought hard for a second before adding, "Sometimes in life, it's okay to leave things unsaid."

"Is that a lie then?" Confusion spread across the child's visage.

Shelley knew Samuel was trying to work out all that she had taught him over the years and grasping to make sense of it. She hated dropping adult realities on him at this age, but he'd been through so much mentally with the demons he was facing that she thought he might be able to handle it. She hoped. "We won't lie to him. If he has any suspicions about what's going on, we'll come clean and not make anything up, I promise. But he might put a stop to getting you help if he finds out. Sometimes you just have to keep the peace."

Samuel nodded slowly, indicating that he didn't completely get it, but would trust his mom. "I'm scared, Momma."

She hugged him again. "It's okay to be scared, my love. I'll be there with you at every step." The boy buried his face into Shelley's neck and she could feel the dampness of his tears. She cursed Claude for what seemed like the millionth time in their marriage.

Samuel and his family lived south of the City of Buffalo. Gates Psychiatry, located north of the city in the Town of Amherst, was in a large brick building that housed various practice sections, including an inpatient ward. The outside was pleasant looking with neatly trimmed lawns and a concrete path that led to a courtyard with benches. Further, in the distance, the trail led towards tree-lined woods. The place oozed serenity, and even at his young age, Samuel could sense it. Not even the appearance of a woodsy area scared him; this was not like the dark forests off into the distance around his home. It looked like elves and fairies could live in these woods.

Patrick was waiting on the sidewalk in front of the building, having taken a metro bus there. Before going in, Shelley had no choice but to tell him what had happened to Samuel this afternoon, even though she didn't want to. She could easily predict his reaction, and she was right on the money. He was irate. He tried to jump in their car and drive right over to the Steiner's. She asked him what he would possibly accomplish if he did that. Either beat up the little shit or give his parents a piece of his mind, or both, he answered. She told him the obvious: none of that would make a difference for that clueless family, and he would do better being here for his little brother since it was his suggestion. Patrick reluctantly agreed though he said he wasn't off the idea of going over there later. In reply to this, Samuel won the argument, as he begged his brother not to. It wasn't going to help him at school for everyone to know he couldn't fight his own battles. Patrick still wasn't pleased, furrowing his brow, but for now, he relented. So the three of them made their way up the stairs to enter the building, their first idea of a solution for their situation unfolding. Patrick had his arm around Samuel as he pushed open one of the double doors with his other hand, which pleased Shelley, and she smiled. While he didn't have a father there for him in these times, Samuel had the next best thing: a surrogate one whom he loved and trusted dearly.

The waiting room was just as eye-pleasing as the outside. Bright vibrant yellow and orange flowers that Samuel didn't know the names of sat in vases on end tables around the room, and the chairs were leather, cushiony. Pastoral artwork depicting farms and rivers were on the walls, and the whole feel was consistently peaceful, calm-inducing. Shelley checked in with the receptionist, who was the same person she'd spoke to on the phone, a kind lady named Tanya. This twenty-something redhead had the ideal personality type to interact with people: pleasant, engaging, and soothing as the first contact here. Shelley liked her a lot, and it gave a fantastic first impression. She was told the wait would not be too long.

While they sat there, Samuel tried to be relaxed by the positive environment, but his fears were returning. Not his typical terrors of a monster jumping out of the wallpaper, although that was there. But the dark certainty that no one could help him. That there was no possible removal of this threat, and all this guy would do is assess his brain. Yes, they came from dreams, which originated in his mind, but they were real now. He knew it. The feeling of doom was starting to overwhelm him. He began doing something that was a bit of a nervous habit for him, spinning his right leg around and around the floor. He made it about ten rotations when he felt a hand on his leg. Patrick.

"Just breathe, kiddo," he said. "I know it's been a long day."

He turned to the left to look at his older brother, the usual hero worship in his gaze. "It's not about this," he pointed to his bruised and swollen face. "It's…" He stopped for a moment, thinking. Then continued, "I just don't know." He actually did know but didn't want to say it. His brother had gone out of his way to get him help, and Samuel didn't want to sound ungrateful or pessimistic.

"If this will work?"

Patrick is so smart. "How did you know?"

"Telepathy," Patrick said with a wink. "I bought a potion from Ames the other day. I can read all minds now. You know that pretty receptionist over there?" He nodded towards Tanya. "She's in love with me."

Despite the pain in his body and fear in his heart, Samuel broke out in laughter. Some of the other patients looked over and frowned at him. He tried to stifle it, but it just made him laugh all the more. Soon Patrick was chortling with him. Shelley looked over and started to frown just like the others, but couldn't hold it, and she let out a chuckle of her own and covered her mouth.

At least I have them. When the laughing ended, Samuel asked Patrick, "What if it *doesn't* help?"

"Then we'll try something else, a fortune teller or a faith healer or whatever. This is the first logical step. Mom talked to my future wife over there when making the appointment and found out about this guy. He's not a typical head shrink; he's all into what they call homeopathic and alternative ideas. Have no idea what that means, but it's apparently cutting-edge stuff. It's worth having hope, buddy."

Patrick always makes things sound better. Hope? I like the sound of that.

CHAPTER 4

T he Zen atmosphere continued to translate in the doctor's inner room. The personal office took on the feel of
the waiting room - the paintings, the comfortable furniture - and brought it to another level, with a mini Japanese
garden and running artificial brook next to the man's large
oak desk near the window. The glass looked right out on the
courtyard that Samuel was so impressed with earlier. He and
his family sat mere feet from the therapist in a sectional leather sofa. A wingback chair made of the same material was to
the left of the sectional. The couch was extremely comfortable;
Samuel's achy body felt like it was being hugged by the pliant,
leathered back. He noticed the chair was pushed a little ahead
of the couch, not far from the front of the desk. *For getting
up close and personal.* The boy thought this would make him
afraid, but it did the opposite.

Dr. Hector Santiago exuded calm and warmness. Samuel liked
him instantly. He didn't look old: he had dark black hair and
a cultivated goatee, which made him appear hipper than most
doctors the boy had met before. Dr. Santiago was in his early
40's with a slightly darker complexion reflecting his Hispanic
roots, and he was trim. He was dressed casually, no rich looking three-piece suit and tie, but a simple purple vertically
striped button-down shirt with the collar open. This helped
present a relaxed approach that filtered its way to his new
patient. Most importantly to Samuel was how Hector smiled,
which lit up his face beautifully. Shelley Redden's first impres-

sion of him was of attraction, which she was ashamed of since she was here to help her son. But the man was a looker. Patrick, too, was impressed, but with the calm bedside manner Santiago provided within just a few moments.

Dr. Santiago had immediately noticed Samuel's physical state, and that is where the questions began. After it was explained, he did not immediately require a call to the ER but did tell Shelley that she should take him to the family doctor the next day just to be sure. Then the story commenced. Samuel was excused to a side room with a TV and books to entertain himself so Shelley and Patrick could speak freely. After the door was closed, his family told Hector about the nightmares, about the gorillas, about the whole thing. They clearly explained the marks and injuries Samuel told of, apparently inflicted by the gorillas that only disappeared when they looked at him. Most of the time, Dr. Santiago just made notes in his notebook and nodded occasionally. But when he heard about the disappearing wounds, he said, "Hmm." Shelley wondered what that was about.

After they were done, she found out what the utterance was reflecting. "Where's his father?"

Shelley and Patrick exchanged a knowing glance. Patrick spoke up. "He can't handle this, doctor."

"I want you guys to start calling me Hector. I'm a Doctor of Psychology, but I'm also a licensed counselor. And counseling will be my main role here, and I have all my patients call me Hector, so please."

"Okay," Patrick said. "Well, Hector, Dad doesn't know we're here. He's old school, stuck in traditional ideas of manliness. He can't accept Sammy has an emotional problem."

"I understand. Now Mrs. Redden..."

"If we're calling you Hector, you have to call me Shelley." She blushed a tiny bit when she said this.

"Of course. Now, Shelley, I'm not disbelieving your explanation for Samuel's bruises today. But the way he came into the office, coupled with his assertions of injuries during the night, I have to ask. Does your husband lay his hands on Samuel?"

This took Shelley aback. *I should have thought this was a possibility.* "Hector, he's old fashioned like Patrick says. So a spanking is not completely unusual; Claude comes from the days when corporal punishment or showing a child the back of your hand was a trusted parenting approach. And he never let that go. But he's never taken it further." Because he's too aloof now, she sadly ruminated. With her older kids, though, he had really pushed the envelope. She was hoping this explanation was convincing enough to prevent a visit from Child Protective Services, as that would end the ruse and involve Claude.

"I believe you. But I had to cover my bases." Hector pushed the notebook aside and adjusted the John Lennon glasses he wore. "Now comes the important question. Do you tell Samuel you believe these things are real? I must know what you've reinforced."

Patrick sighed. "We've never told them the gorillas weren't real. At least not me and Mom. It just felt horrible to do that, to disbelieve him outright. And clearly, something real is happening to him, Dr., I mean Hector. He wakes up in so much sweat that it looks like he just had a swim. And he often pees in his jammies, and it's only when he has the nightmares."

Shelley nodded. "Back to my husband. Claude yells at him, telling him to grow up and that these things aren't real. But Patrick and I have never agreed with that. All my other kids are moved out, and we've never told them about this situation, and we've only recently let the school know. My sin is one of avoidance, but I never talked down to him, never condescended his pain."

"Excellent," Hector said, "other providers would probably say we need to quash this fiction right from the start. But that's not smart. He has to trust me, so I will proceed as if the gorillas are real. Then I can dig deeper into where this comes from and develop a plan of attack. Okay?"

"That sounds smart," Shelley said.

"Cool. I like it," Patrick added.

"All right," Hector said, smiling warmly at both of them. "Now, I need to talk to Samuel alone."

After Samuel returned to the room, Hector asked if he would be all right if his mother and brother stepped out to the waiting area so he could get to know him better. Despite Samuel's instant liking for this psychiatrist, being left alone with a man he just met thirty minutes ago still made him on edge, along with his trepidation of telling his greatest secret and fears. It was clear Hector noticed this feeling even as Samuel nodded yes since when he sat down on the chair adjoining the couch, he reached into his pocket and pulled out a stack of cards, which instantly got Samuel's attention. To his immediate joy, Samuel could see they were superhero cards. Like baseball cards, but instead of photos of athletes in a batting stance and a list of career stats, these had drawings of Batman, Superman, Captain America, Spider-Man, and others, and on the reverse side were a paragraph or two about their origin stories. Samuel smiled broadly. Hector nodded to Shelley and Patrick, excusing them. Shelley hugged Samuel and Patrick patted him on the shoulder as they left.

When the door closed, Hector asked, "Who's your favorite?" He spread out the cards on the coffee table in front of them, like a dealer at a casino.

"Can I?" Samuel didn't want to just touch them. *I don't want to be rude.* Hector held his hand out towards the cards in an affirming way. Samuel took his finger and separated them further apart, clearly looking for someone specific. *There he is.* He put his finger squarely on this card. It said Daredevil, The Man Without Fear, and showed an acrobatic hero in a red devil costume.

"Daredevil, huh? Why?"

Samuel was sure Hector knew why, but he answered the question, "I would love to not have fear." Samuel thought for a moment and added, "Plus, how amazing is he? A blind superhero!"

Hector flashed his charming full-teethed smile. "Yes. He kind of provides hope, doesn't he? Not giving up when that horrible accident blinded him, and then using his gifts to help others. And all the tragedy he's faced and overcome. Like his father being killed for standing up for his dignity and not throwing that fight. And all those crazy things that happened with Elektra? Her becoming an assassin, being killed by Bullseye, dying in Matt's arms, and then being resurrected? Wow. I could never deal with that much sadness. He's strong. It's nice to see someone being strong, isn't it?"

Samuel was stupefied, transfixed. He had leaned forward, listening to Hector's deep but caring voice. "You know about Daredevil?"

"Of course! And not from reading this card. I've been collecting comics since I was a boy in Mexico before my parents moved me here. I'll bring in some of my collection, and you can read them."

Without knowing it, Samuel had been brought out of the world of terrors and gorillas and into the hopeful, exciting world of superheroes, which he loved. "You bet I would! I read comics too, but I don't have many Daredevils. Thank you, Dr...."

"I told your family to call me Hector. Please do the same. I'm your friend, Samuel, not someone to boss you around."

"Okay, I will," Samuel said with confidence. He felt himself coming out of his shell. His first impression of this guy had only improved. *He doesn't talk to me like I'm a baby.*

"And here." Hector took the Daredevil card from the table and held it forward. "This is for you." He handed it to a wide-eyed Samuel.

"Thank you, Hector!" Samuel exclaimed, carefully taking the card from him and looking at it some more.

The doctor gazed at the happy boy and thought about how a child can survive the worst of this world, including night terrors brought about by an absent father or whatever else was causing these nightmares. "I want you to keep this card in your pocket or nearby at all times. When you get scared or feel like life is being too hard, look at it. Look at the wonderful artwork on the front and appreciate the artistry and coolness of it. But make sure to read the back. Read about Matt and the obstacles he's overcome. And then think about all we talk about here and be reminded of how you can be strong too."

Samuel grinned and said, "Sounds good. I promise to do that."

Now Hector cleared his throat and said, "Okay, Samuel, now that we're friends and we have all these heroes looking over us here," he gestured to the table, "I want to talk about what's been going on with you."

Samuel cleared his throat. *Here we go. And I'm scared again. I hope he stays nice.* "All right."

Hector was perceptive, reading the nonverbal signals instantly. "Don't be frightened, Samuel. Look at the card if you have to. We'll start easy. Do you remember when the gorillas first came?"

Samuel's heart warmed immediately. *He didn't say nightmares. He believes me.* But the boy was disappointed that he didn't have a great answer to the question. "I don't know." He then squinted his eyes, furrowed his brow and tried his best to think back. *I don't want to let him down.* "Maybe a few months ago?" he added after a couple moments.

"That's a great starting point! Let me explain something to you. If we know where, when, and how something started, we can begin to figure out how to stop it. Now, do you remember if there was something big going on in your life around that time? No rush. Take your time and think about it."

Samuel let his eyes roam to the ceiling and began the thinking process. He sat there like that for thirty seconds or so, with his face crinkled in concentration. "No, I don't think so. Until the gorillas came along, my life was pretty normal."

"You mentioned a few months ago? That would have been in summer, right?" Hector asked.

"Yes," Samuel said, nodding. "I'm not sure, maybe it's a guess. But that's the feeling I got when I just thought about it. If that makes sense?"

"It does. Why do you think summer came to you?" Hector had been doing this for about 15 years now. He always made it conversational and never a rote rehearsed thing. The questions came with no thought at all. Experience told him what to do.

"Umm..." Samuel again put his thinking cap on, as Ms. Jeffers always called it. And an idea came almost instantly. "Because it was hot in my room?" His eyes lit up with understanding. "Yeah, it was so stuffy when they first came! We didn't have an air conditioner then. It must have been early summer. Patrick put one in our window in August when we had that scorching heatwave. We still have it in there. He said we should leave it in for a little while longer since some warm weather might come back. Pat is smart that way."

Something about this kid's personality particularly appealed to Hector. Again, he was always impressed with young ones who obviously had some kind of trauma, and yet their innocent outlook on life still permeated them. And Hector was positive of one thing already: this child *had experienced* a form of trauma. He wasn't sure if it was abuse yet. His mother and brother certainly didn't fit the mold; they were obviously loving, supportive, and gentle with the boy. He believed the explanation about today's bruises, and the fact that they weren't afraid to bring Samuel in and face Hector's questions about the damage alleviated any fears that they were involved. But he still wondered about the father. Whenever he heard a wife say something about "old fashioned", it set off alarms in his head. But he wasn't confident about that yet. He was pretty sure that there was some kind of emotional abuse from the father, but something told him there was a physical element somewhere. Also, the harm could have originated somewhere else. He needed to figure this out; there was no going forward without addressing it. "Do you remember what else you were doing that summer?" he asked. Being a therapist was part detective, chipping away and digging for the clues to find an answer.

"Mostly playing outside, watching TV, swimming in our pool." Samuel did an intriguing thing here. His face went a bit blank like he was in a daze, staring at nothing. Before this, his eyes were attentive, engaged. Then he said, "Oh yeah," waking up and returning to active mode, "there was recreation."

"Recreation? What's that" Hector looked down and for the first time since starting with Samuel, wrote in his notebook. He had an eidetic memory and didn't like writing while his clients talked, but that blank stare and pause were significant, and he wanted to make special note of it.

"I think it's called town recreation, but Mom just calls it 'playground' since there's a jungle gym near where they have it. It's at our church. They must let the town put it on. I don't know."

Hector put the top of the pen against his mouth and nibbled it a bit. A nervous habit. He told his wife that it helped him think. "Do you have fun there?"

"Yes!" Samuel exclaimed. "We play baseball, basketball, four square, and there are crafts too, which isn't really my thing. My favorite part of the day is lunchtime when we go over to Mary's, the corner store across the street. We buy candy and these cards like your superhero ones, but these are *Star Wars*. They're a couple of years old, left over from the last movie, but my friends and I just started collecting those. We sit under the tree near the priest's house, and we either look at each other's cards or trade. The lady who runs the store is kind of a crank, but it's worth it."

Hector smiled again. He thought this sounded quite nice. But he had to dig deeper. "It's all good times there then?"

That empty look passed across Samuel again, and this time, he actually spoke while in it, a dreamy voice. "Well, there's Bennett."

Hector thought Samuel was in a kind of trance phase, a rare

state that happened when some children remembered abuse, and he knew he couldn't hesitate, had to get at this fast before it ended. "Bennett?"

"He's the camp fix-it and clean up guy. He's mean." Samuel physically shuddered, which gave Hector a start, and then his eyes became focused again. It was like he was emerging from a waking dream.

Hector looked at the clock on the wall. It had been an hour since he started the session with Samuel's family. Time was up since he had others waiting. *That's disappointing; we're getting somewhere already.* He was pleased, though. He knew what the next step was.

Night was upon this part of the world, and Dr. Hector Santiago was still in his office way after the rest of the staff had departed. He had just finished writing and reviewing the notes for Samuel Redden, which Tanya would type up for him the next day, but he remained drinking coffee and thinking. This case had affected him more strongly than any other first session Hector could remember in the many years of his practice. His rationalization was that he'd taken an initial liking to Samuel. But he knew that was bullshit. This was far from his first child case, and he almost always felt a kinship with young people. It was more than that.

His thoughts kept flowing. *Regression therapy makes sense as the next step. I definitely feel there's something significant buried deep here, to do with the town recreation and probably with this Bennett character. But it's even more than that. Something about this child, something special: the blankness that overcame him was remarkable. It was like he was in another place, another time. Now that I think about it more, it goes further than a simple trance state. Yeah, I know, my domain deals with the mind and should re-main in science, and people always laugh at me when I take it fur-ther. But I genuinely believe spirituality isn't captured in a church but inside the human soul, and it's the duality, the mind, and the soul, that gives us a real revelation.*

"Are you saying the gorillas are real?" his rational mind inter-jected. *Let's not lose our license here and become a fortune teller.*

No. I'm saying there's something more. I don't know what it is. But I have to keep my mind open, or I will never help him. This is not some cut-and-dried case of a sad kid whose father doesn't love him. I need to peel the layers apart.

BOOM!

Hector Santiago was not a timid, fearful man. But when he heard this noise, he felt like he jumped about ten feet in the air and came back hard into his chair. *Well, maybe more of a men-tal leap, but what the fuck?* He got up from his seat and looked around his dimly lit office. The noise definitely came from the room, but it felt like it resounded from the whole area, not just one place. And he could have sworn everything did move and shake like an earthquake had struck his inner office alone. He stood up warily and walked around, looking in every corner of his sanctuary. He peeked under the furniture, up at the ceiling, and finally made his way to the window. His imagination was running rampant now as he gazed across the courtyard into the peaceful woods. He could have sworn that he saw multiple shapes gathered outside the trees, taunting him.

Come on, Hector, this kid has really gotten to you too much. He raised his hand and waved to the distance. "Good night, apes." He turned and walked out of his office and proceeded to lock up and activate the security system. All he wanted now was to return home to his lovely wife and two precious sons. When he got to his car, he looked back to the woods and saw nothing. *Get some sleep, my boy.*

It wasn't until weeks later, after the tragedy that had befallen Dr. Santiago, that a passerby finally noticed the massive hole on the siding above the window outside his office. And the weird cluster of hair that resided in the cracks.

CHAPTER 5

I t was the following day, the weekend. Saturday. Samuel was outside playing. It was an unseasonably warm early fall day, and he was wearing tan shorts, which he had already gotten a share of grass stains on. Samuel was busy role-playing Indiana Jones. Not far behind his love of *Star Wars* was Indy. Right now he was in the spacious back yard, pretending he was Dr. Jones in the opening scene of *Raiders of the Lost Ark,* running from the rolling boulder with the golden idol in his hands (Samuel using a big toy block as a prop to hold). A little over a year ago, Shelley had bought him that movie on VHS, and he still thought of it as one of his favorites. He loved the action, and now with his experiences with the gorillas, even the scene when the Nazis' faces burned up from the ark seemed not as scary. He'd probably watched it fifty times at least. He really wanted to go see *The Temple of Doom* last year, but his mom said he wasn't old enough for this darker installment. Patrick told him about that one, though, and he was counting the days until he was old enough to check it out. While he played, he made sure he was far away from the looming woods, forcefully making himself not to look at them. It wasn't an easy task since the trees surrounded three of the four corners of the house. The front part was the biggest and scariest, but luckily those trees were far in the distance. But they still terrified him; he somehow just knew that was where the gorillas escaped to, so he was glad he wasn't near that section. He was mostly playing near the above ground pool in the back. He was flailing his arms out with his pretend whip, and wincing a bit since his stomach still ached, when he saw his father come out of the house and climb up on the deck that was at the front of the pool. The man sat down in a lounge chair and began sipping a bottle of Budweiser. He was wearing a dirty white undershirt and dark green work pants. That second part of his attire might have seemed weird on a warm day, but Samuel was pretty sure he never saw his dad wear shorts for some reason. Claude looked over at his son immediately. Samuel was a little scared of his father and didn't want to deal with him right now; he was having fun, and Dad always had a way of taking that away with his attitude. But there was no hiding, and Claude Redden called out, "Samuel, come here." His heart dropped. Claude was the only one in the family who didn't occasionally call him by his nickname, Sammy. As with everything, his dad was all business, almost military in everything he did. He never served, but Samuel thought he would make a good drill sergeant like in the movies. He even had the appropriate buzzcut.

Please, God, don't let him be too mean. I just want to be left alone to play. Samuel knew he couldn't delay, so he left the safety of his make-believe world and slogged over to the deck, climbing the wooden ladder. He cast an idle glance at the surface of the pool, seeing a few early fallen leaves on its surface. Claude was always late in closing the pool up after summer. Samuel's mom had to continually remind him several times after early September. He turned to his father and reminded himself not to let anything slip about Hector. Mom and Pat had given him a kind lecture about that on the car ride home the other day. "Yes, Sir?" *Show respect, and maybe he'll make this quick.*

"Sit down," Claude said in his deep, gruff voice. It wasn't often that anyone heard Claude speak in anything but this timbre; there wasn't a lot of kindness there. But surprisingly, he toned it down a tad when he added, "Come on, son, sit for a bit with your old man and enjoy the nice day."

What? Is this my dad? Samuel wanted to think the beer in Claude's hand was a clue, but this was far from the only time he'd seen his dad drinking in front of him, or loaded for that matter. So he had no idea what to think of this moment. "Sure, Dad." He plopped down clumsily in the other plastic summer chair next to Claude and looked straight ahead, afraid, not sure of what to say.

"So this fight?" Claude asked.

What's he talking about? Samuel then quickly puzzled it out. *Oh. Of course. Steiner. Not sure I would call it a fight, though, more like a thrashing.* He was pretty sure his father hadn't uttered a syllable to him since yesterday's excitement, the beating and the appointment Claude knew nothing about. Samuel hadn't even thought it surprising that his father didn't want to talk about the bruises until now. At an early age, the boy had learned that Claude Redden had two moods: raging hot anger and indifference. The indifference was more prevalent lately. Clearly, though, Shelley had mentioned the incident to her husband. Speaking of Mrs. Redden, she had followed Dr. Santiago's advice and taken Samuel to his regular doctor, and there wasn't anything to be overly concerned about. Dr. Connor did provide some ointment to put under his eye and rewrapped his stomach, not seeing a need for x-rays, and he said he would be "right as rain" in a few days (the doc was an elderly man who loved his old clichés). So there wasn't much to dwell on or talk about. But still, a caring father would have probably at least addressed it. And now his dad finally did want to talk to him about it. It gave young Samuel some hope that he wasn't utterly invisible to the man. "Oh, right," Samuel said. "It was the Steiner kid." *Stick to the facts.* "I'm okay."

Claude nodded his head and glanced out of the corner of his eye at Samuel. He wasn't one for eye contact either. "Tell me about the whole thing. I see you have some battle scars, and that's good. But I want to know more."

Samuel swallowed. He never got many words in with his dad without correction, so this would be a first if he didn't interrupt him. *I don't know what's happening.* But despite his confusion, he went forward, even though his voice got a bit shaky at times as he told the whole tale. No, not exactly the entire story. He stopped before getting to the glowing hand. He hadn't even had time to think about that since he wasn't sure it really happened. So he ended with, "I got extremely pissed off, Dad. I balled up my fist, and Steiner looked surprised, maybe even afraid. Then Mr. Bosworth came out and shooed Jake away." Samuel paused for a brief second after the minor curse, but his dad didn't change his emotionless expression.

"Oh, the fag?" Claude inquired. Samuel was young, didn't know much about the world. But he knew what fag meant. And how it wasn't a nice thing to say. But he didn't want to get into an argument with Claude, so he just nodded. Claude took a couple swigs of his beer. He then turned his chair to face his son, which was another surprise. The elder Redden usually kept a healthy distance from Samuel and rarely gave his full attention to the kids. Unless he was raging about something. So Samuel had a chance to look more closely at his dad than usual. Claude was a prototypical factory worker type, a large man, with strong arms and lines in his face from the stress of the intense physical work he did. His features weren't fine like Samuel's, so that must have come from his mother. When the man twisted his chair around, it groaned underneath his girth. Truth be told, Claude looked a little comical in the tight seat, but Samuel would never say that. "Tell me this, Samuel. If that fairy hadn't interrupted, would you have acted on your anger? I want the truth."

Again, this was not something Samuel had thought about. Dr. Santiago had told his family what he planned, regression therapy (hypnotherapy to the lay person), and Shelley and Patrick tried to explain that to him as best they could. He was nervous about this unknown path and what it might lead to, and it occupied a lot of his thoughts over the last 24 hours. Samuel had very efficiently compartmentalized the Steiner skirmish's ending, both his temper and even amazingly the wacky thing with his hand. He wanted to give his father a great answer, though, as this was the first time he ever had anything close to a heart to heart with him. He furrowed his brow as he thought and then answered, "I sure was mad. I felt like I wanted to kill him."

Samuel wasn't sure, but he could have sworn his father had the slightest of grins on his face, but it was hard to tell; he wasn't sure he'd ever seen him smile before. At least not with happiness, without bitterness. "Good. I like to see it. You've never shown much of a backbone. You need to start standing up for yourself. And maybe then you'll stop having these ridiculous nightmares."

This made Samuel's heart drop. *Just when I think he's getting to be on my side.* He thought of trying a different avenue than he ever had before. "Don't you have nightmares, Dad?"

Claude had a stern look that held both impatience and exasperation in it. "Of course I do. But they're just nightmares! You toughen up and move on. And wait until you're an adult, with important responsibilities; that's where the REAL nightmares come from. From banks wanting the mortgage payment when you're a bit short, to your car's muffler going out, to an ass boss breathing down your neck. Not fantasy world apes. Got it?"

"Yes, Sir, but..."

"But nothing! I need you to grow up."

"But I'm eight-years-old, Dad." *Ooh, I may have gone too far.*

When he peeked over at his dad, Samuel realized he had indeed gone too far. There was red spreading across Claude's face. The gruff man's next words came out in what sounded like a growl, and Samuel thought he wouldn't mind facing the gorillas at that moment instead. "Showing some backbone does not mean you're disrespectful to me, boy." He stood up, switched the beer to his opposite hand, and roughly grabbed his son by his right arm. As he started to yank him towards the ladder for God knew what, Samuel's heart began to beat heavily. But then he heard it—the voice of his rescuer, his mother.

"Claude." Standing a few feet from the bottom of the ladder was Shelley. Samuel had never seen her like this. It took him a moment to place what he was viewing in her, and then he realized it was fury. Not just being a little angry at something, but the same kind of emotion that he had felt with Steiner. Her lips were pursed, her body rigid, and her eyes glaring. When she said her husband's name, it came out not as a high-pitched upset sound like he had heard from her before but a quiet, resolute, almost whisper. So was this next part, "Let go of him."

While today was what Samuel considered a day of firsts, this next one was the most surprising. Claude looked flummoxed, taken aback. His grip actually loosened a bit, and his facial expression was one of someone trying to figure out some complicated formula. Samuel knew he shouldn't be happy about this, but it made him feel wonderful. *I think I hate him.* "What did you say to me, Shelley?" Claude hissed.

Shelley stood there unmoving, and while she appeared resolute, Samuel knew she must have been terrified inside. He had never seen Claude strike her, but he always thought it was possible. "Sammy's been through a lot this week, and he doesn't need to be manhandled by you. I heard the end of that conversation, and all he was trying to do was get some sympathy from his father. Now *let him go.*"

Claude sighed and pushed his son away roughly towards the end of the deck, making Samuel just miss tripping over the step gap. He clumsily rammed up against the wood structure, hurting his shoulder a little. Shelley beckoned for him to join her with a hand signal. He scurried down the ladder, the relief of this escape lessening his heart's thudding, but it was still far from still. "You coddle him and coddle him, and then coddle him some more. You and Patrick. I thought maybe that bruhaha this week would put some hair on his chest, but no, he's gotta go back to those stupid baby nightmares."

Samuel wanted to yell, "They're not baby nightmares! I'd like you to face those monster gorillas!" But instead, he found himself latching onto his mom as she put her arm around him. He wasn't proud of it, but he was still quite intimidated by the man. "What did he last say to you, Claude?" Shelley asked, starting to sound like Ms. Jeffers.

"This disrespect..."

"Oh, for God's sake. You're the one that needs to grow up. You're like a child yourself sometimes. A man child stuck in another decade. I ask again, what did he say?" Shelley was firmly buried in the protector's role and didn't lose her imposing stance, but deep inside, she was bemused by the words coming out of her mouth.

The startled look on Claude's face became almost comical. To complete the school metaphor, he actually shuffled his feet slightly, like one of Samuel's classmates getting the 9th degree from one of the authority figures. "He said he was eight." Claude just about puffed this out.

"And he is. He's not going to have hair on his chest, literally or metaphorically. And if the only avenue for you to talk to your child is to be proud he got beat up, then I literally don't know what to do with you." Here she paused, and her voice got a little softer, "Claude, I appreciate all you do to provide for us. But being a provider is more than just money and toughness. It's caring and being there for us emotionally. And being approachable."

"I won't do this in front of the boy," Claude said brusquely. Samuel could tell the anger was returning to his dad; he had recovered from the shock.

"You're right," Shelley said, "We'll talk later."

"If I feel like it," Claude said, tossing the empty beer bottle to the ground below. He followed this by jumping down from the deck, completely bypassing the stairs, somehow landing as gracefully as an Olympic gymnast despite his size and alcohol intake. He then proceeded to stalk towards them. Shelley pivoted her body so Samuel was as far away from his father as possible.

"For fuck's sake, Shelley," Claude said while brushing past her and making his way to the front yard. Samuel could hear him enter the house, stomping around and cursing loudly, and just seconds later come out, slamming the screen door. This door didn't close all the way since it was old and needed to be snapped in just right; it merely rattled into the frame and out again. No sound then for a second, before the eldest Redden's footsteps resounded out again and Samuel could hear banging, knowing Dad was bullying the door closed. More obscenities rang out, at a rapid-fire pace. Then dramatic tromping down the porch steps. The ancient Oldsmobile started up, and then Claude was gone, driving up the dead-end road. *Probably to East Eden Tavern.* Samuel was far from ignorant about where his dad spent most of his time.

Shelley turned, looked down at Samuel, and in a faux-cheerful voice said, "Who wants a popsicle?"

◆ ◆ ◆

Night. It was now Samuel's dreaded time period. But this time it felt like it could be one of the okay ones. Patrick was out with friends, and Dad was still gone, but Mom was home, watching the 10:00 news. So no stupid babysitters. The night light was on, and its soft illumination shone shadows on the wall across from his bed. These were not scary shadows, but the proof of his protection. Samuel wasn't asleep yet, though. Thoughts were racing through his head, more than there should be for an eight-year-old in a generally stable home environment. There was the upcoming hypnotherapy, which still scared him. And then there was the conversation with his dad earlier, which was the more pressing matter for him. A child wants the love of his father.

Why can't he accept me as I am? I'm never going to be a "man's man", I'm never going to be a tough guy, I'm never going to be a weight lifter, I'm never going to be any of these things. But I'm his son. That should automatically make him love me. He's the biggest bully I know.

Tears formed in Samuel's eyes. And he gripped his hands into fists under the covers. He wanted his father here so he could swear at him. *Maybe that would work.* He shook in his anger. Then he felt a warmth down below. And it wasn't the embarrassing pee in his pants that often happened. Lowering his head, his heart skipped a beat. The glow was back. He pushed aside the covers, and not only were his hands, both of them this time, giving off that radiant hue, but it was now moving up. The shimmer encroached into his arms and wasn't stopping, continuing its upwards journey. It scared him. No, it terrified him. Now instead of venting at his father, he just wanted to scream in terror. *It's going to eat me alive!*

Instead, the electricity in the whole house was affected. As Shelley watched the local weather report out in the living room, the TV started to blink in and out. And her reading light flickered. She looked around in confusion.

In Samuel's room, the same thing occurred. But to his night light. He gasped and whispered, "No." The little Spider-Man plug-in started to buzz, and then it went out. At the same time, the glow began to recede back down to his hands. He suddenly wanted it to stay, even if it spread over his whole body. The warm feeling it gave him - like he was standing near a camp-fire - was something he was learning to enjoy, a sensation of love and safety perhaps. But more importantly, he knew when the phenomenon was gone, he would be plunged into the dark-ness. "Stay, stay!" He shook his hands, trying to make it expand again, but no luck. It was still slowly drifting its way down until there was only a tiny pinprick in his right pointer finger. And then that was gone as well.

Samuel's panic suddenly stopped, though, when his quick young mind latched onto something. *No worries. I just remem-bered. Pat also put that tiny lamp back on the table.* Last week after the big nightmare that prompted action, Patrick not only plugged in the night light but retrieved the lamp his father had dumped in the basement. He figured with the door mostly closed, Dad wouldn't see it. And in actuality, Claude rarely came in there anymore. Aloofness had replaced strictness. Hope renewed, Samuel charged over to the end table, wasting no time. Being a clumsy kid and with the darkness as heavy as usual now, he was glad there was nothing on the floor in the middle of the room. He reached the table, whacked his hand against the lamp, causing it to start toppling off its pedestal. Miraculously, he managed to catch it before it went to the ground. His heart felt like it was going to leap out of his chest. *Oh, my God. A last-minute save by the goalie!* Still holding the lamp, not bothering to place it back where it just stood, Samuel fumbled for the switch. *Got it!*

Nothing.

The weird power surge had taken the lamplight out too. Samuel sucked in a deep breath, trying to keep himself under control. *Even Mom doesn't like me to get out of bed to bother her at night, but she'll understand. Especially now. She must have experienced this outage too.* But she hadn't. Her electrical issues stopped at a stutter and a flicker. Without thinking twice, she had gone right back to watching the kindly newsman talk about another local business closing. After placing the lamp on the floor, not wanting to risk it falling off the table, Samuel took a few quick steps towards the door leading to the hallway. With no windows or light in the outside hallway, the darkness was deep, so he made sure to hold his hands out like Frankenstein so as not to ram into anything. He swept his hand around the wooden door before finding the knob. *Here we go.* He turned it.

The door didn't open.

He tried again.

No luck.

The panic Samuel had been able to suppress earlier now firmly gripped him in its grasp. The cold perspiration, rapid breath, and shakiness began. But he knew he had to keep trying. He had to get out of there. He wiped his hand on his *Star Wars* pajama top, rubbing it on See-Threepio's face, thinking it was sweatiness that was causing the knob to malfunction. He quickly tried turning it again, but while he could feel the handle turn, the door stayed put. He pushed against the frame, and it still wouldn't budge. *What? No. Please. God. No.*

There's no God here, my boy.

What was that? Samuel turned in a circle to look around the room. That was when he saw it, a dark bulge rising near the window. The sickly green color was creeping its way around that area. It didn't seem as strong as usual and didn't allow Samuel to make out many details, but the shadows then spread to all corners of the room. This shading made it look like the shape's essence covered him, the long talons and sharp teeth visible in funhouse-like grotesquery.

Oh no, they're here.

Just one of us, Samuel Redden. But the one you need to fear the most. I'm known to my servants simply as Leader.

With a start, Samuel realized he heard this voice, the grating, inhuman, almost metallic sound *in his head*. And it was receiving his thoughts too, as he hadn't spoken anything aloud since this started.

I'm not going to harm you tonight. One day, yes, we will eat you alive. Heh. And you will feel every bit of it as we devour you. But today, you will not be attacked. Consider yourself lucky. Now let me know you understand with your thoughts. Scream out, and we won't kill you but will do worse to your mother. And later Patrick.

I understand. How do I hear you in my head? Am I losing my mind?

No, but you may wish you had when this is all over.

Samuel now made a forcible effort to hide his spiraling out-of-control internal thoughts. It wasn't easy given his age and emotions, but he tried his best. He felt violated and didn't want this monster to access so much of him. All the while, he kept a constant eye on the shape, making sure it wasn't moving. And he knew he had a rare opportunity to find some things out. He released some thoughts: *What do you want? Why did you pick me?*

This is not the time for answers, just warnings—about the psychiatrist. You must not allow him to perform the hypnotherapy. Or he will pay. You don't want the Santiago boys to lose their dad, do you? You liked him, we know that.

In his hopefully shrouded thoughts, Samuel could not figure out how they could know all this. Could they listen in on his conversations? Or just read his mind? His feet started to feel wobbly, and he could sense his bladder letting go, so he roughly sat down on the floor. He held his head in his hands and secretly tried mentally calling to his mother to come and stop this intrusion. *Please, Mom. Save me.*

Stop the sessions, Samuel, or we will accelerate our plans. Tell me you will, now.

Samuel removed his hands and raised his head. *Okay, but how?*

DO YOU THINK WE CARE HOW? The voice roared loudly in his head, and Samuel was terrified that the shape in the corner would definitely jump towards him now. **Tell your mom you feel better, make something up, just do it.**

Samuel was about to affirm this when he suddenly got mad again. He felt that insatiable rage building up, an echo of what he experienced on the street the other day. *I'm just so tired of being a victim. This fuckface and his friends have terrorized me, and now he wants me to stop getting help. And he's threatening that nice man.* The boy sensed that stirring in his hands again, but looking down, they weren't flaring up yet. But it gave him an idea, a question that needed answering. And he was feeling another strong emotion, one he couldn't put his finger on since it was another new one. Then it occurred to him. It was bravery. And he managed to keep all these thoughts from the creature. He was sure of it.

Can I hurt you?

WHAT?

There was still intimidation in that verbal thought, but Samuel believed there was something else too, something he was intimately familiar with: fear. He held his hands out to the creature, making fists. *What's up with these glowing hands? Do I have some kind of power? Can I harm you? Is that why you're after me?* In the corner of the room, the night light began to flicker. But Samuel didn't notice this.

But the gorilla must have. No more mind communication came Samuel's way. All that filtered towards him was an audible noise this time. It was a growl, an animalistic, hungry sound. The shape lurched one step towards him, and Samuel didn't feel strong anymore. He felt tiny. But the next second, the form was gone, and the lamp that he had put on the floor turned on, casting a bright light all the way to the lower far wall. He could see that his night light was fully back on, too, Peter Parker's red mask reflecting tiny beams off it. Samuel slowly made his way to his feet. He was surprised to find his legs worked as he stumbled towards the door. He had a feeling about what would happen next. He turned the doorknob, and, yes, it opened.

"Sammy? Are you ok?" his mom called out.

I don't know. I really don't know.

CHAPTER 6

It was the next day, Sunday afternoon. Samuel was spending time at his friend Peter Darwin's house. Peter's family lived a couple streets over, and after the last few days, it was nice for Samuel to get away from his homestead a bit. It was another beautiful autumn weekend day: the sky was a deep azure, birds were still around, dive-bombing each other and chirping, and a few dropped greenish-brown leaves were skipping around the ground in the slight breeze. Indian summer was here, and Samuel knew it wouldn't last long, so he was reveling in the mid 70's temperature, glad to go without a jacket or long pants. The forecast indicated this would last until Monday. Behind the two boys were East Eden's ever-present woods, but not being in his own backyard, they didn't seem as evil to Samuel. Still, by habit, he kept his eyes from lingering on them and was glad they were facing away at the two-story cape cod house. For most kids, it was a perfect day for sports and running around. But Samuel and Peter had different interests. They were sitting at the back of the yard under a huge weeping willow tree, their legs crossed with comic books spread around them. Samuel was reading a Batman and Peter a Spider-Man. They had just traded the two. Samuel was having a hard time focusing on Batman fighting Ra's Al Ghul, however; there were other things on his mind. He put the book down and looked over at his buddy.

Peter was as prototypical geek as one could get. He had horn-rimmed glasses that looked like they belonged to an older sibling twenty or so years ago. He was thin, lanky, tall, scarecrow-like, already a few inches taller than his next highest classmate. He sported longer hair than most of the kids his age, a sable mullet that was uniquely him. And he was a goofball. Always ready with a pun or spouting old 60's clichés, like "daddy-o" and "far out". He was almost like a man-out-of-time, so much that Samuel once told him he should change his name to Steve, for Captain America. Even his t-shirt, with an image of the Who album, *Who's Next*, on it, was something an 80's kid wouldn't typically wear. And the iron-on image was faded out to the point you could barely see Keith Moon's face anymore. But Pete didn't care.

Samuel put his comic down and looked at his hands. *Can I tell him? How much?* Peter noticed that he had stopped reading and asked, "What's wrong, Reddy?" He was the only one who called him "Reddy," and even though Samuel wasn't a fan of it at first, it had grown on him. He wasn't close enough to anyone else at school to even rank another nickname. "Don't like that Batman? I got some other groovy ones we can trade instead."

"It's not that," Samuel said, "I think I have something to tell you."

"You think?"

"There's something to tell. I'm just scared to."

Peter put down his comic now and patted his friend on the shoulder. "You know you can tell me anything. Lay the score on me, brother."

Samuel laughed. "You're so corny."

"Affirmative, Sir!" Peter stood up and gave a mock salute before dropping back down to the ground in a humorous manner, long limbs all akimbo. They had clumsiness in common, but Peter always seemed able to make it look purposeful like he was proud of it.

Samuel got quietly serious for a moment and then began. He told Peter. Everything.

◆ ◆ ◆

After he was done with his monologue, Samuel sat there quietly for several seconds, his hands gripped tightly together. Next to him, Peter made no sound, and as Samuel listened to the ambient noise around him - the chattering birds, cars passing on the street nearby, Mr. Jackson's weedwhacker revving next door - he wondered why he ever decided to tell. His stomach had started feeling funny as soon as he said the word "gorillas", and he now felt another one of those cold sweats forming on his brow. *He doesn't believe me. I just lost the only friend I have.* Samuel then reluctantly glanced surreptitiously at Darwin. Peter had a faraway look on his face, his head tilted up towards the heavens. After a few seconds of this pose, which seemed an excruciatingly long time for Samuel, a huge grin spread over his buddy's features. "This is amazing," Peter whispered. Then he followed that up with a diametrically opposite tone, exclaiming loudly, "I knew it! I knew there was more to this world than all this surface stuff." He gesticulated around with his gangly arms as he said this, reaching out broadly and accidentally bumping the tree bark but not paying any attention. "The world has to be bigger than all the things our parents worry about." Peter always spoke this way, with a better vocabulary and thoughtfulness than the typical eight-year-old. Samuel felt like it rubbed off on him as well.

Samuel took a deep breath out, not knowing if he ever felt more relieved. He made special note of the last thing Peter said, which went straight to his heart because of the lecture his dad tried to give him about reality the previous day. He'd found someone who understood, someone who didn't minimize the deepness of his otherworldly problem. *Thank God. But there's one thing.* "This isn't fun stuff, Pete," Samuel said, trying to sound as somber as he could. "I really think they want to kill me."

"I know, dude," Peter put his arm around Samuel. "But we can beat them. You have those powers, right?"

"I don't know what this is," he said as he clenched and unclenched his right fist a few times, "I don't know anything."

"Well, I think we should find out. See some experts or something."

"That's what I'm doing. Talking to Hector and all."

Peter shook his head. "No, my man. Not a head shrink. We should see a psychic or somebody who knows of the supernatural. Too bad Rod Serling isn't still alive."

Samuel chuckled despite himself. "That show is like 30 years old. Don't you have any new references?"

"Nah, the old stuff is always better. Plus, *The Zone* is deep and timeless. At least that's what Dad says. I watch the reruns with him and don't always get it."

"But I thought you were a genius." Samuel smirked out of the corner of his mouth.

Peter made a false shocked face before uttering, "Just let me take the knife out of my back and then we'll move on." Peter dug away behind his neck and Samuel couldn't help bursting out laughing. *He's such a piece of work.* "Here's another thing to consider with your dilemma," the young hippie said, continuing with all solemnity. "What that gorilla said last night. That he would hurt this shrink or your family if you continue. We may have to try something else just to save lives."

Samuel nodded. "Right. But how did the gorillas know what I'm doing? Spying? Can they read my thoughts at all times? Do they know what we're talking about right now?"

Peter got the most severe and pensive look on his face, which in typical situations would make Samuel want to laugh; it was rare that Darwin was anything but goofy and fun-loving. But it was not funny now. Peter looked around the yard for a moment or two, not appearing to be locking onto anything specific. *He's lost again somewhere in the Peter-Verse, the place where his big brain makes his computations. He's always been so smart, especially with science.* After another minute or two of this, Samuel wondered if he should shake his friend. But then Peter just grinned happily, his normal jovial state returned. "No. I don't think so," he finally said. "If I had to guess, I would say they have some sort of connection with you, and when they get close, they touch your mind. You're probably like them in a way but on the opposite side. The good side. And you're not less powerful, just more pure, noble.

This is the best thing I could have done, confiding in Pete. He gets this stuff. I'm more rational than him; I need to consider the other side, the magical side. It was Samuel's turn now to smile as he pivoted his head to look more closely at his unorthodox friend. "Thanks for believing me."

Pushing up at his spectacles, Peter simply and genuinely said, "Always."

I may not have any other friends, but I picked this one right. "Okay, so what now? Tell my family that I'm okay? That I don't want to see Hector anymore?"

"Yes, Kemosabe. Get out of it any way you can. I would not underestimate these monsters. In the meantime, I will hit mystics-are-us and try to find a new avenue. Fun!" He held his hand out for a high five. Even though Samuel didn't want to minimize the situation's seriousness, he couldn't resist slapping it. *I feel hope. And I can't let anyone in my family get hurt. Or Hector and his family. I won't. It's Peter and me alone for now.*

Samuel picked his Batman comic back up and began to read again, allowing himself to enter a fantasy world that wasn't so threatening.

◆ ◆ ◆

Samuel decided to approach Patrick first about backing out with Hector. He knew that it was his brother's idea to have him see Dr. Santiago and that Mom initially showed reluctance to take the problem outside the house. She would be easier to sway; it made Shelley nervous about sharing family information, especially the way Dad was. And being his roommate, Patrick was the one who more directly saw the result of Samuel's nightmares first hand; he would need more convincing.

Samuel was never more right.

"Absolutely not," Patrick said sternly after hearing the request. They were in their bedroom Sunday night around 8:30, a few minutes before Samuel would have to get ready for sleep. Each was relaxing on their own bed, Patrick looking at a hockey magazine, the Buffalo Sabres media guide with captain Gilbert Perreault on the cover, and Samuel fiddling with but not really playing with his *Star Wars* figures.

"Why not?" Samuel asked.

Patrick put his magazine down on his lap and sighed. "You're smarter than this. We're finally starting on the road to getting you some help. Why would we just stop now? Anyway, the appointment is tomorrow at 4:00. It's too late to cancel without us paying a fee; we're not exactly made of money, you know." He now pushed his periodical aside, dropped his feet to the floor, and studied Samuel with a look that was a blend of seriousness and confusion. But it also had that expression that most little brothers were used to, disappointment.

I didn't think about the money. I feel like such an ass. But if it means my family's lives, it's worth the loss of cash. The best way to do this is to tell some kind of truth. "I'm sorry about that. But I don't think this will work. He doesn't believe they're real, the gorillas." *Wait, did I just say that? There goes the truth already. I think Hector believes me. Oh well. Desperate times.* "I know they are. You've told me you believe, but I don't think he can. Doctors aren't allowed to think that way. So it's really just a waste of money."

Patrick didn't answer right away but looked up at the ceiling. After this beat, he said, "This won't be easy to hear, buddy. What I really believe is you *think* they're real."

Samuel's heart sank. "So you don't really believe me?" *I'm getting off track, but how can this be? How can he say that?*

Patrick didn't take his eyes off the peeling paint above him, as if afraid to look his brother in the eye. "I'm not saying there's no such thing as the supernatural, but I think we all want to believe in something bigger than us, whether it's something good like God or something evil like the Devil, demons, or… killer gorillas. And you're young, little chief, it's easier for you to believe in things that…that…"

"Aren't real?" Samuel was getting angry now, and his voice broke a bit.

Patrick was able to force himself to face Samuel. "Maybe. But I also think that what you're experiencing is real enough. Something is attacking your mind, and it's having effects on your actual body. I don't doubt that. Don't get upset, buddy."

"I am upset! You were the only one who believed me." *Until maybe Hector. But now I'm even doubting that. Luckily I have Peter.* Samuel could feel the sticky liquid sign of tears starting to blot his cheeks. *This hurts, but I can't get distracted. I have to get out of this appointment. Dr. Santiago is so cool. I hate to think what the gorillas would do to him. Or God, his kids.* "I won't see Hector anymore, Patrick. I don't care if everyone thinks I'm crazy. These things are real! No hypnotism or head probing is going to save me." Then he added more quietly, "Or you guys."

Patrick didn't seem to hear that last part. Or didn't feel like questioning it. He got up from his bed and came over to kneel before Samuel. "No one thinks you're crazy. But this is serious, what it's doing to you. I promise you, if the therapy doesn't work, we'll try something else. But it can't hurt, especially the hypnotism, even if the gorillas are real."

"If?" Samuel sniffed.

"Come on, listen to me. I told you I don't have trouble with the supernatural and that I can see something is happening to you. Nothing's changed. I'll consider any avenue, a voodoo doctor if that's what it takes to help you. But we have to start somewhere!"

*I hate it when people older than me start debating things.. I just can't outdo their logic. Maybe it **is** all in my head, and the gorillas can't hurt Hector or my family.* He quickly pushed aside this thought. *But no. It's real, all of it! Could I tell Hector that I'm scared, and maybe he'll at least not try to hypnotize me? Maybe that will make the gorillas happy? God, I just don't know!*

Samuel still wanted to counter Patrick's arguments and fight, but all he could do was drop his head into his hands and begin weeping audibly. Patrick wrapped his arms around him and said, "It's okay, Sammy. Please stop crying. I'll talk to Mom about how much this is upsetting you. That's all I can do. But I think we have to at least go to tomorrow's appointment. Then maybe we can stop. MAYBE."

Samuel peeked up from Patrick's shoulder, snorting in his discharge, feeling a smidge of hope. *It's progress, I guess, but probably still not good enough.* He wanted to say this out loud so his brother would know this wasn't settled as far as he was concerned. But Samuel felt exhausted mentally, and he simply said, "Ok, Pat."

◆ ◆ ◆

Several hours passed. It was fully dark outside, and Patrick had gone into the living room to watch Letterman. Samuel was alone and far from sleep.

He knew he had to talk to *him* again. Leader. He was scared to death to try, but there seemed to be no stopping the following day's session. He had to find out if the gorillas would relent if he successfully begged out of the hypnotherapy and future visits. Samuel had talked to Mom when she tucked him in for the night, and she basically agreed with Patrick. She wanted to at least give Hector the courtesy of showing up one more time. She wouldn't brook much of a discussion given the lateness of the hour.

So after lying in bed awake for the last four hours thinking about all this, Samuel finally left his bed and crept to the end table lamp, which was on a low setting (the night light was off). Dad still hadn't noticed it, thankfully. Samuel reached over quickly before he could lose his nerve and switched it off, which plunged the room into the deep blackness of living in the country with no street lights. His heart did its typical lurch whenever the dark came. He swallowed and tried to steady his nerves. *I have to be strong. This isn't just about me anymore. I have to do whatever I can to save my loved one's lives.*

He backed up carefully, knowing there was the desk with the office style chair just behind him. He had this all planned, mapped out before he switched off the light. He dropped into the waiting chair he had earlier pushed in the perfect place and closed his eyes. He took a few deep breaths to keep himself under control. He was now ready to release a thought to the monsters. If Peter was right, a connection had to be made to begin the telepathy.

I'm here. We have to talk.

Silence.

I tried. But the best I can do is go to the appointment and beg Dr. Santiago not to do the hypnotherapy and then see if we can stop completely. Is that okay? Will you leave him and his family alone? And my family?

Nothing.

Hello? Where are you? The lights are out, Patrick isn't in the room, and we're in the bedroom. The rules are all broken. Come on. Samuel could hear the fall crickets outside, but nothing more. It was perfectly still and calm around the window. Usually, he would have rejoiced for this and celebrated finally getting a good night's sleep. But not tonight.

He got up and walked as carefully as he could to the window. This was not part of the plan, so he really hoped he did not leave any big toys on the middle of the floor that he would kill himself on. But luckily, he made it with no delays. The top section of the window had an open view - since he and Patrick forgot to draw the shades earlier - so Samuel expected a repeat of many nights, a furry blood-speckled face staring back at him, baring its horrific teeth.

But when he gazed outside, all he could see was the dark and the shape of some trees swaying in the faraway woods but not movement around them.

Now he was angry. He did some non-audible screaming in his brain, *COME ON! ANSWER ME!*

Finally, he stopped with the effort, frowned, and cursed. "Shit." It wasn't going to happen. That was clear. He looked down at his hands. They weren't glowing, not that he thought that would help. But it only confirmed in his mind that all the supernatural were dormant this night.

The excitement had loosened his bladder a bit. So he tiptoed his way back to the lamp, managed to turn it on smoothly (he had been practicing), and stepped to the door. This was the one time Dad wouldn't yell if he left the bedroom; he hated it when he wet the bed. Not that it would even matter now: Claude still hadn't said one word to him since the drama on the deck. Samuel pushed away any thoughts of his sadness and opened the door. *No problem there either, like the other night.* He walked briskly down the hallway to the bathroom door, which was on the left side of the hall just past the closet where Mom kept his old toys. Their house was ranch style with everything on the ground floor, which made it easier for late night tiptoes. He could hear voices on the TV and Patrick chuckling as he entered the john. Samuel switched on the overhead light and immediately took care of his business. He hiked his pants up, stepped to the sink next to the toilet, and washed his hands. He looked at his face in the mirror, his mussed-up hair and sad face staring back at him. *I failed.* Knowing he shouldn't linger in case Dad suddenly came in - the bathroom door oddly had no lock, so they always had to tell each other when going in there – he turned to go. As he reached for the door, he could have sworn he heard a booming noise coming from the direction of his bedroom. *They've come!*

He ran down the hallway, not caring how much noise he made this time. *I need to catch them before they leave.* If Samuel had a chance to step back and listen to his thoughts, he would have realized how crazy that sounded. He was actively seeking out those who wanted to murder him. And why would they leave? And how would they even come with the lamp on? But rationality was gone, so he didn't ask these questions. All that mattered was he needed to have this conversation.

He slipped into the bedroom and shut the door, again probably louder than he should. His eyes darted around, but there was no one there, no shape, nothing. Disappointment returned as he realized that it was wishful thinking hearing that noise. He so wanted to protect his family and Hector that he was imagining things. *Just like Patrick thinks I am.* So Samuel resigned himself to go to bed, even if he couldn't sleep.

He began to walk to his bed, but then he noticed something. There was a heaviness in the air, a humid feel that wasn't there earlier. His eyes landed on the window, the all-familiar opening to the world of the gorillas. He noticed it was now dew-covered, and he was positive it wasn't that way before. And it looked weird somehow. He knew he shouldn't risk it, whether he wanted to talk to them or not, but he went the last few steps to investigate.

Then he saw it.

In the dewy, wet window, words were written there, right above the air conditioner. Samuel almost cried out and was glad he didn't, not wanting to wake anyone, especially Dad. And honestly, he was immobilized, stuck in place, not able to even mutter. He felt like his whole body was paralyzed, and that included his mouth. Stuck in another nightmare.

The words said: **TOO LATE**. Then they slowly disappeared.

*It **was** him, answering my call.* Samuel peered out the window, having no doubt that he'd view either huddling apes or their forms rushing back into the woods. But there was nothing except his mother's hedges and the pine trees lining the yard.

But as the humidity retreated and the room returned to its more breathable autumn night state, he knew they'd been there. And he had his answer.

Monday arrived, the start of a new school week and the day of the appointment. Samuel went to school but had a hard time focusing on anything but those words in the window from the night before. When Peter tried to talk about their mystical attack plan at lunch, he nodded his head and heard the words, but didn't really digest them. And he just toyed around with the broiled hot dog and mac & cheese that the lunch lady had spooned onto his plate, barely eating. He didn't even tell his buddy what had happened in his bedroom. Samuel just felt like he was in a waking dream, existing in a distracted daze. And he was glad Ms. Jeffers didn't call on him in class that day, as he was not competent mentally to tackle times tables, vocabulary, or any scholastic concern.

Finally, the school day ended, and he found himself walking through the front door of his house. He barely remembered the hike down Siegel Road and didn't look around cautiously for Steiner like he usually did. When he came into the kitchen, he wasn't shocked to see his Mom at the table with a completely white, sick-looking face. When she said these words, he didn't even react, "Honey, you can't go to your appointment today." She paused. "I have no idea how to tell you this, but...but...Dr.

Santiago..."

"He's dead," Samuel said.

"How could you...?"

Then Samuel dropped on the floor, and all went dark.

CHAPTER 7

The story was covered by the media, on TV, radio, and print. But it was mostly glossed over, like the fifty-word mention on channel 7's *Eyewitness News* by the ever reliable Irv Weinstein, while he shook his head in sadness. And this small paragraph in the local newspaper, *The Buffalo News*, from page five in the local section:

Downtown Psychiatrist Found Dead

Dr. Hector Santiago, age 35, a local psychiatrist and counselor whose Amherst practice Gates Psychiatry received various APA awards for the quality of service and community involvement, was found dead. His car was discovered at the bottom of one of Zoar Valley's gorges Monday morning, not far from his hometown of Gowanda, after his wife reported him missing Sunday evening. The vehicle apparently crashed through the guardrail, plummeting 350 feet, tearing apart the car, and killing him immediately. The state police believe an animal made him go off track, probably a deer, causing him to lose control of his Trans Am. He leaves behind his wife Marta and two sons, Juan, age ten, and Salvatore, age five.

That was what was reported to the news agencies. Some information and opinions were withheld. The authorities didn't understand how they never found a dead deer or another wild animal that could have caused Dr. Santiago to go off track. It was night, but the roads were dry, and no blood beside his own was found on the car. The damage to the vehicle prevented seeing the noticeable dent of a buck. No alcohol was found in his system postmortem, so his faculties shouldn't have been impaired. It was as if he was assailed by a phantom. But easier for them to suggest hitting a deer than a ghost or boogeyman. The police didn't share these questions with anyone outside the department, including the Santiago family. And the inquiry was filed away in the cold case boxes, never to be reviewed again.

But Samuel Redden knew what happened.

He spent days walking around his house and school like a zombie, barely acknowledging anyone but stopping to pay attention when Hector's name was mentioned, either by these reports or his family. Shelley figured this behavior was because of his sadness for Dr. Santiago, which was partly true, but it went much further than that. Samuel knew he was responsible. He was just as culpable in the death of that nice man as the bloodthirsty gorillas. If only he'd tried harder to convince Patrick to cancel the appointment. But he was just a little kid! Why was life so unfair?

This was the train of thought that went through his head during these few days. He went to school Tuesday but was quickly sent to the nurse when Ms. Jeffers became concerned with his lethargy and bloodshot eyes. Shelley had to pick him up around lunchtime. The next morning, his mom tried to let him stay home, which led to a massive argument with Claude that she ended up losing. So when Friday's school day ended, Samuel went directly from the front door and collapsed in his bed, not wanting to even eat. He didn't know he could be so exhausted. The boy learned a truth that adults with anxiety and depression learn much later in life: emotional exhaustion is often more trying than physical.

Samuel wasn't sure how long he was asleep when he heard his mom calling him, saying Peter was outside waiting to see him. It wasn't quite dark yet, so he imagined it was around six or seven. Turning in his bed and looking at his Superman battery clock on the end table, he saw he was in the ballpark but a little later than expected, 7:25. He didn't want to get up. He hoped to just lay there forever and never move. But his mom was knocking on the door now.

She's worried about me. She wants me to rebound, to get active again, talk to people. But she just doesn't get it. And she'll never know. I'll make sure of that.

So he got up reluctantly. He glanced back over to the end table and looked at the Daredevil card Hector gave him, lying there, wrinkled up a bit since he had been clasping it often when thinking about that poor man. He sighed sadly and had to forcibly push himself to walk out of the room. Peter was the one person he was willing to see. The one person who understood. That was the only real conversation he had all week, telling Peter Wednesday when they were outside at recess about what really happened to the doctor. He told him everything then: how Patrick and Mom refused to let him cancel the appointment, how he attempted communication with the creatures, the writing on the window. And he shared his sadness and guilt with his closest confidante. He managed not to cry, as that was the last thing he needed in front of the whole third grade. But Peter had known how much it was hurting him and did him the favor of not providing any suggestions or platitudes at that time, just listening.

He found Peter sitting on the same deck overlooking the pool where Samuel and his dad had their "heart to heart" almost a week ago, which felt more like a lifetime away. Darwin was at the edge of the pool, his long legs dipped in the water, his shoes and socks discarded nearby. Samuel pulled up one of the lawn chairs and dropped into it. The seat allowed him to be a little above the tall Peter and provided the benefit of avoiding direct eye contact. He stared ahead at the inner tube floating in the pool, listened to the sound of the water pump, smelled the chlorine, not really wanting to talk yet. And despite Peter's loquacious personality, he again was good enough not to speak until Samuel did.

Years later, Samuel realized this was the week when Peter Darwin actually became his best friend, and more than that, like a brother. He was exactly what he needed at that time. His family and teachers kept trying to get him to engage, but Peter allowed him time. It meant the world to him.

"I'm not sure I'm good company right now, Pete," Samuel said, after about five minutes passed. He kept looking ahead. "I don't really want to play or read comics or do much of anything. And I don't want to talk about it anymore." Thinking back on the conversation Wednesday at school, Samuel remembered how the only thing Pete did say to him was that it wasn't his fault. That he had to stop with the guilt. But Samuel just couldn't. *I destroyed that family.*

Peter nodded, and his long hair swished around his neck. "Got it, my man. As long as you're not blaming yourself any-more, so we can move on."

Samuel sighed, finally glancing down to meet Peter's almond-colored eyes. *Can he read minds?* "I was just thinking about that. But it *is* my f…"

Peter cut him off. "Do you want to continue with our plan or not?"

"Of course I do," Samuel said, "but I never wanted it to happen this way."

"That's obvious because you're a good guy. The gorillas are the bad guys, and they did a shitty, evil thing. They're to blame, not you. You tried to save Hector. No way can we shuffle on to the next step if you're stuck on the guilt."

"But…"

"No buts, you butt."

For a moment, there was silence between the two of them, and then Samuel burst out laughing. Peter then joined him, and both of them could not stop, tears rolling down their faces. It was the first emotional release Samuel had had in a long time. It made him feel good. He didn't turn around, but if he did, he'd have seen his mother looking out the window with a smile on her face.

"Butts are funny, right?" Peter said in between his almost hiccupping laughter.

This made Samuel keel over with more intense chortling. *Like Mom always says, "It's the simple things…"* He finally stopped laughing. "All right. Moving on, ok?"

Peter gave him a mock bow. "Yes, my liege."

Samuel smiled but managed not to start laughing again. "Have you figured anything out? What we do to tackle the supernatural stuff?"

Peter nodded. "I found someone."

"Someone?"

"She's a psychic. Her name is Madame Takari. She's in downtown Buffalo."

An adult would have turned their nose up at this suggestion. But Samuel Redden was eight-years-old and thought this sounded pretty nifty. One question gave him pause, though. "How can we do this? Is she really going to just see two kids without parents being there?"

"My dad, bro. He'll bring us in and leave us for the hour or how long it takes."

"Your dad? Really?"

"You remember Dad, right? Where do you think I get all my wonderful eccentricities? He's totally on board with the Madame."

Oh yeah, it's true. Mr. Darwin is a real flower child. He was actually at Woodstock. "He's still an adult, though. What did you tell him?"

"Heh, I just told him that I wanted to get in touch with my inner child and thought it would be far out to talk to a psychic. And mentioned after what happened to your shrink that you could use the distraction. Smart thinking, right?"

"You're amazing. Okay, when?"

"She has Saturday hours. No point in wasting time, right?"

"Nope. The gorillas won't wait. All right! Let's do it."

"Low five, baby!" Peter held his hand out towards his hip, and Samuel slapped it.

I hope this works. If so, you're going down, gorillas. You killed someone who was nice to me. He didn't deserve it, but you do. You deserve all the pain coming to you.

The City of Buffalo was the second-largest in the state. Nestled on the eastern end of Lake Erie, it basically pushed up to the border of Canada. A century prior, it had been a bustling port between the Great Lakes and the Atlantic Ocean.

THE GORILLAS ARE COMING

But Samuel's hometown had fallen into hard times. Two types of people would give you an answer as to why. The superstitious type would say that when President McKinley was assassinated in the city at the Pan-American Exposition in 1901 that a curse had gripped the area. But the more even-keeled would point to 1982 when Bethlehem Steel, in the satellite City of Lackawanna, one of the area's biggest employers, shut down much of its operations. Now Buffalo was knee-deep in economic turmoil, close to a depression state. If you traveled around certain parts of the urban crawl, it honestly looked like a ghost town, almost like some post-apocalyptic zombie flick. But Samuel liked the city, especially downtown, maybe just to see and hear more activity than on his dead-end road. The architecture was beautiful, though he couldn't say what he liked about it, and it was cool down by the boat harbor. Today, they were in one of the city's beaten-down, almost forgotten parts on the East Side, an area that his never tolerant father called "the black's shithole ghetto". But Mr. Darwin was such a different sort that he had no problems bringing them down there. "The establishment cronies might have a problem hanging on the streets, but not this Daddy-O," he said as he maneuvered his multi-colored hippie van to the corner of the street. Yep, Samuel knew where Peter got it from.

Madame Takari's shop was in a nondescript brick building right in the middle of the struggling business district. It was neither attractive nor dilapidated. Unadorned would have been the best word for the exterior. The only indication that it was a place of business was the following in block letters on the window of the door:

M.T.
PSYCHIC INTERVENTION

Mr. Darwin (Robert) escorted the boys to the door. The apple definitely didn't fall far from the tree. Mr. Darwin looked like he stepped right out of the Summer of Love: the full and long black rock star hair, holes in his jeans, rarely seen without a concert tee on (Led Zeppelin's *Houses of the Holy* today), and now walked down the sidewalk as if he were Mick Jagger strutting to *Start Me Up*. He was tall, 6'5, clearly the one who passed on that genetic trait to Peter, though not as awkward. Despite his counter-cultural looks, Robert was far from a burnout. He had a job at Radion Labs in Amherst, doing some kind of work with cell growth; Peter never could explain it to Samuel. Almost as soon as the door to Madame Takari's closed behind them (accompanied by the sound of chiming bells above it), the elder Darwin was immediately beckoned deeper into an inner sanctum by a thin hand sticking out through those hanging beads that Samuel thought previously were just something on TV shows and movies. Robert told the boys to stay in the empty lobby, and they sat down. This was a very different waiting room than Dr. Santiago's practice. There was a strong smell of incense. While there were pictures on the walls, they weren't of scenic pastoral images: they were psychedelic conglomerations of lines and stars that Samuel could only stare at for a couple seconds without feeling dizzy. The chairs weren't incredibly comfortable and clearly old, a design style you'd see at your grandma's house, an olive green- colored acrylic, and the one Peter was sitting in had the stuffing sticking out. But Samuel liked it. It felt real, simple, not trying to be fancy. Speaking of Peter, the smile never left his face, and Samuel guessed Robert was the same behind the curtain. This indeed was their kind of place. Far out, you know?

While they were waiting, few words were spoken; Peter even closed his eyes for a bit, and Samuel wondered what universe his friend might have landed in. At the same time, Samuel was feeling the fear again. Despite his admittance to Peter that what happened to Hector wasn't his fault, he knew that his nightmare reality was changing to involve other people, which scared him as he knew it was dangerous. And while he believed the supernatural avenue was the right one to take, he wondered if this Madame Takari was for real. He was only eight-years-old, but he knew there were hoaxes in this world, people who take advantage of the gullible. If she was that, he hoped they could see through her.

After about five minutes, Robert returned, told Samuel and Peter that all was good to go. He had paid the Madame for a half an hour of her time, and they could see her now. And she was groovy, man.

"Are you coming in, Dad?" Peter asked.

Robert stepped forward, ruffled his son's hair a bit, and put his arm around him. "No, my little hippie. This is yours and Sammy's spiritual journey." He winked at Samuel, and suddenly, the child felt a painful pang in his heart. *Why can't my dad be like this?* Robert continued, "And it is truly your journey together now. You're like Batman and Robin, Frodo and Sam, Han and Chewie. You're a team now. Dig it?"

"I dig!" Peter exclaimed.

"Dig," Samuel added, but in his heart, he was even more frightened. If Peter was indeed linked to him and his path, what chances did he have to survive? He couldn't handle anything happening to his pal.

"So go in, my heroes, and I will take a cool walk around the hood. See you when I see you." And with that, Robert put his sunglasses on and glided out the door.

Peter grinned at Samuel. Young Redden managed to smile back despite the thoughts pressing against his troubled mind. Peter then nodded towards the inner sanctum of Madame Takari and the welcoming beads.

Here we go.

◆ ◆ ◆

Madame Takari was the smallest woman Samuel had ever seen. He wondered if she was even four feet tall. Even though they had much growing to do, the two kids were taller than her, even Samuel. She was a middle-aged Asian woman of Vietnamese descent, with raven black hair, and she had the brightest red dress on, something his conservative mother would never wear. It appeared to sparkle, and then Samuel realized there was an actual gem on her necklace that created this illusion. She gave each boy her hand as they introduced themselves, and her skin was silky smooth, with long manicured nails on her fingers (colored black, which gave contrast to her dress). Her face was warm, welcoming. Samuel guessed her age was somewhere in the '30s. Samuel's fears almost melted away immediately. But his thoughts quickly turned to a negative realization: I felt the same with Hector.

Madame Takari asked them to sit in the two chairs facing her, the same type of worn seats as in the waiting room, and Samuel could see hers was no different. The inner sanctum was oddly bare. There was a string of lights around the room's border, similar to Christmas lights, but with a variety of nontraditional colors like purple and pink. The small, low desk she was sitting at had more incense burning in a couple candles. On the wall behind her was a single solitary framed picture; it was a map, and after Samuel squinted to read the words, he realized it was of Vietnam.

She smiled as she noticed him looking around. "I keep it simple in here." Her English was perfect, unbroken, and he immediately felt guilty for thinking she would sound something like the stereotyped singing Siamese cats in *Lady and the Tramp*. He may have been young, but he wasn't a baby and knew TV made stuff up. Her voice was so melodious, he almost felt like he would fall asleep if he continued listening to its tranquil music. "Keeping it unadorned allows us to focus on the quiet, internal, and the expanding universe," she added.

"That's smooth, milady," Peter said.

Madame Takari smiled. "You are the spitting image of your father, lad."

Peter crossed his fingers in a steeple and nodded, saying, "Namaste." *I'll have to ask him what that means.*

Madame Takari locked her eyes squarely on Samuel now, and he had a hard time keeping the gaze as her dazzling blue eyes were like looking into a raging ocean. "All right, Samuel. Robert gave me the reasons for why you two are here, but you can't fool me. You are the sole reason for our lovely visit." Samuel and Peter looked at each other with shocked faces. "Young Mr. Redden, your attention, please," Madame continued, breaking their puzzlement up with one of Ms Jeffers' favorite phrases. Samuel glanced back at this wise woman. "Tell me," she added. "Tell me all."

So he did.

After Samuel finished telling of the trials that had gripped his life lately (and he was kind of sick of describing this, to be honest), Madame Takari took a moment to herself. She closed her eyes for a while and was breathing so quietly that he wondered if she had fallen asleep. It was like Peter's meditations/trips, but she was so still, like a statue that had existed in that chair for hundreds of years. After what seemed like hours for the ever impatient and frightened Samuel, but was really two minutes, her eyes flashed open quickly, and she said, "You speak the truth."

"How can you tell?" The relief spread through Samuel's mind and, in turn, his body. It felt like getting handed a gallon of water after walking through the Sahara. *An adult believes me for real!* And unlike with Hector and Patrick, it was the truth this time.

"Samuel, I am attuned to the spirit world, and I can spot a phony from a mile away." *Ha! To think I was having the same thoughts about her coming in.* "This is all happening to you."

"My family thinks it's in my brain." He paused for a moment before continuing. This hesitation happened earlier as well during his story oration since it was hard to say the name. He swallowed and added, "Hector might have thought it was real, but I'm not sure if he was telling the truth." *Thanks to Pat, I'm questioning it now.*

She shook her head no. "Well, they're wrong. The gorillas are attacking through your mind, but they are real. I have no doubt. They can affect our world, hence your temporary marks and the damage to your room that is miraculously cured. The murder of that dear psychiatrist Hector clearly shows their impact on reality. It most likely does not serve them to be revealed to anyone but you yet, so they control how long these shreds of their trespass, evidence, last. You're a child and were born with belief. Unfortunately, the adults in your life have instilled doubt in you. I can't blame them since they're trying to protect you, but they're not helping. But before moving forward, I need to know these creatures more intimately."

"How will you do that?"

"It's a simple thing," Madame noted. "All I need is to touch the lifelines on your palm, and I will make an otherworldly connection."

90

"Okay," Samuel said, "but I'm scared." He wasn't planning on revealing his emotions to this person who was so recently a stranger, but it just came out.

"You can do it, Reddy. I believe in you, buddy!" Peter exclaimed, reaching out and giving Samuel a half hug.

Madame Takari's eyes latched onto Samuel's, and this time he didn't feel like looking away. There was a kindness there he had never experienced. "Fear is a natural response to this world, Samuel. You're brave for admitting it."

She's wonderful.

"I'm ready," Samuel said, smiling.

Madame beamed back at him. She then reached forward and turned Samuel's right-hand upside down. She then took those long nails and ran them along his palm, which tickled him. But that pleasant sensation changed quickly. Suddenly, she reached out with both hands and grabbed his arm hard. It actually hurt a little bit. When Samuel looked up to her face, he noticed her eyes were closed, and something else was happening to her. She began to shake as if in a seizure. *This isn't supposed to be happening.* Her tremors increased to the point where she looked like she was vibrating. He looked down at his lower arm and noticed it was turning red; the color was running up to his t-shirt sleeve, and the pain was getting intense. He was wearing a *Muppets* t-shirt and could see Kermit's face twisting as his body was wrenched. He was amazed at how those little hands could be so strong. "Please stop," he whispered.

He looked over to Peter pleadingly, and his best friend wasted no time, jumping up and running over to Madame Takari, his long legs taking him there in an instant. He started to shake her hard, not saying a word, but his face was strained in a grimace. Abruptly, Samuel felt that tight grip ripped from him as Madama Takari was hurled backward and slammed into the back wall. Amazingly, the chair came with her and she didn't change position, but hitting the wall didn't stop the shaking. Samuel knew he and everything else in the room were still but watching this nice lady vibrate like the superhero Flash made him feel like he was experiencing an earthquake. It was déjà vu from the experience in his bedroom sometimes. The picture of the map fell, landing on the floor next to her, shattering the glass frame. Samuel couldn't help it; he let out a little scream. Peter stood transfixed with his hands at his side as if in a dream.

This continued for a solid minute. Samuel wanted to run but couldn't leave this poor woman alone. The guilt came back. *If she dies because of me...* But he still didn't know what to do.

Finally, it subsided.

Madame Takari exhaled in a deep breath and slowly opened her eyes. The blue in her irises looked like it was diminished. She murmured something in another language; Samuel wondered if it was Vietnamese. Her hair was damped in sweat, and her skin was as white as his Mom's pristine sheets. Her body then shuddered, but Samuel was sure this was from within, not whatever that force was. This powerful psychic, who exuded so much life just a few minutes ago, appeared to Samuel as he imagined he was after the gorilla visits, shaken, disturbed. She looked in an unfocused way at Samuel and said, "I won't abandon you, my boy. But I must make arrangements."

"Arrangements for what?" Samuel asked.

"We must purge these unholy monsters from your brain. I will explain more later, but now I am too exhausted. But if they manage to escape the hold you have over them and break into our world, all will be lost."

CHAPTER 8

Samuel and Peter sent Robert back in to see the Madame at her request. While they waited in the van, he spent another twenty minutes with her alone. Before she asked them to send the elder in, Madame asked if she could share a little of Samuel's situation with Mr. Darwin; she said it was the responsible thing to do. She promised to skirt the whole truth of the matter; she would tell him that Samuel was facing a metaphysical attack from the recent trauma of losing Hector and needed Robert's involvement so an adult was in the loop. She knew Samuel's family was a no-go but could tell Pete's dad was more open. The two grownups had this conversation, and Robert agreed to return the following morning with the boys. He was actually excited about the karmic influences of the universe affecting the children.

Earlier, after recovering her faculties, Madame explained what she "saw" to Samuel and Peter. She said that during her touching of Samuel's lifeline, she glimpsed both wonderful and terrible things before the evil stopped her. But the terrible was more at the forefront right now. Samuel was special in ways she didn't completely understand, but he was too young to handle this threat. The Gorillas started in his nightmares, in his head, but they were now forcing their way through to our world. So she must, in essence, erase them from Samuel's brain. If he couldn't think of them, then he couldn't dream of them, and they would not threaten our world.

Samuel was a good kid, so he didn't immediately think of himself. Later in the van, as Robert merged them recklessly onto Interstate 190 for their thirty-minute drive back to the burbs, young Redden said, concerned, "But what about Madame Takari? Tomorrow morning isn't soon enough! They will kill her like they did Hector." He knew he was probably saying too much since Robert didn't have the whole story, but the infinitely open-minded hippie only smiled in the mirror with a knowing look. *He may not know about the gorillas, but he understands that big things are going on here.*

"Nope, cool dude," Robert replied, his head bopping up and down to Dio's *Holy Diver* blasting away from his tape deck. He dug in his jeans pockets and took out a carton of his Winston cigarettes and stuck one in his mouth before adding, "That groovy momma is Wiccan. She told me she will have a couple of her cool sisters over within the hour to cast a spell in her place, the business downstairs, and her living abode above. She may not be strong enough to defeat the evil forces assailing you for good, but she can keep them at bay for a day."

"Wiccan? Like witches?" Peter asked his father. "That far out stuff is real?"

Robert looked back over his shoulder, smiling at the boys who were sitting on the long passenger side tie-dyed upholstered bench. He lit his cigarette with the car lighter and opened the window to puff out a mist of smoke. He knew it was an ugly habit, but he always tried his best to spare little Pete the second-hand effects. "There is more in heaven and earth than is dreamt in your philosophy, hip Horatio," he remarked with gusto. Samuel and Peter, not exactly Shakespearean scholars, looked at each other with confused expressions at this paraphrase. "You boys need some culturing," Robert continued, "but for now, just know that all is good. Tomorrow it gets real."

◆ ◆ ◆

Night again. It was 10:30. Samuel was under the covers for the evening but couldn't fall sleep. There were no visits from the gorillas, luckily. The lamp was off this night, but the night light was doing its job. But his mind was racing.

I just can't believe that it might be over for now. I can live a normal life? He wasn't sure he'd ever been as excited as he was now, not even on the many Christmas Eves that had passed over the years. He felt like all his emotions should be positive, but something was nagging at him. It was his hands, not only the mystery of it but the power that he sensed when he felt that heat and illumination. *I'll miss the rush it gave me. I won't remember it, will I?* He knew his parents' basic memories had faded as they got older, and his situation was even more extreme: it sounded like the Madame's powers would remove all trace of remembrance of these fantastic happenings, the good and the bad. Then he had a sudden thought. And it was an impetuous one. *I need to try to talk to him again. Maybe if he realizes they will be banished, he will give me answers.* Yes, this was not a logical decision by the youngster, but kids rarely take time to realize the logic of things. He got up from his bed and walked directly to the night light in the far corner, his will resolute, not thinking of all the failures previously experienced in this room.

He immediately bent down and started to move his hand towards the little switch. But he stopped there. Or maybe something stopped him. *Holy crap, what am I doing? I'm giving them a chance. A chance to just kill me. Stupid.* So Samuel resigned himself to the fact that his golden hand mystery would remain one for many years, maybe a lifetime. He decided that being a kid was just okay for now. That it would actually be wonderful.

He returned to his bed, briefly looking at the usually ominous window halfway through his steps and grinning. *You won't be able to hurt me anymore, you fuckheads.* It doesn't take much to rally a child, to light the fire of hope in their hearts and instill confidence, even for an awkward, nervous one like Samuel Redden. And he thought this was more than a little possibility of salvation: this sounded like a real solution. He believed in the Madame.

He slid under his blankets again, laid his head down, and gripped his Scooter stuffed animal to his chest. He tossed and turned there for another couple of hours, thinking about the following day and the session. But he eventually did fall asleep. And he dreamed.

This wasn't Samuel's typical dream of killer gorillas and impending death. This was more what someone would call an ordinary dream. He wouldn't remember it for thirty-five years. But if he had, he would have realized that someone out there wanted to give him answers. He was in the deep woods across the street from his house. Where *they* ran to. He should have been terrified, but he wasn't. The woods that he could see in every direction were dark here, scary, something out of *Grimms' Fairy Tales*, but his attention was fixated on a specific structure. What he was looking at in his immediate area was both frightening and fascinating. And the fascination overruled. It was an old gnarled tree standing alone in a clearing. It spoke of ages gone, ancient and forgotten. And Samuel felt like it wanted to talk to him. So he approached. He walked around the tree several times, marveling at the knots shaped into its bark, making it almost look like some alien creature. Then he stopped. He could have sworn in one of the larger weathered gaps that eyes were looking out at him. But as soon as they appeared, these round pinpricks of light were gone. He thought about those eyes for a second. They weren't evil and foreboding, but caring and thoughtful, and also in a way trusting, like cow eyes. They actually reminded him of how Madame Takari looked at him. "Hello?" he said. He thought his voice sounded weird, but he pushed that idea away quickly; his focus was still on what was happening. "I won't hurt you." He thought it might have been some small animal in there, and he was sad that he had frightened it away. He reached out with his right hand and touched the tree's rough surface near where he saw the eyes. And then it happened. He felt heat, and his hand started to glow. "Ah, this," he said. He looked at it and made a fist, wondering what he could do.

"The shiny hand! It's back again, Daddy-O!"

He jumped at hearing the voice and looked to the left of him. Robert Darwin was standing a few feet away, with an excited expression on his face. But in the next instant, he realized this thin, long-haired hippie was his old friend Peter grown up. Not sure how he knew, but there was no doubt in his mind. That made Samuel look at his hand again, and he was surprised to see that the appendage was actually larger than it should be, with more lines of age in it.

Samuel awoke. Like many dreams, this remained with him for a few minutes. So he had time to think, *was that the future?* Then it was gone. He was asleep again.

◆ ◆ ◆

October 2nd. Samuel awoke again a few hours later at 6:00 A.M. and was unable to go back to sleep. So he got up, took a bath, and got dressed. He picked his favorite t-shirt to wear this time, the *Return of the Jedi* movie poster one, with Luke's hands holding his lightsaber. He thought he would need the courage that Luke showed standing up to the Emperor. Han might have been his favorite, but he needed to be a noble Jedi today. He was at the kitchen table, finishing his Lucky Charms cereal around 7:30 when his mother came into the kitchen and asked him why he was up so early. He explained that Peter's dad was taking the three of them downtown again, this time to the science museum. These were agreed-upon lies. The day before, they had gone to the park. He felt pretty horrible lying to his family like this, but he decided it was a necessary evil. His mother especially was too grounded in the real world, and the only supernatural she would allow was of the Roman Catholic Church. Speaking of the church, she grudgingly let him skip 10:00 mass to have fun with his friend. She knew after everything he had gone through, he needed it. Before he left, he gave her a big hug. *Things will be better now, Mom.*

Robert and Peter arrived five minutes later. They were supposed to be at Madame Takari's promptly at 8:00. The three *men* - what Robert called them all now since they were no longer boys in going through this trial - didn't speak much on the way. Instead of his typical 60's and 70's rock and roll playing on the van sound system, Robert had on some sort of far eastern instrumental music to get "in the mood."

After they pulled into the same spot as yesterday, a half block away from the Madame's, Robert put out his current cigarette in the ash tray and turned to face the youngsters in the back. "Once again, this is your thing, my men. Yours alone. But I'm sending positive vibes your way from out here in the wide world." He put his fist out to Samuel. "This will work, Sammy. As sure as any Oracle's prediction. This lady is absolutely the real deal." They fist-bumped.

Peter opened the van's sliding door so the duo could jump out, and they proceeded to walk in step towards the building's entrance. Samuel felt chilly, and it wasn't just that it was starting to feel like proper fall weather outside, crisp and breezy. His nervousness was making him shake a little. He zipped his aqua-colored jacket up a bit and tried to ignore the fluttery feeling in his stomach. Before they reached the door, Peter said to his friend, "Well, this is it. Dad's probably right, and it will work." Peter looked pensive for a moment.

"What is it?" Samuel asked.

"Hope this doesn't make me a lowdown buddy, but that was kind of fast. I thought we'd be these magical adventurers or something. Now we'll just be normal kids, I guess. Oh well."

Samuel smiled. "I was thinking the same thing last night. I actually almost invited the gorillas into my room to find out more about my hand thing. So don't feel bad."

Peter put his arm around Samuel. "We're still cooler than anyone else at school, though, dude. Especially the dumb jocks." Peter had learned this term from his teenaged cousin and liked to use it loosely about any kid they knew who was better than them at sports, which was a large majority really. "Even if we forget all this as planned, we had this time that no other kids ever will. And we'll still be best buds."

Samuel felt warmed by this thought and encouraged by his goofy but caring pal. "Forever," he said, nodding.

Peter flipped him a thumbs up. "Let's do it."

Samuel opened the door to Madame Takari's. The bells above the door rang like a wind chime. She was about two inches from the entry. She couldn't have had a more serious expression on her face. "Let's begin, my friends," she said.

Before following the Madame, Samuel closed his eyes and said a brief "Our Father", hoping the prayer that his mom told him to say each night before bed would finally work this time.

Samuel and Peter were seated in the exact place they were the previous day. The room was slightly different now. Above them, at junctures all over the ceiling, hung down plant-like objects. They reeked in an overpowering odor, and Samuel wondered if at least some of them were garlic. He was right, and there was also sage, dill, rue, and thyme. He observed statues placed on various tables all around the space. These comprised a diverse collection from multiple religions and faith systems in the world: Jesus, Buddha, and some of the pagan persuasion (Earth Mother, Greek goddess Hecate, Norse god Odin). Samuel only recognized two of them for sure, Christ from his upbringing and Odin from his comics, although Buddha wasn't completely unknown to him either; he couldn't put a name on the meditative Enlightened One, but he recalled seeing a similar sculpture in Robert's yoga room. He looked around at the solemn, carven images for a few moments before the mystic began to talk to them about what would happen. She repeated the basics of what she had told them the day before. That it was necessary to purge the memory of the gorillas from Samuel's brain to keep them from breaching into our world. She would involve Peter in the spell as he would need to forget too. Then she would have Robert come in separately to have a chat. This was an old Wiccan spell that would eradicate the gorillas and their whole world from his mind and leave them in a sort of limbo.

Samuel had questions that needed to be answered before they started. "Ma'am, did you see anything about me in your visions? Something is happening with my body right now," he held up his hands, "and if you banish the gorillas, I'm afraid I'll never know what it means."

Madame Takari nodded. "Yes, I know of your gifts, Samuel Redden, very intimately now after touching your lifeline. But it's best you do not have this knowledge yet. One day you will face this challenge and rise to it with all that is inside you, but you are too young now."

Damn. "Okay, I'm sure you know best. And if it means I can be free of the monsters, I sacrifice this," Samuel looked down and wiggled his fingers now resting on his lap. "Though I thought I was an X-Man or something. That would have been cool."

Madame Takari brought back her warm smile. "You are truly brave." She looked at Peter now as well. "Both of you. But it's time to exile these unholy monsters until you are ready." She paused before adding, "And the responsibility belongs to you as well, Peter Darwin. Together you will face them in the future." The kids looked with surprised expressions at each other. "I will reveal that much," she continued. "Your friendship will endure, and it is your unity that one day will beat the creatures."

"Cool," Peter said.

"Groovy," Samuel added, winking at Peter. Which made the young flower child break out in laughter.

Madame Takari then glanced at the clock behind them on the wall. It was another item that looked like it came from the Orient, its face covered with symbols Samuel did not understand. "But now we must start, for my sisters' spell is wearing off within the hour. I don't believe the gorillas can attack in the daytime, thanks to your rules, Samuel, but we must do the rite with darkness in the room, so haste is required."

The Madame got up, entered the reception area, and Samuel could hear her locking the front door. When she returned, she closed two black curtains together across the threshold leading to that other room, jangling the beads as she did this. "Join hands, my brothers, and be united in the flesh along with the soul," she instructed. He and Peter did not hesitate one second doing what she asked, and Samuel was pleased that his pal's palms were sweaty too. Madame Takari soundlessly walked to the far wall, turned off the overhead light switch, and closed the drapes covering the sanctuary's two windows. It was now completely dark, and a fear shuddered through Samuel, but he pushed it back with logic. *Like she said, it's daytime. They have no domain here.* But another jolt of terror hit Samuel as he sensed a presence behind him.

"It is only I," Madame said. *She moves like a spirit. I had no idea she was right there.* "I must be behind the two of you to perform the ceremony." Then she breathed in deep and placed her two hands on the kids' heads. She began to chant in a language Samuel was sure wasn't Vietnamese this time. It made him feel peaceful, though, so he closed his eyes while reminding him-self to not fall asleep, daytime or not. While the gorillas were now clawing their way out of his mind and into the world, they first started as dreams and nightmares. That was still where they derived their power. While he thought about all this, Peter was humming beside him, maintaining his Zen.

Suddenly, even though Madame had turned off the switches, the lights began to flash on and off. Samuel sensed this and opened his eyes, and it was unnerving seeing the room con-tinually blink out of reality and then return again. This made him want to run; it was causing his stomach to ache in fear. He tried to shut all this out, but his eyes were stuck, forced to watch. Only a few moments had passed, but it was torturous in its intensity. It didn't feel like the real world anymore - more like he was experiencing some kind of unholy purgatory and half-life. Then he could have sworn he saw something gather-ing in the corners of the room each time the light flickered back on. Shadowy hirsute figures. *THE GORILLAS!* Soon he heard a buzzing and deduced that it was a communal growl from the monsters. They were trying to push through despite the pro-tections. *The darkened room probably let them come, but they're*

THE GORILLAS ARE COMING

limited since it's daytime, so they're using this light show to scare us.

"Oh, boy," was all Peter said. *Well, at least I know it's not my imagination. But their appearance here just proves the Madame is right. They're coming through to our world more easily now.*

At that moment, Madame Takari spoke in a voice that didn't even sound like her own. It was loud, angry, commanding, and Samuel wasn't sure who he should be more afraid of, the gorillas or her. As a result of her incantations, the sporadic lighting ended. Now back in the blackness, he could not see her, but she had her hands up and was sprinkling some kind of fluid in the air from a vial she had hidden in her pocket, letting it land on Samuel and Peter's heads. "BE GONE, CREATURES OF THE NIGHT. BE GONE FROM THE MINDS OF THESE INNOCENTS. BE SENT TO THE NOTHINGNESS THAT YOU DESERVE. BE STUCK IN THE DARK PLACE, NEVER TO BROACH THE LIGHT!"

She now dropped the vial and latched onto both of their heads tightly, and Samuel felt a pain like he'd never experienced before. It was as if someone had stuck a live wire into his cranium. It radiated from his head down to the tips of his toes and gave a sensation of burning, of fire. Looking over to Peter, he could see his friend going through the same agony, his face red and twisted in agony, gasping for air. Samuel was sure he didn't look any better himself and heard a whimper escape his lips, a beaten dog sound.

Madam screamed, "Don't let go, my heroes! It is almost complete!"

So Samuel and Peter gripped each other more tightly in their pain throes. Samuel wasn't sure how either of them wasn't screaming and thought briefly that maybe they were tougher than the bullies at school knew. He felt like he would crush Darwin's hand he was holding so firmly, and both of them were now trembling with the effort. But Samuel also felt comfort in that they were going through this together. *If I was alone, I would be taking on all this torture. It's split between us.*

When Samuel thought he could take no more, he heard it all around the room: inhuman screams, animalistic hungry howls that he had to fight with all his power to not cover his ears from. In his brain, he then heard, **WE WILL FIND A WAY OUT, SAMUEL REDDEN, AND YOU WILL PAY FOR THIS AFFRONT MORE DEARLY THAN YOU CAN IMAGINE!**

Then silence.

◆ ◆ ◆

Now all that was left in the room were two shaken and bewildered boys and a proud-looking woman in a mystic's shop. This lady turned on the lights so the kids could see her better. *Where am I? Who is this person?*

"What's going on? Who are you, groovy madam?" Peter, in his own way, voiced Samuel's question.

Madame Takari grinned at them kindly and simply said, "Let me get your father." She moved like a cat, pushing aside the curtains to the adjoining room and leaving the building.

In the interim, Samuel and Peter just stared at each other, finding no more words. Within mere minutes, Mr. Darwin returned to the shop with the Madame to finish his part in this story. She asked the youngsters to go wait in the car, to which Robert nodded. They left. Then Madame Takari did an individual rite of removing anything the elder Darwin remembered from the last few days. When he came to, she explained that he and the boys had come to have their palms read, and everything was cool, dude. He should explain this to Samuel and Peter as the experience had left them a bit fuzzy too.

Over the next several days, Madame Takari and/or her sisters paid visits to Samuel's mother, brother, father, Ms. Jeffers, the receptionist at Hector's office, Steiner, anyone who knew or experienced anything regarding Samuel's nightmares. They posed as salespeople or prospective patients, whatever it took. An innocent tap on the shoulder or touch on the hand was enough to do a simpler version of the spell.

The existence of the gorillas was eradicated from all knowledge in this dimension.

For now.

Samuel Redden was indeed granted that normal childhood everyone wanted for him, and then he transitioned to be a college student, working person, a husband, and father. And despite the trials and tribulations of any person living in this fallen and damaged world, his life was unremarkable. But evil like this is hard to keep down.

The gorillas would return.

INTERLUDE ONE – THE MEETING (2015)

Madame Takari hadn't changed a lot. Her hair was gray now, and she walked more slowly, but she still had her business. And her powers. She was currently taking out the garbage behind her place when she noticed a stirring behind the dumpster. A person not as attuned to life's permutations as she wouldn't have sensed it, but she was constantly cognizant of all existence in both this world and beyond. She smiled.

"Hello, Madame," a figure spoke. It was a sweet voice, almost song-like, and seemed to reverberate from a great distance.

"My old friend," she said. She dropped her refuse in the bin and then embraced this person who kept out of view of the nearby street light. The shadow now bent from the wall behind the dumpster and appeared to be the size of a giant, though a rational person would have called that an illusion. But Madame also looked up as they hugged; again, however, a sensible mind would argue that she was a small creature. "Is it the anniversary again?"

"You know that, but I appreciate the small talk. It is a lonely existence I live when I am apart from you," the visitor said, sadness underlying its honeyed tone. "Three decades today."

"Amazing. Time continues to flow quickly, too much like the sands of an hourglass. And I apologize for not seeing you in a while. I'm sure you wish to know how he is."

"Of course. I can only sense so much."

"His life is still filled with love and family. The little one is such a joy to both of them. She's in middle school now, even starting to notice boys. The marriage is still stronger than anything life throws at them. He continues to feel a bit aimless in his work, but we both know that will one day change. Most of his life is blessed, which warms my heart. But now he's just months away from the event."

"Yes. The biggest tragedy of his adult life. I wish we didn't have this foreknowledge. Oh how it will devastate him. It often racks me with sadness." It whispered this last part, the verbalism cracked with even more profound emotion.

"And yet puts him on the path," Madame said while sighing. "If I had it in my power to stop it, I would, but he must proceed to his destiny, for what comes next." Silence from the dark corner, but she knew her ally was agreeing. Madame Takari suddenly felt crestfallen, exhausted. "He deserves a lifetime of peace. At least his human struggles are normal, somewhat expected. But what about *them*? I really shouldn't try it again? Maybe that will hold them back longer. I could visit him just as we did his family; he wouldn't remember me."

"No," the being stated strongly. "There is nothing we can do to stop the wheels in motion now. It's almost his time for rediscovery no matter how hard or tragic it will prove to him or this world."

"Yes, of course I know. And we'll be ready. To aid him again."

She stepped closer to the other, touching its chest. "Will you stay longer? We can make sure no one sees you."

"No. I must not be reckless despite my longing." The head dropped.

Madame moved her hands to the individual's face, stroking it. "You're right. My love goes with you." She got on her tippy toes and kissed its forehead. She then turned to leave and wind stirred garbage in the alley. She looked back longingly.

But the silhouette was gone. The Madame returned to her back door. And the gorillas continued to wait for their chance.

PART TWO –
EVIL HAS MANY
FACES (2020)

CHAPTER 1

Samuel Redden awoke. He was sweating. As the fog of sleep cleared from his mind, he realized he was shaking as well. He reached over to the nearby end table, turned on the lamp, grabbed his cup of water sitting there, and took a big gulp. *Man, I guess I had a bad dream. I don't remember ever having one that intense, though.* He sat up and took a big breath. He figured it was about her. Sandy. It had been five years since she died, and while he was mostly able to keep the sad thoughts out of his conscious mind, there certainly was no control over the unconscious. He figured something had slipped through. *I just hope I didn't cry out or anything and wake up Amanda. She's a lot like her old dad, not able to get back to sleep if waking up at...* He then pulled his cell phone over from the same table and noticed the time, 3:15. "Well, shit," he said, "probably not getting any more sleep tonight."

He put his feet on the floor and cast his eyes around the dark room. There was some light cast from the street lamp outside, but it was a room of dark shapes. One for the dresser straight ahead of his bed with its framed family pictures on top, one for the ajar closet door in the same corner, its opening like a maw, and finally, the windows themselves to the right, dull eyes that looked dumbly over the living space. Accepting that he needed to find something to do until getting ready for work, Samuel went out the door and down the hallway. The bathroom was only a few feet away, so he went in there, relieved himself, and then looked in the mirror. Looking back at him was a forty-three-year-old who looked older than his years. His face had lines in it, and the eyes contained bags under them. He still had the brown hair from his childhood, but it had started to develop into a receding hairline, so he had it buzz cut once a month. Back in his bedroom, he had his glasses in their case, both for distance and for bi-focal use. Usually, he would be wearing them. He was not a bad-looking man but was a much cuter child; he didn't exactly age well. Or maybe he was just unspectacular, ordinary. Like many, life had taken a toll on him, but that wasn't the only explanation. Once his teen years hit, he hadn't stood out in the looks department. Girls had never gravitated to him, but that part had to do with his shyness and awkwardness too. There had been Sandy. *But she was special.*

He again pushed away thoughts about his lost wife and began wondering about that dream. There was an aftereffect, a fear, like it was more important than a simple nightmare. *I feel like I just experienced something significant, went through a kind of ringer.*

He was going to dive into it more mentally, as he was one of those people who tended to stew on things. But even he knew it was a waste of time. *If I'm not going to sleep, I might as well read until I need to get up.* So he walked further down the hallway to the next door, his den, his refuge.

After a few minutes, he could hear her crying.

It was muffled but unmistakable. It filtered under the bedroom door all the way down to where he was reading his book. It was a good book, a Richard Bachman (A.K.A. Stephen King) novel about a sadistic game show, the one they made into that bad Arnold movie, but the noise from the other room broke any chance of concentration. There's something genetic that pulls a father out of whatever he's doing when he hears his kid cry. It touches something deep, even more profound than the level of the heart. It rattles your being. It goes back to the days when she first woke up in the middle of the night, needing to be fed or comforted. Every few years, it was something different: falling off her bike when she was six, raging over the 75 on the Algebra test when ten, even simple things like tearing up the first time she watched *Forrest Gump*, her favorite movie. And, of course, the big one, the loss that shook their lives to the core.

But Samuel still couldn't go to that emotional place right now. Not just because of the pain it would cause him and how it could send him deep into the recesses of melancholy but also because Amanda was hurting, alone in her room. Soon she would start to hold it in and begin to sob, and then it would worsen as she tried not to cry. He needed to go to her. She may not need him: it could be a YouTube video from The Dodo about a rescued dog, but it was his job to check. He knew he could cheer her up, even though it seemed like more of a magic trick now that she was fifteen. They were still infinitely close as father and daughter, but as school demands, boys, and puberty dominated her life, problems were more challenging for him to solve. *But no one ever said parenting would be easy, right? It sure as hell hasn't been since…nope, not going to do it.*

Samuel pushed himself up out of his cushy desk chair as its wheels rolled it back a couple inches. Even though he knew he couldn't fall back to sleep, he felt exhausted. *God, sometimes I feel more like 60 than 43.* The bones ached, reminding him of the two minor back surgeries from back in the day, bringing with it arthritic tightness. He put the library receipt inside the page of his book where he left off and placed it on the desk. He felt the warmth of the furnace vent on the ceiling blow down against his face – he had just turned on the heat before bed when the temperature dropped below 40 for the first time in the fall season. The smell coming up from the basement wasn't the best; it had that burning odor that often accompanied the system's initial cycling.

Going back down the short upstairs hallway in his 1950 Cape Cod, he idly glanced at the various family photographs framed on the wall. A lot of happiness over the years, he thought. Despite the hard times, despite the tragedies no family should face, there had been so many good times. He wasn't a church-going religious man – though he did consider himself spiritual – but he thought it was essential to look at the blessings and acknowledge the optimistic side of life. He'd always been that way, ever since he was a small boy. He had been a happy kid, a joyful type, and even with the depression, social anxiety, and obsessive-compulsiveness that came when he hit his 20's, he still maintained that viewpoint of life. He hoped that he had passed that along to Amanda. So far, it seemed that way. She could be moody like most teens now that she had hit that age, but overall she was still so pleasant to be around, fun to be her friend.

He reached her door, which was across from his own bed-room, and knocked gently. Another character trait here. Samuel had always been a quiet person, unobtrusive, and it was probably those features that allowed him to approach his daughter no matter the time of day or night. She never felt like he was butting into her business. "Yeah?" he heard her feminine yet slightly husky voice call out. She then cleared her throat, probably trying to get herself under some kind of control after the crying.

"It's Dad, sweety."

"Who else is it going to be? Harper's knock has a little more nail to it." The sense of humor. Another thing he loved about her. Harper was their Saint Bernard mix, the valued third family member in their household.

113

"Heh. Can I come in?" Again, the absence of pushiness.

"Sure, Dad."

He opened the door and entered. Amanda was a cleanly person, yet another way she took after dear old dad, so he was not greeted by the sights and smells of the typical teenager sanctuary. No food containers lying around on her desk, no random pieces of clothes strewn around the room, no excessive coating of dust on the windowsill. Books were organized on the shelf in author order by the last name. She had some school papers and books along with her tablet on her desk, but no junk or garbage strewn about the surface. And the clothes were in the hamper, even though the sleeve of a shirt stuck out of the top. It smelled good, but Samuel wasn't sure of the aroma. Probably some combination of her perfume and Glade. She had posters or pictures tacked up around the room, a nice variety of topics. There were musical stars (Lady Gaga and Adele), book ones (*A Wrinkle in Time, To Kill a Mockingbird, Harry Potter*), movie sheets (*Crazy Rich Asians, John Wick, Wonder Woman*), TV show themed (*The X-Files* and *Game of Thrones*), and inspirational sayings with bright bucolic visuals and animals ("Life's an Adventure," a cat "hanging in there"). Her bed was pushed against the far wall, and that was where she was, laptop propped on her lap.

"What's up? What are you doing up so late?" she asked, looking up from the computer.

Samuel could see the telltale signs of crying, her eyes swollen red a bit, barely discernable moistness to the cheeks, something a passerby on the street might not notice or even a casual friend, but he was her father.

"Had a dream, a weird one, I think," he said, "can't get back to sleep." In his fifteen years of parenting, he learned to not jump into things, not appear threatening or judgmental; that way, she would be more comfortable to talk.

"Yeah, sleepless night for me too."

"Is that why your eyes are red?" Some would think that was a bit much, but Samuel knew this relationship. It was time.

"I know you heard me, Dad."

He walked further into the room and sat at Amanda's desk, pivoting the office chair on its wheels (a twin to his seat in the den) to face her. "Do you want to talk about it? Anything serious?"

She pushed her laptop off her. Amanda was a pretty girl, with an oval face, long auburn hair that curled at mid-neck, fairer features. She was more like her mother than Samuel in this area; his visage had darker, sharper lines with his brown hair and subtle green eyes. Amanda's blue irises were large, bright, thoughtful, and they now beheld him for a moment. "It's Kyle."

Kyle Green was Amanda's best friend. They had been buddies since kindergarten. With Amanda being his only child, Samuel never got the chance to have a son. Kyle was the closest he would get. Samuel (and Amanda) had spent countless lunches, dinners, evening outings at the Green household. And Kyle was over to their place so often that he genuinely seemed like a member of the family. So Samuel knew him well. There were the basic facts of the young man: he was also the only kid under his own roof, he was a scholar-athlete, and had a great well of enthusiasm and energy. And the most intimate things weren't hidden from Amanda's dad either. The big one? Kyle was gay. Since Samuel felt so strongly about the kid, his heart skipped a beat when he heard what Amanda said. "Is he okay?" He knew things weren't easy for Kyle; not only was he gay, but he was also a black kid in a neighborhood that was still transitioning out of an old, white demographic. When Kyle came out a year earlier and Amanda had told him, Samuel used the words "double whammy". He added at the time, "Try to find two groups of people more discriminated and bullied than gays and blacks. I'll wait."

After a significant pause, Amanda finally answered his question. "Well, no. He's getting bullied online again."

Samuel sighed. Online bullying. With all the benefits of the internet, he didn't want to sound like an eighty-year-old, but he often wondered if the negatives outweighed the positives. Especially for someone like Kyle. "Tell me."

She looked down and started to twirl her hair with her fingers, a nervous habit she had since five-years-old. After about ten seconds of this, she said, "It was on Twitter. All he did was retweet something about white privilege and institutional racism, and some MAGA assholes started in on him. You can imagine what they called him when they took a look at his profile. We reported them, but the damage was done. I talked to him for a few minutes, and he was crying, Dad." Amanda put her head in her hands for a minute, which Samuel saw as a very adult thing to do. But kids nowadays had to grow up so much faster, he knew. And Amanda was always mature for her years. He also knew that she was trying to stifle back more tears and be tough. Again, Kyle was like her brother, which was hard on her, but life had taught her to be stoic, strong.

"You know you don't have to do that with me, right?" he said. *No sense in ignoring it.* "I know we both try to be so strong-willed, but if we can't be vulnerable with each other, what's the point of it all?"

And then it came. The floodgates opened. Amanda burst out crying with deep sobs, her body shaking like a small rowing boat in turbulent waters. He knew it was time to step forward more. Samuel moved to her bed and sat next to her. He didn't reach out but didn't have to. Amanda crumpled towards him, wrapping her arms around his waist and burying her wet face into his shoulder. "Why are people this way? Why such hatred? I don't think I'll ever get it." The words came out muffled, breathless.

Honesty. It's the only way we've operated. "I have no goddamn clue, Mandy." He didn't often use this pet moniker since he loved her full name. It was more from her childhood, but in sensitive moments like this, he found it appropriate. "It's always been there. I can only say that people who want to stay in power over others are usually weak in heart. So they need to prop up themselves by attacking those different from them. It's tribalism, and it's getting worse daily. But it's never exactly been good for certain groups of people. Especially blacks, LGBTQ, Hispanics, other minorities. And that's an abridged list obviously. Sometimes I both bless and curse that we're the typical white-looking family. We're lucky, but I'm often embarrassed by our race."

A moment or two of silence as he still held her. Then she posed some hard questions to him, "Yeah, I know. But how do you stomach it? Does it come with age?"

"It's never acceptable, no," he responded. "But like your mom and I always taught you, you do what you can. You try to make a difference in the world with your attitude, your positivity. But it does get frustrating when you can't change small-minded people quickly. Or ever really." He let escape a wry, frustrated laugh. "I don't want to sound cynical with that last part."

"No, it's hard not to be."

"That's the key, though. You fight with all you have to not be broken by this world's hatred. And you help people and be better than the close-minded. Be content with what you control."

After a couple minutes of quiet, something their family had always been comfortable with, he came back to the critical part. "Is he better now? After you talked to him?"

"Still not great. He's pretty shaken." She sniffed loudly, finally pulled away from her dad, and just stared into nothingness.

"It's late, but maybe tomorrow he can come over for breakfast?" Samuel said. "Not to pull him away from his family, but seeing you might help." He knew Kyle's parents, David and Shayera, shouldn't be overruled in being there for their son. When Kyle came out, they were as supportive as parents can be, the surprise notwithstanding. And they didn't really view it as a complete surprise; there are hints parents pick up on. For one, Kyle's interest in girls when he hit puberty was indifferent at best. Samuel thought the reason he got along so well with the Greens was that they too were understanding and open-minded about what kids go through. Their parenting styles and world view definitely matched up. So he didn't really want to butt in tonight, as David and Shayera could definitely help Kyle with what he was going through, and Samuel knew they also were a close family and would talk about it. And they most definitely would be the ones to talk to on the racial side of things more than Amanda. But sometimes teenagers just need to be around those their age.

"Really?" Amanda said. "I think that would help him a lot."

"Let me call David when I get up."

Amanda wrapped her arms around Samuel's neck. She smiled widely and this transformed her face radically, morphing quickly from crestfallen to something dazzling, as if her skin couldn't contain the joy within. He adored her smile since it reminded him so much of Sandra's. He hugged her back tightly, feeling his fatherly duty was now completed, another success-ful mission. "Thanks so much, Dad," Amanda said.

"It's my job."

◆ ◆ ◆

It was several hours later, 7:15, Tuesday morning. When he'd entered the kitchen, Samuel noticed the date on the wall calendar, October 2nd, and had a stirring about that for some reason. Then he realized it was their wedding anniversary. *How could I have forgotten?* He felt terrible about himself all of a sudden but tried to stifle the feeling.

He had just finished walking Harper, which was always a chore as the dog could never quite learn how to calmly walk at his side. After returning, he took a shower and was now preparing his breakfast, a simple bowl of granola. He currently had his gold-framed glasses on, which rarely left his face when he was awake. The dog had retired to his bed in the living room, and Samuel was standing at the sink. He looked out the window to his driveway and the awakening activity of his city street. The morning routine, along with Amanda's problems, had shaken off some of the effects of how he had woken up last night. But it was still there, like a thin film of residue that made his mind a little fuzzy and weird. He was still confused by the intensity of whatever the nightmare was, even if he couldn't remember it. Samuel knew that he was the very example of a type A personality and it wasn't like him to let go of things quickly. He had to analyze situations and happenings deeply. He had gotten better over the years – he used to take it to the extremes of fixation in his highest OCD days. When he first owned a home ten years ago, he was pretty much a wreck. He sometimes woke up in the middle of the night thinking the house was going to burn down, and it didn't help that when they bought the place they needed a complete electrical upgrade. His extreme fears took everything up a notch; he was always checking things, moving objects away from outlets, and searching electrical topics frequently on the internet. Sandra once asked if he just wanted things to go wrong. That was harsh but made him wonder. But it wasn't easy for him to turn his mind off. He was much better now, though. He had learned from an old counselor that being driven by fears and overactive emotions often led to bad decisions or even self-hatred. So he tried his best to let go. Still, he'd be thinking about last night for a while, trying to pry it apart and remember specific details even if it was impossible.

"Dad? Earth to Dad? Are you in the Upside Down or something?" Samuel turned quickly and saw Amanda under the archway that led from the kitchen to the living room and the upstairs stairwell. She was wearing a beige sweater and denim jeans, one of her standard dress combinations for school.

"How long have you been there?"

"A minute or so. I called your name a couple times. Are you okay?"

He grabbed his cereal bowl and put it on the table in the center of the room. "Yeah, I just keep thinking about that nightmare or whatever it was last night. You know how I am. Do you want me to fix you breakfast? Hey, where's Kyle? Did he not want to come?" Samuel had fulfilled his promise and texted his friend at 6:30; David always left for work early at his law firm, so he knew it wasn't rude to send the early message. Green said he would pass the invite along to Kyle.

"Yes and no," Amanda said, "He wants to get a quick bite at Paula's Donuts and maybe come over tonight. His mom is going to drive us. I only have a few minutes. But I'll grab some power bars for a snack later." Amanda went over to the cupboard and started rummaging through the items. After a few seconds, she found the snack packages and then took a seat at the table across from Samuel.

"You said you don't remember the dream?" she asked. She had that look on her face: that look where Samuel knew he was about to be grilled by his fifteen-year-old daughter.

"Nope," he said. "Didn't you say you had to leave?" he smiled.

"Oh, no, you're not getting off the hook that easy. Why do you think it's bothering you so much?" Amanda had a sixth sense when Samuel was about to get moody, whether it was about a simple setback like overdrawing the checking account or more significant issues, thinking about her mother the most prevalent. And she had a soft gift of broaching it and helping him through it, as he did the same for her on many occasions.

"Fine, I'll answer your questions, counselor," he said, still smiling so she knew he wasn't mad. "But I don't think it's about your mom since I know that's what you're getting at." She shrugged. "It was just odd; I don't remember having a dream quite like that. I was in a cold sweat and shaking, my mouth dry. It was like…"

"Like what, Dad?"

"Like I was just attacked mentally. Like it was more than a dream. It was weird, hon."

"Are you under a lot of stress at work?" She crossed her fingers together, her attention 100% on her father, no typical teenage distraction or daydreaming there.

"You know banking is always stressful, but no more than usual. I haven't been waking up in the middle of the night thinking about deadlines like I was a few years ago. It's been a pretty even keel of stress." He laughed at this last part.

Amanda didn't join him in laughter. "Do you think it's because of the date? It being your anniversary?"

Damn, even she remembered. Samuel didn't want to tell her that he forgot, so he just said something which was probably still the truth. "Maybe subconsciously. I don't know."

"Well, if this keeps happening, you might need to talk to a counselor again. Promise me you'll take it seriously if the dreams recur."

"Sure." Samuel looked lost in thought for a moment. For some reason, when she mentioned seeing a counselor, the name Hector popped into his head, and he had no idea why. His most recent therapist was Barbara.

"Okay, so this *isn't* normal. You look like you're stranded in another world again," Amanda said. An expression of worry and consternation had invaded her usual perky features. She had helped her dad with his many bouts of self-doubt and anxiety, but this behavior was something new, and she couldn't hide her concerns about this.

"You're right. I don't know what this is," he said, "but of course, I won't take it lightly." A car horn beeped outside. "Ah, saved by the bell. There's Shayera and Kyle." *I really need her to go. It's unusual for me to feel that way. Usually, talking things out with Amanda makes me feel good. Now I just feel scared.*

"Geez, Dad, you always tell me avoidance is not a healthy way to deal with things." She took one more deep, investigating gaze at Samuel, more the perspective of a disapproving parent than a child. "I may want to talk more about this later, tough guy."

Samuel laughed. "Sure. Just don't ground me."

Amanda blew a raspberry, stood up, walked quickly around the table, and kissed him on the cheek. Near the kitchen door, which led to the porch, she grabbed her book bag off a small table they kept there for such items and called back, "I love you. Even when you're silly."

"Love you too," he said, "*especially* when you're silly." She giggled, always a joyous sound to his ears, right before she went outside to the sound of Shayera's horn honking again.

"Coming!" he heard Amanda yell out. "Time for Paula's!"

And I do love her. No, adore her is more like it, more than anything in the world. She's so selfless, turning her attention to me more than she should. But she's so on the money here; something is off. I feel funny inside, almost light-headed. All this for a dream?

But Samuel had to leave his morning oddities aside and get moving so he wasn't late for work. He began shoveling the granola mixed with almond vanilla milk into his mouth, pushing the darkness aside for the moment.

CHAPTER 2

Samuel worked at M&T Bank in downtown Buffalo. He ended up staying in his hometown. While the idea of living somewhere else, mainly somewhere warmer, appealed to him, he was quite the homebody and wanted to stay near his mom and extended family. And it worked out well, meeting the love of his life there and having his precious Amanda. Workwise, his path had taken some unexpected twists and turns. He went to college as an English major, eventually landing on the idea of being a high school teacher given his love of books and reading and his hope to share this passion with the young minds of the world. But while one good thing came from this, meeting Sandra at Buffalo State College, the teaching career could not get off the ground. He struggled in his initial forays as an educator, not just the responsibilities of the role but also making ends meet since he couldn't find a permanent position. He had moved out of his mom's house to an apartment, thinking he'd have no problem surviving on his own, and was greeted rudely by the reality of being an adult. So he decided he needed to find different kinds of work. That led him into the world of business and to eventually working his way up through M&T. He started as entry-level as you could get there, mailing statements, but kept progressing step-by-step until he ultimately became a banking officer in charge of corporate trust accounts. As he often mentioned to Amanda, it was at times intensely stressful, being the one approving multimillion-dollar transfers and being in charge of making sure his accounts were in compliance with the trust docu-

THE GORILLAS ARE COMING

ments. It took a psychological toll on him occasionally. But a couple years ago, he had spoken to his supervisor about his mental health, and the department valued him enough to give Samuel less of an account load and less complicated accounts. So while it still had its moments of stress, he had reached a decent place.

He was currently in his little cubicle on the 7th floor of the bank's corporate offices, his face staring at the computer screen, his hand furiously working the mouse. He was going through some PDF docs of the next day's general obligation bond closing for a school district in PA, making sure he had signed everything he needed to electronically. The G.O. paying agent work was better for him than the standard trust agreements, more grunt work really, just making sure the transfers were set up and not having large amounts of clauses in the documents that could trip him up. That was part of the concession, to give him more accounts like that. He did have a decent eye for detail and enjoyed the routine or checklist of setting up these accounts, making the transfers and closing calls, and then just setting up the ticklers on the accounting system for the payment date setups. It was almost noon, and hearing his belly grumble loudly, Samuel knew his body was not so subtly telling him it was nearly time to eat. That creature of habit he was, he always had lunch at 12:30, so he knew it was a bit early but waking up in the middle of the night last evening had thrown his system off a bit.

He also had about ten texts from his best friend Peter Darwin he knew he should get around to. The texts were mostly cryptic: "We have to talk, Daddy-O" or "I remember", things like that. Samuel was just so busy this morning that he didn't even have time to type a simple reply. He figured the Who had announced another reunion tour. Nothing important. He planned on touching base with his buddy during lunch.

"Did you hear about that weird attack last night?"

It was his co-worker in the cubicle across from him, Vincent. They weren't exactly friends, but Samuel had a fondness for most of his fellow employees, and Vincent was always fun to talk to, mostly about sports but sometimes current events as well. "What attack?" Samuel asked, starting to rummage in his backpack for his packed lunch.

Vincent swiveled around in his chair. He was a couple years older than Samuel, with three kids and a wife, a good family man. He had the slightly tannish look of his Italian roots, and Samuel was a bit jealous how he kept his boyish appearance at 50. He tended to be more anal than even Samuel was at work, always needing things to be done in a certain way, which Samuel learned when he used to be his assistant. This similar personality trait most likely led to their ease with each other, even though words were never spoken about it. And both were hard workers, focused for most of the workday, throwing in the small talk here and there, though. "It was out in the country in the Southern Tier," Vincent continued. "Some yokel was torn apart. It was vicious, sounded like a dog attack, but the fur they found on-site was apparently from some kind of wild animal they haven't been able to identify yet."

Suddenly, Samuel's heart had a sharp pain, and darkness assailed his mood again. He had to remind himself to breathe for a second and actually needed to grab the end of the desk. He felt a tiny bead of sweat forming on his brow. *What the hell?* It seemed to him like an extension of his uneasiness from last night and this morning. *Did I already know about this somehow? Did I read about it last night before going to bed?*

"Are you okay, buddy?" Vincent asked, his face registering some surprise and concern.

"Sure," Samuel said, wiping his brow. "Just hungry, I guess." *Way to cover there.* "What time did this happen?"

"I think it was the middle of the morning, like 3:00 or 4:00."

Right around the time I woke up. Oh, come on, Samuel. Get real. You're jumping to conclusions. "Vin, I do feel a little weird actually. I'll take an early lunch. I think I'll go over to Hoyt Lake and sit on one of the benches there since it warmed up a little today. Not many more days for hanging out outside. So I might be a little late if Ronny asks." Ron was his supervisor, who was not one to track lunch breaks, but Samuel figured he would be safe about it. *I need to get myself under control here.*

"Of course, Sammy. Take as much time as you need. You look like you saw a ghost."

Samuel just nodded, grabbed his cell phone and bagged lunch, and left quickly, wanting to get to fresh air as soon as possible.

Vincent looked after him as he left with a now puzzled expression. He would never see Samuel Redden again.

Hoyt Lake was part of the Delaware Park system. It was one of Samuel's favorite places to go during lunch hour. He was a thrifty guy and always encouraged his daughter to be the same, so it was rare that he ate out for lunch. So there he sat on the park bench with his bagged lunch of egg salad and Cheez-Its, looking out on the sizeable man-made lake that rested in the middle of walking and bike paths amid beautiful trees. The part that always amazed him was that this little piece of nature existed right in the middle of the city of Buffalo. It was about a forty foot walk from the street parking, and although you could still hear the occasional traffic noises, you were mostly insulated from the hustle and bustle of the city. It was also his and Sandra's favorite park to spend time in. This brought a little sadness on, and this instant melancholy welcomed back the fear he had felt in the office twenty minutes ago. So he tried to get himself to focus back on his sandwich and the serene water lapping against the bank. He had managed to calm down on the drive over here, and he didn't want to welcome the uneasiness back to his mind.

But it was hard; his anxiety continued to fight against him. He was holding his cell phone, which was opened to the web story of the attack out in Springville. He was afraid to look. He wasn't sure how he knew, but he was positive only terrible consequences would be found in that account. And not just in the event itself but within himself. And this time, he didn't think he was jumping to conclusions, something his brain imbalance sometimes did. So his conscious mind forced itself to retreat away from the potential horror and into a pleasant memory.

He was in his second year at Buffalo State College. Oddly enough, the university was just a few miles from where Samuel now sat. He started as a computer programming major but quickly learned that was just not how his brain worked. He had gone to a community college previously, not earning a degree while slogging through his computer classes, planning on obtaining a bachelor's degree once transferring to Buffalo State. Early in his 1st year at the new school, he made the decision to switch to English. Now at that point, he wasn't sure what he was going to do in that area of study, perhaps teach, but he knew that he loved to read, and that was all he could focus on at the time. He never liked any of the part-time jobs he had as a kid and wasn't convinced of what could possibly bring him fulfillment in that area. So he chose a new major, not one encouraged by his mom this time, but something he would enjoy studying.

Speaking of Mom, Samuel still lived with her and commuted to school during these years. It was just the two of them: Patrick had gotten married and moved on to start his own family. Samuel's introverted character was also a contributing factor for not dorming; he wasn't sure he was ready to deal with a roommate and the party scene. So he made the thirty-minute drive back and forth in his hand-me-down Ford Escort, Shelley's old car. After he switched his major, he enjoyed college more, and on this particular day in the spring semester was walking through the student union on his way to the book store in a pretty good mood. It would soon get even better.

He arrived at the store and saw the inevitable long line for the early semester book buying crush. He sighed, but it still didn't ruin his upbeat attitude yet. His OCD was in full bloom at this point of his life, however, so he did start to analyze just about every angle of this situation while entering the line. How long would this take? Would he be late for class? Was he ready for the discussion of Whitman? It was just the way his mind worked and still did to a certain extent. But before his brain could veer into over -analyzation (as he used to call it), he noticed the girl in front of him in line.

There was nineteen-year-old Sandra Crowell. She had silky red hair, shoulder length but presently tied in a scrunchy, active green eyes, an attractive figure, not thin, not overweight, but shapely. She was wearing a Nirvana *Nevermind* t-shirt, the one with the submerged baby chasing the all-mighty dollar, along with blue jeans, her LL Bean bookbag slung on her back. The shirt was a bit retro, given that Kurt Cobain had died three years prior in '94, but Samuel appreciated that she wasn't wearing something trendy. It reminded him of Pete in a way. She was currently looking through her purse and mumbling under her breath. She seemed put out.

Being true to his social awkwardness, Samuel looked around and wondered if the people ahead in line, which included much more attractive guys, would say something to her. He could never remember even beginning a conversation with the opposite sex through his high school years. Occasionally, one would say something to him, and while he could hold down a conversation, his heart would beat like a jackhammer the whole time. To this point in his life, not far from the age of 21, he'd never been on a date, never kissed a girl, never had the guts to be aggressive on that front. When he was thirteen, one of his brothers, Jeff, had a man-to-man talk with Samuel, encouraging him to speak up to girls. He argued that often less attractive boys get dates just because they took the step to speak and that he should come out of his shell. Easier said than done, though. It's not a simple thing to alter one's interior makeup.

So Samuel was shocked when he heard his voice say, "Are you okay?"

The girl swung around and looked right at him. Her eyes were intense, burrowing into him a bit. He actually flinched, and he thought afterward that this endeared him to Sandra. He wasn't some pushy macho man trying to make a move; he was a nervous kid just noticing a girl struggling. He was sure his intentions weren't *that altruistic* - she was a pretty girl, and he was instantly attracted to her - but his awkwardness put her more at ease.

"Oh," she said with an effeminate but lightly breathy voice that Samuel instantly was charmed by, "I left my pocketbook in the dorm. I'm such an idiot. How am I supposed to pay for this book? Guess I have to go back."

"What book is it? What class?" Still talking to her with no stuttering or fumbling, Samuel felt like he was in some sort of

THE GORILLAS ARE COMING

haze. A good sort.

"It's for an American Lit I class. Norton's Intro to Lit or something."

Samuel smiled internally. He took that class last semester. He could talk knowledgeably about it. But why was he so comfortable? Something about this girl? "I took that in the fall. I think it's only $25 or so." Textbooks were a lot cheaper back then.

"Well, $25 is more than zero." She smiled. She actually smiled at him. And what a smile it was. It lit up her face, forming the most adorable dimples. He had that fuzzy feeling that people get when the attraction really starts to kick in. His stomach was doing aerobics. He'd never really felt this yet in his insulated life. "Off I go…" She turned to leave.

"Wait," he said. He almost grabbed her arm but thought better of that. This was another thing that probably endeared this strange boy to her. "I can help."

"What?"

"I can pay for it. You can pay me back whenever. I'm around the English building a lot. Or you can just buy me lunch." What did he just say? He wondered what alien force had taken over his body.

She looked hard at him again, probing, trying to figure out if she just gained a stalker perhaps. Maybe she wondered if the sheepish act was just that, an act. "I don't know."

"I get it," Samuel said, " You don't know me from Thoreau." He doubted this joke would land.

But it did. She giggled. And it was unbearably cute to him. "You're really just too nerdy to be trying to pick me up, aren't you? All right, Mr.…."

"Redden."

"How about a first name, Mr. Redden?" Again, that smile. Samuel thought he might buckle right there on the spot.

"Samuel."

"Hi, Samuel. I'm Sandra Crowell." She held her hand out. He took it, noticing how soft it was, and shook, trying not to clasp too hard but also not hold it like they were on a date or she was the queen of England. "I'll let you buy my book, but I will pay full price, whether it's lunch or not. And I'm not committing to that yet, you got me?"

"Of course." He realized even if they didn't go right to lunch now, they would have to share phone numbers. Without knowing it, he'd gotten himself a girl's number! Again, he wondered what the hell was happening.

"Okay, Samuel, let's see how long this ungodly line will keep us occupied. You an English major?"

"Yep. You too?"

"Oh God, no. Just taking this as an elective. Not sure what my major will be yet. Maybe Human Services or something in business; I have no freaking clue."

"I was pretty clueless too. My mom wanted me to be a computer major, but that was a disaster."

"You close to your mom?" Samuel just realized this girl was already getting personal with him. And physically, she had her back facing the front of the line now and kept stepping backward as they moved. She was giving him her full attention and had even inched a bit closer, to where their feet were almost touching. Something that crystallized in their years together was that Sandra was quite the opposite of him. She was aggressive and not shy. Amanda seemed to have a nice balance between these two personalities.

"I am. I'm the youngest of seven kids, and they're all moved out. I still live at home with her." If he was reading the man's man book of dating, this would have been a no-no. But he just found it easy to talk to this Sandra.

"That's cool," she said deadpan. There was no judgment or scoffing there. "I'm in my freshman year here, and I'm doing the dorm thing. I'm not local."

"Where you from?"

"Russia actually."

"Are you serious? You don't have an accent."

She let out a full-throated laugh at this. If her smile was beautiful, her laugh was exquisite. It was melodic, lilting, musical. "You're a little gullible, aren't you, Redden?" She punched him lightly in the arm. If he knew anything about flirting, he would have realized they'd crossed this threshold.

But he simply felt embarrassment at his stupidity. He actually blushed a barely noticeable amount. "I'm a little slow sometimes," he said timidly.

The fact she was still beaming at him should have been a sign that it didn't matter; his naivete was actually helping. "No, I like it. I'm from Chicago."

"Chicago, eh? This must feel like hicksville in comparison." Buffalo was still fighting through its twenty-year economic depression that was present during Samuel's childhood. There had been talks of developing the city's greatest asset, the waterfront, for years, but partisan differences and feet-dragging had so far prevented that. Years later, that would change, but in the mid-'90s, Buffalo still wasn't exactly a destination.

"No, it's fine, quaint. I like the quiet. I'm not a party girl, Samuel Redden."

He was quite pleased by that answer. He then put himself out on the metaphorical ledge emotionally by trying another joke. He'd always felt stupid when he tried to be funny conversing, so it seemed a risk since he was apparently doing well with her. Even at that moment, he felt fear grip him, thinking Sandra would suddenly give him a weird look and turn away. "Well, darn, you don't know what you're missing," he said. "I'm out on the town day and night." He smirked and hoped whatever success he had stumbled into kept working.

She laughed again. Samuel found this sound acutely seductive. The book line was really moving at this point, and she glided back a few more feet. She really appeared so graceful, like a ballerina (or maybe he was just completely taken already). He warned himself to not be smitten. He had no chance. "Can I get honest here? Don't know why I would say this," she remarked.

"Go ahead."

"I really haven't made any friends in half a year here. I'm social, yes, but I just find the party scene exhausting. Always have. I like real people, you know? Some students feel fake here. It's like they're preparing themselves for mindless corporate America already."

This may have been the moment where Samuel fell in love with Sandra. She had a mind too. She felt like the kind of person that would never put up with bullshit.

"I don't make friends easy either, Sandra."

"Call me Sandy."

The queue had finally moved to the end, and the young acned male clerk behind the counter, obviously a work-study student, had to give Sandra a clearing of the throat to get her attention. Samuel pointed, and she smiled sheepishly. It was time for the exchange of money. When Samuel handed her the cash, he felt an electric jolt when their skin touched again. Being so inexperienced with girls, he knew he was aroused and hoped it wasn't showing at the time. He even stole a glance down at his pants to check for a noticeable erection (all good there) and looked back up quickly. He at least made sure he did this when she was turned away asking the clerk for the book.

A few minutes later, they were in the hallway outside the bookstore about to part ways. He sure didn't want to.

"Where you off to? Class?" he asked.

"No, I have a break until 2:00. You?"

"Back to class for me. English Lit 2. Chaucer time. Do I sound excited?"

She giggled yet another time. How often had girls laughed at his jokes before this? Ever? Does she really like me, he wondered, not wanting to hope. "Sounds wonderful. I think I might pass on English as a major, guy."

They now stood there in complete quiet for several seconds. This wasn't yet the comfortable silence of their relationship. The main reason for the uneasiness was Samuel's social ineptitude. He wanted to say something, maybe not ask her on a date, but something to make her like him even more. "Well," she said, "better let you get to it."

"Okay." He was a little sad now. He began to walk away. He

tried to keep his head up and not look like Charlie Brown.

"Redden, are you forgetting something?" She said with a somewhat raised voice behind him.

He turned so fast he almost lost his balance. Thankfully, he didn't.

"I haven't given you my number yet. How am I supposed to get in touch with you, morse code?" Another thing he grew to love was her sarcasm; somehow, it was never mean like some people. "I do want lunch, bookworm."

He smiled broadly. He was pretty sure this was the best moment of his short life to that point. Knowing his previous luck, he had a strong feeling that he would never see her again, book debt or no. But she actually wanted to get together!

Since this was before the prevalence of smartphones, Sandra pulled out a sheet of paper from the notebook in her bookbag and scribbled down a number. He went over and put his hand out. But she tucked it in his side jacket pocket and zipped it closed, which excited him intensely. "Don't want you to lose it. Just so you know, I'd like to go off-campus. I'm really sick of the food here, if that's good with you."

That sounded like a real-life date to Samuel, but he didn't want to jinx it by overthinking. "Sounds perfect!" They looked at each other eye to eye. Samuel did his best not to glance away awkwardly as he usually would. "See you later," he added after a moment. This time she was the one to walk away (after smiling one more time), and he tried not to stare at her back end as she strode off confidently. It was hard, though. She was so beautiful.

After a full minute of being lost in a daze, Samuel finally began to walk off towards the union's exit doors. He thought about how he'd just been traversing these halls forty-five minutes ago in what seemed like a whole different period of his life as if years had passed. He was going out with a pretty girl! How did that happen? But he found he didn't care how. He tried to keep his head out of the clouds and not skip around like a five-year-old. But the spring in his step was noticeable. He made it outside to the school's courtyard on his way to class, but before long had to stop. He's legs actually felt a little rubbery, so he sat down in front of the fountain halfway to the library building. Once he was down on the concrete surface, he actually pinched himself on the leg.

Samuel's mind returned to his surroundings in the park. *What a great memory.* Not like a few years ago, when she was undergoing chemo. When she was emaciated, weak, in agony until the end.

No, stop. You have something else scary to focus on now.

Samuel looked at the news article on his smartphone. And was never the same again.

CHAPTER 3

S amuel's mother had a subscription to *The Buffalo News* when he was growing up, delivered to the house daily. And after he moved out, he read the online version of this periodical and others consistently. He liked being knowledgeable of what was going on not only in his town but in the world. So he had probably read thousands of news stories by the time he got to this one. But there had never been a story in his forty-three years that provided such a gut punch and irrevocable life changes as what he read now:

Man Dies of Animal Attack

(Not the most shocking of titles, but what followed quickly brought it all home for Samuel.)

Reginald Samuels, thirty-three, was found dead behind his house, in the woods of Springville. The state police on the scene indicated he died of an animal attack. He had various punctures and scratches throughout his body, concentrated mostly around his throat and stomach. The police described the scene as gruesome and would not provide much in the way of details, except to say while a dog or wolf attack would be the most obvious culprit, the animal hairs left at the scene brought that into question. When asked what he meant by that statement, Detective Stanley Grover indicated, "The fur was not consistent with that of a canine." The police department refused to share any more details, so The News located the local who discovered the body. We have edited much of his description of this shocking attack as it was graphic, but the gentleman, one Harlan Tilley, said of the fur, "That was no dog. Or wolf. Or coyote. The hair was black, tinged with silver, and there were big clumps of it. It was almost like an ape did it."

Samuel didn't need to read any more after this. Instantly his brain overloaded with memories. Recollections of a terrified eight-year-old boy who was having horrible nightmares about killer gorillas. A child who thought they were real. His family didn't believe him but did finally try to help. And that ended in the death of a kind counselor named Hector. Finally, some people did accept the otherworldly reality: a beloved friend and a mystical lady. And the monsters were erased. But not eliminated. No, they were back now. And this time he had to face them.

Samuel passed out.

Samuel's eyes opened. He looked around foggily. A group of people stood around him: several teenagers with skateboards (clearly playing hooky), a lady who looked dressed for jogging, and a family of four, two parents and two young children. He glanced around, unsure for a moment, and then remembered where he was. He must have fallen off the bench since he was lying on the grass with his lunch and cell phone spread around him. His head ached, and he touched the top of it, feeling a lump. But more so, his heart ached, and he knew why, but he couldn't deal with that now. He sat up a bit and leaned his back against the bench. The husband told him to be careful. "How long have I been out?" Samuel asked.

One of the teenagers said, "Just minutes, dude. What the hell was that?" The wife tsked at the language, saying there were kids present. The majority of the high schoolers either scoffed or laughed.

I need to tell them something. "Just been feeling under the weather," he said, which wasn't a complete lie. "Can some of you help me up?" He wasn't sure he could manage on his own yet. He dusted some grass clippings off his polo shirt and grabbed his phone, sticking it in the pocket of his khaki pants. The husband and the jogger were the ones to step forward, each latching onto an arm. They eased him back to the bench and gently guided him down to sit. The wife wanted to call an ambulance, but he said he was okay. He told them he would be fine alone now, and even though the adults protested a bit, he managed to convince them.

So he was by himself again. Samuel took a deep breath. He knew a further breakdown was coming, but first, he had to take care of business. He called work and let Ron know that he wouldn't be back in the office today. Family emergency. *I'm getting good at these half-truths already.* He then tried to keep himself under control while he collected his thoughts. Only a minute passed before his phone chimed. He glanced at it. A text. *Peter, holy shit! Peter was there. He knows. What an idiot I am. If only I would have read his texts earlier.*

Samuel dialed his hippie friend's cell. "Jesus, brother, what the hell took you so long?" the voice said on the other end of the line.

Samuel sighed. "I was busy at work. Then I saw the article at lunch. They're back." His voice broke at this last part. "Damn it, Pete, they're back. I remember all of it."

"Me too, Reddy. Are you all right?"

"Well, I just passed out at Hoyt Lake. Must have banged my head; it hurts like a bitch. And…"

"You feel like you're losing it?"

"Yep."

"I'll be right there."

Twenty minutes later, Peter arrived. If you knew his father, you would have sworn you were staring at Robert Darwin, unaged since 1985. Or at least a strikingly similar-looking brother. Peter's young growth spurt never stalled; he was fully grown in his mid-teen years to a statuesque 6'3 and was a little more scarecrow-like than his pops who had some meat on his bones. He also had the familial long black flowing hair (no more mullet, though), and he no longer wore the horn-rim glasses, changing to contacts. Also slightly different from his clean shaved father, he sported a Van Dyke beard; he always said it perfectly fit his bohemian lifestyle and Democratic socialist leanings (he was an avowed Bernie Bro). His raiment was absolutely Robert inspired, though. He was wearing a psychedelic Grateful Dead skull t-shirt; concert tees were his clothing of choice when not at school and he had hundreds of them. Over the shirt, he was wearing his old 80's jean jacket, which further demonstrated his reluctance to let go of the past. Clearly, he had taken the day off, although Samuel didn't make note of the lack of dress clothes. Peter had obviously matured mentally over the years, becoming a beloved local high school science teacher, but his mannerisms and vocal style were almost the same as when he was a kid. He was also the one person Samuel could count on outside of his wife, daughter, and mother, including the rest of his immediate family. Peter remained single over the years. He had his share of relationships, but none lasted more than a few months. "Bachelor-style for life, my cool cat," he often said. He had become an uncle of sorts for Amanda; she thought he was the most amazing person. *And now I'll need him more than ever.*

Peter plopped down on the bench next to Samuel with the weirdly awkward yet controlled way he always had. He wasted no time in putting his arm around his buddy and pulling him close. Samuel let him; these two were never macho and were consistently expressive in their fondness for each other. Samuel actually leaned in a bit; he wanted to cry, to let it all out, but most of his being was still in shock at this point. The two of them stayed in this position for a couple minutes before Samuel straightened out, and Peter removed his hand and started tapping on his lap to a beat only he could hear.

They both stared out in silence for a good five minutes at the lake, even the loquacious Peter clearly not knowing what to say. It was a bit of a callback to their conversation overlooking his mom's pool those many years ago, though neither made the connection with everything going on. Samuel finally asked, "What was it like for you?"

"I'm stringent in my early morning daily routine, as you know. I was watching the morning news on the old rabbit ears set before going out for my constitutional and yoga, but I was stopped in my tracks by the tale of unholy murder in the burbs." If Samuel were looking at his friend, he would have noticed how Peter's face had an unsure look before he had said this. It was reminiscent of an old favorite movie of his, *Star Wars,* when Obi-Wan paused when first queried by Luke about his father. "I knew as soon as I heard the name," he added. "Did you make the connection?"

"What connection?"

"The poor dude's name is Reginald Samuels. Or was. Pretty much your name reversed, Daddy-O."

Damn. I didn't even realize. "I knew something bad was coming even before I got far into the story. As soon as Vincent told me about the attack earlier, I just felt it. But the foreboding started earlier than that. I had a nightmare last night and woke up feeling out of sorts. I didn't even notice the significance of the name. I was just plowing through the article, accepting that I needed to get to the end of it, to the revelation of the simian hair. I couldn't look away, couldn't run from it. Like I was caught in a wave that was going to plummet me down to some destination below, knowing where it would lead. To horror."

"Poetic, my dear Frost acolyte. You never lost that English major groove. But yeah, I felt the darkness as soon as I heard the name. But after that porcelain pretty TV host finished the story, my psychedelic brain went down a trippy lane in past mode. I saw it from the point when you told me about the beasts until that cool Madame Takari banished it from our heads. This is a bad beat, Kemosabe."

Samuel looked down to his lap, the comfort Peter had provided him when he arrived slowly dissipating. He felt like the terror gripping him now was a tangible thing, stalking him, wanting to take his heart and smush it to pieces. *As the gorillas want to do.* All this made his situational depression and anxiety, which always seemed like the end of the world, feel like child's play. He exhaled loudly and quivery. "I figure we're the only ones who remember. Not even my family."

"Nah. They had their feet planted firmly in the real world. Their naivete is maintained, I'm sure."

"Or maybe they'll have some vague recollection of me having nightmares and will decide not to pursue it. So what now, Pete?"

Peter looked away from the lake and gazed upon his oldest

friend. "We finish what we started. It was only a temporary fix, but we did figure it out quickly last time. We move fast again."

"Madame Takari said if they get free, they would threaten our world. It's happening. And people will suffer greatly because of it. Because of me. Back then it was Hector and now someone I don't even know. A true innocent."

Peter grabbed Samuel on each shoulder and turned his buddy to face him. Samuel reluctantly looked up. "Not this Catholic guilt revue, Sammy my boy. The only ones to blame are those unholy beasts. We couldn't have expected the block to hold forever. It's time."

"Time for what exactly?" Samuel just wanted to go home, bury himself in his covers, and hide forever.

"For you to fulfill your destiny and banish these hell monsters forever." Peter was bopping his head up and down excitedly, looking like a giant mutant chicken.

Samuel shook his head. "This isn't fun, exciting, or a movie, Pete. This is fucked up."

"Do you think I'm acting silly? How long have we known each other? I'm always like this."

This allowed Samuel a small laugh. And he was grateful for it. "Okay, Van Helsing, how do we kill these demons for good this time? Try Madame Takari again? If she's still around." At the mention of the mystic's name, Peter's eyes wandered, but Samuel was too lost in his racing thoughts to notice it. "And what the hell do I tell Amanda? She's going to want to commit me just like my family did. And she has more of a sense of my mental health problems."

"You know Mandy's stronger than that. She's open-minded, just the way we raised her." Samuel let a tiny smile escape when Peter said, *"we raised her."* But he had to admit this was true; after Sandy died, Peter stepped in as a kind of surrogate parent. "We'll tell her together," Peter added. He paused for a second before continuing, "Good call on Madame Takari. But this is going to be a team effort, and I think we need both sides of things, the unreal but reality too."

Sometimes he's exhausting. "What do you mean?" Samuel asked.

"I know a guy." Peter stopped for a dramatic beat, looked up at the heavens with dancing eyes, and appeared wistful, enraptured. Then he glanced sideways at Samuel with an almost sinister smile. "But before I tell you about him, let me say what I think. The gorillas are more aggressively in the real world now, correct?"

"Uh-huh. As this poor guy can attest," Samuel said as he took his phone back out of his pocket and held it up.

Peter didn't acknowledge the guilt bubbling up in his friend again. "Yes, they are unholy dream creatures as the Madame mentioned back in the wild '80s, but the more they break through to our reality, they have to obey the laws of physics and science to an extent too, I'm sure." He beamed again, showing his exceedingly whitened teeth. "So this is where my cool dude comes in. He's a gorilla expert, a primatologist."

"Like Diane Fosse?"

"Yes, but even more larger-than-life. You gotta see the man to believe him. A few years back, I met him on a jungle expedition in Africa, that summer trip I did with my kiddos. He was the guide. This wasn't some cushy safari cruise, though: it was deep in the veldt with the hero protecting us, guiding us, teaching us how to interact with the gorilla tribe. He speaks their language, brother, knows their ins and outs. He's accepted in their world. Do you know how hard that is?"

"I can imagine," Samuel said.

"Oh, but you can't imagine, not really. I've gotten together with him several times since then, true science bros. He's just outta sight. Wait until you see him!" Peter leapt up and began to pace around, gesturing with his long arms, so excitedly as if he couldn't contain the energy that wanted to burst out of his pores. "He's the real deal." That last part was one of Robert's favorite witticisms.

Samuel reached a hand out and grabbed Peter by the arm when he passed by again. "Slow down. What pray tell is this legend's name?"

"Carter. Just Carter, man."

Samuel had returned home. It was only 3:00, and Amanda wasn't back from school just yet. *I'm glad. I'm not ready for that conversation. I need the time to collect my thoughts.*

So he decided to take a shower. It was rare for him to take two in a day, but he felt dirty, sweaty, just gross, after the afternoon drama. Once he was in the shower, feeling the slightly burning water cascade over his body, it felt great, and he knew he had made the right decision. He always loved extra hot and long showers, even if the experts will tell you that it's not good for your skin. He'd undergone those two back surgeries in his thirties, minor discectomies, and the heat made his bones feel refreshed over the years.

It was a solid twenty-five minutes before he stepped out of the shower. The room was ridiculously steamy. He felt like he was stuck outside on a humid and foggy day. *Maybe I made it a little hotter than usual.* His bathroom didn't have a venting fan, so he typically opened the window to alleviate the dampness in there, but this time he'd forgotten with everything else on his mind. So after putting on the fresh pair of clothes he had lain on the floor, a Buffalo Bills t-shirt and red sweat pants replacing his business casual wear, he cranked the window open. He thought he would brush his teeth again as well. So he wiped the mirror over the sink with a towel. That's when he saw it— the face.

Looking back at him was not the visage of a slightly balding, baggy-eyed white man. But that of a gorilla, the huge head filling the reflection. Samuel felt like someone had slammed a sledgehammer into his chest, and he found breathing difficult. He had mostly outgrown asthma, but he remembered the exercises and now did those deep inhalation and exhalation repetitions, almost like a reflex. He wanted to look away from what he was seeing but could not. The image he was faced with was worse than he could even remember. The mirror's steam residue broke up some more and the gorilla was revealed in better detail. It turned its back to him, showing muscular silver shoulders as it flexed like a bodybuilder. It then swung back around and pushed up closer to the glass, displaying dripping red spots around its jaw, and Samuel knew what that meant. Its eyes glared with baleful inhuman rage. It growled at him and bared its teeth. He could have sworn they were fangs, even though cerebrally he knew simians didn't have teeth like that. Then his mind flashed back to the experiences in his bedroom during childhood, how the ape's champers always did look like something a vampire would have. The buried memories had come back like a flash a couple hours ago, but his subconscious must have held back certain specific details. Now that his brain was unveiling more of what he had lost, another fact registered, and he wondered if he would hear telepathic thoughts in his head from the creature. Instead, shockingly, the face disappeared, and words appeared in the lightly dewy mirror. They were written in red.

WE FOUND YOU.

He then had yet another recollection, that of the message they had given him the night of Hector's murder. That time it was written in his bedroom window, not a mirror, but it all felt like a terrible attack of déjà vu. Samuel whimpered and turned to the bathroom door. But he felt like something was holding him back, as if his feet were in cement. He knew this wasn't a new phenomenon either; everything about the nightmare world had returned with a vengeance. "No!" he exclaimed. He pushed with everything he had, knowing it was more mental exertion than physical, but his legs began to ache, and he hoped that was a good sign. He could hear noises behind him, like a bunch of animals sniffing and grunting. And he could smell. That horrible manure stench permeated the room, worse than ever given the small size of his bathroom. He gave up trying to run for the door but did manage to collapse on the linoleum surface and proceeded to put his arms around himself, now in a completely fetal position. And he rocked himself back and forth, cried and moaned. A terrible thought occurred to him. He wanted to die. He wanted it to be over and to be with Sandy again. Then he immediately flashed on Amanda's face and felt a clawing guilt. So he just closed his eyes tightly and begged for deliverance.

Samuel wasn't sure how long he was locked in the child-like position. But he looked up at a point, and no longer did he feel mired in a nightmare scenario. He glanced around, and the room was no longer humid and steamy (or smelly for that matter), and the only thing reflecting in the mirror was the opened shower curtain across from it and the tiles of the bath wall. No words written in crimson. *They can still remove their im-*

prints on our world just so I can question my sanity. His temples throbbed, the stress bearing down on him. And even though the danger seemed to have passed, his senses were still in overdrive, so when the door opened, he got ready to jump away, knowing he would be able to move now. Then he saw the light pour in from the hallway, and a tall, long-haired hippie dude burst into the room. And Samuel's heart surged with relief.

"Reddy!" Peter dropped to his knees and took his friend into his arms in such a loving way, more like a mama bear would be with her cub than a "normal" friend would ever embrace their pal. Again, some would be surprised at their closeness, but they never cared what others thought of them.

"They were here," Samuel croaked.

"In the daytime?" Peter asked, looking dismayed.

"Yeah. I guess. I don't know," Samuel shook his head. "I saw one in the mirror somehow. I can't do this, man. I can't do it. I can't." Samuel began to cry again and buried his head in Peter's shoulder.

"Sure you can. Remember your hand? Your fist? When Steiner was bullying you?"

Samuel looked at Darwin through blurry eyes. More flashes, this time of a little hand projecting a great light and revealing a burning fire within. *My brain must really have wanted to ease me through this. That was the one thing that happened that was both amazing and positive. I want to remember THAT PART.* "Oh yeah!" he exclaimed. Right there, he sounded like an excited child, for a second no longer the broken shell lying on his dusty bathroom floor.

"We'll find out what that means. We'll figure it all out. You and me. Like before, my brother." Peter exuded a special kind of confidence that made Samuel want to kiss him.

Then Redden heard another voice. A female voice. "Dad?"

He looked over in the doorway again and saw Amanda and another person there. This other one was a young, handsome black teenager with deep hazel eyes and carefully coiffed short hair with braids on the top. He was wearing a blue jacket with red stripes on the sleeves with the name Spartans on the back, a school junior varsity jacket. Underneath was a preppy green polo. It was the combination of the somewhat nerdy and athletic that partly defined the kid. *Kyle. Maybe he decided to stay tonight to take us up on last night's invitation. How long ago does that seem? A million years?* Amanda had an extreme look of fear and worry on her face. It made Samuel sad to have caused this. He knew it wasn't merely seeing her dad being cradled by "Uncle Peter"; it was his appearance. Even though the shower helped refresh him, the incident took all its benefits away: he was white as a ghost, shuddering, with a wild look in his eyes. Kyle was staring at him too, but he just appeared confused.

Samuel's parental instincts kicked in, and he pushed himself gently away from Peter and stood. He was wobbly on his feet, so Darwin jumped up to steady him, his long arm wrapping around Samuel's back. Amanda didn't move, transfixed and still as a statue.

Samuel tried to smile at the young girl, wanting to comfort her, but only managed a crazed grimace. "We have to talk, baby. We really have to talk."

CHAPTER 4

*H*ow *do I tell her this? How?* The four of them were grouped around the kitchen table. Samuel and Peter were sitting on the archway side that led to the living room, and Amanda and Kyle opposite them nearer to the outside door. To their right, late-afternoon embers of light permeated through the window over the cluttered sink, lighting the brown table's edges in red. Harper had maneuvered his large frame underneath and lay at Samuel's feet. That was comforting. Kyle insisted on staying, and Samuel figured the reason was his concern for his friend, but there was also that fondness for Mr. Redden as well. At first, Samuel objected, not wanting to bring another innocent into this mad world he and his loved ones found themselves in. But Peter talked him into it, saying something about needing as many spiritual warriors as they could muster. Samuel thought himself crazy for allowing it, but he later cut himself some slack considering where his brain was at that point; he just couldn't think straight.

The first thing he did was make Kyle swear he wouldn't tell anyone, not even his parents. He knew this was a horrible thing to ask a fifteen-year-old kid, and if this request ever got back to David and Shayera, it would destroy a friendship that had developed over ten years. But if by some miracle Amanda and Kyle both believed what Samuel was about to tell them, then they had to keep the circle closed so people didn't start causing problems like getting medical professionals or the authorities involved. To his credit, Kyle didn't hesitate or show anything on his face that indicated he was concerned about the promise. He simply nodded his head in the affirmative. *Maybe at a certain point, kids like to keep secrets from their parents, to have something all their own.*

Samuel had made a pot of coffee and now took a sip. He wasn't a big java drinker, usually just a cup in the morning and maybe one more at work. And he knew caffeine wasn't the thing to calm his frazzled nerves. Still, he felt like he needed an object nearby to fixate on and touch. Plus Peter liked to guzzle the stuff. Kyle only enjoyed the sweet Starbucks style alternatives, so he was nursing a Coke, while Amanda, always health conscious, had a bottle of water in front of her. He let a long sigh before starting. "Amanda, remember how I felt off-kilter this morning?"

"Yeah, Dad," she said. Samuel could tell she was trying to not appear worried and project strength, as she so often did. Her eyes were focused and solemn, but she was completely calm, not fidgety or jumpy. But he knew she was bracing herself for bad news, and that made him sad again. Life had already taught her the hard way that it's not all roses and quick resolutions like a sitcom. He knew there was much more to come, and he so hated to put her through it. *She, of all people, deserves a break from tragedy or trials.*

"I still don't remember the exact details of the nightmare I had last night," he said, and then hesitated a second before adding, "but it was about gorillas."

"Gorillas?" she asked dubiously. "That's random." Kyle was silent, his eyes moving back and forth between Samuel and Amanda, almost like he was watching a match at Wimbledon while taking occasional slurps of his pop.

"Not so random, my fair maiden," Peter said. "Let me jump in, Reddy, since I know how hard this is for you. Baby girl, your daddy and I went through a thing thirty-five years ago. It was far out but also scary. It all came back today. And not just memories; *they* are literally back."

"Can the two of you stop being cryptic? Can you just tell us?" Amanda shot back, clearly flustered and a bit testy. *She's not used to me being cagey.*

"Of course, dear," Peter said, "For me, it started..."

"No, I'll tell," Samuel interjected. "It's my responsibility, Pete."

"I dig it. You're such a prince," Peter said, "I'm here if you need me."

Samuel smiled back at his oldest friend. "Thanks." He then looked at Kyle quickly before fixing his gaze upon his daughter. "It started in the summer of 1985. I was eight." His nervousness overwhelmed him, and for the first time since she was born, he couldn't maintain eye contact with Amanda while speaking. He stared at his coffee cup and continued, "At first, I just thought they were nightmares..."

It was thirty minutes later. The story was told. The night terrors, the creatures, the glowing hand, his family intervening, meeting Hector, the telepathic conversations with the monsters, Hector being killed, bringing Peter in, Madame Takari and the spell, and finally ending with the murder last night. Samuel continued looking down the whole time, speaking like a robot, his eyes appearing to be in a daze, not even blinking. But he got through it. And then he looked up. Kyle appeared amazed, like he just went on the roller coaster at Darien Lake and had the time of his life; he was actually smiling and couldn't sit still in his chair. Amanda was the opposite, severe and intense: if Samuel had watched her during the telling, he would have seen the worried face return, but now it was gone again. There was a resoluteness in her countenance even more than before; Samuel could tell she wasn't burying her fear at all now. He didn't know if that was good or bad.

"Anything to add, Pete?" Samuel said.

His friend's hands were steepled as if in prayer, and he had his eyes closed this entire time. Samuel was sure he had been meditating but also listening at the same time. His eyes now slowly opened, clear and confident. "Comprehensive, my brother. I'll just say this. We need you two. We're getting expert assistance, and not a shrink this time since your dad is telling the truth about the monsters being real. I've seen and heard the reality of it. But as the Beatles said, all you need is love. In my gut, I feel companionship will win the day."

Silence filled the room. Samuel let it, not wanting to say anything more. He pushed nervously at his glasses, adjusting them on his nose. *Even if Amanda has dealt with this in her own way, it's a lot to take in. Give them a couple minutes.* So he did.

It ended up being close to two minutes of multiple sips of drinks and thoughtful expressions. Samuel was starting to get anxious again. Even though he was terrified to tell his story, he calmed down while he did it, finding it therapeutic to put it out there. But now the moment of truth was here. *She doesn't believe me. She's going to start calling people to get me help, have an intervention or something. I can't deal with this.*

"Dad?" Amanda finally said with no hitch in her voice.

"Yes, honey?"

"Can I curse?"

All four of them burst out laughing. It was much needed, cut the tension in an instant. Samuel wasn't sure why she had to ask for permission, given his leniency in this area, but the give-and-take sure helped with the room's atmosphere. "Yes, you can use all the foul language you need," Samuel said after catching his breath.

"Okay, that's good," she said, smiling. "So first off, what the fuck, Dad." She was still smirking warmly, so he knew not to get riled up. "Secondly, I believe you." Kyle was nodding happily next to her, so Samuel figured he did too.

"Why? Not that I want you to question my sanity, but how can you believe in this, sweety?"

Amanda put her hand under her chin and rubbed it, and Samuel knew she was trying to word this next part correctly. "You're the most down to earth person in this world, Dad. You don't even like to go on vacations since you're so opposed to adventures." Then she chuckled. "If Uncle Peter here came up with something like this, then I would disbelieve. Sorry, Uncle Pete." Darwin nodded understandingly. "But you'd never come up with a story so out there just for the hell of it. You're not quite that imaginative. And another thing. We don't lie to each other. We never have."

I raised her right. "But you believe they're real? Your grandmother and Uncle Patrick felt that something real was going on with me, but they couldn't accept the supernatural or that the gorillas were anything but nightmares. Now don't just accept it because I'm your dad. You were taught to question things. Even if you have some doubts, I think we can still move forward together."

"You're right. You always encouraged me to think critically." She paused. "So let's just say I land somewhere in the middle. I have to maintain some sort of scientific balance here. I believe something is affecting you, but not in the way your family did. Because I can acknowledge the supernatural more than they can, *X-Files* style. But I'll be the Scully here, okay? Be your real-world anchor but at the same time willing to welcome the unexplainable." The *X-Files* might have come out when Samuel was a teenager, but both of them had discovered it together the last few years on Netflix. Dana Scully was one of her inspirations.

"I think we'll need that balance. Although Peter's animal expert buddy will probably be the same way, even more questioning, I'm sure," Samuel said. He had briefly mentioned the esteemed Carter when he finished with his narrative.

"Nah," Peter said, "he'll buy it all."

"Really?" Samuel asked. "A scientist? Why would he?"

"I'll let him answer that." Peter winked knowingly. In a way only *he* knew.

"All right, I'll look forward to that." Samuel was not exasperated with Peter in this non-answer; he knew his buddy and that sometimes he had to take things on faith and patience with the flower child. He now turned to Kyle. "I don't even need to guess about you, kiddo. You've looked like a child in a candy store this whole time."

Kyle flashed his pearly whites, lighting up his face in a way that would have made the 10th grade girls (and some boys) at Buffalo School 46 blush. "That's exactly what this is to me. The candy equivalent for a teenager!"

Oh no, he's not taking this seriously. "Kyle, this isn't anything fun. It's scary. More than one person has died over the years. And I worry about you. I have a responsibility to your parents, who are two of my closest friends."

Kyle put his hand up before Samuel could go further. "I'll take it seriously, Mr. Redden. Let me tell you why I'm excited about this. The world we find ourselves in now is crap: so much hatred, abuse, inequality. But we need to have a world to make it better. These things have hurt you, and now they're hurting people in the world. I can't stand for either of those. I hate bullies."

Although he still thought Kyle was treating this like some comic book or video game in his mind, Samuel nodded. "Good enough, but if I tell you that you need to step away, you step away, understand? I know I can't really ask my daughter to do that, but I can with you."

"You got it, boss," Kyle said.

Samuel looked around at the group he had around him. "Well, I guess a team is developing here ." He thought for a second and then added, "I'm glad. Before Pete entered the picture, I felt so alone when I was younger. I need the support."

Amanda pushed her chair back, stood up, and came around to Samuel and Peter's side. She hugged her father hard. "Of course you do. We got you, Dad."

Samuel felt tears welling in his eyes and grasped tightly to Amanda. Peter leapt up and did a little dance that kind of resembled the Macarena. Kyle glanced questioningly at Darwin, and Samuel was sure he thought it was the silliest white man dance, but he proceeded to dab in the science teacher's direction.

Samuel was sitting in the den at his desk and staring straight ahead, thinking. He had just hung the phone up after calling his supervisor Ron. Working at the bank, they had a calling tree for contingency situations, so he had Ronny's home number. He didn't really want to call him at his house, especially after 10:00, but he thought it would be better than phoning in the morning and springing this surprise then. He would have contacted him earlier, but he had to get up his nerve for it. He told Ronny that he had some family issues and would need to take an FMLA leave. He expected questions and confusion, but Ron was a good guy, so he was mostly worried about Samuel's welfare and asked whether this came up suddenly and if he could help. Without giving out any details whatsoever, he simply said he would be okay (probably a lie) and that this situation had been brewing for a while (not a lie).

After saying goodbye, Samuel was relieved that the task was done but also felt adrift, now left without a regular 9-5 routine. That was never a problem for him in the past, even when he was out of work for extended periods over the years: when he had the two back surgeries and, on another occasion, a month-long mental health break. He was a hermit at heart and was always able to keep himself busy either by reading books or comics, watching movies or TV shows, or when he was younger, playing video games. But this felt different. He couldn't just veg out; he needed to form a plan to finally fight these creatures. He knew the first step was meeting with this Carter guy but was that so great a plan? *I wish I had a clearer idea of how in the world to do this. I'm so scared. And that's precisely what I can't be. They want me afraid.*

He heard a light tap on his door. "Come in, Amanda," he said.

She entered. It was getting close to 11:00, so she was dressed for bed, with a long t-shirt (a Buffalo Bills Josh Allen jersey tee) and gray sweat pants. *Similar to how her mom used to dress when sleeping.* The thought gave that old twinge of ache in his heart. He had come a long way to converting his sadness about Sandra to positive memories, but he figured all the drama of the last couple of days was bringing back the melancholy. "Heading to bed?" he asked.

"I am. Kyle's in the other bedroom playing *Fortnite* online. I think he might be up awhile, but I'm exhausted."

"Is he doing all right? Seems like a lifetime ago that he had his problems with those bullies, even if it was just last night," Samuel said, repeating his thoughts from earlier out loud.

Amanda dropped herself into the loveseat that was across from Samuel's desk in the corner of the room. She shook her head. "That's just like you. You're besieged by childhood nightmare figures, and you're worrying about Kyle."

Samuel laughed. "I can be selfish, you know. I'm really just trying to get a handle on the last 24 hours. And maybe thinking about Kyle's issues helps get my mind off this madness."

"I get it," she said. "Since you asked, he's doing better. That's the bullshit part of it. He's been bullied so much that it's just like another day." A second or two passed before she added, "Dad, can we talk for a few minutes? The little group round table was fine, but it wasn't us, you know? You and me connecting one-on-one like we always have."

As usual, she understands what I need in the moment. He smiled pridefully. "Thanks. That would be really nice."

"You can take the credit. You raised such an intuitive and wonderful daughter." They both laughed, and for a second, it felt like there was no impending cloud of disaster overhanging their lives. "So this might be such an obvious and maybe silly question, but how are you doing, Dad?"

It's a good question. "Not silly. I think I'm in the shock stage. Like this is an actual dream, and it's way past time to wake the hell up. And I was just thinking before you knocked that I have no idea how to proceed here. A gorilla expert will be great, but how do we defeat dream creatures forever? You know how I am. I need a routine, a plan in life. I'm not like your mother, who could just figure things out on the fly." He suddenly put his head in his hands and muttered, "I sure wish she were here right now. I could use some of that free spirited mentality."

These comments affected Amanda deeply, and Samuel could see it in her newly downcast face when he took his hands away. And he knew it wasn't sadness for herself but feeling terrible for her daddy. But she didn't wallow in it and said, "I'll bring that energy for you. You know I'm a little more like her than you in that way."

Samuel grinned. "But not as sloppy. You're cleanly like me." This made Amanda laugh, and Samuel thought again how much he loved that happy sound, especially now. "You're the best of both of us."

"Thanks." She paused again for a moment before saying, "Did Mom know about any of this? I know the answer is probably no, but maybe picking up signs from you, like the mental health stuff?"

"That's probably about right," Samuel replied. "She knew something was a little off with me. But that spell or whatever you want to call what Madame Takari did was strong. You hear about burying things in someone's subconscious. But I think even then, there are echoes of what happened to someone. For me, it was like it never happened."

"But in the same way," Amanda interjected, "it's not like it really didn't happen, right? You experienced it, your mind, your body. Something had to remain."

Samuel thought for several seconds. "Yeah, that's why I think you're right about my mental health issues, my anxiety and OCD. I don't think that's completely caused by the world or some chemical imbalance. It's probably a kind of aftereffect of the experiences with the gorillas. And…"

"What?"

I'm not sure. Samuel wrapped his fingers around his nose like he was going to sneeze, perusing his thoughts. He was like that for a good minute, and Amanda was about to speak up when he said, "Déjà vu."

"What about it?"

"We all get a déjà vu sensation once in a while. I had one in the bathroom earlier after all this came back. But I think there have been times in my adult life where I have that impression of feeling something from before. An emotion. And not the typical idea of 'I've been in this exact situation physically before,' but a stirring that speaks to something deeper. It's been so strong, but I could never place the origin of it. Not typical déjà vu at all. It often shook me, but I couldn't put my finger on it. And it usually came out of nowhere, not when I had an experience with real-world gorillas or something."

"That begs another question," she said in a wondering voice, "why are they back now? How'd they break through? If it was a dream you had of the killer gorillas that opened the door, what put it in your head? And is there more to it than that?"

She's so smart. I never even took the time to think of the why. "Awesome question. And one I have no freaking clue about. It's not the only one." He let out a sad laugh. "I guess this will be where Madame Takari comes back into it. Maybe she can touch my hand and figure it out."

"Have your hands started glowing?" Amanda was covering everything.

He looked at his right hand. "No. I wonder if that was the one thing that was part of my imagination." He then hesitated before continuing, "But I doubt it. Maybe I haven't really interacted with the monsters yet. That experience in the bathroom was more like a message from far away than an interaction, if that makes sense. Plus, it was daytime. I think they bring out whatever that glowing, burning phenomenon is." He sighed. "I just don't know much of anything."

"You will," she said with a smile. "No, *we* will. You have all of us here for you: Uncle Pete, me, Kyle, these experts. And whoever might join us along the way."

"We should keep the circle small," he said.

"Sure," she said as she stood up. "But don't refuse any help that comes along unsolicited." She strolled over to him, leaned in, and hugged him. "I'm ready for sleep. It's been quite a day. Good night, Daddy."

When was the last time she actually called me Daddy?

She began to leave but turned around right before she finished opening the door. "Oh, I almost forgot." She reached into her sweat pants pocket and pulled something out. She tossed it to him.

He caught it. And looked at it. A night light. It had Jasmine from *Aladdin* on it. He chuckled. "This was yours, right?"

"Yep, and now it's yours unless you need a more manly one."

He shook his head and tried to hold back the emotions, but he knew his voice betrayed him. "No, it's perfect."

Amanda smiled again and it hit Samuel how much she looked like her mother in that moment. It wasn't just the smile this time, but the kindness in her eyes as well. "Only good dreams, tonight. I love you."

"Love you too, baby girl." *With her at my side, we will win.*

Samuel was now sitting up in his bed, his therapeutic pillow behind him, bracing his somewhat aching back. He had been reading a bit, *The Running Man* again, but despite enjoying the story before, he just couldn't get into it right now. He put the book on his lap. His mind was still racing. He didn't take any additional meds to help this, as he wasn't sure he wanted to go to sleep. The lamp on the end table was turned on along with the night light plugged into the far wall, but he didn't want to chance it. They had started in his nightmares, and that is where they were coming from again.

But rather counterintuitive to his precautions, he wondered, should I invite them to talk, just like I did as a kid? *Maybe the glowing hands will return.*

Immediately after thinking this, he realized it wasn't a great idea. He thought they meant business this time, no more talking, just killing. He needed to protect himself until the whole group was assembled and they had a plan. In the morning, he and Peter were going to meet the primatologist. That was a big step, or at least Pete thought so. Until then, he was just left to his thoughts and maybe eventually sleep and, hopefully, no dreams.

He thought it might be a good idea to think of some positive things, so he returned to Sandra.

It was the night of the dinner. What turned out to be their first date. Which was the next big step in the most important and only romantic relationship of his life. It was a night he would never forget.

He went into it trying to stamp down expectations. He tried to keep telling himself that it wasn't really a date at all. Sure, Sandra agreed to meet him and even chose dinner, but a pretty girl like her probably had many suitors. She just wanted to have a decent meal, pay him back for getting her the book, and move on with her life, never to see him again. He needed to just focus on enjoying himself and not jump too far to conclusions about any future ramifications. That was easier said than done, especially with someone who had so little experience with girls.

The restaurant they were meeting at was on the main road that the college was on, Elmwood Avenue. Even though the city had been dying since the '80s, this strip was a hot spot, and perfect for the college, artsy with many cool little shops selling everything from clothing, wall posters and art, books, you name it. And, of course, there was a bar on just about every block for the party crowd. Most important for this night was the great variety of restaurants from fast food to higher end. He picked something in the middle, Danny's, a slightly upscale version of a burger joint. He had called Sandra a few days earlier to tell her where to meet and managed to dial down his nervousness enough to not stutter or have too much of a shaky voice. He thought himself irrational to be so stressed about the call; he talked to her just fine at the book store. But this was different for two reasons: one, he was approaching her about a date (or a date-like situation), and two, he was never comfortable on the phone. But he got through it, and everything was set.

All during the day of the date (because in the end, that's what it turned out to be), he thought he would die with nervousness. It was in his college days that he had begun to recognize the generalized anxiety he had about every little detail in life, but this was at a whole another level. His mom tried to get him to relax by talking to him during the day, but her words couldn't change how he felt. He could even sense the apprehensiveness behind her brave front as he was her baby, and there was always a layer of overprotectiveness there. He was meeting Sandra at 5:00, and the seven hours since he woke up were the longest of his life to that point. He was young and hadn't experienced much in the way of trials yet, and if he knew the terror that he would face years later during his dinner mate's chemo treatments, he would have told himself to buck up and enjoy it. But perspective is also not something you can automatically instill into someone; life is a participation sport.

Samuel arrived at the restaurant at what he thought was early, 4:30, since he couldn't handle hanging around at home any longer. He had tried to pass the time by working on homework, playing Madden on the Playstation, or watching TV, but nothing was cutting it. He figured he could give the hostess his name and hang out in the unseasonably moderate late January night and see if the cool breeze would relax him. But when he got there, lo and behold who was sitting outside but Sandra. They had a friendly hello with smiles, and something unsaid passed between them when they locked eyes, which told Samuel that Sandra was feeling the same nervousness as him and had the same plan he did. He had noticed at the book store and learned more fully after a few dates that she was a lot more sociable and easy-going than he was, so it certainly wasn't a general fear that made her come early. She later told him it was a specific anxiousness about the dinner with this new guy. He sensed a bit of this, if not the whole story, when they looked at each other, and it both set him at ease and also made him excited since he began thinking this was maybe more than just a "payback" dinner for her too after all.

Sandra was dressed simply but elegantly in a white top, green wraparound sweater, and a black skirt that showed some leg but wasn't skimpy enough to let the mind wander too much. He was glad that he wore a polo shirt and black dockers under his winter coat instead of one of his superhero shirts and jeans. They seemed to have landed on a casual dressy mode for the evening. But she had a little more makeup on than in the store and her hair looked bouncier, shinier. And there was a faint scent of perfume, a lavender aroma. Samuel idly noticed this, but with so much nervous excitement buzzing inside of him, he barely registered the significance.

They were seated in the restaurant's back corner, ending up a few feet from a fireplace, which was perfect for setting the mellow (romantic?) mood. They both sipped their water while waiting for their drinks, root beer for him, and a 7 Up for her. Samuel asked how English Lit 2 was going. Sandra sighed and stated her disdain for poetry.

"I get it," he said. "I much prefer stories or even plays over poetry. I can sit there for a good twenty minutes pouring over the individual words of verse, trying to see how they fit together, what it all means, and get pretty frustrated."

A sly smile formed on her lips, again revealing those dimples that made his heart rate increase. "Well, if the genius English major can't handle poetry, why the heck am I even trying?"

Samuel laughed. "Genius?"

"Okay, maybe I exaggerated a little. Smarty pants?"

"How about Mr. Average?" Samuel was never a grade A student. He had to work his ass off to even make the merit roll in his primary education days. But he had been doing much better since changing his major in college. Closer to A's than B's. He was thinking about this, getting lost in his thoughts as he was wont to do, his inexperience with girls not allowing him to see that Sandra was really just diving into this line of conversation to flirt with him. But the clueless person he was, he explained this all to Sandra and asked, "How about you? What kind of student have you been?" Being rebuffed by his lack of understanding didn't turn her off, though. She grinned, shaking her head a bit, kind of digging his naivete. He didn't catch on to this at the time either.

"About the same. I actually have a high IQ and SAT scores, but I have to be really engaged with something to find it worth my time to get good grades. I'm a searcher, Samuel, my boy. Explains why I haven't found my major yet."

The flow of the conversation hit a gap there. It was the end of small talk about school, and they hadn't yet moved on to the next topic. It would typically be in these occasions where Samuel would crumble, his nervousness taking hold, where he would find himself trying to find something, anything, to talk about with the other person. But not here. This was the first instance of comfortable silence that they would enjoy the rest of their relationship. For a solid minute, they just locked eyes and gazed. But not in a creepy way; they were simply in the moment with each other in a way Samuel didn't know existed. When the minute passed, she said a little under her breath, "All right, enough about school. Time to dig deeper, Redden." Samuel finally was able to sense something about her. She was just as surprised at the thing that had passed between them as he was.

But before they could start a more in-depth conversation, their waitress, a young girl clearly their age and probably a Buff State student too, stopped by with their drinks and took their order. They both wanted to try the specialty this restaurant was known for, Kobe beef burgers, something neither had eaten before. They were equally intrigued whether it was as tender as promoted on the menu (it was). Samuel got the mushroom burger and Sandra the bacon cheeseburger. When the waitress walked away, he said, "So what do you want to know about me?" Again, he was still a little amazed at how easy it was to talk to this pretty girl. And impressed that she moved so quickly between the boring everyday talk to more important life issues.

"Tell me about your family."

This was an easy one for him. He was lucky enough to grow up in a family that didn't have a ton of drama (the most significant exception would be his childhood experience, which was wiped from his mind). They had their challenges like any family, but they weren't the kind of group that held grudges or went long times not talking to each other due to anger. It was a close, loving unit, something he was still to this day grateful for. "I mentioned before that I'm the youngest of seven, right?"

"You did. Seven! Wow, your parents kept busy, if you know what I mean." Again that crafty smile. And finally, this time, Samuel got it. And he was a little rattled. He sure didn't know how to deal with her forthrightness.

Samuel finally let out a chuckle after a couple seconds and said, "You got that right. But don't gross me out here thinking about that! They were Catholic, and back then, people just had more kids; it was the way. Now it seems three or four kids are the max."

"I'm an only child." Sandra looked a little wistful before she added, "I'm a bit jealous. I did get spoiled being the lone kid, but you lose something not having brothers and sisters around. Probably why I'm more social than some, making it up with friends. What's the breakdown with your brothers and sisters? You have both?"

"I do. Four brothers and two sisters. The thing about it is I was ten years after my last brother, so there wasn't a lot of me play-ing with them. In a way, I was a bit of an only child too, until later that is, when I got older and we hung out more."

"Oh, you're just trying to make me feel better," she said as she flashed that heart-stirring smile, not the playful sinister one, but the warm and inviting gleam.

This made him blush a bit, but either she didn't notice or didn't comment on it. Probably the latter. "No, seriously." Again he seemed to not know how to respond to her playful approach. "I guess that makes us both the babies of the family, huh?"

"Yep. You were quite the surprise, weren't you? Mom and Dad probably both still spoil you."

This is where Samuel had to mention something that always made him uncomfortable to talk about when he was younger. His father. "My Dad is actually not around anymore. He and my mom got divorced when I was ten. I rarely see him."

"Oh crap, I'm sorry!" Sandra grimaced in embarrassment.

This type of reaction was exactly why it always made him feel weird talking about Claude. He hated for people to feel bad about it. "Don't worry about it, Sandy," he said quickly, remem-bering to call her by the nickname even though that made him a little nervous. "Lots of kids have to face a divorce, you know? But..."

"What? Tell me." She actually put her right hand on top of both of his resting on the table, which he thought was ridicu-lously (but wonderfully) forward, and it made him lose all train of thought, experiencing the sensation of her physical warmth. She could sense the difficulty of the topic for him, and this touched him deeply. The range of emotions surging through him now was a bit disorienting.

He took an intake of breath before answering, collecting him-self. "Well, he was a hard man. One of those old-school dudes who expects dinner at 5:00 and can only talk manly things with his boys. I was never manly." He realized what a dating faux pas this could be, but she didn't seem to care, her tender eyes not even blinking. "As sad as I was to have a broken home, I wasn't upset to not have him around anymore. He did quite a number on my mom too. She hasn't even dated since he left."

"That sucks. Did you see your dad at all after the divorce?"

"We didn't see him a lot even when they were married: he was either at work or the local bar. And after they split, that dropped to once in a blue moon. He wouldn't come to our house, but I would visit him at his downtown apartment every once in a while. Now that I'm older, I don't think it's even worth the effort. It's odd, though. He seems like a sad, beaten man, but I still can't have sympathy for him. He didn't try for us."

"You shouldn't feel bad about that," Sandra said, her voice low, confidential. "From the sound of it, you don't owe him anything."

Samuel smiled. "Thanks." He sorely wanted to stop talking about his father, so he transitioned to her. "What about your parents?"

She shrugged her shoulders. "They're cool. Well into their fifties now. Dad always talks about retirement. He's worked for over 20 years at the phone company. He can get an early retire-ment there. The world is changing now, so I don't think he'll keep up with the technology. Mom is the one..." She stopped talking and appeared to be looking for the right words.

"Issues with Mom?" Samuel glanced rapidly down at their hands, which were still touching, and he wondered if he should shift his on top now that she was taking a turn sharing. But he felt clueless, so he just left it.

"She just gets on my last nerves. I don't know if it's a female thing, but we butt heads much more than with Dad. She's the main reason I'm here at the dorm. She..." Sandra paused again as if realizing she was about to share her own deeper internal life with pretty much a stranger.

"It's okay. You don't need to say anything you don't want to."

Sandra wasn't looking at Samuel but off to her left at the flickering flames of the fireplace. She appeared mesmerized by the crackling blaze for a moment before continuing. "It just makes me sad. We were so close when I was younger. Mom is a restless soul. She's always worked part-time jobs, like at fast food places and department stores just so she can get away from the house. And she doesn't have to since Dad makes good money. Don't get me wrong; I don't begrudge her independence, but it seems like avoidance sometimes." She looked back to Samuel and definitely had a sadder visage than before. "You talked about divorce. I wonder. Sometimes I wonder. She takes it out on me sometimes."

"I'm sorry." Samuel hoped he sounded sympathetic and at the same time, wondered how he had found himself talking so intimately with this sweet girl.

"Wow," Sandra said, staring intensely at Samuel. "What is it about you, Samuel Redden? I just feel like my life is an open book or something. I'm never this way. And it's not because you opened up; it just felt right. I'm an outgoing person, but this stuff," she pointed to her heart, "I never share that."

Samuel felt like she was reading his mind. He almost told her this but then thought it would be a bit too much. He smiled. And if he genuinely did have telepathic ability, he would have known she found his smile heart-rending as well. He was more attractive at this age, less worn down by life: his fuller brown hair was curly, and his green eyes stood out under the prescription glasses he started wearing in his teen years (Sandra later said she loved his nerd spectacles). But these positive features typically weren't fully revealed, opened up, until he smiled. "Females have always felt comfortable with me," he said after a beat, "and I with them. I think it's the absence of that manly man stuff I was talking about. I don't come across as threatening to girls. But.."

"It's held you back," she said, "from dating and romance."

Samuel let out a nervous laugh. "Yeah."

"Until me."

"What?"

She grasped his hands tighter, and he realized that at some point, he had stopped thinking about their clasped fingers. "That won't hold you back with me." Samuel felt excitement in every pore of his body. "Promise me something?" she asked.

"Of course."

"That we'll always be this real with each other. It's so freaking refreshing."

Samuel hesitated for a moment as his mind raced. She was talking about the future with him. Things were moving so fast that the dazed feeling from before resurfaced. He finally said, "Deal."

The food came shortly, and they enjoyed the delicious burgers and then talked more. About so many different topics, personal and otherwise, that Samuel was amazed. He had finally found someone he could actually comfortably converse with and be himself. It was perfect.

◆ ◆ ◆

It was close to seven o'clock when they left the restaurant.

"It's early, " Samuel said, "Want to go walk the strip and get ice cream or something?"

"Let's save some things for date two," Sandra said. "Plus I'm a bit emotionally wiped out from our conversation," she added as she laughed.

Date two. Samuel couldn't wipe the smile off his face. But he suddenly got nervous. He knew that he should probably kiss her, but he was terrified. Talking was one thing. Getting physical was a whole different matter. Intimate contact was foreign to him outside of family embraces. And kissing a beautiful girl? He felt lost again.

He didn't have to worry. Sandra stepped forward and gave him a gentle yet passionate kiss that lasted a few seconds. Even though there was barely a tip of her tongue that touched his, Samuel felt such a rush of sexual energy heretofore experienced in his life. Their hands latched again and she gently caressed his knuckles with her nails. She had a faint taste of cherry on her lips and her warm breath sent chills down to his toes. The lavender smell was stronger in close like this, and all his senses felt overloaded. When they parted, he knew his smile was probably comical.

"Call me tomorrow, Mr. Average," she said, laughing a bit, "or

I'll come after you."

They would regularly see each other over the next few weeks, with the physical intimacy increasing each time until one night several months later when Sandra invited him to her dorm room. Her roommate was gone for the weekend, and they would be alone. This was when they first made love. He said goodbye to his virginity but more important than the carnal exchange was the giveaway of a heart that was already hers.

Samuel returned to the present. He realized he was crying. *I have to get my emotions under control or the gorillas will crush my heart into a million pieces. I just miss her so much. It never goes away.*

But as he curled under his blankets and brought his pillow down to his head, he realized reflecting on good memories was a powerful thing. He fell right asleep. And no nightmares came his way.

CHAPTER 5

T he next day, the meeting with Carter, the much-bally-hooed gorilla expert, was set at the nearby Starbucks in the morning. Samuel figured this was as good as any place since it was the closest to his house, although Peter wasn't thrilled with what he called the chain conglomerate capitalist scum monster establishment. He much preferred Paula's Donuts, the local chain, or even Tim Horton's. They were driving in Samuel's Acura when Peter uttered this in disgust. Samuel simply nodded his head and said, "Of course I agree. But the frappuccinos are fantastic."

He said this mostly to rile his buddy up, and Peter knew it, so he responded with a grin, "Great, when all the local shops are dead, they can thank you, Daddy-O. You have much to learn, young Padawan."

After getting to the Starbucks, Peter insisted that they wait outside on a bench until Carter arrived. He said that someone's entrance truly defined them; pro wrestling had taught him that. And Samuel just had to see Carter's unveiling first-hand. *There's no way this guy lives up to the expectations Pete is setting.* Samuel knew he needed to capture all the details, though, for when he gave their report to Amanda and Kyle. He was permitting a lot of leeway here with the kids, but letting them skip school was not something he was game for. Peter had his obligations at Buffalo City Honors, his school, but he had banked quite a few personal days from the previous year and planned to take as many as needed in their quest here. He loved his students, but it still didn't scratch the level of devotion he had for Samuel. Darwin didn't have much in the way of family in the area: Robert had died of lung cancer a few years back, his mother was retired to Florida, and his two sisters lived out of town, one in Syracuse and one in Colorado. Plainly put, the Reddens were his family.

The two old friends weren't currently engaging in any further conversation. Samuel was nervous about meeting Carter, but not because of his legendary status coming in; he was just that way with all new people. He was fingering the left sleeve of the long-sleeved t-shirt underneath his jacket. His young self would have been pleased with the decal on the shirt, a Star Wars image of the main characters with the number 77 on it; he still embraced his childhood interests. The rubbing of the fabric was simply a nervous habit, one of many the man had. And Peter was doing his Zen thing, looking up at the sky, the birds, or something Samuel just couldn't see. But suddenly, a big smile broke across Darwin's face, and he closed his eyes. It was like he was re-living a wonderful moment. Samuel didn't notice this as he was in his own little world, but Peter, in an almost worshipful whisper, said, "Behold. Carter."

Samuel didn't see anything and began to look around, but then he heard it. The squealing of tires as a jeep barreled into the parking lot. The sound made him instinctively stand up from the bench. The vehicle was eye-opening but not for anything glamorous. When he saw it, Samuel's first thought was the Jeep Wrangler from *Jurassic Park* that the staff drove around. But its condition was more like the tour cars AFTER the T. rex started attacking them. There were several large dents on both sides, and it was mud-caked all over. The windshield even had a crack on the passenger side. It looked like the guy just pulled out of the jungle. Samuel had felt that Peter was overplaying the living legend concept and the potential impact of the man's arrival. It just seemed like typical Darwin overexuberance. But he had to admit this was impressive already. *And I haven't even seen the man yet.*

Then the wait was over, and Samuel got a look at the person, and he thought the jeep paled in comparison. Laboring out of that not so large vehicle was one of the most enormous individuals he had ever seen. Carter was probably somewhere between 6'5 and 7 feet tall. It wasn't just the height; he was built wide (but not fat) with solid rock muscles, gargantuan hands, and legs that looked like tree stumps. He was wearing cargo shorts and a camouflage colored muscle shirt, which highlighted these features (and showed an element of toughness in the low 50's temperatures). He was a black man with a bald head, and Samuel thought he looked strikingly like the deceased actor, Michael Clarke Duncan. Except more imposing than what he saw on the movie screen. And seeing him helped stamp down the ever-present fear of the gorillas hurting those around him, as he thought this mountain of a man could probably tear even the biggest of the creatures apart.

"Holy shit," he said under his breath.

"You can say that again," Peter said, laughing. "Didn't I tell you so?"

"Oh, you told me. Sorry for doubting you."

Peter jumped up from his seat, leaving Samuel and striding with a cocky strut over to the approaching Carter. Samuel wondered if that walk was inspired by the confidence exuded by his colleague. He happened to see others in the parking lot walking to the coffee shop turn and gawk as he imagined he was doing. "My man," Peter said, "I told Reddy over here that you would make an entrance, and you definitely still got it."

"Darwin, you white scarecrow, of course I still got it," Carter said. Samuel thought the voice was just as impressive as the physical form and fit again the comparison to *The Green Mile* actor perfectly. It was borderline Optimus Prime-sounding, though more human than mechanical, deep and so masculine. *He should be doing movie voiceovers.* And Samuel wondered if the man had any weaknesses. The reunited friends embraced, with Carter lifting Peter off the ground. Samuel wasn't sure how the behemoth wasn't crushing Pete's ribs. *He must be used to modulating his strength around us ordinary folk.*

The two of them disengaged, and Carter turned his steely eyes, which were probably considered dark brown but appeared almost black, in Samuel's direction. He lumbered the last few feet to him. "You Redden?"

"That's right." Samuel extended his hand to Carter. "Samuel. Nice to meet you, Mr. Carter.

"Just Carter," the man said, repeating Pete's mantra. They shook, and Samuel winced, readying for his little bones to crack. Carter let out a deep guffaw. "I won't hurt you, friend." Then his face changed to deadly serious, and Samuel wanted to take a step back. "Unless you piss me off, that is," Carter said before morphing his features quickly to a friendly grin. Peter slapped Carter on the back, and both of them laughed, sharing this moment while Samuel tried to recover his composure. Carter nodded to the coffee shop's door. "Now, let's go and have some watered down mocha, and you can give me your story. Darwin just told me some weird shit was happening, and you needed a primatologist. Can't wait to hear more."

He's won me over already. There's something about him beyond the impressive appearance. And not just the confidence he oozes, either. There's a tangible power, a strength, that surrounds him like an invisible aura. You can feel it. We need that.

Peter patted Samuel on the shoulder and winked. In their

years of friendship, they had developed a kind of non-verbal shorthand. So Samuel just gave the hippie a head tip that basically translated to: "Okay, sometimes you have a good idea, you freak of nature." And he immediately followed this up with a gesture he often had to give his buddy, a pointer finger warning that said, "But let's not get ahead of ourselves."

Peter just extended his arms leading Samuel to the doors to the coffee shop, almost wacking an exiting scowling elderly lady in the process, his confidence not wavering.

Ten minutes later, they were seated at a corner booth of the Starbucks with their drinks in front of them, a chai tea for Peter, a pumpkin brewed iced coffee for Samuel, and a blonde roast with a tiny bit of cream for Carter. Samuel immediately recited his tale for the second time in 24 hours. He hoped this was the last time. It was exhausting reliving these traumatic moments. Carter fixed him with his hard, unwavering stare during the whole time, and Samuel at times had to look away from the intensity there. The listener gave no indication or reaction during everything said: no nodding, "Uh huh's," or anything like that. Samuel knew this story by rote, so while he told it, he was paying close attention to Carter (when he could manage it) but could get no read on him whatsoever.

Samuel looked down when he finished talking, needing to take a more extended break from Carter's attention. It was intimidating, to say the least, but he was glad he did so well for most of the time, not wanting to be rude or appear weak in front of this larger-than-life figure. He took a sip from his barely touched joe, and when he glanced back up, Carter was biting his lower lip with a pensive face. After a couple moments, he said, "So you think a gorilla guru will help with all this, is that right?"

He thinks I'm crazy. "That's what Pete thought," Samuel said sheepishly, before adding, "and I don't think it could hurt," not wanting to just blame someone else for his decisions. Samuel then quickly spat out the all-important question he had been asking just about everyone, it seemed, "Do you believe me?"

"I believe something." No hesitation.

"What does that mean?"

"I believe you're not lying. I'm a human lie detector, brother, and you're telling the truth," Carter said. Samuel's memory didn't immediately latch onto the fact that Madame Takari had said something similar all those years ago. But Peter remembered. "And obviously, anything about gorillas piques my interest," Carter continued. "But you'll have to forgive me if I don't jump right into this world without some pessimism."

Of course. I guess I couldn't expect everybody in my group to just suspend disbelief here. It's crazy. "So I'm telling the truth but only because I believe it, right? Like my brother." Samuel hoped he didn't sound too bitter, but he didn't want another Patrick situation.

Carter shook his head negatively. "No. I don't think it's that simple. Not much in life ever is. There are clearly mental elements here but physical manifestations as well. It's complex, but I won't jump to ANY conclusions."

"I can accept that," Samuel said, " as long as you're still helping us."

"I am," he said quite simply. These two words made Samuel's heart swell with such gratitude that it surprised him. *But I need this guy. I just know it.* Carter went on, "If only to educate some more people about beautiful gorillas. That has to be my role: the natural world and my know-how about primates. But on the more spiritual side..." The big man started massaging his chin. "I've spent a lot of time in Africa. Amongst the apes, of course, but also with the human tribes there. And Africa is special." He had a wistful look on his face. "Magical, you can say. I've seen things. Things in the overpowering beauty of the sunset. Things in the ceremonies of the native people. Things told to me by shamans. Times my life has been spared when I thought a pride of lions would eat me alive. There's more to this world than just my science. So I'm open."

Samuel was impressed yet again. *He's a three hundred pound poet.* "I'm happy to hear all that," he said.

"But," Carter added quickly, "I don't kill gorillas. I've often carried my trusty shotgun on trips deep into the jungle and sometimes had to defend myself. However, I never like to hurt a living animal, except the white Republican big game hunters who come out there thinking they're going to get a trophy. But gorillas are peaceful, family-like animals that may defend themselves but don't hunt humans. I won't hurt them. I want to find out what makes these gorillas, if they do indeed exist on some supernatural plane, tick. I will ingratiate myself with them as I do their real-life counterparts, and there will be a peaceful solution."

Peter sighed loudly, the first noise he had made in almost a half an hour. "No, my old ally. These evil cats may have some features of actual gorillas, but they are not the real deal. You couldn't have missed the groove that they have fangs for teeth and long Freddy Krueger claws. And they can walk comfortably upright like us homo sapiens. Even if they are some bizarre offshoot, they've made their murderous intentions clear. Not groovy. And if you need further convincing, here's another example: Sammy now notes seeing a silverback jumping into the fray. He didn't meet one when he was a wee lad. Why?"

"Educate me, oh, wise one," Carter said sarcastically.

"Because they come from his nightmares and not reality. He didn't know much of gorillas when he was young, so he didn't know about the silver-hued leaders. Now through documentaries or movies, he has increased his deep knowledge, so his adult mind has brought this dude..." Here, Peter paused and looked to Samuel. "What would you call him, Reddy?"

With no hesitation, Samuel said, "King."

"Okay, Sammy brought this King into our plane of existence as an adult. Before, it was just a huge black-haired version. Still not a cool cat but different."

"Fine, but what does that prove?" Carter asked while he took a deep sip of coffee, his vast hands dwarfing the tiny Starbucks cup.

"Goes back to my earlier fine point. These things may have elements of real gorillas, based on the conceptions of Reddy's mind, but they are also majorly skewed too, not of this world. They are monsters. They are bloodsucking vampires that want to destroy not only us but our world. Big Daddy, your knowledge about how they work and how we can approach defeating them will be invaluable, but they are more than you can imagine. I may have problems with our government's overlords, but let's take one cue from them: no negotiating with terrorists. And that's what these low down things are." Peter punctuated his argument with a drumbeat pounded out on the table.

Most people would have been fascinated by this science teacher who looked like he teleported from the 60's making this argument, but Carter clearly knew him well since he had no visible reaction. He just said, "That has to be proven to me."

"And when it is proven, since it will be, will you take action?

Because this is one time where I don't believe in 'make peace, not war.' Will you help protect us if need be? And destroy them? Send them back to Hades?"

Carter rubbed his bald head and looked up at the ceiling. He was most obviously struggling with this. Samuel could swear there was a pained look breaking through. He was not just a tough guy, this Carter, he had a heart. Samuel was sure that was a good thing – he needed someone who felt, not some uncaring robot, but they needed to get past this part.

"Okay," Carter finally said reluctantly, "if I'm convinced they are so different from real gorillas and pose a threat to us or others, I will do the humane thing and put them down. That's all I can give you right now."

"I think we have a détente," Peter said while looking sideways at Samuel, who was on his side of the booth. Samuel nodded his agreement. "Thanks for having such a wise, open mind, big boy."

"Don't call me boy, boy," Carter snapped back, but Samuel could tell it was in a teasing way by the slight smirk on his face.

"It's much appreciated," Samuel finally chimed back in. "Now where do we start?"

"First of all, I need to get a hotel in town. No way I'm staying in Darwin's bachelor pad. More like bachelor sty." Carter said. This was another one of those moments of tension release, and all three men laughed, Carter's the most booming of course. Peter held his heart with his right hand and put his left in the air, an impression from the old show *Sanford and Son.*

"After that important step for my comfort, we will need to begin specifically with you, not the threat yet," Carter continued.

"What does that mean?" Samuel asked.

"The whole supernatural idea is out of my purview right now. And I'm not a psychologist. But I know that if you did somehow create these gorillas in your brain, we have to start there. And where it began is most obviously fear. Fear is a powerful thing. We have to tackle that if we have any chance here. I can't get into how you possibly created these beings; you'll have to talk to your psychic friend about that. But I know that you have a terror of gorillas or creatures that look like them. It doesn't matter to me when that started, but I guess it was when you were a kid. We have to defeat that emotion first before we can even think of stopping the actual threat."

"Makes sense," Samuel said, "but how?"

"You meet a gorilla or two. The real ones." He smiled kindly, and Samuel thought he was having a memory of his interactions with simians. "I have a cool relationship with most zoos in the country, and yours is no exception. I'm not a big fan of zoos; these animals should have room to roam, you know, but if they're going to be held in captivity, it's important to me to know their setup. The Buffalo Zoo isn't half bad. I'll set up a meet and greet where I will take you inside the enclosure, and you can interact with the gorillas, learn that they aren't bloodthirsty monsters. That will help remove any blocks to facing whatever this is."

"That's groovy, my soul brother," Peter said. "I dig."

"I thought you would," Carter said, shaking his head in what was fake exasperation. "But what about you, Redden?"

"I agree it's groovy," Samuel said, grinning over at Peter, "it scares me, but it sounds perfect."

"Woo!" Peter exclaimed. "Let's commune with some apes!" He

said this a bit loud, which brought some looks their way.

"Sorry, folks," Carter said with his forceful timber, "Just an overeager hippie."

Later, in the early evening, Peter Darwin made another visit to an establishment. He returned to the section of the East Side that he and Samuel had so fatefully visited thirty-five years ago. The section of Buffalo that Madame Takari's shop resided had, like much of the city, seen a renaissance. Now instead of boarded-up storefronts, there were all kinds of shops, everything from ice cream parlors, pizza restaurants to hardware stores. Most were locally originated, although a chain or two could be spotted along the way, mostly food places like Mcdonald's and quite a few Starbucks looking almost exactly like the one they met at in North Buffalo. As Peter strode around the gentrified neighborhood, he bemoaned some of the loss of character even if it was safer to walk at night. He stopped outside Madame Takari's, which was almost like a remnant on the street. It hadn't changed much at all over the years. It wasn't beaten down; it just maintained its nondescript look, though the brick was now slightly more weathered. Peter smiled. It made him feel good that something still had class around here.

He opened the door, hearing the pleasant sound of the jingling little bells from above. And Madame Takari was awaiting him a few feet into the reception area as if she sensed him outside. Even though five years had passed since our last check-in with her in the alley, she somehow looked the exact same age, a bit aged but somehow maintaining the appearance of abundant energy and strength. "We meet again, my friend," she said.

Peter reached out and embraced the lady. At his height, he had to bend over to grasp her slight form. If Samuel Redden had seen this exchange, he might have thought it weird for these two to embrace like long lost friends. But Peter Darwin had always been physically affectionate. So any questions would be easily pushed aside.

Madame Takari led the science teacher through to her inner sanctuary, which also not surprisingly looked and smelled exactly the same: the beads in the entranceway, the string of colorful lights, the incense burning, the map photo. There was some disrepair to the room that wasn't there before: brown wet spots on the ceiling, chipped paint, and the floor creaked more. Peter figured she had more important things to worry about. The two of them sat. Oddly, the chairs were newer looking, not as beaten up but still had the muted acrylic upholstery, as if she went to a garage sale and asked for the same style. "So the time has come," she said. She held her palms up in front of her on the desk, beckoning Peter to speak, "How is he?"

"He's as cool as someone can be after having the weight of the world thrust upon his head." Peter had a sad look on his face, quite unusual for his personality. "I feel dirtied, like good ol' Charley Schulz's Pig-Pen, but on the inside."

"So you still kept your word to me and did not tell him?"

"No. He thinks my noggin was awoken at the same time as his."

"It was necessary, Peter," she said with her kind and understanding tone. "When he finds out I released you from the spell when you turned 21, there will be bitterness, and earlier in your relationship you wouldn't have been able to stick together to eventually win the day. But you must wait a little longer so he gets his thoughts right and hope your lifelong friendship will be enough to survive this." Then she winked at him with a twinkle in her eye. "And you know what I saw of your destiny through the flux of time: you two as expected have stood together all these years, no matter the trial. That kind of bond is hard to topple, though the waves of this evil flood will be your biggest test."

Peter sighed, a deep sound of sadness that his students wouldn't have recognized from him. "That's a good low down, little lady. Otherwise, I would have laid the truth on him a long time ago. He's like a brother to me; I won't see him hurt any more than necessary." Peter thought for a second before adding, "I only agreed to have this knowledge because you made it clear to me the dire and tenuous nature of the situation. Hindsight has helped me understand that I needed to keep an eye on him, to help him avoid the dark thoughts, especially when Sandy died. And to censor ape images when I could. You said he wasn't going to be ready until 2020. Until now. I believed and trusted you. And here we are."

She reached her tiny hands out and laid them gently on top of Darwin's. "I am sorry it had to be this way. Do you still trust me?"

"Always," Peter said, his usual smile returning. "You never steered this cat wrong."

"Good," she said, nodding. "And you've been a dear friend to me these many years. Without you and our other confidante, I would probably have lost my mind, no matter how strong my abilities are."

"And when do we bring T into the mix?"

"Not yet. You have engaged the primatologist?"

"Just as you foresaw, Madame. He's taking us on a visit to meet some real gorillas at the zoo to help Reddy with his fears. I'm glad you didn't show me everything, as that is a coolio plan and worth the surprise!"

"Obviously, you couldn't know all, or it would affect what you would do." At this, an extreme dark countenance came upon the Madame, as if a storm cloud wrapped around her; she suddenly looked older than her age, ancient and tired.

"Lordy, Madame, are you ok?" Peter was taken aback.

The shadow passed. "I am fine. After you visit the apes, you must bring Samuel back to me. I must help him do regression therapy as was originally planned by that poor Hector. He must face the creation of the monsters. I will not let you bring in another professional; the threat is too great. I will take the risk. And perhaps, at that time, we will reveal the truths to our golden child. Hopefully, his anger with you will be lessened if I am with you."

"I'll think about it, my love. As cosmically connected as Sammy and I are, it might be preferable to do it without you. But I appreciate the nifty offer."

Madame Takari stood up, came around the table methodically, leaned down, and kissed Peter's forehead. "Of course, my beloved Peter. Now go. Prepare yourself. Meditate, rest. We will all need it. And in no later than a month's time, bring our Samuel back to me. I've waited long enough to see his face again."

CHAPTER 6

I n terms of quality, The Buffalo Zoological Gardens was one of those middle-of-the-road zoos. It wasn't state of the art and progressive like those in San Diego and Toronto, but it wasn't in shambles either. Like most of Buffalo, money had been put back into it recently, so there were newer exhibits such as the sea lion cove and a rainforest experience. The gorilla enclosure was completed about four years ago, not a caged area but a habitat that tried to give the apes more space and try to recreate their jungle home. It wasn't as good as the wild, obviously, but at least it attempted to consider the apes' needs.

Carter was telling Samuel and Peter this as they walked through the zoo grounds towards the gorilla house. It was the next day, Wednesday, 5:00 in the afternoon, after closing time, and they would be the only ones there besides the staff. Still no Amanda or Kyle with them; while school was let out at this time, Carter indicated the fewer people, the better for the apes. Looking around, Samuel caught glimpses at some of the other animals in outside cages. He especially noted the impressive lion and the adorable combo of rhino mother and child, the last of those his favorite whenever he and Amanda came here. But he couldn't appreciate the environment as much as he would have liked since his heart was beating a little heavy and his stomach was in knots. He did his best to continue listening to Carter's lesson. Peter was especially quiet to his left. He, too, was checking out the animals and seemed quite at peace here with nature all around him. The Buffalo Zoo was located right next to Delaware Park, and even the most jaded person would admit the neighboring trees provided a scenic backdrop. Samuel was glad for no Peterisms right now. *It's a mercy. I love him to death, but I don't need the noise at this moment.*

Lost in these thoughts, Samuel was surprised that they had already arrived at the gorilla habitat building. It was a bit more modern (and larger) than some of the other brick buildings they had passed. There were glass windows lined at intervals along the shiny steel frame, which looked into the informational lobby area before you reached the habitat. Walking through the large double doors, the three of them were quickly greeted by Jerry Sanders, the simian caretaker, a balding, slightly paunchy man with a mustache. It wasn't a kind greeting. He was clearly grouchy and ignored Samuel and Peter completely.

"Still not thrilled about this, Carter, but I guess when you have pull with the powers that be, you can do anything." He stood with his hands on his hips. He was not a large man, so he was most obviously dwarfed by Carter. But he wasn't backing down one iota; if the two of them were the same size, they would have been close to being nose to nose.

Carter let out a bellowing laugh. "Sanders, you white whale. Back yourself off a bit there. I'll give you the respect of acknowledging your concern, as long as it's for the gorillas and not for your ego. Not completely sure which it is right now."

Sanders' face turned red. "Of course I'm worried about the apes! And our liability too, you ass. Something you're lucky you don't have to consider being the roving tour guide." *Did he just call Carter an ass? Wow.* "You might think you're this big bad gorilla adventurer, but this is my exhibit, my animals. Bringing a member of the public into here," at this, he nodded his head in the direction of Samuel and Peter, "is unethical and dangerous."

Carter only smiled, showing no agitation at all. "I'm a scientist, not just a tour guide, and you know it. Secondly, How long have we known each other professionally?"

Sanders, exasperated, shook his head impatiently; his temper did not abate one bit. "I can't remember. Years," he said in clipped tones, sounding as frustrated as a businessperson running late for a meeting after being stopped on the street by someone asking for change.

"What do you know about me? Am I known for recklessness? For putting myself, people, or most importantly, simians, in danger?" Carter asked. Samuel was amazed by Carter's continued patience, although he could see a small crease in his forehead that might mean this was starting to change.

"No," Sanders muttered.

"Then you need to return some of the goddamn respect my way. I'll be in the enclosure with Redden the whole time. I'll shield him if necessary and pull the plug if it goes wrong." He now reached out his elephantine hand and planted it on Sander's shoulder, and Samuel wasn't sure if it was a token of comfort or a threat. Perhaps both. "Now lead the way or get out of it. Oh, and one more thing, you might want to temper that tone of yours."

Sanders pursed his lips and said, "Fine. We'll go inside. And if you push it too far, I'm coming in and clearing you out. And make sure you never set foot in this zoo again." *Holy shit, the balls on this dude.* Samuel turned to Peter, and his friend just arched his eyebrows a bit.

"Are you done? Huh? Are you fucking done?" Carter hissed with a hint of anger finally, but it was still controlled, even-keeled. But it felt like when you could sense something in the air before a hellacious thunderstorm. Samuel actually wanted to step back from his resident gorilla expert.

And Sanders must have felt it, too, as he actually did step back in the end. "Let's go," he mumbled.

The threesome followed the zookeeper through another large door, which, unlike the outside world's opening, had no panes to peek into. This allowed the patrons a pleasant surprise at what they found inside. If the outer hall/mini planetarium they had just vacated impressed them (and it did, though Samuel had little time or interest to marvel at the architecture and flora, multimedia, or plaques with information about the gorillas), the next room was way more eye-opening. It was a wraparound glass enclosure, which gave a 360-degree roundabout to search out the gorillas. The inside looked like he was viewing the African veldt; it was slightly steamy and hazy (obviously humidity controlled), with tall artificial trees that reached up to the fifty-foot ceiling, sections of lush grass, and even mini stone mountain structures. There were the standard hanging tires for play, which kind of ruined the feeling a little, but Samuel imagined the apes enjoyed the living area for the most part. Like Carter was getting at earlier – it wasn't exactly like running free in the jungle, but maybe the next best thing.

Samuel could see no gorillas presently.

Carter now turned to him. "Okay, Redden. What we have in here is a family of mountain gorillas. Gorgeous creatures who once faced extinction, another reason I don't mind them being out of their natural environment. I am, above all, a conservationist. Here's what we have done to make this go smoothly. We have moved all the apes to what's called their staging area, where they get looked at by the docs. Once you and I get in there and are ready, Sanders will let Amy in. She's the mama gorilla. I thought interacting male to male wouldn't be a great idea; they can sometimes sense a challenge no matter how

THE GORILLAS ARE COMING

timid you may act. And since Amy won't be with her family, my hope is any defensiveness will be absent. She may think it weird after a couple minutes that her family isn't with her, but they routinely go into the staging area at different times, so I hope the few minutes will be enough to let her engage with you. And remember, I'll be with you. Try to stamp down your fears. She won't hurt you, understand?"

"Got it," Samuel said. *I can't do this. I can't do this. I can't do this.* He wished Amanda was here with him. But Carter wouldn't allow it. He told him there was no way Sanders would have permitted any more people than he grudgingly had. Carter even had to push for having Peter nearby; he knew a little emotional support was good, so he insisted on the hippie's presence. Plus, he didn't know Amanda since they hadn't had the chance to meet yet. It was an issue of trust, he said. He wouldn't budge on this.

"All right," Carter said, staring hard at Samuel as if he were an art critic scrutinizing a painting, clearly seeing the fear, "let's do it."

Peter reached out and put his hands on his buddy's shoulders. "I so envy you, Daddy-O. This is going to be transcendent." *I'm sure he sees how scared I am too. We know each other too well.* Peter smiled and nudged Samuel gently, resembling a mother sending her child to his first day of kindergarten.

Samuel slowly followed Carter towards the passageway's side corner, where there was a solid steel access door. They entered a small room, which was mostly bare besides a shelf with some unmarked boxes on them. "Let's call this a buffer area. It's to give the workers more than one way to get to the animals besides the back staging section," Carter mentioned, but Samuel barely heard him. His mind was starting to flash on childhood memories of cowering under his covers. He heard a loud noise, waking him from his daze, and saw that Carter had opened another door made of the same alloy across the room. The gorilla habitat was now open to him. Swallowing, he walked through, wishing to go anywhere but there but also not wanting to let down Carter.

Once inside, the humidity hit him like a slap to the face. It started an instant sweat. He looked around in amazement; he felt like he had just entered a movie, like *Tarzan* or *The Jungle Book*. *It's like another world.* Then he heard another loud thud of steel securing against the frame behind him. Carter had shut them in. *Oh, God.* "Let's walk for a bit, Samuel," Carter said. *That's the first time he's called me by my first name, I think.* As they walked in the Africa re-creation, Carter kept talking gently. *For such an intimidating looking guy, he's being extra sensitive here. I like to think he's concerned about me, which might be true, but it's probably mostly his gorilla mode. He's becoming Zen-like in here; he probably feels this is where he belongs. Peter would be proud.* "It's important to have you tour the whole area before we release Amy. That way, your smell is all over here, and she can feel you belong, that you're not a threat."

Samuel nodded as he walked around with his guide, noticing other elements to the living area, including a cave for shelter and shrubbery. He actually felt like he was on one of Carter's safari tours, exploring another continent. That didn't significantly improve his mood much, but he worked extra hard to focus on the man's words now. *If I don't listen, that could be trouble. Terrible trouble.* "No sudden movements. That's vitally important. You cannot risk posing any kind of threat to her. She has children, and even if they're not in her immediate area, she knows they are not far off. And this is her home." Samuel noticed Carter didn't say what would happen if she believed he was a threat. The big man then followed this up by saying, "Your fear. You have to be so careful with it."

Easier said than done, my friend. "I know," Samuel said, and he realized his voice wasn't incredibly confident.

"I understand it's impossible to be unafraid given your history. But you HAVE to do your best to not show it. You probably heard people say this about dogs, and it's true for most in the animal kingdom…even humans," he chuckled, "fear is easy to sense. Your perspiration, your posture, everything. Try to suppress it, man."

"Okay, I will." They had now come all the way around to where they started off. Samuel could see a nervous but still testy-looking Sanders and a smiling Peter at the glass window. Carter dug in his shorts and pulled out a phone. He tapped on it for a moment and then held it up towards the onlookers. *How does he manipulate that thing with his monster fingers?*

"I just texted Sanders," Carter said. Samuel observed the caretaker pull his own phone from his baggy brown pant pocket. He looked down at it, frowned, and then walked away from Peter.

"It's time, Redden. I'm going to step away."

"WHAT?" Samuel's heart leapt into his throat.

"It will do no good if Amy sees me, someone who is completely comfortable with her and gravitates to me. I need her to socialize with you. I won't go outside the enclosure since Sanders would have a coronary. It would be preferable, though. She'll probably still smell me some. But I will hide behind one of the larger trees that I observed halfway down the roundabout, so she will see you first. I'll be far enough from the staging door but still generally close by."

Samuel began to stare out in front of himself in a stupor, seeing nothing.

"REDDEN!" Carter screamed at him.

Samuel came speedily out of his trance-like state, hard to ignore that booming vocalization. "Sorry."

"You will be if you keep this up, and so will I. You know yoga?" Carter's easy-going timber was edged with a little frustration now.

"Some," Samuel said.

"Practice breathing in and out deeply." There was another clamorous noise, and without turning towards it, Samuel knew it was the staging area door. It was similar to the others he had entered from but three times larger and broader, so the sound reverberated even more around the whole habitat. "I'll be around the corner," Carter blurted out with much more speed than his usual careful enunciation. He moved away just as fast, like a fleeing (but towering) cat. Not quite running but moving his large frame so swiftly that Samuel was shocked. Then he was gone from sight, and Samuel was alone. *Breathe. Like he said.* He did it. With his asthma history, he knew breathing exercises well. Yoga techniques always seemed to him a form of this. So he began his deep breathing and tried to settle the shaking that was starting in his hands. He did this for a couple seconds before considering looking up. *You're stuck here. You have no choice. Look up, Samuel.*

He did. And with great effort, he twisted his body to face the staging area door.

And there she was, the gorilla.

Amy was a few feet from the entranceway, so she had moved that distance in the time he was doing his exercises. She was in the shadow of one of the large trees. As normal gorillas are wont to do, she was on all four limbs, not standing upright like his monsters. That made him feel slightly better instantly, his mind latching onto the idea that this was not something that immediately wanted to tear him limb from limb. It helped a little, but not entirely because he was still looking at a gorilla, and that deep source of terror and pain doesn't go away easily; logic is a valuable tool but hard to access in instances such as this. If he was allowed an utterly rational analysis, Samuel would have noticed the beauty in this creature. She was just under five feet tall at full height, weighed approximately two hundred twenty-five pounds. He seemed to remember Carter saying something about Amy being a mountain gorilla, a rare thing for people to see up close. Her hair was black but dotted with a brown, almost reddish hue. Her eyes were bright, alert. He knew it wouldn't be long before she spotted him. She was actively sniffing the air.

It seemed like hours waiting like this, but Samuel knew it was probably only seconds. Then it happened. Amy, the Gorilla, saw him. Her ears went up a bit, and she let out a small grunt. His heart started thudding at that sound, but he tried to keep his already questionable composure. *I'm failing, though. I'm sure she can sense every ounce of panic I'm feeling. If Carter were near me, he would be yelling at me to get it under control or move slowly away, maybe. But I'm alone here now. And I honestly can't move. I feel like I'm in one of my nightmares again, that old stuck in mud sensation.*

Amy started to advance, crawling slowly towards him on all fours. She continued to sniff and make those occasional snorting sounds. Samuel could smell her now and was relieved it wasn't that manure/bloody stench of his monsters, but a more earthy, dirty aroma, like when his doggy had been playing in the mud. Amy closed the distance in half between herself and Samuel, who was near the glass. He thought it happened incredibly fast but also acknowledged he'd lost all sense of time. She then stopped. She pushed up from the ground with her hands to rear back on her legs and then let out some cries. It began as the sound many heard watching nature channels, an "ooh, ooh" type utterance. But she quickly transitioned to more of a howl, like a yell of extreme emotion, be it fear or anger. Samuel could then hear banging on the door from the staging area, and he figured it was likely her mate wanting to help her. *Please don't let him break through.*

Then everything Samuel had been worried about came to fruition. Amy dropped back down to the artificial earth and charged at the human invader in her territory, the quadruped propulsion causing the terra firma to shudder lightly underneath his sneakers. Samuel sure wanted to run, but he was still stiffly rooted to the spot, feeling completely helpless. He couldn't even yell, he couldn't scream. But he was now visibly shaking like a leaf, his chest was burning intensely, and he wondered if a heart attack was coming. The epinephrine was surging through him, and feeling this chemical reaction, his mind flashed upon the cortisone shots he used to receive when he had his childhood asthma attacks. If he could have pulled his eyes away from the creature bearing down at him and looked to the glass behind, he would have seen Sanders screaming into his cell phone like it was a megaphone and Peter with a rare drawn, concerned look on his thin face. From this vantage point, Carter was still nowhere to be seen.

Samuel finally felt released from the bonds that held him, and he dropped to the ground. He curled in a ball and held his hands over his eyes. It was yet another déjà vu moment, this one more recent from the other day in the bathroom. And not only that but flashes of his childhood experiences bombarded him too. Gorillas walking throughout his room (upright), bloody mouths filled with fangs, dagger-like claws flexing, the smell of dung, the growling, him shaking under his blankets while peeing his Underoos. Then he felt something soft on his head. "Patrick?" he asked, completely reverting to his eight-year-old self. Thinking his brother had returned to him, not questioning how that would make any sense that he would just show up here (even though he still was nearby with his own family in Eden). But when Samuel gradually and carefully opened his eyes, he didn't see his older brother, but a weird sight. The gorilla was there, but she was petting his head. He looked up through blurry eyes, "What?" he gasped.

Then Amy took Samuel Redden into her arms and embraced him. He felt love and safety in those soft, furry limbs. The tears of fear that had taken over him when he flashed on his childhood dried on his face as he buried himself into the hair of this caring creature. He didn't take any time to reflect on the encounter's bizarre nature but only lost himself in the friendship he felt now. But he did hear Carter, who apparently had rejoined him. "Amazing! Her motherly instincts took over when she saw you terrified, Samuel. Just look at that. You had me worried there, buddy, but these animals are so much better than we are." If Samuel had looked up, he would have seen a large black man with the sweetest look on his face, caught the profound love this man held for apes. Carter reached out his hand, massaged Amy's neck, and looked over with a haughty smile at Sanders, who had even begun to grin. Peter Darwin was headbanging with a vengeance.

This is the best I've felt since all this began. Is there hope?

A few hours later, they were gathered at a new location, Carter's hotel at the Buffalo Marriott in the heart of downtown. When Samuel entered his new companion's suite, he knew his mouth was wide open in shock. He first wondered where Carter got this kind of money but was also surprised anything this elegant was in his backyard. Though he admitted he was always a Budget Hotel guy on trips. The lodging's size was one thing, over 400 square feet, but everything just looked so spotless and pristine. Walking through the door, you found yourself in a room that some corporate board rooms wouldn't compare to. There was a long desk running from the middle of the room to the near wall, and on the other side were all kinds of plants, namely geraniums and cactuses, around a series of windows with popping beige shades. When you took a right from that space, an archway led to a voluminous kitchenette with a modern fridge and gas stove along with quartz counters that held various amenities, including a cappuccino maker. The ample cabinet space would make any family of four happy. Passing through the conference area, the bedroom was unveiled next. A king-sized bed with the silkiest coverings was pushed against the far wall, which faced a 70 inch TV screen. The standard end tables were there, but they were made of polished veneer, along with a smaller circular table near a leather divan off to the side. Straight ahead at the foot of the bed was a long picture style window that gave a breathtaking view of Buffalo's inner harbor area, especially at this time of night with the brilliant lights all around. The carpet throughout was a shiny white, almost silver one, that actually sparkled. Around the corner from the windows was the most oversized bathroom Samuel had ever seen, with golden fixtures, a glassed-in immaculately clean shower, and also a clawfoot tub sizable enough to even fit Carter. Unsurprisingly, the toilet shined too. And there were several pictures on the walls of every room that caught your eye, photographs of Buffalo architecture along with Renaissance style paintings. Peter's first comment upon seeing it all was, "I guess we know who the king of Africa is. And it's not Eddie Murphy." He really couldn't give any kind of popular reference within the last twenty years.

Carter only uttered, "I may like to get dirty when out in the jungle, but this brother needs pampering when inside."

After they were all done oohing and awing, this became officially the first meeting of the club since Amanda and Kyle were there too (and dumbfounded by both the suite and the man). They were all sitting around the long table now: Samuel, Amanda, and Kyle on one side and Carter and Peter opposite them. The threesome gave the teenagers an update on how everything went today. Amanda actually got misty-eyed when she heard about Amy's embrace of Samuel. He knew this was twofold, not only the love of her dad and her worry about him but also passion for the animal kingdom. Kyle was into it too, but it seemed like he was more focused on Carter than the actual story – he kept gazing deeply in the man's direction whenever the primatologist spoke and seemed raptured by his bass articulation.

"That's truly amazing, Dad," Amanda said as she sipped coffee. At Peter's urging, they had picked up donuts and coffee from Paula's on the way back. There were also bagels and several little cream cheese containers, as both Amanda and Carter were not fans of sweets. "Mr. Carter..."

"Just Carter, babe," Kyle joked. Carter nodded, and Peter laughed.

"Carter. So you continue this, right? More visits to Amy?"

"Exactly, smart sister," Carter said, grinning with warmth. *He likes her. Who wouldn't?* Samuel felt deep pride. "We'll reinforce the relationship with Amy and as your dad gets more comfortable, maybe even introduce him to the rest of her family if that tight-ass Sanders lets us." Kyle snickered at this and clapped. *Yep, he has a crush. Can't blame him. Carter is truly a specimen.* "My goal is to achieve no fear whatsoever with gorillas. That will provide him confidence when we face whatever these things are."

"Thanks for helping him," Amanda said sweetly.

"For sure," Kyle added, "you're a godsend. You should have

seen Mr. R. a few days ago. He was a mess. I've never seen him like that, and it worried me." Kyle now glanced at Samuel with a look of care that could only be interpreted as love, and it touched the older man's heart. Samuel smiled and nodded his head at the teen. Further words weren't necessary to convey anything else.

Carter reached out and gave Kyle a personalized handshake: first the full hands, then pulling back and latching fingers, punctuated by releasing and doing a fist bump. Immediately afterward, Kyle looked down, knowing he was blushing. "My pleasure," Carter said with a knowing expression of joviality, "I have a feeling my most incredible adventure in the domain of apes is about to begin. This is a good thing."

Peter interjected, mumbling a bit through a mouthful of maple bacon donut, "But remember, Daddy…"

"I know, Darwin, they're not apes, they're monsters. It will still be an adventure, though."

They all nodded or uttered agreement to this.

Samuel looked around at each person at the table and felt another swell of emotion. *All these people are willing to go to war for me. Why?*

Of course, Amanda could tell her dad was stewing about something. "What're you thinking, Dad?"

He paused for a second before answering, knowing that he needed to word this exactly. "Okay, I want to be really clear here. None of you, even Peter, understand what you're dealing with. I do. These things are primal, powerful, not even made of real-life stuff. It's going to be hard to win. Chances are they will attack, and it will be awful. Some of us could die. And winning is a questionable thing, no matter how we plan. I don't know if I could have it on my conscience if I didn't warn you all and something happened. So this is your last chance. I completely understand if any of you want to back out." There was silence for a good minute after he said this.

Peter then spoke up, "What do you want here, buddy? An oath?"

"I want you all to consider this right here and now and decide."

"I'll go first," Amanda said. "Are you fucking kidding me?"

Samuel audibly gasped, his neck actually cracking as he urgently craned to look at her to his right. He never heard her speak that way to him before. It was especially jarring after she asked for permission to cuss the last time the gang talked. The rest of the group was completely silent, although he noticed Kyle lay his hand on his friend's arm. "Mandy," Samuel began to speak.

"No, I talk now." Her face was strained, tears were welling. "Where do you think I'm going to go, Dad? You're all I have. I'm not fucking losing another parent." She held her head low. A part of Samuel wanted to reach over to her, to embrace her, but as always, he knew his daughter. He needed to leave her be for a moment. *What an ass I am.* She looked up, and now her face was downright intense; she wiped hard at her tears. "I'm not leaving you alone. And you're not sending me away. Not in some stupid masculine attempt to protect me or something. Our love will beat this thing."

I love her so much. Samuel nodded his head. "I know. I'm a dick. I should have excluded you from my request. I knew you'd never abandon me. I just worry. But it's you and me to the end, babe." She smiled at this, brightening her whole countenance, and Samuel once again saw Sandra in her. He felt tears at the edge of his eyes. "And if your mom were alive, she'd be with us too. She would have believed me right away, and she probably would have strangled those gorillas to death so we wouldn't even need a plan." He laughed at his own joke - something Patrick always told him not to do when he was little - but so did Amanda. The feeling in the room loosened up a bit.

"All right, dude," Peter said, "do you seriously need me to answer this?"

"I do," Samuel said. *It's the only way I won't kill myself if and when some of them die.*

Peter only shook his head from left to right. "Nothing has changed in thirty-five years. You and I - with help, of course - banished these unholy creatures once before, and this time we will do it for good. You're my brother. Maybe not flesh and blood but in our souls. I will gladly lay down my life for you. In an instant." He saw Samuel starting to interrupt and waved his hand. "No, no more guilt shit. Mandy said she had no one else; do you think that's not true for me? I have no soul mate at home, no little chickees. My only other friends think I'm a joke. You've stuck with me through this crazy deep journey, and I'll always do the same with you." When Peter finished, he looked off past Samuel to the right and appeared to be looking out the series of windows to the skyscrapers outside. Samuel could have sworn that Peter had something else to say, and he looked like he was re-living a bad memory or that he actually looked guilty about something.

"Pete? What is it?" *No one else picked up on that.*

"Later, Reddy. Not now." It took a second before he brought his eyes back to his friend.

"Okay," Samuel replied. "And thanks."

Carter spoke up. "Hell, I felt a nice moment with you in that habitat, Redden, but I still barely know you from any other white dude out there. But..."

"But what?" Amanda was the one to ask.

He looked at her, then right back at Samuel. "I have a good feeling about you. You have a strength that you just don't even understand, and I'm not just talking about this glowy hand mumbo jumbo. It's real, and it's powerful. And like I said, the adventure beckons me on all planes: physical, spiritual, you name it. Plus, look at me." He pointed at his pectorals. "If I get killed, it will be impressive. No guilt for you there."

Samuel smiled at Carter, notably impressed with that answer. *I don't think there's a moment where he doesn't knock my socks off.* He then turned and looked at Kyle. At this teen who had faced so much hate already in his life. This young man who had all the potential in the world and an incredibly bright future with his intelligence. Samuel worried about him the most. He had his own family. He didn't have to do this. "Kyle, do you understand the risks?" he asked. "I mean, your parents, your future. Why? I know you already told me you hate bullies and that we mean the world to you. But is that worth your life? Every part of me wants to talk Amanda out of this." He saw her fidgeting. "I won't, sweetheart, but if anything happened to you, my life is pretty much over. But I know I can't stop you. But Kyle, you have a real choice to make here."

Kyle answered almost immediately. "Mr. Redden, do you remember several years ago when those racist assholes who lived over on Bryant Ave. called me 'nigger', and you told them off?"

Samuel did recall the incident. It was the Smith family. There were six of them: the parents, four kids, and a grandfather. They had since moved down south. But they were the worst when they were around. They flew their confederate flags and were known for their use of the N-word and horrible beliefs about blacks, using words like "animals" and "shooting them down in the street." And they had a lot of guns. Prototypical white trash. They pretty much personified everything Samuel hated. When they were nine, Amanda and Kyle were playing in the street near the Smith house, a dilapidated Cape Cod with peeling paint surrounded by grass as high as a country field, and the elder, a 70-year-old dinosaur, told her to stop playing with that nigger. Amanda came crying home. Despite Sandra trying to prevent him from going over there (this was a year before she passed), Samuel raced over and gave the Smiths a piece of his mind. He couldn't believe the things he said to them. He called them racist lowlifes and told them that if they ever spoke that way to Kyle again, he would kill them. He was shaking with anger. He never thought twice about this family having military-type ordinance in their house and how he could get his ass kicked or even killed. He was lost in his furor, insistent on defending that sweet kid that his daughter loved so much. It was an anger, a power he never knew he had welling inside. Now he kind of knew where it came from. "I remember," was all he said.

"Well, when I went home that night and told my parents, they were, of course, pissed too. If they had been around when it happened, they might have done the same thing you did. All my dad said to me after I recounted the day's events was, 'Kyle, we have prejudiced people in this country. Beyond that, there are ugly racists like the Smiths. And some people aren't racist but aren't anti-racist either. Last, of all, that rare breed we call allies. Those out there, too few if you ask me, who actively have their stomachs turned by injustice and discrimination, no matter what group of people we're talking about. That's Samuel Redden.' My mom added, 'We had a feeling, but this confirms it. He was willing to die for you, son. Don't ever forget that.'"

Samuel was crying now, and he could hear Amanda doing the same. He never knew any of this. He happened to glance over at Carter, and the strong man had his head turned away. Samuel couldn't imagine exactly what he was thinking as a black man, but he knew the emotions must have been extremely strong. "So now is my time to be there for you, Mr. R.," Kyle continued with a quivery voice, his own wet eyes locked onto Samuel's. "I'll be right by your side." He moved his right hand and squeezed Samuel's upraised left palm. "It's not just my friendship with Amanda. You're the greatest white person I've ever known. Screw that. You might be the best person I've ever known. Well, besides my parents." He grinned. "I'll fight for you."

Samuel sighed a wheezy breath, swallowed deeply, wiped his eyes, and looked around at this madcap group: the skinny hippie scarecrow, the mythical African hero, his lovely daughter, and this brave youngster. "All right. Thank you so much. I will do everything in my power to protect all of you. I don't know exactly what's happening, I don't know how these creatures can exist, I don't know if I have any kind of abilities to fight them, but I won't ever take your loyalty for granted."

In classic Peter Darwin style, he stood up, saluted Samuel, and summed up as only he could, "I guess we got those Musketeers topped. There's five of us!"

Samuel smiled and then laughed with the rest of them. But his only thought was, *God, don't let any of them die.*

CHAPTER 7

T wo weeks passed. Samuel made several more visits to see Amy, and in his mind, felt like they were actually becoming friends. Carter didn't make an effort to disagree with this. And true to his word, the primatologist introduced Samuel to Amy's family: her male mate Jeremiah and their little children. They had two offspring, both born in captivity: Santino, a male juvenile, and Lola, a tiny baby girl whose beauty made Samuel's heart actually ache. There was a slight adjustment with Jeremiah, as he initially protected his territory as a male naturally would, but it didn't take too long with him either with Carter's involvement. There were anxious moments when Jeremiah beat his chest and stalked Samuel, but the human did much better with his fear, even with that intimidating sight. And Amy actually pushed her husband away at one point. Even Sanders had come around to seeing the benefits for both man and ape in this developing relationship. He had come so far as allowing Amanda and Kyle to come a couple times to watch. And Samuel was pretty sure seeing Amanda's huge smile watching him play with the little gorillas was one of his favorite memories ever.

But now it was 3:00 in the morning at the Buffalo Zoo. Samuel and his friends were fast asleep - the elder Redden luckily still not dreaming - as were most of the animals at the zoo. It was utterly dark at the wildlife park; the workers shut down all lights in both the inside and outside areas in order to recreate the sundown hours for all the animals. Inside the habitat, Amy was curled up under a cluster of trees, her two children buried in each armpit, with Jeremiah snoring next to her, sleeping upright against one of the arboreal re-creations. Their peaceful sleep was suddenly broken by a smell that they all sensed. The scent was weird. It seemed similar to the simian aroma, but there was something in it, something foreign. And they didn't like that part. It smelled like danger. Instinctively, Amy scooped her little ones up in her arms and ran them over to a cave formation about twenty feet away. When she returned, Jeremiah was moving to the glass and growling. What Amy saw confused her much. A muted green glow had pervaded the dark in the viewing area. And there were gorillas in that space, a whole band of them milling around the glass. She quickly joined her mate and reared back on her haunches. She then realized what her confusion was: these gorillas were walking completely and comfortably upright like men. She couldn't understand how that could be.

Breaking through the cluster of gorillas outside the glass was the largest silverback Amy had ever seen. Jeremiah was a silverback, but he was dwarfed by this huge specimen. As she looked more closely, she was even more confused by the blood that spotted this one's skin, with the predominance coming near its jaws. She understood their own lives, typical of the existence of all gorillas, which were those of limited violence. Sure there were tribal fights, standoffs, but it was unusual to see lifeblood covering a fellow ape like this. And the crimson spots around the mouth perplexed her even more; it was almost like this gorilla had torn the flesh of some animal, a rare thing for her kind. The amount of the matted viscous substance indicated it probably came from a large prey, unheard of. Also, something appeared different about the tips of his teeth too. They were shaped oddly, but she couldn't see this clearly in the puke coloring. She found all of this not just weird but horrifying! She looked over at her love and while he was acting as a male of her breed should, getting as upright as he could and starting now to beat his chest, she could sense his disquiet as well. Amy was quickly becoming terrified for her children.

The gargantuan silverback, who stood well over seven feet tall and weighed above 600 pounds, pushed his arm at each side, which immediately cleared his group a few feet from him. Then Amy experienced an obscene sensation. She knew Jeremiah felt it too, given his wide-eyed reaction and stopping his pectus thumping instantly. This invader was speaking to them in their heads! She understood his communication perfectly. While what was said wouldn't be understandable in human terms, the sentiments communicated were as such:

I AM KING. YOUR MALE POSTURING ISN'T NECESSARY, TAME, INFERIOR ONE. YOUR LAME DISPLAY POSES NO THREAT TO ME.

Jeremiah simply made a head tilt, that gesture many dog owners would recognize. He was desperately trying to figure out what was happening here. Amy knew she was doing the same. But gorillas are smart animals. She quickly figured out how to return a thought. *What do you want?*

YOUR BLOOD, LADY. YOU HAVE BEEN SULLIED BY YOUR RELATIONSHIP WITH HUMANS. ESPECIALLY WITH THE ONE CALLED SAMUEL REDDEN. YOUR NEW FRIEND. YOU MUST SERVE AS A MESSAGE AND A LESSON TO HIM THAT HE CANNOT OPPOSE US. THAT HE WILL ONE DAY SOON BLEED AS YOU WILL.

At this threat, both Amy and Jeremiah returned to defensive mode, he banging his chest again and she making a howling noise. All Amy could think about was her babies, how if anything happened to her and her mate, they would be prey to this monster, so she hurled herself at the glass in a brave gesture rattling it.

IMPRESSIVE, SHE-APE. BUT IT'S OVER FOR YOU NOW. COME NOW, MY FOLLOWERS. WE FEAST. He opened his arms in a sweeping welcoming gesture and then sprung forward to the glass with such speed that even the posturing Jeremiah took a step back. Then the two real-world gorillas saw something shocking. On his hands were not standard nails like a human or ape would have. This creature had claws somehow. He put these weapons to the glass and began to scratch. The sound was piercing, unbearable. Amy and Jeremiah both covered their ears. The other visiting apes mimicked their leader precisely, leaping to the glass and scratching it themselves. After a minute of this, King growled for them to stop. Then he lunged. The glass crackled in response to his full weight. He hurled himself at it again, and its reinforced foundation shattered. Shards flew out and cut into the skin of Amy and her love. They grunted in pain and looked down in bemusement at their bleeding fur. King's sycophants followed his lead and went at other parts of the glass until there was a large enough hole for them all to enter.

Amy truly knew fear now, and so did Jeremiah, terror like they had never experienced. And letting this emotion in was a giant mistake. They did not realize how this was just as appetizing as the smell of blood for Samuel's dream gorillas. But she and her partner were still strong, prideful animals, and they knew they must protect their family, so they pushed through the fear and moved forward, ready to fight.

It didn't matter.

◆ ◆ ◆

Samuel Redden was awoken by something. And unfortunately, it broke him away from that dreamless sleep. The culprit was a noise in his bedroom. It was his cellphone on the end table vibrating. This was the kind of thing that always gave him terror. He grew up with a healthy fear of death, especially the potential of losing his mom after Dad left, and that was probably a bit extreme for a little kid. But he was sure it came from that feeling of abandonment, no matter how nasty Claude was to him. It actually caused an extreme case of OCD in his 9th year. He would go around the house, placing items, books, papers, and toys in specific positions, thinking that his mom wouldn't die if he did that. This gradually transitioned to his more manageable overthinking mode, even though it was still tough being a perfectionist when he felt like such an imperfect being. Samuel now found it eye-opening the year (1986) and age (9) this all began. No coincidence there; it was clearly an aftereffect from his initial experiences with the apes. And later on, after what happened to Sandra, he had an elevated reaction to the phone going off, especially in the middle of the night. He understood it was somewhat irrational; he knew Amanda was in the other room, sleeping, and her safety was his biggest worry. But it was still there. He even sometimes left his phone in the other room just to avoid it. But tonight, he had it with him right before he fell asleep and forgot to silence it completely.

After the initial jolt to the heart hit him, he managed to calm himself, took a deep breath in, and answered. He noticed the time, 5:00. It was Carter on the other end of the call. "Redden, I'm coming to your house right now with Darwin. We have to go over to the zoo."

With his mind still foggy with sleep, this statement didn't register. He took a moment to process it, but he still didn't understand. "What? At this time?"

"Yes. Sanders called me in a panic. It was hard to make out much of what's going on from his muddled jabbering, but it sounds like something bad happened."

"Something bad?"

"To the gorillas." Carter allowed this to settle in with Samuel for a moment. "Be ready in 15."

It's them. They've done something.

Samuel jumped out of bed. His feet were unsteady, but he still ran awkwardly to his dresser for some clothes, trying to block out all his ugly thoughts.

They went to the zoo in Carter's jeep, which was a tight fit since Peter was along and Samuel also insisted on bringing Amanda. But while there wasn't a lot of legroom, it was just enough space, with the four medium-sized bucket seats. Samuel knew he would need his daughter for emotional support despite correctly anticipating Carter's objections, so he had roused her as soon as he was dressed. She'd wasted no time getting ready, breaking out of her fog more quickly than her dad, like an army cadet springing out of his or her bunk. Her apprehension of the situation and the urgency of the timing helped limit any questions, and Samuel was glad. When Carter arrived, he had a spirited conversation on his porch with the man, but he eventually won the argument when noting how they had to stay united in this venture. He didn't dare wake Kyle and cause a conversation with David and Shayera, though. While they drove over, not a word was spoken, not even from Peter. The silence was difficult, uneasy, but Samuel knew there was nothing to say. At one point, he started the nervous habit of wiggling his right leg, and Amanda sitting next to him, placed a hand on it. He sadly smiled at her.

As Carter pulled into a parking space at Buffalo Zoological, Samuel agreed with him that Amanda should at least stay in the vehicle while the threesome went to the gorilla refuge. Their silence continued as they shut the car doors and walked through the parking lot, to the unlocked entry gates, and finally down the path to the habitat. Sanders was waiting on the sidewalk leading to the building. He looked terrible. His eyes were bloodshot, and Samuel was sure that the man had been crying. He also looked pale and in shock, staring un-focused up into the sky even after they greeted him.

Carter tried to get his attention again. "SANDERS!" Not many could have ignored that booming exclamation. But Sanders was still unresponsive.

Carter took his large hands and actually shook the little guy a bit. Far from his full strength, but enough to wake up the zookeeper. "Sorry. It's bad in there," Sanders finally said quietly. Then his cloudy eyes cleared up a lot when he noticed Samuel and Peter. *That's the second time he's treated us like we're statues.* "What are they doing here?"

"This involves them," Carter barked, testy already, and Samuel knew he was finding it hard to stay his usual calm self with the idea of gorillas endangered.

"Listen, I get that this man has bonded with the gorillas," Sanders said, more his pert self, "and I can also understand you wanting him to know." Samuel bristled at being talked about like he wasn't even there. He was also most obviously on edge and felt like hitting the smarmy jerk. *Keep it under control.* Sanders continued, "Not sure why the hippie is here, though. But neither can go in. Carter, it's ugly. I haven't called the po-lice yet. Or my bosses. I have no idea why I even contacted you first. Maybe to have another gorilla person look at it." With this, he let go of that perturbed stance and looked lost again. He spoke low now, a shaky whisper, "That scene...it makes no sense. Why would someone do this? I need to wake up. This can't be real. " Samuel made special note of these last remarks and wondered about his nightmare gorillas and how far their powers reached in the world now.

"I get it, man," Carter said in a more understanding voice. "But I think this involves my friend here. We need to see this together. I honestly can't explain more than that." Samuel made no note of Carter calling him "friend," something he would have been overjoyed at a couple days ago. But not as much now. His thoughts were firmly focused on what they were going to find in there.

Sanders just nodded dejectedly now and stepped aside, shuffling his feet. "It doesn't matter, I guess," he whispered. This expression of utter defeat from the previously unwavering guy put an extra layer of unease into Samuel. Then the caretaker added in a mumble, more to himself than to anyone else, "I just don't get why the security cameras were all blurry and muffled. I guess I better make those calls." He walked away while a knowing, worried look passed between Samuel and Peter.

Carter stepped forward and opened the door to the entranceway, holding it open for the others. "I don't know if I can do this, Pete," Samuel said to his oldest friend.

Peter put a hand on his shoulder. "We're with you."

Samuel stepped through the door and instantly gasped. His eyes had immediately gone straight to the inner door that led to the sanctuary. It was ripped off its hinges. He then saw its remains lying against a far wall. The door was bent as if it had been twisted by Superman. He followed Carter, who moved briskly forward, and felt like a zombie as he trudged through the new opening with Peter right behind him. What he saw in the viewing area made him whine a little under his breath. Shattered glass was all over the floor. And in the glare of the recently switched on lights, there was something that stood out even more. Dripping crimson on a section of the protective glass wraparound structure. Blood. The yawning hole with its shards sticking out looked like a monstrous maniacal mouth. He began to move forward quickly, unable to stop himself and unheeding Carter's warnings to be careful. He too felt like he was dreaming again; reality took on the foggy half-existence that his nightmares were made of. When he reached the glass and the massive crevice in it, he managed to snap out of the waking muddiness. But he was still in a nightmare.

It was a carnal house inside the habitat, truly a murder scene. Blood was splattered on grass, trees, bushes, the cave in the distance. And just inside the sharp, toothy crevice was Jeremiah. He laid spread-eagled. At first, Samuel wondered why he was confused by the mishappen form. Then as he stepped a bit closer, it became more than obvious. The male's head was gone. The pool of blood that oozed from it formed a puddle on the ground.

Samuel started to breathe hard but forced himself not to hyperventilate. He could hear Carter and Peter behind him saying things, but it was all mumbles to him now. *I have to see Amy. Then I can completely lose it. And I will.* He stepped carefully through the jutting shards in the hollow and tiptoed gingerly around the gorilla that seemed so majestic and powerful when he visited. He didn't want to look at the body fluid running towards him from its pool in the grass, but he had to so he wouldn't step in it. His eye instantly moved to the cave formation twenty feet away. There was a sizeable furry hump prone there as well, the shape half in and half out of the opening. Carter laid a hand on his shoulder, but Samuel somehow shrugged off that firm grip and then ran to his first simian friend.

He reached her. And then wished he hadn't. Amy's head was intact. But there was a vast crater in her stomach area. It looked like someone had made an incision and placed a home-made bomb in there. He could see some spaghetti-like pro-trusions, clearly what was left of her intestines. The gaping wound actually started just below her neck and went all the way down to her legs, so he could see the chest cavity as well. Or what was left of it. It looked like they had ripped her heart out.

As they have mine.

Samuel was all ready to let himself collapse and just lay on the ground, never to get up again. But a thought occurred to him. It was a horrible thought that he did not want to explore. But he had to. He turned to Carter, who stood a few feet away with Peter. Carter looked like someone had killed his imme-diate family. His eyes had a dismayed look that was far away, maybe thinking about every gorilla he'd loved. After a second, he blinked and bit at his tongue, obviously trying to forcefully return to the present.

"Where are the kids?" Samuel asked.

Carter just shook his head. *He ran into this blind just like I did.* "Maybe we should go," the big man said. Samuel heard some-thing new in his brave primatologist's voice: fear.

"Reddy, listen to the smart dude," Peter added, his voice quivering and his hands held in fists at his side. *He values all life. This is going to do a number on all of us for a long time.* "This is not a good scene."

"I must know all of it," Samuel said. He stepped over Amy as she was blocking the whole entry and sucked in a developing cry when he looked at her again. He stumbled further into the cave. Immediately he gagged. The smell that reached his nose was noxious, the tangy stench of blood. Floodlights cast illumination down from the ceiling, and he instantly wished they were still off. Somehow the ruddy gore in here was more plentiful. It made his mind flash on that scene in the movie version of *The Shining*; it looked like someone had released a flood of blood in the place. The sticky goo was dripping from the roof and covered almost every inch of the surface below his feet. But he couldn't see bodies. Then at the far end of the cave near the wall, he glimpsed something—two dark spots. The light was dim back there, so he barely made it out. He walked towards the objects, stepping wide to tiptoe on the only dry spots he could find. When he got there, he became perplexed again. All he could see was fur. But he kneeled down, and there were bones spread throughout. The realization was dawning. Amongst the fur and blood, he saw several silver hairs.

He turned quickly to his companions, who were now deep in a stupefied state. "He ate them. The silverback, the leader. He fucking ate the babies!" Samuel screamed this last part before rocking on his knees and vomiting out his dinner of pork chops and mashed potatoes.

Samuel, Peter, and Carter made it out to the parking lot. They were all walking in a stupor. The cool night air froze the sweat that had broken out all over Samuel's body. This would have felt good in a normal situation, but now it only made him queasy again. He genuinely saw nothing in front of him as he walked to the jeep. It was like a gray haze had taken over the world, and he was sure it was no real fog, and indeed, the lamp-posts were casting their unimpeded nighttime illumination. It was his eyes, glassed over and blurry. But when he got to the jeep, the door opened, Amanda came out, and he saw clearly. Her face quickly morphed into concern. "Dad?"

Behind Samuel, Carter said, "They're real. I thought I believed you, Samuel, I really did. But this? What is this? God, I killed them."

"What did you say?" Peter asked, his scarecrow form lost in the shadows further back.

"I killed those beautiful gorillas," Carter choked out. It was hard to tell exactly in the dull light, but Samuel thought tears were rolling down the strong man's cheeks.

"No, it's my fault," Samuel said. "They're my creation. What's wrong with me, guys? How can my mind create such horrors?"

"Dad," Amanda repeated, this time not an interrogative. She certainly had questions about all this. But she knew to hold back. Then came the imperative, gently mouthed, "Come here." Samuel collapsed into his daughter's arms. He thought he would begin weeping like Carter. But he just laid in her arms as she kneeled down with him to the garbage-strewn parking lot surface. *This is getting to be a regular position for me.* He noticed Amanda's body vibrating like a cell phone and felt heavyhearted for her before realizing he was the one shuddering. Carter also took a knee and held his head. Peter Darwin, the pacifist, looked up at the heavens and glared with an expression never seen from him before. An ugly sneer. Caused by hate. A deep burning hate. He wanted revenge.

CHAPTER 8

O ver the next few days, the group took a break from each other. They all agreed it would be smart to take a breath and relax. And mourn. Samuel still talked briefly with Kyle when the teen visited Amanda, but beyond telling him of the tragedy, the contact was mainly casual and non-business. It was rare even before this crisis for the older Redden to go a few days without hearing from Peter, so when his friend finally reached out, he was glad to see him. They were now sitting outside on his covered deck overlooking the backyard, and this time Samuel's mind did make the connection of that past conversation between the two out on his mom's pool deck after Hector died. As a gust of slightly cooled air brushed the back of his neck, it even occurred to him that it was the same time of year, the dividing line crossed from the mild end of summer to the crispness of full autumn. *It all comes around, doesn't it?*

While just taking some days to process what happened was not a cure-all, Samuel was getting by now. He focused hard on his mental health and avoided when he could thinking about Amy and her family. He had his doctor up his anxiety meds and took it upon himself to eat well, exercise, and just rest. He and Amanda finished doing a MCU movie marathon, and that was fun to get his mind off things. Though all this helped, he still had bags under his eyes and felt exhausted. Sleep was hard to come by now. He thought on one level that was a good thing.

Peter didn't look much better. His skinny face appeared haggard, strained. Despite being the same age as Samuel, he always had a more youthful appearance, as if he hadn't aged much in the last 20 years. But he now looked older, world-weary. It was almost like the scene they witnessed at the zoo had zapped his faith in the world. The two of them sat watching the birds for several minutes before Samuel finally said, "How's Carter doing? He's the only one I haven't seen since..." *Since the massacre.*

"He's dropped off the grid, buddy. I tried to text him a couple days ago to no response. As hard as this has been on all of us, and I know how you always gravitate to the guilt thing, brother, I think it's had a special effect upon our main man. He loved those animals like they were his own flesh and blood. It did something to him, and I'm not sure what the result will be."

Samuel nodded. "Seems weird coming from me, but he should try not to blame himself. It was a good plan. It helped me a lot. I guess while I accepted my nightmare monsters were in the real world now, I didn't truly understand the true extent of it. It's all so disturbing. You and I decided long ago that they can't read my mind all the time. So they must have been following me, stalking me, which isn't a much better thought. They bided their time and acted on the situation when they thought they could most do the damage. It was a message, Pete. To me. That there's no hope. That they could kill any of us at any time." He sighed.

"But why wait then? What's with the methodical process?"

"To torture me. To break me down mentally before killing me and everyone I love. God."

"Right." Peter paused before adding, "Daddy-O, it's time to try my plan."

"I thought your plan was Carter." Samuel looked over more directly at his friend. They were on opposite sides of the deck, Peter on the outdoor couch with his long legs propped on a little glass table, and Samuel across the way on a lawn chair, his back to the sliding glass door that led to his tiny dining room.

"Part of it, buddy. But kind of a small part. That's in no way to put a negative whammy on my old African explorer friend. But there's a big aspect of this we haven't rapped about. The beginning."

"What do you mean?"

"How it started," Peter said. "We have to go forward with what Hector planned on doing. Regression therapy. But he was most likely a doubter. We know better. We need to seek out what originally made them come to you—the connection. There are the luminous hands, which might be the how, the gateway, so to speak. But what was the trigger?"

I hadn't thought of that. "But endangering another psychiatrist," Samuel said, "I can't do that."

Peter didn't reply right away. He actually took a minute or two staring off to the left, his eyes absently passing from Samuel's lawn to the driveway, his face looking more strained than Redden had ever seen. "Pete?" he asked.

Peter returned his focus to Samuel. "Do you remember at our little oath swearing when you noticed something about me, and I said we'd jive about it later?"

Oh yeah. I'd forgotten all about that. With what happened to Amy's family, that conversation was lost to me over the last couple of weeks. "Now that you mention it. What about it?"

"I have a secret, compadre. I feel as low as climate change de-niers must when they look in the mirror."

"Okay," Samuel said. *This is weird.*

"There's someone else who could do the regression and not a shrink. A certain someone who has a level of protection." He stopped again for a solid twenty seconds. "Madame Takari."

"Oh, she can do that?" Then a thought occurred to Samuel. "How do you know? You've seen her?"

Peter stood up, walked over, dragging the small table over to the front of Samuel's chair, and sat awkwardly upon it. He pursed his lips and then laid a hand on his buddy's knee. "I've been meeting with Madame Takari regularly for 35 years."

Samuel heard what Peter said but didn't wholly conceptualize it. *Wait, what?* "I don't understand. You just remembered the gorillas, like I did."

"That's a negative, partner," Peter said with a sad voice, a dis-gusted sound. "I had to pretend that part."

What is happening here? "She did that brain wipe thing to both of us. I was there!" Samuel's voice was rising in intensity now.

"Accurate. But right after the lady did the whammy on me, she put a post suggestive thought inside my noggin. It laid in there coolly until my 21st birthday. It forced me to visit her place of business at that point, though I had no idea why. She then removed the spell so all was recollected, and my world was shaken like the stands at a Metallica concert."

"But why?" Samuel leapt up and began pacing the deck, flex-ing his fingers, another nervous habit.

Peter didn't take much notice of this, knowing Samuel's ticks, plus he was still lost in his own mental world, the pupils of his eyes a bit dilated, extra aware, but not in the direction of his friend. "She wanted me to keep my peepers on you and report back," he said quietly.

"WHAT?" Samuel yelled uncharacteristically. He stopped moving around and then became the opposite of his frenzied self, standing completely still against the far railing, resembling a carven sculpture of a nondescript man, unfeeling, blank.

"Please calm down, fellow Musketeer," Peter said in a wavering outtake of air as he now shifted his body around to take in Samuel.

"Oh, stop with the hippie shit and just talk like a regular person!" Samuel shouted. At this, Peter recoiled back like he was struck with a blow. "Have you been lying to me my whole life? Are we really friends?" The appearance of deep hurt on Peter's face would have customarily moved Samuel but not now. "What is all this about? How could you not tell me?"

No jive jargon from Peter now. He was dead serious. "I've always been your friend and would have been without Madame's involvement."

"You don't know that, Darwin." Samuel never referred to Peter with just his last name, and it surely didn't go unnoticed.

"I know it in my heart. Listen to me, Reddy. Madame cares for you, worries about you. That is why she did what she did. I was never happy about it."

Samuel unclenched a bit, coming back to sit on the couch slowly. "My whole life has broken down in the last month. And now you lay this on me. You betrayed me."

"I know," Peter said with a sigh that sounded more like a piti-ful dog whine. He twisted back around but not fully, as if afraid to get too close to the raging Samuel. "All I can say is sorry. And to answer your earlier question, it was for your protection. The Madame needed to be aware in case the gorillas came back pre-maturely. And we wanted to give you as many happy years as possible, brother."

"You're not my brother!"

"You know what, Samuel? Go fuck yourself." Now it was Sam-uel's time to flinch. "I've been living with this secret for 25 goddamn years! It hasn't been easy. If I loved you any less than a brother, I would have bailed, okay, asshole?" The words were angry, if not loud, but Darwin's stiff posture and downcast ex-pression still was one of defeat, not fury.

Samuel looked long and hard at his childhood friend, the one who never left him. "Fair enough," he said, "but we're not okay. I have a long way to go with this."

"I don't blame you one bit. But we need to focus, all right? You need to see the Madame. All I said here was true and important about the regression therapy. And it doesn't just come from her. I know a thing or two about the transformative power of meditation and the deep wells of a soul." The hippie style was fully back now, and Samuel was kind of glad for it. "We have to stop putting off facing your inner demons. It's these buried issues that created the low-down dirty creatures."

"Of course I'll go," Samuel replied. "Despite my anger at you and her, she did help me all those years ago. So I trust her abilities if not her master manipulation here." Samuel stared intensely at Peter for a long moment, which actually made his free-loving pal drop his eyes. "No more secrets, okay?"

"A-okay, old pal."

"And you'll tell me everything? Twenty-five years is a long time, a lot of information that has been withheld from me."

"Yes, of course. I will let Madame lead the way, though. A lot of it is for her to tell. But I will fill in any gaps that are left."

"Let's hope she doesn't conveniently forget anything." The bitterness still threatened to overwhelm Samuel. "I'm going to have some strong words with her about all this. Any appearance of protecting me now has to end. I have to be armed in all ways, especially with information."

"As always, you're a wise one, Sammy," Peter said, gazing back up at Samuel. "And try not to be too hard on her. She's a wonderful woman. I've honestly come to love her over the years." Samuel did note how Peter redirected the focus of his concern to this other person, not on himself, which impressed him. *Peter is the same person I've always known, even with this. But still.* "Again, I'm so..." Peter tried to continue, but Samuel cut him short.

"Not now, Pete. I want to be alone."

Peter had left, but Samuel remained on the deck. He was having a hard time dealing with his emotions, but he knew he had to get them under control. The more of a mess he was, the more vulnerable he became to the gorillas.

I'm just so angry. I get what a danger I was to the world. But why did Madame Takari bring Pete into this? Couldn't she have someone else look over me? She's cast a dark spot on one of the things in my life that was always a sense of safety, my friendship with him.

How am I supposed to trust her now? When I need her the most? God, I hate all of this.

Looking out at his small yard, he returned to his past.

Seven years had gone by since Samuel and Sandra first started dating. They had been together since that dinner at Danny's. Both went through their academic and career attempts and had remained a couple through all that time. Samuel tried his hand at teaching English but couldn't handle it. It started going wrong in his second student teaching placement. His first had been pretty good. They were middle schoolers, 7th grade, and despite some exuberance of energy that was sometimes hard to deal with, he had a good rapport with them. It helped that his cooperating teacher, Mr. Maker, ran a tight ship coming in, and he didn't leave Samuel alone with the students hardly ever. It actually gave him a false sense of control.

His second arrangement was awful. This cooperating teacher, Mrs. Randolph, honestly threw him to the wolves. It was 9th grade, and she often left him alone with the unruly students. It didn't go well. Spitballs being shot around the room, kids calling him names, and disrespecting his authority constantly. He was in his early twenties and still had a babyface, so they didn't feel like he should have any say over them. And it was hard for Samuel, with his easy-going personality, to suddenly become the tough guy.

This took a lot out of his self-esteem and damaged hope for this career he often dreamt about. He wanted to have inspired conversations with young minds about the classics of literature, but he wasn't sure he could ever get to that point with his classroom management issues. This was when his mental health difficulties became more clarified for him, although he didn't take it seriously at the time. These struggles continued when he actually tried to start his career after graduation. He couldn't find a full-time teaching job and had to do the dreaded substitute teaching in the fall. This was basically his second student teaching gig times 100. There was no cooperating teacher to help him through the rough disciplinary patches; he was alone with the ungrateful creatures the whole day. He got to the point where his heart sunk just hearing the phone ring in the morning knowing that they needed him. And it was worse when he heard the sick teacher's name, knowing that certain classrooms would be hell. He was not enjoying it.

But earlier that summer, Samuel did have a good break, finding a part-time tutoring job at a local college, Erie Community College. This was better. It was more what he imagined when he got an English degree, working with students to refine and edit their papers for writing classes. He even got the occasional question about stories for lit courses, which he loved.

What led him away from the teaching field was when he wanted to get his own apartment. It was a big step, finally moving away from his mom, but he felt like he finally needed his general independence and, more importantly, privacy with Sandra. And while this felt really good for Samuel, he also realized his two low paying jobs were not going to pay the rent. So he took a typing test at a temp agency and found he could type over 70 WPM, benefiting from the keyboarding classes he took in high school. This moved him away from the world of education, which partly made him sad, since he wasted a lot of money on the classes in college and burdened him with a sense of failure. But on another level, it gave him a sense of stress relief as he ventured into the business sector. He found himself doing varied job roles at a couple companies: first as a print operator and graphic design assistant at a statement manufacturing plant and then mailing out account statements for M&T Bank, which led to full-time work there in both operations and administration. There were times he hated his work; it felt so soulless and not what he ever intended to do. But certain positions gave him contentment, mostly when he was in the Reorganization Department (Reorg for short) in Trust Operations where he felt part of a team and found the repetitive work of balancing ledgers suitable for how his mind worked. And during these times, he found it just lovely to not hate getting up in the morning to go to work.

And all during this time, Sandra had set on her own path of discovery with a career. There was no hesitation in her deciding to stay in Buffalo with Samuel. Workwise, she found her calling and didn't need to jump around as much. And it had all the makings of irony. She became a school teacher. She started working in elementary special education but later had positions in middle school science. She was passionate about helping kids and spreading her fountain of knowledge out to those who needed it. While she didn't take to the English courses in college, she became an avid reader too eventually, and Samuel liked to think that he had something to do with that. This led her to seek out a way to use this passion, and the year she became sick, she was about to take a new position at a local school as a 6th grade ELA teacher. Samuel was enjoying talking with her about the different types of literature she was going to teach. They discussed it constantly.

Most importantly, they had their tight union no matter the individual struggles. They were much in love. This brought them a deep happiness, a filling of a hole in both their lives. About a year and a half after finishing their undergraduate studies – Sandra was two years younger than Samuel, but they finished the same year – the two of them moved in together, got a larger three-bedroom place in downtown Buffalo. They had the typical ups and downs of a couple. Still, the connection they formed from that first day in the college book store remained, and they had an understanding and excitement that lasted well past the infatuation-filled dating period.

But Samuel had always been a fearful being. And while death and losing his loved ones was top of that list (another irony, this one cruel, given what would happen), there was apprehension in making changes and rocking the boat, so to speak. Even after their seven years together, he wasn't ready for marriage or for Sandra to go off birth control. She wasn't exactly a traditionalist: she was liberal and free-thinking, but with her love of children, she wanted kids. And Samuel was reluctant, thinking he didn't want that: he had enjoyed spending time with his many nieces and nephews, but that was easy when you didn't have responsibility for them. Since he had gotten out on his own, he found himself losing more and more patience with screaming neighbor kids and liked his independence.

Finally, in this seventh year, Samuel's childbearing thoughts led to Sandra breaking up with him. He was heartbroken. After being a loner and socially awkward for his young life, having Sandra was so important to him; she was the one person he felt completely himself with, even more than with his mom or Peter. Losing her made him feel adrift, lost in the ether of life, and his mental health took an even deeper fall during this time. This was when he finally talked to his doctor and got himself on meds. He actually took a couple weeks off work for mental leave, and this gave him time to think a lot about what he wanted in life. He still wasn't sure he wanted kids or even marriage, but he needed Sandra.

So on this hot mid-July day, Samuel asked Sandra to meet him. She reluctantly agreed, not acting too happy to hear his voice on the phone. She would later confess to him that she was thrilled and also shaken to hear his voice and ended up crying. He asked her to meet him at their old stomping grounds, Buffalo State College, and he was sitting on the bench near his old bus stop when she walked up. A few minutes earlier, looking around at the vine-covered buildings, he'd felt a deep nostalgia and wistfulness for this time in his life when he was young and idealistic discovering the classics of literature and engaging in intellectual debates. But that sense of the past was miniscule in its power compared to the very sight of Sandy; his heart was a flutter just glimpsing her approach. She was dressed in a white Kerry/Edwards shirt with a small American flag and Democratic donkey image (2004 was an election year) and casual fit red shorts that went only about halfway between her hip and knee for this sweltering 90-degree day. Samuel always hated the heat and actually preferred snow over this kind of humidity but seeing his old flame's legs made him feel like it was one bright spot. He, too, was dressed down for the weather with black jean shorts and a *Lord of the Rings* shirt showing the tree of Gondor. His eyes took her in entirely, relishing it after missing her so. The years had been kind to Sandra; she didn't look all that different from the 20-year-old girl who stood in front of him in the bookstore line. All through their time together, he felt like he aged more exponentially than she ever did. When she got close, he still marveled at her striking green eyes and sunlit red hair, but her face looked different, drawn, sad. He wasn't used to that. She was never one to go overboard with makeup, but her natural beauty was now muted by her expression. It wasn't typical; Sandy was happy go lucky, the yin to his yang.

"Hi," he said.

She sat down next to him but not too close. "Hello." It wasn't a warm greeting, but he thought it sounded more sad than mad.

"I know this might seem a little corny to have us get together where we first met, but you know by now that I'm a corny guy."

No laugh, no reaction, not even a smile. Sandra just nodded her head. Samuel realized he had his work cut out for him and also knew it was his fault. They had a big blow out at the apartment right before she decided to leave him, sincerely their first big fight. He always had an angry side, a festering temper, but rarely was it shown to another person; he kept it well buried - *along with other things*, his present self realized - and limited his moments of screaming to alone times. Well, he let it all out that day, and it was ugly. He had raised his voice to its zenith, shouting at her at one point that if she just wanted to be with him for vows and to have kids, then she never loved him to start with. He figured he would begin there. "I'm sorry about how it ended up. I wasn't nice."

"No, you weren't," she agreed, "but you were expressing your feelings. If you don't want marriage and kids, that's that. Not sure what else there is to say, Samuel."

He started to run his hand through his hair, which was still there in volume, not beginning to recede yet, and curly (somewhat messy even). "I don't think it's quite that simple. I'm just afraid."

"Of what?" her voice was testier now. "I just don't get it."

"Have you given any thought to my family background? My dad was not a good person. My closest example of a husband and father is him. I guess..."

She finished his thought, something she often did. "You're afraid if you change our relationship, we'll morph into your parents. And what? Be destined for divorce too?"

"I think so." He let out a weak sardonic laugh. "And now I sound like a character on those corny Lifetime movies. I've always tried not to be dramatic. But I'm just terrified at change. I don't know that I can be a good husband or father."

She now turned her whole body on the bench towards him, and when her knee bumped his leg, a swell of excitement came over him. "But, Sam, you were an awesome boyfriend and partner!" She was the only one who ever called him Sam. "You are not your fucking asshole dad and never will be. Hell, our biggest fights before the end were just you throwing my stuff out." This was the whole tidy vs. pack rat discussion. "And it's not like I don't have some baggage too, my mom, you know. But it's like suddenly you didn't believe in *us*, believe we can take the next step or face the next challenge. That's offensive, buddy."

Samuel had never quite thought of it that way. "I understand," he said thoughtfully and with slight exasperation with himself. "That's also on me. And these weeks apart have allowed me to look closer at myself. I got on mental health meds and took a short leave at work. I think my fears had to be addressed. And I've at least started to talk about them with someone, a professional. I'm seeing a counselor now. His name is Jake, and he's great at getting me to ask the important questions." He moved his hand forward and then pulled it back. "Can I touch your hand?"

This made Sandra laugh, that old pleasant sound, not tinged with frustration or anger. "You can, nerd."

He smiled. He reached out and took her hands in his. "I'm sorry. Will you take me back? That's all that needs to be said."

Tears started to form in her eyes. "I want it so bad, Samuel. I was a wreck without you. I've been crying more than ever in my life. But..."

"But what?"

"I haven't changed my feelings. I want a kid. I know I'm only in my mid-twenties, but time goes so fast, and before you know it, I'll be looking back and thinking I shouldn't have waited."

"Sandy, I wouldn't have dragged you out here if I wasn't willing to fight my worries and apprehension and plunge forward with you."

"An English boy to the end," she joked, and despite herself, a slight grin creased her features. "Plunge ahead?"

He giggled again. "Yeah. And the way to do that is…" He now paused, reached into his pocket, and pulled out a small jewelry case. She gasped. He opened it, revealing a small diamond engagement ring. "It's not much, but you know our budget and debt. Let's do this all at once. I don't care which happens first, getting married or pregnant, but I want to spend the rest of my life with you."

She looked down at the ring, a sparkle now in her teary eyes. It was almost like her whole face had changed to that vibrant, happy go lucky look. "This is amazing. But I'm going to make you ask, Samuel David Redden."

He grinned broadly. "I get it. Say the words and take the step. Okay, Sandra Ann Crowell, will you marry me?"

"YES!" She actually screamed this, and some passerby summer students took notice of them. This was the first moment Samuel had even sensed other people in the area, given how deeply into their conversation he was. Usually, public displays of affection weren't his thing, but he didn't care now; he took Sandra in his arms and kissed her deeply.

Samuel returned to the present. He stared out at the patchy yard, the few trees that ringed it, a less scary image than his childhood woods. *We would have a lot more happy moments after that one before the sadness began. We only got ten years of*

marriage, but I would say our ten years were more joyous than many couples that are together for 50. I just wish she were here right now. All this is about to get even worse, and I need her strength. Where will I find that?

CHAPTER 9

T
he next day, Samuel and Peter ventured to the East Side to meet with Madame Takari. Peter had finally gotten a hold of Carter the previous night to tell him of their intentions. The primatologist was okay with it, saying that the spiritual and psychological aspects were not his thing. He also was still working his way through what he saw that night at the zoo, even if he wouldn't admit as much to Peter. But Darwin could hear it in his voice; Carter just didn't have the same confidence that his flower child friend was used to. Peter said it was a bit off-putting.

He was driving Samuel in his Hyundai electric car and often tried to engage his friend in conversation. But Samuel wasn't having it. It was partly the anger still remaining from Peter's revelation the previous day, but was also thoughtfulness at seeing Madame Takari again. He had mixed emotions: he remembered liking her a lot as a child, but what she put Peter up to made him think she was more of a manipulator than he previously thought. And to be honest, this part, the otherworldly aspect, made him feel overwhelmed. He was surely glad to move on from thinking about Amy all the time, but the bigness of the spiritual side was often too much for him. Real-world problems can at least be thought through a bit, but the gods and devils, demons and angels, good vs. evil type exploration freaked him out a bit. He grew up in a Catholic household and had family members who were evangelicals, but he'd fallen away from that life. A lot had to do with the ideals certain

Christians embraced, such as anti-LGBTQ+ stances and aligning politically with the right, which at its extreme embraced white supremacy. It made him sad sometimes to think about. He often wondered what Jesus thought about this whole movement that sprung out from his short days on earth. Especially the wars fought and people killed in his name. And for Redden, even though he enjoyed the church life at times, he was always a doubter, wanting to use logic in addition to faith. But Madame Takari had opened up a realm of possibilities to him last time of a world beyond this one. The question of where the gorillas came from and what the glowing hands of his childhood meant were almost too much for him to consider. But he knew the luxury of ignoring that was ending soon.

As the car pulled up to the curb in front of the brick façade of the psychic/Wiccan's business, memories flooded back to Samuel. He flashed upon riding in the van with Peter and Robert and remembered his initial introduction to the Madame. And like in the days after the mental explosion in the park, he had more images come back to him within the moment, needing the active engagement. He had previously recalled Madame and how she purged the idea of the gorillas. But he'd safely compartmentalized the first meeting when the gorillas invaded the sanctum shaking the whole room. But everything was back now. It was surreal arriving here as an adult. He stepped out of the compact car, and after Peter came beside him, said, "Is this the only building in Buffalo that hasn't been updated? I feel like it's 1985 again."

"It's character, Reddy, character."

Samuel wondered whether it was character, a retro thing, or if revitalization efforts failed to go into certain neighborhoods where the lower-income people lived, namely people of color. But he did notice the new shops all around, so maybe the Madame was just unique. These ruminations had to wait as Peter was nudging him towards the door. Samuel noticed that the paint of the old block letters on the glass (M.T., Psychic Intervention) were almost completely faded out. Then he pushed the door open and heard the familiar chiming above his head. The déjà vu sensation was so intense here that it made him feel a little dizzy. It wasn't just the musical sound that continued the mental journey back in time, though; he noted how everything was exactly the same inside the place as well. There were the psychedelic pictures on the walls, the smell of incense, and he would have bet even the paint was the same color (purple). The chairs were the only updates that he could tell. And he was sure the retro motif would be duplicated when he entered the inner sanctum. He laughed. "Has she changed anything besides the furniture?"

"No, my man, Madame Takari values tradition, consistency." As Peter said this, long black colored fingernails pushed aside the beads ahead of them, which was the first accoutrement Samuel's eye had come upon when making his previous judgment. Out stepped the tiny Madame Takari. Samuel had a really random thought that he looked forward to seeing her stand next to Carter. He observed the slightly aged features in her dusty-colored hair, the way she moved, and some wrinkles, but again, the passage of time hadn't affected her as much as he expected. Back to his thoughts about time standing still, he noticed her wearing a borderline gaudy red dress and wondered if it was somehow the same one from all those years before. Or maybe she was trying to create a mood of stability for him. His first feeling upon seeing her was comfort, of being reintroduced to someone who greatly helped him. But then his conscious mind put up a wall, remembering the slight that had dominated his thoughts the day before. So he pushed back a smile and an urge to step forward to her. He just quietly said, "Madame."

Takari did not reciprocate this standoffishness - she beamed magnificently at him and closed the few steps between them, holding out her hand. "I have waited patiently for this day, Samuel. It is not a happy time for the universe, but I believe it will be a proving ground for you."

Samuel reluctantly took her hand, "I wish I felt the same fondness towards you. But Peter told me something yesterday, and it kind of changed a lot of things, ma'am."

Madame looked knowingly at Peter. "It was time, deep lady," he said, "he had to know."

She nodded. "Of course. Let's talk." She quickly turned and went through the beads.

Upon coming into the inner sanctum, Samuel was not disappointed in what he was expecting, namely the exact look of what was there thirty-five years ago: the map of Vietnam, the ever-present smell of incense, the stringed lights. It perpetuated that odd sense of nostalgia, like he had been dropped physically back into his childhood. As he sat, he tried to focus on his anger. He felt it was his right. And after he turned down the offer of tea, he said, "How could you?"

Madame Takari had her hands crossed in front of her like she was beginning to pray, and Samuel noticed they shook a little. "I had a responsibility to you, Samuel," she said. "I cast a serious, powerful spell, and I had to know you were okay and that you did not remember the gorillas."

"Okay, but couldn't you just cast your thoughts and see me with your inner eye somehow?"

"That's not how this works," she replied. Samuel could hear a little perturbed feeling in that utterance.

"I'm sorry if I frustrate you, Madame," he responded to this. "Even if I accept this concern, why use Pete? You put him in a horrible position. I give you credit for not doing that to him when he was a minor, but he was still young, in college, trying to figure out his place in the world. How much turmoil must that have caused him? It's borderline cruel."

"Reddy..." Peter began, but Samuel told him to hush.

"Yes, let me answer, dear Peter." *Dear Peter? I guess I didn't understand what a bond they must have formed over the years.* "It was a burden for a young man. And it may seem that I turned your best friend into a spy, but while I can't see over distances in real-time, I do see the future. I knew he was to be the greatest friend in your life, except for your lovely wife." She noticed Samuel wince and added, "And my much-belated sympathies. You and your family deserved better than that fate. But Peter was the correct person for this role, with the right amount of empathy and love to watch over you. And it's that, watching over, not spying."

"And?" Samuel said, knowing he wanted to hear one thing.

"I'm sorry for any additional pain this may have caused you, especially at this time. I only wanted to protect you until you were ready to defend yourself, which is soon."

Samuel could see great pain in the old lady's face as she grimaced, and the apology was what he really wanted. *I may still feel dirty about all this, but now is not the time to hold grudges and stew on my bitterness. Too much to face.* "All right, Madame," he said, "you know I'm not happy, but we need to focus."

She smiled broadly, an intimately proud expression. "You are an amazing person, Samuel Redden. I knew it the day I met you, and I still see it. You truly are the Golden Child."

"Golden Child? What in the world does that mean?" he asked, perplexed.

"Not now. There is much you must know about yourself and the larger world you belong to. But I will not be the one revealing this."

"Then who? I'm not sure how I can do much of anything without knowing more about the gorillas, the glow fist, all of it." Impatience and annoyance were replacing Samuel's anger now.

"I understand. Soon you will meet someone who has the right to tell you all you are lacking. But it's still not the time for you to even know about him. But soon. It's a process, Samuel. We cannot skip to the end."

Him? Must she always speak in riddles? But as much as I hate it, she's right. I have to accept it for now. Answers to the metaphysical are important, but we have to deal with the real world events first. But she better be more forthcoming soon. Otherwise, what's the point of her area of expertise? Beyond his flood of feelings right now, Samuel also felt a little weary under the lady's gaze. She looked at him with a love he couldn't return even without the last day's information and her irritating caginess. He barely knew her, but she looked at him like his mom would. It was unnerving. So, looking down at his hands now away from the stare, he said, "So Pete says you can do the regression therapy Hector mentioned. That it's time to discover the origins of the monsters. I'm guessing that's what you mean about not rushing the process."

"Yes, my boy," she said, "it's the starting point before we can explore anything else. All of the events of the last thirty-five years start with that event. Once you have that knowledge, you can be ready for more. It's honestly the biggest step in being prepared to fight them and discover your true destiny."

"You kind of intimidate me with all these comments about golden child and destiny," he said, shaking his head and looking up a bit now, "but what you're saying makes sense. I thought doing the therapy was a good idea when Hector suggested it back in the day, and it's probably overdue. Let's do this."

◆ ◆ ◆

Madame Takari changed the setup of the room a bit. She had the boys push the table that typically stood between them against the wall and arranged their three chairs in a triangle formation with her at the head. She said that she needed to be closer to Samuel to perform the rite. Peter asked if he should leave, but the Madame thought his moral support would help, just as in the past. Despite the previous day's fight and drama, Samuel felt the same. Before she began to explain how this would work, Samuel thought of something that gave him a start. "What about the gorillas? I just remembered coming in here what they did the first time, shaking the room to shit. If this remembrance is truly a key to start the process of beating them, would they try to stop us?"

Madame shook her head. "They may very well. But it's daytime, and your 1st rule still applies. The totemic power of your brother's protection may no longer limit them, but they hate the light. The shuddering room was just a stunt, similar to the haunting appearance in your mirror that Peter told me about. Any time they attacked your mind in the day, going all the way back to your childhood, were mere psychological games. But as an extra precaution and so we can focus, I had my sisters come early this morning to help place a protective spell over the room. Just like we did the night before the purging enchantment. It will hold for as long as this takes us."

Samuel smiled. "Are they all the same sisters? From when I was little?"

"You got it, buddy boy," Peter said, "I've met them all, and they are such wise elders."

Madame let a small smile form, one that indicated a well of love that words would find hard to explain. "They are indeed special. But let us begin. If I were a psychiatrist, I would ask you to close your eyes while playing some sort of nature sounds in the background. You probably remember old TV shows where a doctor would wave a stopwatch back and forth to put their patients in a trance?"

"Yeah, I remember that stuff," Samuel said.

"It may seem like a cliché or just made for TV, just like racial stereotypes, but hypnotists do often use watches or pendulums to relax the eye. A therapist too, like Hector, might utilize this to try to put you at ease and then talk you through the important moment in your past, which you would see in your mind's eye. Naturally, to start, it's necessary to zero in on that point in time where the discovery can unfold. Though with my abilities as both a Wiccan and a psychic, I will not need any such aid to get you there. I just need to touch you physically to help you transport in time, so to speak. While you won't be falling asleep, we still need to get you in a calm state in the here and now." She stood up, went over to the table, dug around in some papers, and pulled out a small rectangular object, her cell phone. Samuel thought the thing looked anachronistic in the hands of this supernatural lady. Then he heard the sound of a running brook coming from the device. She returned to them and sat down. "I believe you told Hector the approximate time when you thought the gorillas appeared?"

"I did?" Samuel thought for a moment, and as if coming to

him upon demand, he did indeed remember. "That's right! It was around the time I was spending a lot of time at the town recreation. Summer. He wanted me to start there."

"Perfect," she said. "Now, here's what my powers will do, and it can be quite a jolt to your system. When I touch you, you will be transported to the most emotionally impactful moment of your time at this recreation."

"Wait a minute," Samuel said, "that's the second time you've said 'transported.' What do you mean?"

"It will be like you're there. As if you're experiencing it all over again. You will have your forty-three-year-old consciousness but will be living it as your eight-year-old self did. Your body will be here, fully functional, but everything in this environment will fade away since your conscious mind will be in that other place. Inside your old body. You'll feel what it feels."

"Woah, deep," Peter muttered.

Samuel just shook his head at his friend but then said himself, "Okay, deep might be about right. So let me get this straight. It will feel physically like I'm going through it again?" *Wow, I hope I can handle this.*

"That's right," she said, "but we'll both be here in the 'real world' to support you. It's essential to do this, Samuel."

He nodded. "I know. Okay, let's do it before I get too nervous."

Madame smiled at him, encouragingly, "Be brave, as I know you can be." She glanced at Darwin, "Peter, my darling, this will not work as the other spell did, so I will ask you to not join hands with Samuel. That might take him out of the experience. Only I can touch him. But feel free to send your positive thoughts to him. That will help. He will be able to sense your warmth, even if he can't hear your voice exactly."

Peter did a sitting curtsy to this woman he had come to love, "Ay-ay, my queen."

She didn't respond to this, now holding Samuel in her intense gaze. "Take my hand, Samuel." He did. "One very important thing before we start. No matter how painful or scary the journey may be, I cannot remove you from the trance. Only you can break yourself free. Otherwise we can cause brain damage. Do you still wish to do this?"

Oh boy. I have to know, though. "Yes," he said more confidently than he felt.

The Madame nodded. "Okay. Now, close your eyes." So he did this too. As of late, it scared him to even close his eyes. He knew he had the night light in his room, but the gorillas were never far from his thoughts. He often wondered if illumination would still protect him as an adult. The Madame just said it did, but his heart was still thudding a bit, and they had only begun. "Shortly, you will feel a weird sensation in your body, and then you will no longer see darkness. You will see your past." *That's not frightening at all. Geez.*

If his earlier interactions with Madame Takari had taught him anything, it was not to doubt her words. So when almost instantaneously he experienced a fluttery feeling all over his body, almost like a gentle electric stirring, he wasn't surprised. But still, when the darkness in his eyes turned to a viewable place, he gasped. He thought he gasped not only for the transition from nothing to something but also because he was now looking at images from his childhood. Again, he thought about the longing for days gone by. Nostalgia is a powerful thing, and as before when he entered the shop, he knew it was easy to be transmitted to the sights, smells, and feelings of the past. But this was quite literal. It was as if he was watching an old home movie of his life but in HD. Wistful would be an understatement for how he was feeling. "Wow," was all he could say. This comment he could hear in his mind but not externally in this new reality. He was sure Madame Takari and Peter had heard him say it in the room, though.

He was looking at the old playground down the street from the church buildings where recreation was held. There was the baseball diamond beyond the backstop less than ten feet away, and further down the road, east of the ball field, the swing sets and slides that he so remembered playing on. But there weren't any kids frolicking around the area now, and he wondered why. A different thought instantly occurred to him, and he looked down and saw small hands, his hands. *My God, it's my eight-year-old body. No, seven. My birthday was a month away. But she really **has** transported me.* He was still confused as to the lack of activity. Then he heard a car horn beep, and his body turned around.

Right behind him in the tiny dirt parking lot was the car, a rusty red Buick Skylark. A middle-aged woman sat behind the wheel, and the passenger side door was just being shut by another little boy beside her. Samuel instantly remembered some names, Donny and Mrs. Fredricks. It was a nearby neighbor that he and his family knew. Samuel was on friendly terms with Donny; he was in the group of kids that would sit with him under the elm tree near the rectory and trade *Star Wars* cards. Donny was a pudgy kid, red-haired, and looked like the type of boy that they always made the catcher in the movies. And his mother wasn't much different as Samuel was pretty sure she pushed 300 pounds. *But what I remember the most is how kind she always was to me.* "Samuel, do you need a ride home?" she called out. *Proof in point there.*

Then Samuel heard a voice, and it alarmed him a bit. Because it was coming from his body, and it wasn't his voice. It took him a second to realize it was his younger self responding to the lady. *Damn, I feel like I'm Sam Beckett on Quantum Leap.* "No, thanks, Mrs. Fredricks," young Samuel answered, "my mom is coming to get me." *I still have no recollection of this moment, and I have a fantastic memory for the past.* If Samuel did remember it, he might have known his mother had received a long distance phone call from his older brothers Terry and Jeff who lived in California in the mid-80's, and that was what held her up. She never forgot her baby, so it was unusual.

"Okay, honey," Mrs. Fredricks said as she started to drive away. Donny waved, and Samuel watched them go, their back tires kicking up a swirl of cloudy dust. He knew he couldn't make this body move, but he kind of wished he could explore more of his old childhood haunt. *But I'm confused. How is this an intense moment that brought about the gorillas? Or was Hector wrong? I mean, my mom is probably going to get me soon. Maybe a little upsetting that she's late but how is this traumatic?*

"Hey, you!" He heard a grating voice that broke him out of his analyzation. He found his young self go rigid as his head craned to the sound's source. He could see the church hall in the distance, where they held the annual chicken BBQ and other events and also where town recreation provided the arts and craft classes. Beyond that was the rectory, Father Tim's house. Behind would be the tree where he had such fond memories of trading those cards with his companions, although it was too far out of his view now. Across the street from these buildings - the same side of the road Samuel was on - was the church with the graveyard looming in the background. If he cut through the cemetery and made it through the church parking lot to East Eden Road, he would see tucked behind the rectory East Eden's one establishment, the East Eden Tavern, which consequently was his dad's favorite watering hole. Not that Claude was picky about where he got drunk, but the tavern was just so close by the homestead. And straight ahead on the other side of the street would be Mary's Corner Store, the place where he bought the cards and penny candy with the purse change his mom gave him. He so wanted to go check that out, but his attention was diverted in the other direction. Standing in front of the hall was a man, the voice's owner. It was an older guy who fell somewhere between retirement age and elderly. Samuel would have placed him in his 60's. He was thin as a stick with a graying, receding hairline, a tight, emaciated face that made him look like a walking skeleton. The man was wearing grimy green dungarees with big pouch-like pockets and a red plaid shirt with the top three buttons undone, showing the silver chest hair. He had on big brown work boots that were caked with mud. It was the kind of casual work garb someone who did a lot of outside tasks would dress in. Suddenly, Samuel's heart surged up into his throat and he felt a clinging warmness from his head to his chest. At first, he thought he was somehow experiencing his younger self's emotion in the moment, but then he realized he now remembered this person.

It's Bennett. Goddamn, I remember him! They called him the caretaker at recreation. He took care of the grounds and the buildings and hated the kids. He used to chase us away if there were more than a few of us congregating somewhere or if we were in a place he thought we didn't belong, like under our tree or in the graveyard. Even the counselors were a bit scared of him. Just a look in his beady red-tinged eyes, and you sensed something ugly, dead in there. Wait a minute.

If Samuel's adult bodily functions could have transferred to this place, he would have just lost his breath. Back at Madame Takari's, the other two observed him take a deep, gasping inhalation. Peter began to reach out, but the psychic stopped him with a look. Samuel was starting to remember something else; ironically, it was on the edge of his mind like a forgotten dream or nightmare. But he knew it was dark, terrible, something that was life-changing. And it had to do with this bitter old man.

This is it. The defining moment Hector and Madame Takari were both talking about. And yes, it's undoubtedly traumatic. And there's nothing I can do but re-live it.

"Yo, boy!" Bennett screeched out again in a hissing timber, serpent-like. "You aren't supposed to be here now. Recreation is closed. Go away."

"My mom didn't pick me up yet, Mr. Bennett," young Samuel said, raising his usual reserved tone so the other could hear. "I don't know where she is."

"Is that my problem, you ingrate?" Bennett replied. "Leave now."

Samuel knew it was about a 40-minute walk to his street down the aforementioned East Eden Road, which intersected the one he was on now, Keller Road. Not a short distance for little legs, but still he mentally begged his seven-year-old version to just start walking as far from Bennett as possible, no matter the direction. But he was rooted to the spot, feeling paralyzed, at the mercy of his other body. It seemed like he just couldn't escape the chains of dreams. It was a horrific feeling, a re-living of his nightmare immobility. He felt like a hostage to his own body. Free will was a casualty to this experience. He wondered if he could just break out of this like the Madame said earlier, but he also knew he had to see it through, had to know.

"Are you deaf, boy? Okay, get over here!"

Now is the time to stay still, and maybe he'll just go away. But I won't, will I? And just as expected, other Samuel started to walk slowly in the building's direction, dragging his feet over to the figure in the distance. The pace made Samuel realize he knew even then that this was not a guy you wanted to get close to.

But his mother raised him a certain way, and one thing that stood out was respecting authority. His brothers passed that idea along as well. Claude may have been absent, but his other influences made certain things clear.

As he took the ride aboard young Sammy express, he noted that his senses were taking in everything as it was then. In contrast to his earlier thoughts, it wasn't just a replay of events and interactions like watching a show or even comparable to a virtual reality simulation, but a completely immersive experience. He could hear the wind picking up, whistling shrilly, and rustling nearby tree limbs. The warm, stuffy breeze gave him a feel of sweatiness. He could see the sky darkening in the distance over the downtown skyline, the buildings visible over the trees of the valley even though they were 20 miles away. Usually, this was a beautiful vista, but with the storm clouds forming, it was foreboding. And worst of all the sensations, he smelled Bennett as he approached him. The man always stunk of body odor and garlic. The other kids used to joke about it, but Samuel was consistently unnerved by it. When he got close to the custodian, he heard himself say, "I'm sorry, Mr. Bennett, but I don't want to walk. Don't want my mom to miss me somehow. She could be coming from the other way, town." This meant Hamburg, the larger township to the north, where Shelley did her shopping since Eden was a country place with limited grocery options.

"Oh, you're a mouthy one, aren't you?" Bennett asked.

"No, sir," Samuel replied shakily. He heard a chugging sound and glimpsed an rusty green tractor from one of the nearby farms going north along East Eden Road at about ten miles per hour. The driver, a middle-aged black haired man in blue overalls, waved to both of them. Samuel waved back and Bennett tipped his head respectfully.

But the grizzled old man wasn't distracted for long. "Yes

you are, like most of the brats here," he spat out. Then for a moment there, Bennett appeared to be thinking. "Well, while you're waiting, you will help me. Follow, now."

Bennett turned and made his way quickly and surely to the hall building. He opened the door, not holding it open for the child but letting it slam closed. Samuel knew this was another chance to bolt, but he felt his body moving that way too, always obedient, but still felt the reluctancy there as well. *Each moment this passes, I remember more. But like unraveling the bandages of a mummy, I'm terrified to find what lies underneath.* He saw his unlined young hand push the door open and look around as they entered the hall. It was a mess: cut up paper and crafts supplies like glue and scissors spread all over the many tables. Paper shavings were littered beneath the chairs too.

"What's your name, boy?" Bennett asked as Samuel tried to keep up with his brisk pace now.

"Samuel Redden."

"Okay, Redden, start picking up those supplies from the tables and put them in the baskets that are there. That should be simple enough for a dumb-looking child like you." *How did they ever hire this guy to work around kids?*

Samuel traipsed his way over to the nearest table. These were the long banquet-style types so as many kids could sit down in there as possible. It was the same ones they used for the church dinners. The town probably figured it was economical not to provide their own, but they looked so drab, an ugly brown with much of the varnish chipped. About ten of these were lined up until they reached the far wall. Smartly, the counselors had tacked up some artwork that the kids made through the summer, which gave the room a little more character. He looked to the right and saw the double doors and serving window leading to the kitchen. He remembered putting trays there when he helped Patrick bus during the chicken barbeque.

Samuel began to pick up a pair of scissors, and immediately his clumsiness betrayed him. He wasn't often asked to help with manual labor at home besides cleaning up his room, and whenever his father did involve him, he spent most of the time berating the awkward kid. His nervousness being around the custodian probably didn't help either; he could feel substantial perspiration now on his little hands. The scissors slipped right out of those wet digits and clacked on the floor. This made Bennett take immediate attention and stop sweeping the corner of the room. Even from here, Samuel could see redness spread into that pale face. "Redden!" he screamed. "You klutz! Get over here!"

Don't go. Please don't go. Somehow Samuel knew back in Madame Takari's room, his physical self had begun to exhibit more demonstrative expressions, teeth chattering with deep body shakes. Peter Redden was saying something to him, but from here, it came over as background static, like it was reverberating down a long tunnel or under some body of water. *I remember all of it now. Don't go!*

But young Samuel was cursed with his submissiveness. He sprinted over to Bennett as not to make him angrier, head down with embarrassment. When he got there, Bennett didn't lower his voice in any way. "You're a retard aren't you?"

This was a time before the term was taboo. And to a young boy who was uncoordinated, it was the worst kind of insult. The child Samuel glanced up a bit, and his older self could now feel a solitary tear go down his face, which was the last thing he should have done with this guy.

"Oh, a crybaby retard, huh?" Bennett marched over to the front door and locked it. *No, please.*

When the caretaker came back, he unscrewed the broom head from the stick it was attached to and tossed it to the floor, still holding the handle. "The only thing for crybaby retards is punishment."

Samuel could feel the fear from 1985 overpower him, a clenching feeling tensing the muscles. "No, sir, please," he said. Bennett only laughed as he swung the broomstick and whacked the child on the back. Samuel 2020 could feel blistering pain go through his lower spine. If he were at all mentally present at Madame's place, he would've known that he just fell off his chair as struck by a blow, landing hard on his butt. But he was utterly focused in the past now, so Madame made sure to not let go of his hand. His younger version collapsed in exactly the same way. But this did not stop Bennett. He proceeded to hit him multiple times, once on the head, once on the legs, and worst, right in the groin. The boy was gasping deeply now, crying and babbling in pain.

Then it got worse. Bennett reached down with his thin, skeleton hands, and undid the button on Samuel's shorts, then unzipped. He yanked them down to his knees, and there was not a thing he could do about it, with the pain he was in. Then his underwear was next. At the age he experienced this, Samuel had a minor inkling about sex from schoolyard talk but hadn't been taught about the birds and bees yet, and the idea of sexual attack was nothing the sheltered child knew. So the bewilderment was equal to the terror. Bennett now turned him, so he was lying not on his side as he was, but on his stomach, his face pressed to the dusty floor. The deranged town worker then poked the point of the broom into the small of his back, slowly moving it down.

Someone help me. Madame, please bring me back. But she can't. Only I can. Then why am I still here? I know everything now, right? Wake up, Samuel.

The movement of the weapon stopped. "I can't even stand to look at your bruised little balls and your tiny, pitiful dick," Bennett said. "But your back side isn't much better. You're disgusting. I was going to have some real adult fun with you, but you're not even worth it." Bennett straddled Samuel's posterior and reached out the broom the long way, positioning it under his neck, and began to pull back, choking him. Forty-Three-year-old Samuel noticed from his past self's twisted head that even though Bennett was not raping the boy in the traditional sense, he was getting a masochistic thrill from the hyperventilating figure under him as he pinned him down. There was a bulge on the creepy man's pants rubbing against his back that Samuel could feel through the panic and pain. Soon there was wetness there as well. At some point during this, the rain had started outside and was audibly loud on the steel roof; it reverberated over his pitiful moans of anguish. He could also smell Bennett's body odor in an extreme way here. He thought he would vomit (if he could breathe). Back at Madame Takari's, he was writhing on the floor sucking deeply for air.

After what seemed like hours to both versions of Samuel, but was actually less than one minute, Bennett stood up and spit on Samuel. "Get up and pull up your pants." Samuel did this quickly while trying to regain his breath. "Now get the fuck out of here!"

Samuel ran to the locked door, the familiar sound of wheezing escaping his lungs as the asthma fully kicked in. Normally that would have caused a panicked digging in his pockets for his inhaler, but he just had to get out of there. But when he reached his destination and touched the cold metal door handle and began to shakily and urgently unlatch it, he felt a bony hand on top of his. Bennett had chased him over there. He kneeled and spun Samuel around to him, bringing the terrified kid face to face with his attacker. The smell of garlic was absolutely overwhelming now. Samuel had never used this herb when cooking in his entire life, it repulsed him, and now he knew why. The ugly excuse of a human being uttered, "You tell anyone about this, and I will kill you. Painfully. This little demonstration is but a hint of what I'll do to you. But first, I'll kill your whore of a mom. Kill your pansy dad. Kill your spineless brothers. Kill your scuzzy sisters. Whoever you love. Understand?" The threats were real but Bennett's eyes were full of laughter, of mirth, a mocking display of enjoyment.

Samuel nodded through his sobbing and tears. And as Bennett pulled away, it was not the face of a man the boy saw but that of a blood-stained, hairy beast. A gorilla.

Darkness followed. For how long Samuel did not know. But then a voice brought him back to reality. Madame Takari, "Samuel, awake!"

He opened his eyes. He was lying on a bed in a room he did not recognize. "Where am I?" he whispered.

"Upstairs at the Madame's, Reddy." Samuel looked to his right, his eyes just now adjusting to the people in the room. It was Peter sitting on the edge of where he was lying. "I carried you up when it was over. You were comatose. You had us worried. You've been out for half an hour. This is Madame's bedroom." The hippie reached out to him, handing his friend his eyeglasses. Samuel put them on and gazed around some more and saw the Madame sitting on an easy chair in the corner of this room. There were a series of windows above her, letting in bright light from the Buffalo morning; it bathed her in a luminescence that made him think of the virgin Mary. The room was decorated a tiny bit more than her work setup. The furniture was much more modern, not only the pieces they were sitting on but also an attractive set of filled bookshelves on each side of his host. And he could see scenic framed photos of Vietnam on the walls: the jungles, the rivers, and the villages. Smaller picture displays of people sat on a desk on the other side of the room, some older ladies of varying races he assumed were her Wiccan sisters. There were also shots of children of Asian descent, and he idly wondered if they were the Madame's. But he couldn't focus on all that now. He pushed up on his elbows in the Madame's comfortable bed. He was lying on top of a comforter that made him feel safe. He took a moment to collect his thoughts and inhaled incense, a carry-over from downstairs. "I have to tell you two about my flashback." The area under his eyes felt damp.

"No need, my brother," Peter said, "the Madame was able to experience it right along with you since it was her spell. I'm so sorry." Peter wrapped his arms around his friend, and they embraced long and hard. The emotions overwhelmed Samuel as the trauma recently experienced became a tactile thing, twisting his insides and making his muscles ache. He cried bitterly into Peter's chest and could feel the thin man shaking and sniffing as well. The betrayal Samuel felt twenty-four hours ago was a million miles away.

After they disengaged, Samuel rubbed his eyes hard and then said to the psychic, "Madame, so I took a real-life monster and transferred it to imaginary ones?"

Madame Takari's face was strained, crestfallen, and she at last looked older, withered, world-weary. "Before we go any further, " she said, "I'm so sorry I couldn't save you from re-living that. It was the only way with it being so buried."

"Buried, yes," Samuel said with a dreamy voice. "More like I entombed it deep into the earth's core. I don't even remember explaining the bruises to my family. And the marks were surely there even if I tucked away the emotional part. Do you remember any of that, Pete?"

Darwin thought for a moment and then said, "Not specific-ally, Sammy. But the only mark that would have needed eluci-dation would have been your lovely face. Maybe in some kind of defense mechanism, you unconsciously came up with a tall tale for that? Hit with a ball in rec, maybe?"

"Perhaps," Samuel muttered. "School was out of session. And the recreation counselors probably weren't as proactive in in-vestigating abuse, so the questions were avoided. And I likely ignored the injuries on my body so not to re-enter the trauma. But you'd think Patrick would have seen me with my shirt off. Fuck, who knows?" He shook his head in disgust and motioned towards the Madame. "Please go on."

Madame Takari rubbed the bridge of her nose, a nervous habit that rarely came out, but this was all starting to take a toll on her as well. "What were we saying? Oh yes, the transference. You're absolutely right. You indeed made a mental leap for sur-vival. It was likely easier to deal with a created creature than face the ugliness of your world. But you awakened something inside of yourself: your ability to make the dream world blend into ours. That is what your radiant, blazing hands are - a dis-play of your golden powers, fueled by your connection to that other realm. You have special gifts. In this case, they allowed you to change simple nightmares to something alive. And this is just a hint of your talents, a peek. A lot more will be revealed in detail as time goes along, discoveries that will open up a larger life for you. Soon, I promise. Things I don't even know." *Some answers, at least. One thing I don't understand, though.*

"But why gorillas?" Samuel asked.

"A child's mind will latch onto something, anything, to make sense of real horrors," Madame said. "Perhaps apes scared you more than other things, and you just made them into these monsters, with additional scary features."

"Makes sense. I do kind of recall a zoo visit now. When I was maybe five or six. A male gorilla launched himself into the cage towards me when I was there with my mom." He peeked quickly over to Peter. "This was before they had the habitat setup we just saw. I looked stupidly into its eyes, and he didn't like that. Too bad I didn't remember to tell Carter. But the memory must have been blocked too." Samuel moved his focus back to Madame Takari. "But let's not gloss over..." He paused, swallowed, tried to push certain images out of his mind. He couldn't. "That asshole Bennett and what he did. How do I not let that traumatize me more? People probably have years of therapy to get over sexual assault, and I just now recalled it. How do I use it to move forward to beat the gorillas?" *This is too much, on top of everything else.*

"There are no simple answers, Samuel," Madame said in a caring tone. "But at least it's not buried in you anymore. You can start working on being free of it now."

"I know," Samuel replied, "but again, trauma like that isn't fixed instantly. The gorillas aren't going to give me the time."

Madame only nodded. *At least she's not giving me false hope.* But of course, Peter had wisdom to share, "You process it and defeat it AT the gorillas. They are your Bennetts. Take it out on them."

For all the times I tease him about his free love sayings, this is right on. Not many abuse victims can take out their frustrations on a proxy. Bennett is probably dead by now, but the gorillas are much alive because of me and, therefore, my responsibility. They will feel the rage of my seven-year-old self. "Thanks, Pete," Samuel said, beaming at him, "for everything."

Peter was moved by this; his eyes again glittered with emotion. He knew there was forgiveness from Samuel in that look. No clever witticism came from him in response. He only nodded and pounded his heart.

CHAPTER 10

Several more days passed. The others were told of the monumental cathartic discovery from the past: Amanda and Kyle by Samuel and Carter by Peter. It was quite an emotional moment for Amanda as she cried and embraced Samuel. He gave himself these days to reflect more on this moment in time and the damage it had done in his life. He faced all the emotions: fear, anger, regret. But he knew he couldn't put off things forever, so he decided that they should all get together to get ready for the next step, Madame Takari included.

But before that happened, Carter said he wanted to discuss protecting themselves. He arrived at Samuel's house with Peter. It was 1:00, and the kids were at school, but Carter said they had no time to waste, so this part would have to be without the full team. When he got there, he was carrying a huge duffel bag. He opened the strings of it and dumped its contents onto the kitchen table where they were sitting. Samuel was amazed to see the variety of weapons that were now strewn in front of him. He was not a gun fan - as a liberal, he was staunchly on the side of gun control - so he didn't know the exact types of guns here. Still, he noticed handguns, shotguns, and even those military automatic type weapons (AK 47?), and he especially hated that last kind. But it wasn't only guns that he saw collected where he usually ate his spaghetti. He beheld various baton-like objects, probably what they called fighting sticks, other hand to hand weapons, and to his amazement, archery equipment.

"Come prepared, huh, Carter?" Samuel asked.

"It's not just the motto of the Boy Scouts; it's also mine," the big man said smiling. Samuel was glad to see this full teethed grin and, more importantly, the mood behind it. As tough as he knew the man was, Redden feared witnessing the massacred gorilla family would take something away from the primatologist. He wasn't sure what that would be: *his optimism, his fighting spirit*? Samuel knew there was nothing Carter loved more than gorillas, and the kind of images they saw that night would leave a mark. He knew it firsthand. *He may just not be showing it. He's internalized the experience and using it just like I am my childhood trauma. Or he's seen just as much horror from men out in the jungles.*

"I guess we're on the verge of disowning our 'make love, not war' viewpoints, huh, buddy?" Peter said, his eyes wide at the tools of destruction before him.

"Well, yes to an extent," Carter replied. "As we've learned, these beasts are vicious, so we obviously have to fight with equal aggression. I've definitely moved to that point after what happened." As he said this, Samuel certainly made a note of the quick sad look that went across Carter's face, and he was sure Peter noticed as well. *There it is. Buried just like my issues.* "But on the other hand, I can't realistically teach either of you to be safe gun handlers in the short time we have. So you won't be transforming into Rambo overnight, libs." He rebounded from his momentary sorrowful recollection, flashing another smirk.

Samuel was relieved by this. He thought he perhaps could get over his moral issue with guns, but with his clumsiness, he was sure he would never be able to wield a firearm precisely or accurately. He didn't think Peter would be much better.

"So we're going to be ninja warriors?" Peter asked.

"Something like that," Carter said but then shook his head, "and that's disrespectful to those disciplines to think I can transform you into skilled fighters that quickly either. But it's the best we can do." He picked up one of the shotguns lying on the table, a polished black piece. He got up and aimed it towards the hall archway. "By the way, this is my trusty weapon. It's a Mossberg 500 Tactical. I've used it in the past when I had to, unfortunately, put animals down. It packs a punch and will hopefully put these gorillas away, denizens of hell or not." He placed the gun back down gently. "Okay, boys, time to pick your poison. Redden?"

Samuel pointed to the shiny long bar type item closest to him. "I like the stick." *If I can summon my courage, I can at least hit the things. I just hope they don't get too close to me.*

"Stick, you say?" Carter now picked this up. "You whiteys sure know nothing about weapons." Samuel shrugged, and Peter gave a look that could only say, "duh." "This here is a bo staff. It's unique in that it's made of lightweight metal. So it won't be hard for you to lift and wield but should do damage to the apes if you hit them with the right timing and placement. Take it."

Samuel reached out, bracing and ready for it to drop to the floor with his weakness. It wasn't necessary. It felt as light as a fallen branch he would have picked up during one of his old walks with Sandra at Hoyt Lake. "Wow, you're not kidding about it being lightweight." Samuel stood up and swung it in a circle. The movement had a bit of his trademark clumsiness as he almost lost his grip, but the "whoosh" sound excited him as much as it could for a pacifist.

"We'll practice," Carter said. He sighed lightly. "If I can turn the two of you into fighters, they should give me a medal." He reached out, touching the staff. "There's a button on the side here. See it?"

Samuel looked and saw an almost imperceptible depression with a more noticeable black dot on it. "Yep."

"Press it."

Samuel pressed down and was shocked to feel the staff vibrate in his hands and shrink into a much smaller size, about nine inches, down from its regular six foot length. "I left it at full size in case one of you picked it. But better to keep it collapsed when not in use. This will allow you to stick it in your pocket or belt and move from place to place quickly without tripping over the damned thing. And it automatically locks when closed, so it won't spring open and injure your johnson." *He's just full of jokes today. But he already knows how clumsy I am.*

"I like it," Samuel said, sticking the weapon into his jeans pocket comfortably.

Carter now turned to Peter. "What about you, hippie? What will make you into a lean, mean fighting machine?"

"I always thought I would dig karate, a la Mr. Miyagi, only for self-defense, you know. But if I'm to wield something, I'd pick this." Peter stuck his hand out and touched the bow in the middle of the table. "Call me Hawkeye, Legolas, or Green Arrow; I'll take any of that."

Carter was pensive for a moment, massaging his bald head. "That would take more training than I think we have time for." He pushed his hand around the pile for a bit and came up with something smaller. "Try this." Peter snatched it with his usual gusto. Samuel hadn't noticed this coming out of the bag earlier due to its size. It was a slingshot. *Seriously? A slingshot? Like David in the bible? Incredible what variety of weapons Carter has.*

The smile on Peter's face became wide. "Ooh, I dig it. Bring on the gorilla Goliaths!"

"Yes, and you won't be just shooting rocks." Carter grabbed a small satchel from the table. He extracted a round metal object, like you'd find in a ball bearing, but larger, like a tennis ball. "These things will take your eyes out. If we can somehow get you to be accurate, you can definitely incapacitate the creatures." He then paused. "That's a big if, though."

Carter took them out to the backyard to train. It was what he was calling the express class. There was enough room for the two learners to spread out even with Samuel's small city lot yard. The gorilla expert showed Redden how to hold the bo staff properly and swing it so his full weight was behind it. He had him whaling on the large oak tree in Samuel's yard. Even with his limited skills, Samuel could see how powerful the staff was. He was taking large chunks out of his tree. He wasn't just averse to fighting but also an environmentalist, so he felt terrible chipping away at the tree, but Carter said it was the only way. "Some trees have been around hundreds of years, way longer than you or I," Carter told him, "so they can take it. *" I forget he's a bigger conservationist than I am.*

Carter also set up one of those targets typically used in archery work for Peter (but made of a cushiony material, not wood) and helped work on his aim with the slingshot: how to position both arms to get the maximum pull and still focus on accuracy. Peter started awfully, blasting the projectiles into the fence, the garage, the neighbor's lawn, anything but the target. Samuel couldn't help lose focus from his exercises when one of the metal balls came close to the garage's window. But after an hour, Darwin began to hit the soft surface, making compressed, squishy sounds as they landed. Two hours in, he managed to hit a bullseye, which led to a trademark Peter Darwin celebration dance, arms all akimbo, butt shaking. Carter snapped at him, telling the flower child to stop the nonsense, but a small smile escaped his lips.

As Carter walked into the house with his two trainees at 4:30, a good three hours from when they started, with both Samuel and Peter's arms aching - Carter drove them hard and gave them few breaks - he did utter one concern. "More progress than I could have hoped for in just an afternoon session, so feel good about that, friends. But I fear it's not enough. These are powerful, supernatural creatures. You need to kill them, not just stun or blind them. But I still can't feel good about putting guns in your hands."

Peter opened the sliding glass door on the deck for the other two as he said, "I think the Madame can help with that."

"How so?" Samuel asked, filling up each of their plastic bottles from the purified water pitcher once they reached the kitchen.

They sat down again at the table, and each took a deep swig of their water. "She has powers, you know," Peter said. "I think she might be able to do some mumbo jumbo on the weapons. Bless them like a priest would. Give them an extra kick so we can keep the monsters unbalanced and allow ourselves multiple shots."

"Oh, fuck, Darwin," Carter hissed, "this isn't a *Dracula* movie."

"Isn't it?" Peter asked.

Carter just looked at him stone-faced. "Point taken. Okay. So we all meet tomorrow?"

"Yes," Samuel said. "You, Amanda, and Kyle need to meet Madame Takari, and we have to figure things out, how to end this. I fear every night I go to bed that they won't afford us this opportunity. That they will just come into my room and tear my throat out. Madame thinks the rules still give some protection, but I wonder. They're in this world now more fully, so will the night light even help?"

"Don't worry about that," Carter said. "They won't attack *just you* now."

"Why?" Samuel asked.

"Like we've said before, these things maintain some characteristics of gorillas even if they are mutated, so to speak. And gorillas understand family units. You've surrounded yourself with this group now, this *family*, so they'll want all of us. Plus, it seems like they want to destroy you mentally and spiritually before they take your life. You know what that all means?"

"Uh oh," was all Peter said. Samuel was silent. *They want to massacre all I love first.*

"Exactly," Carter said. "Chances are if we all get together tomorrow, that's when they'll attack. We won't need a plan. We won't need to seek them out. They'll come, Samuel." He couldn't hide a slight look of worry, a grimace of thoughtfulness.

Samuel sighed and put his head in his hands. "That makes sense," he muttered. "And while that's scary," he raised his head and suddenly looked resolute, an intense determination gracing his features, "let's be done with it." He paused and then added, "and it won't be a surprise and no more games like what they did to Amy and her family. We'll be prepared." He then thought for a moment. "What about Amanda and Kyle? Madame can probably take care of herself. They can't be defense-less."

"Didn't they take self-defense, Reddy?" Peter asked.

"That's right," Samuel said. "They'd been taking a self-de-fense/Tae Bow class for several years. But I think it's been a little while. Will that be enough or should they have weapons too?"

"They can't do hand to hand fighting with these creatures," Carter said. "They need something between their skin and the attackers. So I will have them do the same thing, choose their own weapons of destruction when they're back from school. We'll have to use whatever limited time we have to train. And maybe this fantastical Madame can do something to help all four of you. The kids have every right to fight with us, but we are running out of time to get ready."

"They'll be home soon," Samuel said, "and we'll get right to work."

Amanda and Kyle came into the house mere minutes after this conversation. After a quick dinner of leftover rotisserie chicken and salads, Carter did indeed work closely with the team's two younger members. The whole group worked out in the yard under the floodlights cast from the back of the house, the two young charges with their teacher near the rear fence while Samuel and Peter kept practicing their exercises closer to the building. The ritual choosing of their weapons came first. Kyle picked nunchaku (nunchucks) and Amanda a pair of sai, similar to what the character Elektra from Marvel Comics used, a sharp dagger-like eastern weapon. Both of these tools were so dangerous looking, fearsome, but Samuel knew that

MARK BERMINGHAM

would qualify for most of Carter's arsenal. He was a little worried that these were made for more closer up fighting than his staff, but the gorilla expert insisted that he could teach the kids to thrust and move quickly out of reach of the monsters. First Carter showed the two best friends how to grasp the weapons and thrust them out for the most lethal strike. Kyle whacked himself a few times on his right shoulder with the other end of his nunchaku (he was a lefty) while swinging the unwieldy tool, crying out the first time but trying to exude toughness the ensuing instances. He would sincerely pay for it in the morning since the nunchucks were also constructed of metal - luckily, his first few strikes didn't have a ton of power behind them. But he started to get the rhythm down remarkably fast, his athletic background paying off. And Amanda looked incredibly at home with her dual set of daggers, her eyes as focused as they were when she studied calculus or played volleyball. She rarely secured her medium-length hair, but now had it pinned back with an elastic tie so she could keep it out of her eyes. Carter remarked that she was a natural and asked Samuel how he got such a graceful daughter. That brought a lightness to the intense proceedings. The teenagers were quick learners, and while they weren't the same as experienced users of these devices, it was going a lot better than any of them could have hoped.

After the initial lessons, Carter then had those two doing a similar routine as Samuel, using their weapons against a tree. The small yard of the Reddens only had two trees, one near the house and one at the fence, but luckily there were enough for all three of them since Amanda and Kyle took either side of the rear one. Then the big man took it up a level, providing a one on one fight, charging at the kids (an intimidating sight), using the cover of an old steel garbage can to land "gentle" blows and protect himself. He added Samuel and Peter to the mix an hour later, Samuel also fighting in close and Peter a few feet away, using his slingshot. Carter was impressed with all of them, but especially how quickly the two teens learned; he even had them demonstrate their Tae Bow skills, which were not as rusty as they thought they would be since they hadn't taken the self-defense class in a year.

"The younger you are, it's much easier to learn on the fly," Carter said, looking over his sweaty and bruised pupils. He dropped the bent in trash cover with a clang. The five of them were finally finished and walking towards the deck slowly in their battered bodies. They had all worn warm clothing for the crisp fall night to begin, but now each of them was carrying their various jackets, sweatshirts, and hoodies.

Kyle smiled broadly and poked Peter in the gut. "Hear that, old man? We got you beat."

Peter stopped walking and posed like Rodin's Thinker statue, standing still and stroking his goatee. "But we're more wily, methodical, striking when you least expect it, little Gen-Z Daddy-O!" He dove at Kyle, and the two of them fell over, wrestling and laughing.

Carter let out his deep, joyful guffaw, and Amanda turned, put her hands on her hips, and said, "Boys," with fake disgust.

Samuel thought this camaraderie was lovely and smiled back as he went up the deck steps. But he was lost a bit in thought. He had been amazed watching the "kids" - who he always saw as such gentle and loving beauties - throw themselves into the training fights with such abandon. And he knew it was for him, because of him. He wished they didn't have to do this. And he worried.

◆ ◆ ◆

A few minutes later, Amanda was walking Carter to his jeep. Kyle and Peter had already left, the hippie giving the exuberant youngster a ride home. After having tidied up the back yard, Samuel was now picking up the plates they left in the kitchen. It was 11:00, and Amanda didn't know if she ever felt such exhaustion.

"Are we ready?" she asked. She looked back and could see Samuel was looking out at her from the big picture window in the living room.

"No," Carter said, shaking his head. "Too little time, and even the great Carter isn't a miracle man." He tried to smile, but he just couldn't manage it. "But we can't let these things roam our world. We have no time and no choice. It will be tomorrow; I know it. And honestly, could anyone ever be ready for these monsters? Even if we had a fully trained army, it would still be a challenge given their origins."

Amanda looked down and kicked at some stones at the end of the driveway. "I'm scared," she said. Tears began to roll down her face, and she turned her body so her father's view of her would be blocked. Carter moved to embrace her, but she pushed him away. "No, I don't want Dad to know and come out." She wiped at her face. "I'm not scared for myself. I'm scared for him. He's my world, Carter. And clearly, he's more than I ever knew, being able to create these things from dreams, but he's still so vulnerable, so..."

"Soft?"

"Hard choice of words, but maybe accurate. He's caring, loving, not a fighter. He'll have to find anger, hate, and I don't know if he can. Even after discovering the child abuse and wanting to use that as fuel, he still will choose peace if he ever can."

"We'll protect him, little lady, and I think he might just surprise you. I've seen something in his eyes at times. Something strong. Something tough. He just has to tap into it."

She patted Carter's arm. "I'll have faith in that." She turned to go back into the house.

Carter stood there for a moment after she went inside. He thought how strong that girl was and how amazing her mother must have been. And he sincerely hoped he was right and wasn't acting in haste putting weapons into the hands of novices. But he was a man of the wild, and he could sense things. And what he knew for sure was that time was up.

CHAPTER 11

The next day came. It was a Saturday. October 24th. Samuel had initially wanted to have the meeting in the morning. With his doubts about the lingering efficacy of the rules, it was still better to be safe and gather at a time far removed from nightfall, and the kids were available all day being the weekend. But his plans were scuttled. Peter had reached out to the Madame, and she mentioned an important engagement for most of the day. Samuel couldn't imagine what would take precedence over this but then assumed it was related to their defenses. They would meet at 4:30. He decided to order pizza and wings for his team. Not the healthiest of meals, but he figured they needed some kind of protein fuel if the shit was really going to hit the fan. And he also did one other thing – he sent Harper to doggy daycare at the kennel. His dog was always a comfort to him, but he would not put him in danger. The humans now knew the horrors they would face, but Harper was innocent, ignorant. He knew Saint Bernards, while gentle, would defend their people with an unaccustomed aggressiveness, but he still wouldn't have it.

The night before, he took an extra Xanax (and 3 Aleves for the pain from the training session) so he could sleep. He was bouncing off the walls when he came in. Despite her best efforts to hide it from him and put on a brave face, he knew Amanda was bothered when she came back from talking to Carter, but he let it be. He wasn't going to change their relationship now and push things, even with the end of their world looming.

The big day dragged along: two hours felt like several life-times, so he went out and ran errands, did some grocery shop-ping, and took a walk at Hoyt Lake. Amanda offered to come, but he wanted to be alone. So she decided to go see Kyle at his house. Samuel's body was still aching; he had that day after muscle agony, and even though Carter used about one-quarter of his strength, those garbage can shots HURT. But the walk did him good on two levels. It loosened his joints and allowed him to think. Hoyt was always a great place with its scenic paths and lapping lake to put him in an excellent reflective zone. He tried doing all his mental exercises: repeating man-tras, consistent deep breathing, focusing on the exertion in his leg muscles and even the lingering pain in his upper body. It was still hard, though: he felt that dark cloud welling over his life since he knew Carter was right that the attack would occur today. And while he was an optimistic sort, he had a feeling it would be bad. Really bad.

He got home at 3:30 and put away the groceries. He overheard Kyle and Amanda, having reconvened to the Redden house, up-stairs in her bedroom laughing while watching some YouTube video about a best friend dog and deer. He peeked his head in and saw them both sitting up in the bed, faces focused on her laptop. Before Kyle had come out in the days preceding dates and dances, Samuel used to get nervous observing them hud-dled so close under her covers like that. But he should have always known better. They were just as close as two kids could be.

"Hey, Mr. R!" Kyle said excitedly. "Want to watch this with us? Animals can teach us so much about decency to each other. Look at these two divergent creatures, immediately bonding."

"You're right about that, buddy, but no, I'm good. I'm just going to go down to the living room and try to read my book. I'm almost finished with it. It's so much better than the movie.

How are your folks? It's been too long since we hung out."

"Oh, you know, workaholics as usual." Samuel knew this was true. David spent long hours at his law practice, and Shayera was a shift nurse, twelve hours a night, seven on/seven off, and they were two of the hardest workers Redden had ever met. Kyle continued, "When I tell them to slow down, Dad always gives me the 'the look' and his standard line: 'black people have to work extra hard to get ahead, son. And beyond that, a work ethic is something no one can ever take away from you.' I'm sure he's right, but they're too driven sometimes." He said this last part with a wide grin, which showed no matter what he said about his parents, that he loved them more than life.

"You guys want a healthy snack before we launch our cholesterol into the hemisphere with Tony's Pizzeria's greasy concoction?" Samuel asked.

Amanda gave him a small smile, but he could tell a lot was going on in her brain. *This is hard for her to process, but she's not the only one. No time to even handle this. I need to let her be.* "No thanks. We actually had some yogurt an hour ago." She then stared intently at the most important man in her life, immediately reading his emotions. "You need to talk, Dad?" *I'm glad I'm used to being an open book with her.*

"Sure, I can make myself disappear for a bit," Kyle said, looking both of them over, he also being a very empathetic individual and knowing when to give space. "I don't mind, really."

"You're both wonderful, two of my favorite people in the world, you know that, right?" Samuel whispered. Kyle said, "Aww," and Amanda just kept her tight gaze on him. "But, no, I'm good. Just want to lose myself in a fake world for a bit." He turned and left before he could get too emotional. What he didn't see was Amanda turn to Kyle and immediately lay her head in his lap, closing her sad eyes.

When the time finally arrived, and Peter knocked at his door, Samuel was so grateful. He ended up only reading a few pages of his book and just staring around the room for the next hour, overthinking. Impatience had entirely overruled his fear. He just wanted it over with. Carter arrived a few minutes after the flower child. Samuel had the food delivered, and Amanda and Kyle came down when Door Dash delivered it at 4:45. Each person had a deadpan, impassive expression, no one joking around.

The five of them ate in silence while they awaited Madame Takari's entrance. When he and the others had been setting the table, Samuel asked if they should wait for the last of their group, but Peter said that just like wizards, psychics arrive on their own schedule and they should start. While they munched away, Samuel thought how awkward this all felt. He was sure if this were a normal situation, it would be a talkative, jovial dinner. But the seriousness and apprehensiveness continued from all. At one point, he considered offering the adults beer, but immediately reconsidered. Dulling their senses one iota was not a good idea this day. But he wished he could. The atmosphere was tense. Even the garrulous Peter and the normally fidgety Kyle were lost in their thoughts and sitting still in place while the quiet came to feel like an actual physical force around them. They all knew the storm was coming and were each preparing themselves as best they could. When, at 5:42, the doorbell rang while they sipped coffee, tea, and fruit juice, he was sure all of them jumped in their chairs. And they then let out an uneasy group laugh. Even Samuel, who thought he had no humor left in him.

The pleasant tension-relieving moment was short-lived. Peter went to the kitchen door. There were two small windows two-thirds up the entry frame; he glanced in them and could see no one. But Darwin knew it had to be that wonderful, tiny Vietnamese woman, not tall enough to show her face in the opening. When he swung it open, ready to curtesy and kiss his friend's hand, he gasped. It was indeed Madame Takari. And she was covered in blood.

"My lady!" he screamed.

Samuel's heart leapt so fast into his jugular that he had to catch his breath. But he wasted no time in running to the door. He aided Peter in helping Madame into the living room. She collapsed before they could even reach the couch but was able to lean her back against it. The two of them kneeled beside her, and she immediately reached out, grasping and bringing together each of their right hands with her left, so it looked like they were ready to do a cheer. Samuel felt the slippery combination of blood and sweat in her skin and tried not to think about it. But when he got a better look at her whole body, he knew turning off his brain was not going to happen. Her wounds were almost too many to count. Her sweet old face had two deep scratches on the cheek. Her dress, which he initially thought had been one of her garish hues, most likely purple, was now covered in blood, so it was like a child's messy finger painting. And in the holes in the fabric, Samuel could see what looked like bite marks on the stomach and near her breasts. Her legs were equally gashed. But the worst was her throat: she had her other hand on her jugular, and blood flowed freely through the fingers.

Samuel's chest was throbbing with a painful jackhammer consistency now. *It looks like a crocodile or a hippo took a couple bites out of her throat.*

"What happened?" he asked her with a wavery voice. He knew calling for an ambulance now wouldn't do a lick of good, so he needed as much information as he could get. She was not long for this world.

"They came. Spells held for several days but they broke through two hours ago when I was about to leave my shop. They are smart creatures. Even punctured the tires of my car without alerting anyone outside. You can't underestimate their powers, my child. I just made it here in time. I started off as soon as they left me for what they thought was dead."

"You walked?" Samuel was mystified. He guessed it was at least an hour and a half trek to walk from the East Side to North Buffalo.

"Yes, there was some power left in me. I was able to slow the blood flow with some ancient incantations. But I don't have much left."

Then Peter posed the question Samuel should have asked first. "They got you in the day's light, my lovely lady?" *Oh, no.*

She gave a tiny, shaky nod. "Yes. They brought the darkness with them."

Samuel pressed her for more details, "What does that mean?"

"No time," she rasped and then coughed, a liquid hoarse hacking sound. "It all happened so fast. It was this King who bit my jugular after his followers toyed with me. His thoughts were dark, ugly. But we must delay no longer.Bring the young ones to me and your weapons, except for the shotgun. The African warrior can take care of himself. My touch has just given you what protection I can manage, and I must share the rest." Samuel and Peter looked at each other nonplussed, given that they had talked about this idea the day before, but both of them weren't completely surprised either.

As Samuel got wobbly to his feet and ran to the kitchen archway to obey her wishes, Madame Takari turned to Peter with tears in her eyes, "My sisters were butchered. They put themselves between the monsters and me. But I used much of my remaining strength to set fire to the inside of the building so nothing would lead back to Samuel. And to give my beloveds a proper funeral pyre. It was the least I could do. They had no families, just me." Peter leaned his head down to touch Madame's. His forehead was now dappled in blood. He wept.

She said one more thing to Peter, and it was hard for the hippie to hear. "You must take my body away after this is over. Dump me behind my building somewhere. It will look like my sisters and I had some bizarre murder-suicide pact and finished it with the fire. The timing of finding me might lead to questions, but it will be too unusual for the authorities to figure out. I'm known for being the weird witch downtown."

"No, I can't!"

"You must. For Samuel. It will keep the police from suspecting his involvement."

Peter sighed deeply. "You are special. I will make sure to give you the proper arrangements after."

"I know you will, my love." She touched his glistened cheek with her long finger.

Samuel arrived back with Amanda and Kyle. They looked stupefied. When he went to get them, they were rooted to the spot in the entranceway to the living room. Carter was further back in the kitchen, loading his shotgun. Samuel had yelled for them to grab their weapons, but they wouldn't respond. So he had to run to the table himself, snatching the slingshot, nunchaku, and sai (his staff was positioned in his pants belt). Now looking up with a weak grimace at the new arrivals, Madame released her hand from Peter's and reached out, locking onto the teenagers' wrists in turn, first Amanda and then Kyle, more firmly than Samuel would have imagined possible. They both cringed at the cold, sticky touch but managed to not pull away for the few seconds each was held (and the act helped wake them up). It stained them in red, much like Samuel and Peter's limbs were now too, but they were respectful enough to not make a big deal of it. "Now you will have the ounce of protection I already gave your dad and Peter. Please survive, dearies," she muttered.

"Now the weapons," she said. Samuel laid them all at Madame Takari's feet. She managed to pick them up but had to release her right hand to do it. The blood luckily was just dripping now, not pouring out, but Samuel put his hand to his mouth when he saw the gaping wound. Madame squeezed her eyes shut as she held all four weapons at her breast, and Samuel knew it was taking all her remaining strength to bless them. He noticed now that her lips were moving even if no sound came out. After several seconds, she stopped and sucked deeply for air. She beckoned to Samuel with her head. He leaned in close as her voice continued its whispered rasp, "After, Peter must take you to see Terrian. He will guide you to the final steps."

Samuel wanted to ask clarification but knew there were no more answers to come. And he figured he already kind of knew who the person was: Terrian must be the one she head mentioned briefly before. The Madame now looked up at Samuel with adoration in her eyes, the only part of her that remained strong. "You *are* the Golden Child. You will defeat the abominations. With that pleasant thought, I can go to the next part of my journey in peace." She cast a quick glance at Peter and winked at him. He blew her a kiss through his flowing tears, mouthing, "Thank you." Then she breathed her last.

Samuel realized he had, at some point, kneeled back down and taken her cold, lifeless hands. He could feel wetness on his cheeks as well. *No matter how mad I was at her, she was a special lady who helped me immensely. And now they've taken another.* Peter bent down and closed her eyes with his fingers.

There was no time for further reaction, though. The house was suddenly cast in darkness. It took Samuel a moment to recognize why this felt entirely off. Then his mind remembered what time it was when the Madame rang the bell. He recalled it precisely because he had walked by the counter microwave on the way to the kitchen door and took in the digital numbers. It had been 5:43. Which meant it couldn't even be 6:00 yet. And while the year was inching towards the end of daylight savings time and the beginning of earlier sunsets, it still wouldn't be dark until 6:20 or so. And there were no overcast skies just minutes ago either: while a chilly day, it was bright, sunny. But as he now looked outside via the big picture window behind the couch, it was completely dark. He would have sworn it was 9:30 at night out there, evening's murky fingers reaching in to create the gloom inside.

"How?" he asked.

Peter wiped at his face and answered sadly, "The one who might be able to answer that is no longer with us. But I think she gave us a clue: 'they bring the darkness with them.'"

Samuel stood up and noticed Amanda and Kyle on either side of him. They were much more aware looking than before and now holding out their cell phones with the flashlights turned on. It gave a tiny break in the suffocating sable pall. Carter was still behind all of them, though he had moved to under the archway, casting his enormous shadow. His eyes were moving to and fro, searching for predators in the dark. Samuel stared dumbfounded out the big bay window and, at that moment, gasped. As he noticed a moment ago, the area around his home was pitch black, but as he looked around the street, he could see the expected sky, a little cloudy but still with the sun fighting through. There weren't any neighbors in their front yards at this time, the cold probably playing a bit of a role there, but he saw a car go by, and the light glinted off its windshield.

They've darkened the area around my house only. If the Madame was right and they're somehow traveling with darkness now, that means they're here in the immediate vicinity. An idea came to Samuel, something so obvious he kicked himself for not realizing it sooner. There was a light switch just outside the stairwell to the second floor. It controlled an overhead light in the living room. He switched it on, and his heart dropped a bit more. While the light did indeed pop on, it was a dull shimmer and even flickered some. *Whatever the monsters have done, even artificial light is affected.* The others followed his cue: Amanda switched on two lamps on end tables, Carter flipped on the kitchen light, Kyle ran down the hallway and turned on the lights in the bathroom and spare bedroom, and Peter turned the switch in the adjoining dining room, all of them using their cell phones to navigate. Samuel finally tried to activate the porch light, and for this one, nothing happened. The illumination provided from all these sources was so weak that it was only a slight improvement. It was similar to when globes that employ four bulbs have three burned out. At least the flickering had seemed to resolve itself. And they could see each other. Their faces and forms were murky and shaded, but they could tell who was whom and see the shape of the objects around the room. *And we'll be able to see any invaders. Since I can't imagine this is enough light to keep them out.*

He looked around to his loved ones, his companions, his team. He observed the same understanding about the limited lighting in their expressions. Even with the shade, their befuddled looks were clear to see. "How is this even possible? They've never done this before, have they?" Kyle asked.

Who knows? "No. Maybe it's tied to their very presence," Samuel said. "But why now? Why couldn't they cloak themselves before? Unless with each person here they kill, the darkness grows. And killing Madame, a powerful enemy, they've gained that much more of this shadow. This is what they'll cover our world with if they win." They all looked at him with unresolved confusion, but he only shrugged. *Maybe it's intuition coming from that world. Or perhaps I'm just making shit up because I'm terrified.*

Then they all heard and felt it. The house shook like it was being moved somehow. All of them but Carter stumbled or grabbed for anything, the other person, the wall. The primatologist was amazingly still, focused. Samuel thought about that lovely Pixar Movie, *Up.* It was like when Carl's house was torn off its foundations by the balloons and took to the sky. But that was fun, a triumphant moment in the film. This was the polar opposite; it was the feeling of being uprooted, invaded. Another memory came too. It reminded him of that day in Madame Takari's sanctuary all those years ago when she first touched him. But Samuel knew this time the gorillas were here, in reality: it wasn't just some psychic attack.

The shuddering stopped as quick as it had started. Amanda and Kyle were holding onto each other. Peter had his hands against the far wall, under the now jostled family hanging picture of Samuel, Sandra, and Amanda. Samuel had toppled a bit to sit on the end of the couch. Despite looking stoic, unmoved before, Carter was now holding his left hand against the inner side of the living room opening.

Then Samuel saw something out of the corner of his eye, but it was too late. Dark shapes were hurling themselves at the picture window. It shattered, spraying painful shards at the four closest. Darkness took Samuel's vision.

It had begun.

◆ ◆ ◆

Samuel's eyes opened. Only seconds had passed and he was glad to notice that he hadn't passed out but had reflexively protected his face by cutting off his view. But he felt disoriented. He could feel the pain of the glass shards now stuck in his arms and face but couldn't wholly register what was going on. He felt like he lost himself there for a moment but was slowly emerging. He noticed that he had been blown off the end of the couch from the force of the explosion further into the room, landing on his back and jostling his neck. This was painful as well, but the cuts were taking precedence. His glasses were askew on his face, and he quickly re-adjusted them, though the left lens now had a crack in it, just under his line of vision. "Dad!" Amanda screamed, pulling him up. Kyle and Peter were also yanking at him. They had recovered more quickly since they didn't fall. He looked at them and noticed the same cuts on all of them from the glass explosion. Some of the protruding fragments were large and scared him. He was afraid to look at his own body too close. His daughter's frenzied voice had done an excellent job of completely waking him up, and he was able to notice that even though the glass pieces were frightening, no one seemed to be bleeding profusely. He was grateful for this. "How am I?" he asked quickly. "Are any of the gashes deep?"

"No, you're fine, like us. Now move!" Amanda yelled, jolting him further with a shake. The foursome scattered quickly over to Carter, who had emerged fully into the living room, his shotgun aimed. Even as far away as he was, he hadn't completely survived the glass shower either, showing a few cuts on the bare arms coming out of his white short-sleeved shirt.

Samuel followed the direction of the gun to the window, and there they were. His childhood nightmares, exactly as he remembered them. The gorillas were huddled on every side of the couch. They were standing upright in a perverse unnatural way, again not the usual crouch of a worldly ape. Samuel's mind latched onto an image of those Bigfoot videos he saw as a kid. Their dark black fur was matted with blood. And their faces were long, almost lupine like with mouths filled with long fangs, mucous infused drool dripping there. There was a reason he could see all this so clearly: swirling around the apes was a sick, greenish afterglow that was spreading around the room. It was not a bright, pleasant colorful green but puke-colored, lurid. But any concerns about seeing well enough to fight were unfounded now. Though he knew this was *their* light, their power, and would not protect him and his friends. He had a feeling that the dull illumination in his house was being cancelled out by this unholy hue. There was a scraping noise, a horrible sound that went right through him. Some of the apes were stooping down and scratching into his hardwood floor with their hand claws, leaving their mark, so to speak. He felt the physical manifestation of terror spreading up from his dry, tight throat, where it would likely finally explode in his brain, but he managed to push it back. *If I let the fear reduce me to a cowering eight-year-old, I won't be able to fight. And my daughter is here. I'm not letting them hurt her or the rest of my team.* He was able to recalibrate his mind enough to observe that he saw five to ten of the apes, but no silverback, no King. *He's waiting. Waiting until we're at our weakest, like the coward he is.*

Samuel took a quick look at his friends. In the pea-colored backsplash, they all kind of looked like alien life forms in some old sci-fi flick.

Peter had clearly managed to put away his trauma at losing his dear friend Madame. Something Samuel hadn't noticed in his retreat was that the hippie had snatched the four weapons from the dead lady's lap. He now handed Samuel his bo staff, having already given the kids their tools, which they held at their sides. Peter was looking straight ahead as he did this, breathing in and out in a meditative fashion. Samuel could also see an anger in his features that were somewhat foreign to his longtime friend. *He so loved that woman. She was probably a mother figure for him.*

Kyle looked scared, his mouth comically wide open, his forehead creased. Samuel couldn't blame him. And he was shaking a bit. Amanda laid a hand on his arm, and he stopped.

Speaking of Samuel's daughter, she amazed him. Her visage was fierce, intense, with squinted eyes that stared unblinkingly at the monsters. Samuel also didn't fail to observe that she had stepped in front of him in an act of protection in the intervening moments. It made his heart melt. *She's even stronger than her mother, who was the strongest woman I've ever known.*

And in front of them all was Carter, who had almost casually crept to the vanguard, still in a fighting, aiming stance. Samuel found something else that was exuded in every part of the big man's body. A fury. Like an animal, ready to pounce. He was yearning for revenge. There was a kind of heat radiating from him; you could just feel it. *For Amy and her family.* Any questions Samuel had that first time about the man being unable to hurt the nightmare monsters was completely gone now.

And the conversations from the past month with this group about whether the gorillas were real became moot as well. None of them had expressed significant doubts, and in Peter's case, he never even questioned, and after what happened to Amy, it was a lot easier to believe. But now, seeing the unholy creations in the flesh was the culmination of this journey. And they were all still standing with Samuel, unbowed by the madness presented to them mere feet away. Even Kyle's very human response of shock and fear was more under control than most people could have managed; the very sight and sounds of the gorillas were enough to reduce a person to a puddle of fright and cause the need for immediate flight. *I'm so lucky to have them with me. They really are special.*

Samuel stepped up to Carter. He knew who the general was here. "What's the plan?" Amanda had first reached out to stop her father from going past but stopped in mid-motion. The reason? Carter had peeked back, shook his head, and given her a knowing look. She smiled. *This has to do with their conversation last night. And she's proud of me. That I'm keeping my fear under wraps. Well, let's see if I can really make her proud.* Seemingly in response to this, sounds of the gorillas snorting and grunting reached his ears. Before this could shake him up, Samuel forcibly remembered his molestation at the hands of Bennett. He glared towards the gorillas and planned to do what he said before, take all his aggression out on them. He was glad they hadn't had time to train him and the others with guns. He needed the hand-to-hand sensation of whaling on his past.

"The plan?" Carter said. "Samuel, it's quite simple. Y'all stay behind me, and I'll start shooting. But I won't be able to take them all, so be ready to fight. I hope whatever magic that poor lady did will help give you some protection. But - and I say this with all respect - after what they did to her, we probably can't rely on that too much. This is as real as it gets."

When Carter said "y'all", Samuel was sure he caught a tinge of southern accent in the man's vocalization. It provided him an idle thought that he had no idea where the legendary character came from. He let this thought drift away and nodded. But then he said, "We'll stand next to you, not behind."

"Right," Kyle added, stepping up.

"For sure," Amanda said, joining them, taking her position next to her dad.

"This is heavy, man," Peter said at last. Coming up on the other side of Carter, he rested a hand on the gorilla expert's shoulder. "But you're not going to be a martyr. Come together, as the Beatles once told me."

Carter unveiled his toothy grin. "All right. Good luck, friends."

No going back, Samuel thought as he and the rest of them shuffled to the left and right to give Carter room. *Nothing is ever going to be the same now.*

Then a shotgun blast discharged its sound around the room, and he felt it deep in his ears and down his body. And a cry of agony, an inhuman shriek followed.

The gunshot was much louder than Samuel expected, but he managed to keep his focus through the first moments and not let his newness to guns and their effects distract him. He looked over towards his enemies and could see the damage that was done instantly. The first gorilla victim had its head blown clean off, the lifeless eyes staring vacantly as the hairy face propelled forward, plopped on an area rug, and then rolled towards Carter, stopping just short of his feet. He took no notice. The blood funneled out from the hole in the still-standing creature into three directions; it drenched the couch in front of the beast and the two walls to each side. The headless torso then crumpled with an audible thud, its 500 pound body causing a small crater in the floor. *Wow, that's a powerful gun.* After thinking this, Samuel glanced quickly to Carter and noted a brief look of surprise in the warrior. *It's not supposed to be that powerful. Maybe something to be said for confidence, mental mastery when facing monsters of the mind.* The big man didn't waste any time reflecting, though, as he pulled the trigger again. The second shot was also pinpoint, hitting one of the other simians square in the chest. This brute was in front of the couch and had just gotten a bit of a bath from its friend. He had been tensing his body a moment before, ready to charge at the humans, but his comrade's violent murder made him wary and dismayed. The buckshot opened a cavity in his chest that made its insides visible, a now slowing, gushing heart and a ribcage that started crumbling into dust. He fell backward over the prone body of Madame Takari and landed on the couch, ending up in a bizarre sitting position. The other gorillas howled in anger, and several broke away towards the group.

"Spread out!" Carter yelled. "Don't let them corner you!"

So they did as their military leader instructed. And action came quick and intensely now, a blur of activity. Samuel desperately wanted to stick with Amanda, but he understood cerebrally how Carter was right. So he drifted to the right towards the bedroom hallway, kicking the upended living room coffee table out of the way. Then he saw it, the thing that had stalked him for years, an ape from hell coming at him. He didn't have time to think and prayed he wouldn't hesitate. He didn't. With urgency, he depressed the button that released the full length of his bo staff. He immediately followed this up with violent action, swinging the weapon exactly as Carter had taught him, and the whooshing sound gave him more pleasure than ever. He managed to connect squarely on the rapidly advancing gorilla's face, and the thudding noise would have normally given him a queasy stomach. Now, it only gave him satisfaction. The gorilla fell to one knee. Samuel caught a whiff of the beast's manure stench that often assailed his nasal passages when he was little. But he pushed this sensation aside since he knew he couldn't let up. He reared back, put all his weight into the next strike, smashing the gorilla again. And then again. The metal surface of the staff clanged sickly. But he didn't stop. He was screaming now and indeed visualizing

Bennett as he continued to flail away. The bloodlust was indeed upon him. After a moment, he realized the thing wasn't moving anymore, and its brains were spread over the floor. He still wasn't revolted, but he also knew he couldn't celebrate. There were too many of them. He turned to face another. If the Samuel of a few weeks ago could see himself now, ready, brave, snarling, he would have been stopped speechless.

Meanwhile, Amanda and Kyle hadn't gone too far from each other as instructed, just a foot or so, backing slowly together toward the opening to the dining room. The shadows cast by the deck furniture outside the sliding glass door were shaped as perverse, green building blocks. These two had clearly woken up from their earlier stupefaction, not being cowed by the encircling creatures. Kyle cried out, "Take this, you fucking bullies!" He swung his nunchucks in a frenzy, blasting against a swiping gorilla, landing on its shoulders and neck. He wasn't alone; the two kids worked beautifully as a team. Amanda, making no verbalizations, leapt in, biting her bottom lip in concentration, and plunged the right-sided sai deep in the stunned gorilla's throat. Her other hand, not being the dominant one, wasn't quite as strong, but she still followed that up by jabbing this into his groin as well. She pulled the knives out harshly, leaving a dripping trail of blood. The gorilla underwent a spasm before going still. Again, friends at school of these two would imagine they were dreaming this of their two peaceful classmates. Kyle and Amanda both looked beamingly at the other for a second. But it was a second too much. Unfortunately, they didn't see another ape coming from behind, and it barreled into the two of them. But whatever Madame Takari did to them helped blunt the blow, keeping the nightmare claws from penetrating. Amanda only staggered while Kyle landed on his backside. Before the gorilla could press the attack, Carter put a load of buckshot into its back. Like the second victim, this blow hallowed this one out too, and its spine partly split in half before the gorilla fell over face first.

Over in the kitchen, Peter was engaged with a couple gorillas, but with his proficiency with the slingshot, they kept staggering backward from shots of bearing balls. He was in real rapid-fire mode and didn't know if it was his gift with this tool or the blessing of Madame Takari, but he kept burying the metal projectiles all over their bodies, putting depressions in their fur and skin. He hoped he wouldn't run out, but that wasn't a big worry: Carter had provided hundreds of the "rocks," which Peter had in both his pockets and the knapsack, which he had tossed on the kitchen table when retreating here. It was a heavy bag, but despite his gangly form, Peter had strong biceps, always saying, "Feed the body and the mind, my friends." He, too, was caught in the barbarity, screaming gibberish after every shot. In his mind, he was avenging his beloved Madame while at the same time trying to shake off the image of her bloody body. Finally, he managed a kill shot on one of the apes, landing the metal into one of its eyeballs. It made a squishing, juicy sound as it embedded in there. The ape dropped backward, hitting its head on the counter before plopping on the linoleum. The other gorilla screamed shrilly, sounding creepily like *The Lord of the Rings* Nazgul, and charged with inhuman speed. That noise threw off Darwin, and he had his first miss, shooting over its head and breaking through the window over the sink. The gorilla swiped out, and even Madame's protection could not save him from the slash of the dagger-like hand. The longer she was dead, the weaker her spells would become. His cheek was opened up. He cried out, dropping the slingshot. The ape pounced on the hippie, straddled him, and opened its mouth to take a bite, its crimson fangs starting to dip downwards. But surprisingly, it stopped short. Blood began oozing from its neck. Peter had pulled a jackknife from his pocket and plunged it into the gorilla. He carried this around for his camping expeditions and never imagined he would use it in self-defense. But Darwin was proving a resourceful and quick-thinking fighter. He grunted as he used all his power to push the monster off his body before the free-flowing blood could drench him. Still, he got quite a bit on him and now looked like he was wearing one of his red-hued tie-dyed shirts and not the Pink Floyd *Dark Side of the Moon* one he came with. He took a hand and pushed his long bangs out of his face (he hated pony-tails) and prepared himself for more action.

While this was happening, other kills had been completed. In the dining room, Kyle and Amanda had two more destroyed apes near their feet, each having finished one individually. Samuel felled one other, and Carter's marksmanship was un-erring, eliminating five of them. The shotgun blasts and the monsters' howls had become the background noise of the bru-tal scene.

After reloading with the shells he'd jammed in his large pants pockets, Carter roved around the space and dropped two more. The apes weren't showing much intelligence - which made the primatologist sure their simian traits were few - since they clustered together in a pack. But a few of these broke away, spread out, and sped towards him. He pivoted and used the shotgun as a hand weapon, knocking one out, sending it spin-ning in a circle before crumbling near the media center shelf. He then fired on the next, hitting it first in the arm, this limb looking like he was waving hello as it sloughed off. A second shot hit it in the stomach, spilling its intestines. "Same as you did to Amy, you son of a bitch!" he screamed. But the next moment, Carter was back to his vigilance, yelling for Samuel to watch out as three more were loping in Redden's direction. Carter wasted two of them, firing with no hesitation, taking the legs out of the first and another headshot for the sec-ond. But the third managed to reach its quarry. It slashed at Samuel in a flurry of blindingly swift-moving talons making short work of Madame's last bit of protection. Luckily it kept him from being punctured, though. He fell rearwards, and the gorilla simultaneously jumped on top of him. The reek of the brute was overwhelming now. Samuel gagged. The gorilla bit deeply into his left shoulder, and he screamed out in agony. Ten feet away, Carter cursed himself for not getting body armor for everyone. He would not make that mistake again. The pain overwhelming him, Samuel dropped his weapon and winced, bracing himself for another jolt of searing torment, but something made the gorilla pause.

Samuel's right hand was glowing, the bright illumination spreading out from his fingertips and casting its tendrils of yellow into the sick sub light. And he felt a warmth flowing to both ends of his body. The ape seemed terrified by it, recoiling a bit. *It's back!* Samuel started to reach out towards his enemy with this hand, but before he could do anything with it, the gorilla fell over, knocked senseless with one of Peter's sling-shot attacks. The two kids ran over, and while Kyle held the gorilla by the throat with his nunchucks, Amanda pierced its heart.

The luminescence of Samuel's limb dissipated quickly, snapping out like a flash. Then all was still, quiet. The smoke from the shotgun blasts slowly dissipated. The ugly green light was still there.

Peter ripped off a piece of his bloody shirt and wrapped it around his best friend's arm in a tourniquet as he got to his feet. He'd clearly seen Samuel's hand trick as he also tapped Redden's right knuckles before shaking his head in amazement. But there was no time to dive into it, which must have been killing the hippie. Amanda followed the first-aid attempt with a towel she'd retrieved from the bathroom, which she wet in the sink and now pressed to her father's wound as a compress. Samuel looked around and was shocked to see almost twenty dead or severely incapacitated gorilla bodies strewn all over his house. He stood up a little uneasily and took in the status of his loved ones. Even though there were some scratches and cuts on every fighter, his arm was probably the worst of the injuries. *We beat them!* Most of the dead were due to Carter's quick gun work, but the others had undoubtedly done their part. A surge of pride took over Samuel, but a second later the pain in his arm really kicked in. He held the towel tight to it and grimaced.

"Did we win?" Kyle asked.

"Maybe not the war. But it's a victory for sure," Carter admitted, smiling as he came walking over to them.

But then the house shook deeply again, causing all to steady themselves for a second time. Samuel's stomach churned with an uneasy feeling. His eyes immediately went to the picture window. And what he saw took all his hope. There had to be 100 gorillas milling in his yard amid the algae-like sheen. They parted, dropping down, their heads pressed to the ground. Stepping through the gap and into the broken window frame was the silverback.

King had arrived.

CHAPTER 12

King wasn't allowed to continue his dramatic entrance, his saunter interrupted by several explosive reverberations. Carter wasted no time in emptying a whole round of buckshot into the head monster. This gave Samuel some hope seeing their leader jump so quickly into action, not giving the silverback a chance to pounce. But his hope suddenly turned to despair yet again. The shells hit King and dropped to the floor right in front of him with a clattering sound, a similar effect to when gangsters shot at Superman.

No.

King growled once at the shooter, an almost human sound of disgust. Then he turned his head to Samuel, who was stunned by the size of this one. He didn't know if it was its sheer girth or the cockiness that it exuded, but he knew even if the others, the ones he created in childhood, were standing, they would have to look up to see this monstrosity.

King looked to the floor to his right and saw the still body of Madame Takari. He took two long, loping steps to her and kicked her body.

"You son of a bitch!" Peter screamed but made no move, given what had just happened with the gunshots. But he was shaking in a fury.

"You fucker," Samuel mumbled.

King made a guttural sound. Samuel took a moment to place what the auditory response represented before landing on it with further bewilderment. *He actually laughed.*

King now reached out to Samuel mentally, the first time the human had experienced something like this in thirty-five years. And it was way worse. King's "voice" was so deep. Deeper than Carter's. Deeper than anything Samuel had ever heard. Something that sounded like it was created down in the soil, in the earth's hollows, where all kinds of wriggly things lived. **STOP WITH YOUR INEFFECTUAL EMOTIONS AND INSULTS. SHE INTERFERED ONE TOO MANY TIMES IN OUR BUSINESS AND PAID FOR IT. BUT YOU AND YOUR LITTLE BAND HAVE DONE WELL WITH THIS SMALL SAMPLING OF MY MINIONS, REDDEN. EVEN SO, DO YOU HONESTLY THINK YOU CAN HARM ME WITH EARTHLY WEAPONS, EVEN THE ONES PITIFULLY BLESSED BY THAT OLD GYPSY WHORE? I AM SOMETHING NEW. NOT YOUR BABY NIGHTMARE CREATURES. I'M A FULLY FORMED ADULT TERROR. AND BEYOND ANYTHING YOU CAN HANDLE.**

That's why he's such a worse threat. He was created by my grown-up anxieties and failures.

Samuel now turned to his companions, "Can you hear him?"

They all shook their head "no" while not taking their eyes off the enemy.

Why can't they hear your thoughts?

THEY HAVE NO CONNECTION TO ME OR MY KIND.

Samuel looked back to the others. "He's speaking to me mentally. Like the other one did in my past. He says you can't hear him due to me creating them, I guess."

Samuel had a thought. "Where is the old leader? From my childhood? The non-silver one?" he asked King.

The silverback turned his head and grunted. Through the crowd and into the window came another ape. It was crawling on all fours. When it reached King, it licked his feet. It raised its red-tinged eyes to its master, whimpering. Samuel could see a large scar that ran from above its left eye all the way to its mouth.

That's him.

IT TOOK ME ALL OF FIVE OF YOUR EARTH MINUTES TO CHALLENGE THIS WEAK ONE AND REPLACE HIM. IF YOU FELT THREATENED BY HIM, YOU HAVE NO HOPE TO STAND MUCH LONGER IN MY PRESENCE. King then snarled at the deposed ruler, who slunk back away.

That one looked so huge and menacing when I was little, but next to King, it's like he's shrunk.

"What's going on? What's he saying?" Kyle asked. Samuel could see the teen was now working hard to contain his terror, to appear tough, though his wide eyes betrayed him. Amanda just stayed silent but subtly took Samuel's hand.

"That was the old leader he wrested control from. The rest is just bragging and threats. Namely that our weapons cannot harm him. Not good."

Carter looked helpless, casting a sad glance down to his shotgun, which he now held at his side, no longer aimed. *He can't handle not being able to solve this physically. He's a man of action.* "What's the scumbag waiting for then?" he asked.

Samuel could hear King chortle again, but in his head now. He actually pressed his fingers to his temples. The sound was like hearing the grinding metal of a car crash. **WHAT A PETTY, IN-EFFECTUAL INSULT. AND FROM THE MIGHTY ONE, THE SO-CALLED GORILLA "EXPERT". BUT I APPRECIATE HIS GUMP-TION. WHAT AM I WAITING FOR? NOTHING NOW. I WAS WORKING UP TO THIS MOMENT, TO THE CRESCENDO OF YOUR DESPAIR. TO REVEL IN HOW HELPLESS YOU AND YOUR PLANS ARE. YOU CAN'T WIN. YOUR DEATH WILL BE PAINFUL, REDDEN. AND THEN YOUR WORLD WILL DIE HORRIBLY AS WELL. ALL BECAUSE OF YOU.** King actually grinned at him now, brandishing its mouthful of sabretooth tiger-esque teeth. **MORE HORRIBLY THAN YOUR WIFE DIED EVEN.**

FUCK YOU! Samuel released this thought with more anger than he ever emoted in his life. It actually scared him a bit. He started to feel that encroaching warmth rising inside his bones and looked to his hands, hoping his untapped power would come now and save the day. But there was only a small flicker, a spark in his fingertips before disappearing. But to his joy, he noticed King had actually taken a small step back. The creature would remember this later. And Samuel's friends were looking at him with bewilderment. They may not have heard the thought, but they could feel something in the air, the rage as Samuel's face twisted. Amanda winced from the tightening of her father's hand. And Peter Darwin saw the flicker, looking and wishing for the possibility.

King now growled under his breath, angered intensely by Samuel's act of defiance. **MAYBE IF YOU HAD LEARNED TO HARNESS THAT RAGE, YOU COULD HAVE BEAT ME, HUMAN. BUT IT'S OVER FOR YOU NOW. AND FOR YOUR SAD WORLD. SAY GOODBYE TO YOUR COMPANIONS.**

All during the last thirty minutes, Samuel had been so driven by adrenaline. His initial fear of his nightmare creatures being alive in the flesh had been overcome by the emotional surge of the battle. But now, with the imminent attack coming from King, the terror came back. He was facing more than just his childhood monsters now - something more primal, more final: the all too realness of unavoidable death. Even at times in his life when he had the strongest moral certitude of the afterlife, the unknowns of death had always terrified him. He often feared that all the religions were wrong – that there was nothing after this. That we just turn off, go from a functional thinking being to nothingness. It was what his fear of the gorillas on some level represented to him, the final loss of control. Death was the ultimate power of finality. God, *I don't want to die.*

King didn't respond to this last thought but only smiled wider and flexed his claws.

Samuel looked to his loved ones for what he figured was the last time. Tears developed at the corners of both eyes. "He's going to kill me now. And there's nothing we can do to stop it." Each of them handled this in their own way. Peter shook his head and muttered, "No." Carter just glared at the monster in anger and gripped his gun more tightly. Kyle looked lost in his thoughts. And Amanda, not surprisingly, grabbed hard onto her father. He took her fully into his arms.

"No, Dad. No. We have to do something," Amanda said, sobbing, which made Samuel cry audibly now as well, the proverbial floodgates bursting through and his body hitching in misery as he moaned.

He held her more tightly than he ever had in their fifteen years together and stroked her hair like he did when she was little. "I really don't think there's a way, sweetheart." He lifted her head away from his chest. He wanted to tell her how scared he was, but he couldn't make this worse for her. "Be strong as you always have been. The world will need your courage." Samuel lifted his eyes to Carter, the most physically strong of the group. "Take her, Carter. Please."

But Carter just kept giving King the evil eye until Samuel yelled his name again forcefully. Then he broke out of this mental block, dashed over, and gently took Amanda from Samuel, actually lifting her in his arms so there would be no resistance. She screamed, "Daddy!", holding her hands out to Samuel, but the big man held her fast and tight. Samuel cried more miserably.

Carter said this to him, "We won't stop fighting, brother."

Samuel smiled weakly at him. Then he cast his eyes back to King. He was still terrified, but he wouldn't give this horrible creature the satisfaction. *Do your worst, fuckface.*

King lost his smile and then howled, sounding nothing like a gorilla and more akin to a hunting wolf. He took three stalking steps in Samuel's direction. Then he pounced, his dark and ugly vampiric mouth opening its enormous maw. Samuel closed his eyes and braced for the killing blow. But he didn't feel anything. Just heard Amanda scream, "No!" She then muttered, "Oh God."

What just happened?

He opened his eyes and what he saw made no sense. So all emotions were withheld while he tried to puzzle it out. Kyle was in front of him, moving from a standing position to put one knee on the floor. He was holding his neck. Samuel could see blood dripping through his fingers to the hardwood. King was backing away with a look of satisfaction, blood ringing his mouth while he licked his chops. Kyle twisted his head back to Samuel, his mouth agape in terror. His whole throat was coated in red.

What Samuel had missed was Kyle soundlessly coming out of his deep thoughts and running to put himself in front of one of his great heroes in life, placing himself there as a shield. He was so inconspicuous as he did it that the others didn't even notice until it was too late.

This horrible realization knocked Samuel mentally right out of reality. He found himself awakening to a memory. He was at the Taylor Street playground. He was looking around, searching, and then he spotted her: five-year-old Amanda in pigtails and jean dungarees running around with another child. It was a laughing black boy with the cutest afro. It looked like they were playing tag. The thought that instantly came to Samuel that day ten years ago was a simple and wonderful one: *kids aren't born with racism. They are innocent until people dirty them.*

Little Amanda, her hair color then redder than the auburn it would develop into, spotted her dad. "Daddy!" She yelled. And then turned to her playmate. "Come. Meet my daddy."

She took the little man's hand and ran him over. She hugged Samuel. "This is Kyle. He's my friend from kindergarten. I was so happy to see him here!"

Samuel kneeled down and shook Kyle's tiny hand. "Hello there, mister," he said.

"Hi!" Kyle said exuberantly. Then he took a long look at Samuel's t-shirt. It had a *Toy Story 3* print on it. This was Amanda's favorite movie that summer, having seen it three times, so they all bought shirts as a family. Amanda got a Jessie one, Sandra a Rex the Dog version, and Samuel the movie poster with several of the characters. Kyle smiled broadly and said, "Awesome shirt!" He reached his pointer finger out, tracing all the characters: Buzz, Woody, Jessie, the Potato Heads, until he stopped. He pressed hard then. "Rex! He's my favorite. I love dinosaurs!"

Samuel grinned deeply. "I love dinosaurs too, Kyle. And the T. rex is by far my favorite."

"You know dinosaurs?" Kyle said in that shocked kid voice when they realize adults might know something.

"Sure! Another really cool one is the Triceratops," Samuel said. "What about you? Do you have a favorite?"

"Yes! Dad bought me a book with dino pictures when I asked to see *Jurassic Park*. He said that was too scary for me to watch." Smart father. One of Samuel's pet peeves was seeing age-inappropriate kids being brought to certain movies. Kyle continued, "But I love that book. I think the Stegosaurus rules!"

"Oh, yeah, he's impressive," Samuel said. He glanced over to Amanda, and she was just smiling, listening to the two boys talk. She had grasped Kyle's hand again. "Those spikes he has are impressive!"

"You're not playing, sir!" Kyle said excitedly. Samuel laughed a full-throated guffaw. *Could this kid be any cuter?*

"Okay, Daddy," Amanda said, "can we go play some more? Kyle is going to be here a while longer. His babysitter brought him over." She pointed to a young blond-haired teenager sitting on a bench reading a book.

"A few more minutes. Your mom is waiting for us for dinner. Pizza tonight."

"Yay!" she said, pulling Kyle towards the nearby swing set.

Samuel watched them go, feeling quite pleased. And he heard Kyle say to Amanda, "Your dad is so cool!"

◆ ◆ ◆

The sound of sirens brought Samuel back to the present. King tilted his head towards this sound and continued to back away. **WE'LL BE GOING THEN. NO TIME TO FINISH OUR DANCE HERE. BUT IT'S WORTH THE WAIT TO DEVOUR YOUR WORLD JUST TO SEE YOU THIS BROKEN. I HAVEN'T WRUNG ENOUGH PAIN AND GUILT OUT OF YOU YET, CHILD. LIVE WITH THIS FOR A WHILE, AND THEN COME SEE ME ON THE OTHER SIDE.**

With this said, King bounded out the picture window, and he, along with the rest of his multitude, disappeared. Literally. And it wasn't just them: the bodies of their slain comrades vanished too. Their severed body parts and even their blood was gone. Into the ether. Or the dream world.

But unlike in Samuel's past, the physical damage inflicted remained.

Amanda had run to Kyle's side and was holding his other hand, her sobs racking her body. Peter and Carter stayed where they were with very different expressions coming from them: Carter was gritting his teeth with the most intense sneer, and Peter's visage was that of a little boy who had lost his parents at the store, one of sadness, confusion, and fear. Samuel emerged from his daze and bolted around to the front of Kyle, falling to his knees (the sense of déjà vu from his memory was jarring), ripping the towel from his arm and wrapping it around Kyle's neck and hand, pressing hard. He eased him to a lying position. The teen was shaking, almost vibrating. But blood was flowing at an alarming rate. *He's going to die. Because of me.* The sirens were now getting louder. His neighbors must have heard the ruckus. *Oh God, neighbors. Kyle's parents. What do I tell them?*

He looked down to see Kyle gazing into his eyes, the teenager's typical lively hazel iris clouding over and still. "Just hold on, buddy," Samuel said, trying to sound hopeful but knowing the

THE GORILLAS ARE COMING

fear in his voice was unmistakable, "help is on the way."

"Who, the cops? Not much of a comfort for a black kid, Mr. R.," Kyle's words were a harsh whisper, so Samuel had to lean down to hear. "A joke."

Samuel forced a smile for the wonderful kid. "Good one. Just hold on, all right?"

"I told you I'd die for you. But I'm so scared."

Samuel instinctively let go of Kyle's throat, letting the towel flap to the floor. He took this precious child into his arms, holding him like a baby so they could still see each other. "I got you. You're safe."

The body felt superheated for a few seconds like it was burning up, but then it started to cool off a bit. And Kyle's shuddering subsided. "It's okay, Mr. Redden," the injured child said at last, "it's like they say. A peace comes over you. Thanks for always supporting me and tell my parents I love them." With this last request, Kyle Green let out one more raspy breath and left our world.

Samuel screamed.

◆ ◆ ◆

In the aftermath, things became fuzzy for Samuel. The green haze had dissolved, and true night was beginning outside, but, for Redden, there was little in front of him but a mental fog. But luckily, Carter and Peter jumped into action. Peter told the big man of Madame Takari's plan, and the two of them urgently wrapped her body in a blanket and rushed her out to Carter's jeep. Carter said he would take care of dumping the body for two reasons: 1) Peter was known to be Samuel's close friend, and it wouldn't be a stretch having him at the house and 2) it would save Darwin the pain of disrespecting his special lady's body. Peter was eternally grateful for this.

Carter sped off immediately, just missing the police by mere moments. He knew he couldn't get rid of the body right away with Madame's fire started only two hours or so ago, so he drove his vehicle to one of the waterfront destinations, Canalside, which was located right downtown across from the metro rail tracks. This was about fifteen minutes from Samuel's and ten from Madame Takari's, convenient but also far enough away from the latter so he wasn't lingering in her neighborhood. It was also within shouting distance from his hotel, but he figured there'd be no suspicion if an out-of-towner was checking out the city's main attraction. So he pulled his car into a nearby parking lot and sat at a bench twenty feet away with many vigilant looks back to make sure no one was around. It was a chilly night, in the low 40's, which helped: he was basically alone near the breezy waterside except for an occasional jogger. Even the formidable gorilla expert felt a little uncomfortable in his typical light shirt and shorts, but he kind of welcomed the cold. His emotions and feelings were so encompassing at this time, ranging from the sense of failure for these people that put their trust in him to the senseless loss of another potentially great young black life. He sat as still as one of the large rocks down below the boardwalk, listening to the peaceful sound of the water lapping against the bottom of the wooden beams, while he waited for the right time. The park closed at 10:00, so he made sure to leave a few minutes before that to not raise any suspicion. Then he just drove around for another two hours and waited for the stroke of midnight to enter the Madame's neighborhood, finally feeling like his raging thoughts were getting more under control about halfway through that time. He figured midnight was a good time to make his move: night, dark, late enough to maybe avoid prying eyes but not so late that someone could take special notice of a gigantic man toting something big behind a burnt storefront.

Carter didn't want to drive on Madame's street, so he turned off toward the end, ignoring the GPS, and parked on a side street to walk the rest of the way with his burden. Despite his size, he made his way quietly and stealthily down the two blocks, finding the dumpster behind the building in minutes. He took a quick look at the sturdy brick, which appeared untouched from the conflagration within its structure. From where he was situated, he could see a little inside the window that showed into the sanctuary, which was completely blown out. Everything in that room looked black, scorched, unable to withstand what the strong exterior brick was able to. He was sure that special inner sanctum was where she had lain her sisters when setting the blaze, probably with some witch powers. Looking at the yellow police tape surrounding the still standing edifice, he made a mental note at how effectively that lady had made her life's work and loved ones disappear with little hesitation. He went into this union questioning how a psychic/Wiccan could work with him, but all he felt now was respect. Wearing leather gloves that he would later dispose in the river with the blanket, he gently placed the body in the dumpster both to show honor for the dead and not to raise any alarms. Now finally feeling his exhaustion, Carter knew he needed to get back to his hotel asap. He felt dead on his feet and knew the next few weeks would be murder.

Back at the house, Peter took control in a confident way that neither Samuel nor Amanda could manage. The first smart thing he did was hide the weapons in the garage; besides their clothing, these were the only things in the house that had blood on them. And figuring the animal attack on the first real-world victim would work here, he explained to the police that wild coyotes entered the home. Darwin even toned down his 60s speak a little to not let the cops think they had some drug party here that got out of control. He told the stone-faced officers how they tried to fight the animals off, but they couldn't save Kyle. Luckily, unlike during Samuel's childhood, the gorillas were not apparently intent on making wounds disappear, so their bodies backed up his claims. More questions would come, but it seemed to satisfy the powers that be for the nonce.

Madame Takari's case was challenging for the investigating officers (as she assumed it might be). Her body was discovered the next day, well after the fire department put out the blaze. No suspicion came Carter's way; he was a careful man, and no one indeed saw him. And the situation was so wacky, insane, that the police did exactly as expected once they identified the sisters' body, chalked it up to some weird occult rite. The oddity of both Kyle and Reginald Samuel's murders a few weeks apart, namely the distance of the two towns (rural vs. city), combined with Madame's incident, never registered to them as the same case. Even the majority of the gorillas' hair was gone, and the tiny amount that was left intermingled with Rusty's and prevented precise analysis. Samuel figured the creatures didn't need to leave simian proof in his situation – the earlier time that was all done for his "benefit". The cops also didn't bother dusting for fingerprints at the Redden's given the explanation, while Carter's disposal of evidence helped cover the loose ends. Everything seemed to fall in place in this area, at least.

Kyle's parents weren't home at the time, and Samuel later was glad for this as he couldn't handle them coming upon the scene. And they also didn't push the police to follow up on the attack, accepting the premise. This was a break, since if they didn't let it go, things might have unraveled for the team. But the Greens were never ones to rely on the police establishment. And if their friend Samuel, who always had Kyle's best interests at heart, said it was coyotes, it was coyotes.

That night, Samuel and Amanda got a hotel room just off downtown, at the Red Roof Inn. He vowed never to return to that house. He took double his meds, and he and Amanda slept with all the lights on. They cried to sleep in each other's arms.

Peter was true to his word and took care of Madame Takari's arrangements but did it anonymously through an area Wiccan organization. She wished to be cremated, no services, and her ashes were spread outside her store. Peter stopped by one evening at the building and left flowers near the hollowed-out front door, the place where he first entered and met his friend. He also cut off a lock of his hair and dropped it on her remains. They would be tied together for eternity. "Goodbye, my sweet princess, my angelic Rose Takari," he whispered while walking away.

Several days passed, and the police continued to do their due diligence in following up more with Samuel, Peter, and Amanda, asking additional questions, much more so than with Madame's situation. They even talked to the Reddens' neighbors, but not much came from that part of the investigation. While one of them, old Mr. Santora, heard the glass shatter and called the police, he had trouble making out what was going on over at that house. He did acknowledge that he heard animal sounds coming from the vicinity, though, which helped lend credence to the whole thing. What he didn't say was how unusual those howls were. And he, along with several others, held another additional aspect back from the questioners. They had an acute foreboding, a terror that prevented them from approaching or even staring over at that area of the street. The neighbors felt like they were losing their mind a bit with all this, so they might as well let it be. It wouldn't bring that kid back anyway. So the official explanation of an animal attack was filed. But no coyotes were ever found in the nearby woods outside the city, just like the earlier attack. Once again, the group took some time apart from each other, with Samuel and Amanda remaining almost exclusively in their room at the hotel avoiding the few calls from the press about the incident. And Samuel didn't speak to the Greens until the funeral.

CHAPTER 13

T he day of the funeral came. It was Friday, October 30th, six days after the murder. Samuel, Amanda, and Peter went. Carter thought it best he not show up, too many questions about who he was. It was a beautiful service. The Greens were new school Baptists, not the type that fell in with the old political leanings, those who senselessly supported Trump. Their church was almost exclusively black and primarily progressive. It was such a different service compared to the Catholic ones Samuel had attended when younger. It was less a depression causing dirge for the lost and more of a celebration of life, with joyful songs of praise and fun recollections of Kyle's young life. Samuel cried three times at the service, making his sight blurry behind his pair of old brown back up glasses (not feeling the need in all that happened to get the cracked lens fixed in his good ones). The first time was when they entered and they saw the urn with the remains on an altar at the front of the church. Since Kyle was cremated, no viewing had taken place, and this was the first any of them had seen a representation of his body after the bloody shape it was at the house. The second time was when Kyle's father, David, spoke through his own tears about how his boy was the purest example of goodness and light he'd ever known and that this ugly world just didn't deserve him. The final instance was when they sang *Amazing Grace* at the end. Amanda wept for most of the service, her father's good right arm around her the whole time (his opposite one bandaged up). Peter sat on the other side of Samuel, looking uncomfortable in his jacket and tie even though he often wore them at work, and spent a lot of the service with his eyes closed, in deep meditation, reflecting on the cool little dude that had entered his life. He had no more tears to give after the events that took Kyle and his beloved Madame.

After the final part of the service outside in which Kyle was buried, Samuel waited several feet away until all other loved ones left, steeling up the courage to approach the Greens at Kyle's gravesite. When he walked to that site earlier, he could feel people's eyes on him, and he wasn't surprised given the situation. Amanda was currently a few feet away saying a sad hello to some classmates. Samuel was so afraid of how the grieving couple would react to him, given that their child died at his home and that he hadn't talked to them since. *Not exactly the actions of a close friend. They probably hate me.* But his fears were unfounded as when he got closer David wrapped him in his arms immediately with a hug, and they remained that way for a good thirty seconds. Then Samuel also embraced Kyle's mother, Shayera, but for only half as long, as he knew she was never one for physical displays or affirmation. Amanda took turns as well, latching hard onto both of them at the same time while sobbing: these two had been like a second set of parents for her, and their closeness was easily observed. Peter hung back.

"God, Dave, can you forgive me?" Samuel asked, his mouth quivering, after Amanda disengaged from the morose pair. He cast a glance at Kyle's gravestone, a simple one with these words: KYLE GREEN, 2005-2020. It also had a bible quote that even lapsed churchgoer Samuel recognized: "But those who hope in the LORD will renew their strength. They will soar on wings like eagles; they will run and not grow weary, they will walk and not be faint." He swallowed before saying, "I just felt so guilty about it happening at my house. I couldn't face you guys."

David shook his head, and for a moment, Samuel misunderstood the gesture and was further crestfallen, thinking they truly couldn't absolve him. But he should have been focusing on the kindness and empathy in his neighbor's face. "Don't do this to yourself. There's nothing to forgive. You've already had one great tragedy in the last few years, pal. I don't blame you for having a hard time processing this."

The Greens were an attractive couple in the best of times, but their grief made them look older than their early fifties. David was a tall man with a dignified air to himself even when cooking hot dogs on the grill. An offshoot from his career as a defense lawyer, he always carried himself professionally but had a great sense of humor. His hair was cut short with a couple grays showing through the black and had deep brown eyes. He was stooping a little currently, something Samuel never saw in the man. Shayera was a larger woman with a full welcoming face and had a carefully braided coiffe. She now looked like she had lost 10 pounds, though, and there was a haggardness to the usual zestful appearance. They were both dressed in typical funeral wear: David in an impressive three-piece black suit and Shayera with the same color dress but with red rose imprints along the neckline.

"Thanks, Mr. Green," Amanda said, coming a bit closer again and touching David's hand. "We appreciate it. It's not your job to comfort others at your son's funeral." She paused and then added, "He loved you so much, you know that, right?"

Shayera looked deeply at the two of them, then nodded with tears pouring down her eyes. "We do." She put her arm around her husband. "And he adored you both so much as well. I think when your Sandra died, he wanted to be there for you even more. But you were always so supportive; he just felt safe with you."

This comment caused a deep aching inside Samuel, bringing to the surface emotions he had managed to suppress with medication the last six days. He put his hands over his eyes while the tears sopped his fingers. "I'm so sorry. I should have protected him," he said in between hitching breaths.

"Bull shit," David said, latching a strong arm around Samuel's neck. "It was a freak occurrence. I mean, wild animals busting into your house? It was a one in a million thing. It just shows the randomness of life." He hesitated for a second before adding, "I'm not angry about how it happened. Just that it did. But this anger is directed at life, the universe, even God. Not you, Samuel. Not one bit." Samuel could see David was trying to be stoic, but he sniffled hard, like he was sucking in the feelings. *Not that I ever doubted it, but I know better than ever where Kyle got his character from. For the second time, this bereaved man is trying to make me feel better. That's rare. Though maybe it's helping him to focus his energies outward.*

"I feel the same," Shayera added quite simply. "The two of you are like family."

Samuel thought hard for a moment, not wanting to say something stupid and revealing the whole state of things. But he wanted to leave them with something to hold onto. He came up with this: "Whatever happens, whatever I do going forward, I will honor him, his life, his sacrifice. You know he was trying to protect me, right?"

Shayera nodded. "The police said as much. That really shows Kyle's devotion to you and his courage, things we can all be proud of. We'll remember that part fondly, the self-sacrifice. We tried to instill selflessness in him, and now we know we did that right. But guilt has no place here. For any of us." She smiled weakly.

With that said, they all embraced again, and Samuel and Amanda walked away.

"Good job, Dad," Amanda said, looking at the ground as they walked, "it's better they don't know the truth. As much as I hate that. Kyle and I were always about the truth too. But we should continue to keep this circle small. Kyle would want to protect your secret."

"I know," Samuel said as they stopped where Peter was standing, next to the driver's side door to Samuel's car on the road that led from the cemetery. He kicked at the dirt a bit, "but it doesn't make me feel any better about it."

Samuel looked at his oldest friend. "So, what now, Pete? As much as I just want to curl into a ball and never wake up, we've taken enough time. What's the alternative? Just give up and let the gorillas run over our world? None of us will ever do that now, I know, but while we can beat some of them, their multitude is probably too much. And we can't seem to touch King and his power. I want Kyle's sacrifice to mean something, but how?"

"Wait," Peter said. He pointed further down the access road. Samuel could see Carter's jeep approaching. "Wait for the big man. I know what to do next, Daddy-O, but let's not have the conversation twice."

"All right," Samuel said in a slightly questioning manner. Amanda took his hand for what seemed like the millionth time during the last week, but it still helped immensely. It was such a simple gesture, but he needed that now.

Carter's jeep screeched to a stop, and he descended to the ground. For the first time, Samuel noticed how the jeep kind of creaked under his girth. The gorilla expert approached them and nodded to the group. "Okay, Darwin, you got me here. What's the word?" Samuel noticed that Carter didn't look much better than the three of them; his face had lost a bit of that "lust for life" vigor that always filled it.

"Okay, Carter, my main man. Reddy here was just asking what the approach is going forward. How can we avenge Kyle and protect this sometimes beautiful, more often than not fucked up world? Well, the Madame gave us a way forward." He lifted his finger to the heavens as if giving her credit. "Perhaps King is not as invulnerable as he boasted."

"How?" the other three asked in unison. This brought a small smile to all of their serious faces.

Peter said, "Far out, my cool cats. Quite the unified response. I like it. It's as simple as this, my precious ones. Sammy, think back to right before the shit hit the fan with the gorillas at the house. The glorious lady gave us the secret code before she passed."

What's he jabbering about? But then Samuel flashed on the scene right before the apes entered. "That's right," he said, "she mentioned you taking me to see someone?"

"Terrian. He's a wise one," Peter said.

"Who is he?" Amanda asked.

"I'd rather not say anything until you meet him. He's a creature that's hard to properly describe."

"Creature?" Samuel asked.

Peter nodded. "Like the gorillas, he's not of this world."

"More hocus pocus," Carter said, grumbling.

"Come on, my world-weary idol," Peter said, "you've seen enough by now to not doubt things beyond our plane."

Carter rubbed his head. "Of course. I just can't get a grip on how to handle this. It's not my way. You brought me in for my gorilla know-how and my abilities as a fighter. You may have noticed how my gun was doing more damage than humanly possible when mowing through those monsters. That made me step beyond my worldly fixations and latch onto the power of belief in battling these things. But as confident, hell, cocky, as I was, I couldn't put a tiny sore on King. If we can't damage him, the one who leads this pack, what good am I?" Samuel noticed he called them a pack, not a family.

"Your path with us still has a way to go," Peter said, patting Carter's impressive bare-armed bicep. "Terrian will know what to do, how we can defeat them, including King, and what role each of us will play," he added.

"Then why did we wait until now? It could have saved Kyle if we went sooner!" Amanda snapped, sounding angrier than Samuel ever heard her.

Peter sighed, a profoundly frustrated outtake of breath. "I'm so sorry, sweetums. I'm sure my dear lady was going to take us to Terrian right after we met at su casa. But she surely regretted the delay in her final thoughts." He glanced at Carter. "She wanted to give us the time to complete Carter's part of the plan. She respected it; knew our boy needed to conquer his fears first."

All four were quiet for several seconds. "Fine," Samuel said at last. "It's better than doing nothing and waiting for King and his minions to destroy our world. Where is this Terrian?" *I feel like I'm in Empire Strikes Back, seeking out Yoda. It sounds ridiculous. But isn't all of this? It's not fun like in the stories, though. It's too real and too hard.*

At this point, Peter smiled broadly. "He's to be found deep in the woods of Eden, not far from your old house. Sweet Reddy, we're going home."

CHAPTER 14

When Samuel got back to the hotel, he called his mother. She was alive and still living at 1404 Siegel Road. And doing great at the age of eighty-three, generally healthy and quite aware, sharp. It had been a few months since he had visited, even though Eden was only thirty-five minutes from the city. Life had just taken a weird twist in the last few weeks, and he didn't want to burden his mother with the details, given how prone she was to worry and anxiety. He never wanted to even tell her about the "animal attack" or Kyle. But the news reports prevented that. So he just made it clear on the call that they didn't want to discuss the situation when they arrived, hoped to get away from it all. She understood and sounded quite excited when he said that he and Amanda would be staying with her for a few days. She even offered to make room for Peter and Carter when Samuel mentioned they were traveling with some friends, but Darwin planned to hit up some of his nearby cousins as not to overburden her.

Samuel was currently standing outside the hotel room door, having called Mom in the car on the cell. Amanda had gone in right away, saying she needed a hot shower after the funeral drama. The Red Roof had outside access to the rooms, so he felt the now ever-present cool breeze through his non-insulated dress jacket. This was generally his favorite time of the year, but with all the fear and tragedy, he hadn't been able to partake in his joys of the fall: drinking apple cider, going to harvest festivals and picking apples, riding haunted hayrides, gorging on Halloween candy, watching horror movies, and cheering on the the Bills and Sabres with the beginning of football and hockey seasons. The crisp air now just made him think of the encroaching winter and the death of things. He was sure the massacre of Amy, her family, and Kyle played a part in this. And it felt weird living in a hotel mere minutes from his house. But they lacked the will to return to their home still. He was dealing with the insurance company to get the living room fixed. But he wasn't sure he'd want to go back even after that was resolved. He would probably sell. *I can't be in a place where that wonderful child died so miserably.*

Despite the uncomfortable chill, he was hesitating to go in. He had something he needed to discuss with Amanda, and he was nervous to, as he knew she wouldn't take it well. This made his mind drift back to the past for the first time in a little while...

The time was late August 2005, three months after Samuel and Sandra were married. They got hitched less than a year after the engagement but wasted no time getting pregnant, conceiving Amanda in November. Again, they were liberal and not heavily influenced by certain religious limits, and Samuel was glad to make Sandra happy in this area. At this moment in time, he was standing in the doorway of Amanda's room in their three-bedroom apartment. They had upgraded from the little two-bedroom to this one when they got the good news of their impending arrival. And now, here they were, their first night with the baby Amanda sleeping in their home. He crept into the room as quietly as he could. It had taken until about an hour ago, 1:00 A.M., to get the baby to sleep. And he knew from his family members who had kids that his own slumber was a precious commodity. But all he could do was toss and turn for the last hour, thinking about whether Amanda was safe.

He tiptoed to her crib in the far corner and looked down into it below the circling mobile of *Star Wars* ships: X-wing, Tie Fighter, Star Destroyer (he insisted on this, and Sandra finally relented). Amanda looked peaceful and beautiful in her itty bitty rose-colored onesie. She had a little tuft of the red hair that would dominate her early years on top of her soft newborn head. Her tiny hands were held still over her chest. He gently put his right hand on top of hers, knowing he was risking waking her up but not caring. He could feel the steady beat of her newly developed heart, the slow and even rhythm rising and falling from her lungs. And she was actually cooing a bit in this state. He wondered if there was anything as serene as a sleeping baby, its fragile little life without any care in the world excepting the need for food and love.

While Samuel stood there gazing with love at his baby daughter, he couldn't stop the doubts from coming. He wondered how he could possibly do this. How could he give this small, vulnerable life the love and protection she needed? He thought about all the struggles he had keeping himself and Sandra afloat in this modern world. They were deep in credit card and student loan debt. How would he provide for her? And how would keep her from harm? He bemoaned his clumsy and uncoordinated aspects and imagined dropping Amanda on her head. He loved her so much already, but was that enough?

He felt a touch on his shoulder and jerked around, ripping his hand away from Amanda. Sandra was there smiling behind him in the shadow of the night light. Even with the physical strain of child-bearing just experienced, this expression brought that consistently vibrant dimpled beauty to her face. "Oh, baby," he whispered, "I'm sorry if I woke you. You've been through a lot the last 48 hours. You need your rest." He took her in his arms.

"It wasn't you. I'm guessing neither of us could sleep." She also kept her voice to the minimum.

"How is it possible?" he asked. "How can anyone sleep when you know there's this defenseless, breakable little life dozing in the other room. Geez."

"I guess we'll get used to it, Sam. We'll have to. We'll need the energy for her!" She nuzzled her face against his neck.

He laughed and then immediately and humorously covered his mouth, glancing over quickly to make sure Amanda didn't awake. She hadn't stirred. "I suppose you're right," he said, returning his attention to Sandra. But his thoughts circled back to the doubts he was just reflecting on.

As always, Sandra could tell something was wrong. "Tell me," was all she said, pulling her head back a bit and touching his face lovingly.

"I was just thinking about how much of a screwup I've always felt like. We're barely keeping our heads above water financially, and here we are bringing in another mouth to feed. And I'm such a klutz and not technically proficient at anything. Hell, your dad had to put that crib together. What can I possibly offer this perfect baby but struggle and failure?"

Sandra now wrapped her arms around his neck and stared deeply into his eyes. "We live in a screwed up world, my sweet boy. We're not the only ones struggling in this country, and as you know there are those in a lot worse shape. The more and more I think about it, Pete might be right about Democratic socialism being the way to go. But I know how you are. You want to attack yourself for any risky decision, blame yourself for things outside your control. But any issues we have come from the fucked up system. You've always done your best, as have

I, and we've survived. And you overstate your clumsiness and inefficiency. Doing things like constructing a crib or putting up siding are the least important parts of being a good husband or father, and you know it. Let me ask you this, do you love her?"

Tears immediately began to glisten in his eyes. "I fell so deeply in love with her the moment I saw her curious blue eyes looking at me."

"And you'd do anything for her, right?"

"In a heartbeat."

"Well, let me just say this for the record. You're going to be the best daddy in the history of the world. You've already been the best husband and boyfriend. So this is the next step. You sell yourself short."

He leaned in closer to her, and they kissed deeply. When they withdrew, he said, "What did I ever do to deserve someone like you?"

She gave him that old smart ass, ironic grin. "I don't know, but it must have been something awesome." She pulled at his hand. "Come back to bed."

"I will. Just give me a minute."

Sandra nodded and then disappeared with nary a sound. And Samuel pivoted to look back down at the baby again. "I'd die or kill for you, Amanda Redden. It's you and me to the end, pumpkin."

◆ ◆ ◆

Now still standing outside the hotel room door, he realized this very last sentiment was the same thing he said to ten-year-old Amanda after stepping out into the hospital waiting room immediately after saying goodbye to Sandy. He rubbed his wet face, inserted the key card, and opened the door.

"Dad!" Amanda exclaimed. "What took you so long? Grandma not want to hang up?" She laughed. It was nice to hear that, even if it wasn't her standard happy giggle; it was a little subdued. She was sitting with her back to the headboard of her double bed, the one closest to the door. She had the TV remote in her hand. He looked to the medium-sized TV on the table to the right and could see that she had CNN on. Her hair was wet, and she had changed into a long Winnie the Pooh t-shirt and her baggy sweats. He realized she had already finished her shower. *I must have been standing out there longer than I thought.*

He looked down at the cell phone in his hands. "A little. You know Grandma. She likes to chat. But it wasn't just that. I was out there thinking. We need to talk, Amanda."

"Uh oh," she said, "that's never good. Sit." She patted the covers.

He sat down, removing his jacket, placing it beside him, loosening up his tie, and kicking his brown shoes off. His arm ached, and he massaged it a bit. "I'm glad you're coming back home with me. Your grandma really doesn't see you as much as she should. It'll be nice."

"I agree! It's like the one ray of sunshine in the last few weeks. I love her so much. She's such a sweety."

"I know," he replied. "I've known that since I was a little guy when she raised me all on her own. She's a special one." He paused for about 15 seconds, dropping his eyes to the ugly purple coverlet. "About what I wanted to say. I'm going to ask you to do something for me. Something I know you won't like."

"Go on," she replied with a doubtful sound in her voice.

"When we head out to meet this Terrian character, I want you to stay back with Grandma."

"Absolutely not!" Amanda stood up angrily, dropping the remote. She stood in front of him, her hands clenched at her side. "I won't, Dad. I won't lose you. I need to be there for you. I thought we already had this debate."

"We did," Samuel said in a frustrated manner, lifting his head to look at her. "But that was before Kyle was killed. I can't lose you like that."

"And I can't lose you either, dumb ass!" Amanda's voice broke, and he knew she was willing tears not to come.

He stood up and latched onto both of her hands even though she tried to pull away. "It's more than that, honey. I don't know what kind of journey we'll be taking after Terrian. But I do know this. It may be taking us far away."

"How? What?" She was perplexed.

"It's weird. Since I woke up from the Madame's spell, I think I have premonitions or knowledge about things. It's like a muddy picture, though, similar to a dream you forget the instant you're awake. In this case, though, something that happened at the house awakened one of those thoughts. I don't know the details, but I think Terrian might show us how to reach the gorillas in their environment. King said he'd see me on the other side. Not sure if you remember that."

She wiped away the tears that she couldn't halt and nodded. "I remember now. But what does that all mean?"

He removed his right hand from the clasp, and stared at his palm. "Just like with the other parts, the glowy hand and how I managed to give these monsters life, I have no real idea. But maybe we can cross over to wherever they came from. Perhaps Terrian is the one to answer these questions and show me the way."

"Well, if so, I should be there with you!" she exclaimed, her face getting red, the anger surging up again. *She gets that from me. Maybe that's where they come from—the bile inside of me.*

"I need you here in our world," he said calmly, doing his best to not get emotional too. "You have to protect my mom if King sends some gorillas back to our world. I can't leave her alone. That silver fucker wants to rip my heart out and stomp on it before he even tries to kill me. It's amazing he hasn't targeted my old mom yet."

Realization came into Amanda's eyes. "Wow, you're right. But Dad…"

"Promise me. Promise you'll protect Grandma. You're tough. You were fighting those apes like Furiosa or Ripley." He smiled proudly. "You're a badass and the only one I trust with this. It's really not me being protective or sexist in excluding you from the journey. You may have to battle for our world. So many times, I've thought it would be good if this world, especially this inequitable country, would burn. But I don't feel that now. I feel it's worth defending against these monsters."

His daughter looked probingly into Samuel's eyes, and he swore he was staring into the intense glare of his dead wife, his mind circling back to that moment beside little Amanda's crib. It freaked him out a bit, but after a few seconds, she blinked. "All right, fine," she said at last, "but I don't like it."

He hugged her hard. "Me neither, pumpkin. I don't like any of it."

INTERLUDE TWO -
THE DARK REALM

I t resembled a castle in our world, but its stone foundation was covered with a yellowing, pee-colored moss that seemed to have eyes. Deformed crawling critters, which kind of looked like squirrels, small and furry, but all with some sort of divergent aberration, dotted the walls. Some had extra limbs, others were missing heads, several showed off octopus-like tentacles, and the most bizarre of the lot had men's faces but the bodily stripes of skunks. All of these were black as coal and made varying types of inhuman shrieks and guttural groans as they slithered or oozed around the slippery hand-holds. The castle towered high into the sky with spiky spires at the top that pointed out with malice. There was a drawbridge that led to this overwhelming abode. It was treacherous, with giant gaping holes in the wood and some smaller craters where spears poked out. Below it paced the guards, squat red-faced goblins in battle gear brandishing cudgels tipped with blades coated with poisonous giant spider blood. It was up this draw-bridge that now warily walked King the Silverback. The guards merely grunted at him as they knew he had been summoned by the Master. King viewed himself as a creature of fear and dread, but the few times he'd visited this place turned that terror right back onto him. This was the stronghold of that ruler of the nightmare realm, the plane named Sambala.

King opened the tall double doors with their etchings of demon faces, his taloned hand slipping a bit on the long metal bar that swung the doors outwards. As he loped through the entranceway, looking more like Samuel's Bigfoot than ever, he even shivered a bit. Hanging from these rafters were not standards of the realm as one would expect in the storybooks, but the skinned bodies of his master's followers who had failed him. They were all kinds of nightmare creatures: demons, zombies, mean supervisors, but even their victims would feel bad for them now. They were still alive, either moaning or wailing in torturous agony. There were no windows in this room, but all the monsters here could see in the dark, so he couldn't ignore the tortured ones' too aware eyes and mouths through their pink and reddened tissues. He picked up his pace, passed a long dining table with stringy and gooey vittles that he didn't even want to think about. He opened another large door similar to the first. This one creaked, sounding like a child's cry.

At the end of this next chamber was a throne. High windows graced the top of this room, and you could see all kinds of dark storms raging in Sambala. It was as if every dangerous storm cycle existed at once: snow blizzards, lightning and thunder accompanied by hail, tornadoes, hurricanes. It framed this room of intimidation perfectly. All kinds of flying things were also seen in the distance through the stained glassed viewport: dragons, human sized bats, and monsters that have no name. The throne was the only thing in the interminably long room, and sitting upon it was the Master. No one in Sambala knew his name. It was a different kind of darkness in here, one that the world's denizens couldn't see through. It was a doomful, suffocating, absence of light. Except for the throne. It was visible in a paradoxical copper glow. It was humongous both in height and width, with its seat elevated twenty feet above its footrests and ringed with skulls. But the shape filling the space, whose shadow stretched out to every point of the room, was just a black form, like a mist, but with spots of hard edges and protrusions.

King dropped on all fours several feet away from the five giant steps leading to the throne, looking more like an earth ape now as he said mentally, **MASTER, I HAVE NEWS**.

The voice that came back to him was that of a hiss, a sound a snake would make if it could talk. Human ears would not be able to understand the brutal, guttural sounds that emanated. "Stop with the mental projections, King. You know the rule of this land, that my language is the only allowed form in this hallowed, unholy place. Your mental power may impress humans but not me. NOW SPEAK!" These last words shook the whole castle.

King cowered as if he were struck. "My apologies, my lord," he said audibly in the choppy phonation. His vocalization was the same here in Sambala as Samuel heard in his head, though, grating, harsh and made even more so with the coarse serpentine language. But at the same time, it now had a undercurrent of fear.

"The news. Now." The Master said this with dripping frustration.

"I have furthered my emotional attack on Samuel Redden. I invited him here for the final battle." King chose not to mention his failure, that he actually meant to kill the human before the interference from the stupid child and the expected arrival of the idiotic constables.

"YOU WHAT?" Now the room didn't just shudder, but reality seemed to flicker out of focus for a moment, not only in the stronghold but in all of Sambala, causing creatures of all shapes and forms to show the terror that they were supposed to instill.

King backed up slowly, pawing the floor and moaning like a kicked dog. "Have I erred, wise one?" He sounded less like the fearsome entity that had taken apart Samuel Redden's world and more like the typical sycophants in the movies, a Grima Wormtongue or the hyenas from *The Lion King*.

"Have you erred? You've failed me miserably. And after I gave you and your followers a shred of my power, my darkness, to capture the humans unaware. And now you've invited the Golden Child to our part of the dream world? To the realm in which he can fulfill his destiny? How even in your great stupidity can you consider this a good thing?" The Master's form was starting to stabilize now, appearing more like a sable wall than a cloud. It wasn't a positive development for King.

The silverback gasped at the sight but then reminded himself who he was. He was the one that was going to destroy the human world. And his master would reward him. "He knows not of his power. He will just be overwhelmed here, and it'll be easier to ring out every vestige of his hope. And then our victory over the light will be complete." This nightmare gorilla was many things, and cockiness was at the top of the list. He had that back now.

There was a good minute of silence as the creature on the throne ruminated. A sharp formation like a sword projected from the side of the Master's layers and jutted upwards, stroking the top of his structure in a very human gesture. Not that a person could have rubbed his face safely that way. "Okay, ape," he said finally, quietly. "But if it's not as you say and Redden triumphs but does not kill you, I'll have a new wall hanging. Leave me."

King had never moved so fast as he leapt up and charged away, his vampire teeth chattering in his impressive mouth.

PART THREE – THE GOLDEN CHILD RISES

CHAPTER 1

Samuel's ride from his hotel in the city to his childhood home took close to forty minutes, a few more than from his house. But this still short distance was a luxury most didn't get when they grew up, to live so close to a valued parent and the memories of childhood. This particular drive felt a bit different, though. He was seated in the back of Carter's jeep with Amanda, with Peter riding shotgun in the front. As they continued down East Eden Road and finally passed the old closed church where town recreation was held, the traumatic recollections that he'd re-lived recently corrupted his nostalgia a bit. Now that he knew what had happened to him, how he'd buried trauma that had unleashed a force that could destroy his world, it took away the simple, quaint joy of the mostly unaltered country town. A lot of it still didn't make sense to him, but the reality was that the positive images he remembered from his young life had this dark undercurrent now. He shivered as they passed the church, looking back to glance at Keller Road and swearing he could see the ghost of Bennett standing there, unzipping his ugly green pants. Samuel closed his eyes and shivered.

"Dad?" Amanda asked.

Samuel shook his head. "It's okay. I just need a minute." He couldn't see it, but Amanda was digging her nails into her palm, Peter had turned in his seat looking less subtle than the girl, his forehead creased in anger at the pastoral view passing the back window, and even Carter cast his steely eyes in the rearview mirror. They all knew what he was thinking about.

Within a few minutes, they had reached his mother's street, Siegel Road, and through his breathing exercises, he had calmed down. As they turned onto the street, the location spurred a clear recollection, as if a shadowy figure had suddenly emerged from a thick fog. This was another one of those past moments that became available to him that day in the park, but he hadn't fully accessed yet. He was clearly recalling the bully episode with Steiner when he had first felt the glowing hand and its accompanying comfortable warmth.

I just hope this Terrian can somehow provide me with more information about that and this golden child stuff. Madame Takari was just too cagey for my likes, God rest her soul. I'm going to need all the information now. Kyle might still be alive if we had more knowledge. Samuel didn't realize it, but he had just transferred the guilt about his young friend from himself outwards. It was a big step.

Carter turned left, pulling the car into the driveway at the last house on the dead-end road. The homestead had changed over the years. Shelley had the house sided a few years back, so it no longer had a red-painted look but a pleasing baby blue colored edifice. And the pool was gone making the backyard look larger than it ever did when Samuel was younger. With the pool deck gone, she had a new patio version built off the kitchen similar to what Samuel had in the city. He even noticed the little things, like the clothesline being gone from the house's side, where she hung the clothes when he was a toddler. But beyond all that, the surroundings were familiar. Again, though, while there still was a rush of happy reminiscing, he knew that lurking not far was the reality of the gorillas. He looked around and took in the woods, which were far enough away while still feeling to him like they were surrounding his every side.

The trees stood like distant towers against the dull sky, and he wondered if the monsters were milling somewhere out there or had retreated to wherever they came from. He also couldn't conceptualize how the Terrian character could be living in that wild, untamed area.

Before he could reflect much further, he saw Shelley Redden step out to the porch. Samuel knew she had lost much of her hearing over the years (and had been deaf in one ear since childhood), but she must have been looking for them. Amanda quickly exited her side of the jeep and sprinted to embrace her grandmother. Samuel followed her and did the same.

"Mom, it's so good to see you," he said while releasing her from the hug. "Thanks so much for letting us stay for a few days."

"Don't you dare thank me!" she exclaimed. Shelley had aged wonderfully. She finally stopped dying her hair brown a few years back and embraced the silver look, which appeared re-markably dignified on her. She had the expected wrinkles of an eighty-three-year-old, but one would never guess that was her age. She kept active, and while she had some medical issues - a hip replacement, arthritis - she was fit and health concious. She went once a week to a swimming class for senior citizens and often did things with family members, like walking in the park or camping. She was now wearing black stretch pants and a purple sweater and looked as cute as a button. "It's been far too long and even longer that you've stayed over. You two are easy company and a pleasure."

She still favors me, her baby.

Samuel turned and gestured to the approaching Peter. "You remember Pete?"

"Of course!" Shelley said excitedly. She took his hand in the two of hers. "So sorry to hear about your father passing a few years ago, Peter. But I'm delighted that you've come home. And that you'll be visiting your cousins." Peter's cousins were from the neighborhood and known to Shelley. "They ask me about you any time I see them in the supermarket."

"They're cool cats. It'll be groovy to re-acquaint."

Shelley laughed happily. "You sound just like your father. So sweet." Peter bowed to her. Then motioned to Carter, who had been standing at the perimeter of their circle. "This is our compadre, Carter. He's spent a lot of time in nature, so we thought the country would speak deeply to him."

Samuel wondered how his mother would take to seeing this large black man. She had come a long way over the years but was raised by a raging racist, who used to say things to her like, "They have a whole different kind of smell." She took a long time to learn not to call black folks "colored". But she was a gracious woman, who had learned a lot about the dangers of intolerance in the days of Charlottesville and police brutality, so he shouldn't have been surprised when she treated Carter like an honored guest. "Welcome, Carter! You'll love it out here in Eden. So peaceful. Carter, is that your first or last name?"

"Just Cart…" Peter began.

"Last name, ma'am," Carter interjected, smiling a kind, full-toothed grin. "My first name is Michael, but everyone has called me Carter for so long that I almost forget it sometimes!" He stepped up, took her hand, and shook it so gently, considering his power. And the two of them were quite a scene: Shelley was a tiny lady (none of the Reddens were tall) and was dwarfed by the mountain of a man. Samuel finally got that visual he'd hoped for when Carter was to meet the Madame, though Shelley was slightly taller than her.

Peter and Samuel looked shocked at each other and at Carter at the revelation of his first name. He just ignored them. Amanda, standing close to her grandma, just giggled. It was a fun moment for them all, another one of those little moments they had missed the last couple of weeks.

"Michael is such a nice name. Your parents gave that to you, and you should be proud of it. Maybe you should use it more," Shelley said, smiling right back. A small look of sadness crossed the big man's face when she mentioned his parents. It went unnoticed by all in the group except the extremely empathetic Amanda. "Anyways, I'd like to have you come in, and I'll make all of you lunch."

◆ ◆ ◆

While Shelley prepared lunch, Samuel and Amanda showed the others around the house. There were a few more updates here, a remodeled bathroom with a new shower, for instance, but so much looked the same and gave Samuel that déjà vu feeling. He lingered a bit in the back bedroom after the others moved on, feeling stuck in the special place where he and Patrick slept and where the gorillas first attacked him. He was disappointed to realize that the regained memory of the monsters had even tainted the sanctity of this room where Pat used to tell him about Hank Aaron and where he and Pete would wrestle. He glanced up at one point and noticed another new addition, an overhead light. And this made him think of Claude's iron fist rule of the household, and he felt that ancient sense of sadness. When they got to the living room, Samuel noticed Mom had orange stringed lights over the mantle and the ceramic pumpkin she made years ago set up. He then quickly looked at his phone's calendar. *Halloween. How appropriate. I always loved this time of year, but now all I can think about are real terrors.* He knew it would be a quiet night given that kids rarely came trick or treating down his mom's secluded street, but maybe they could at least watch *Halloween* on AMC. Before leaving the room, he again bemoaned the fact that time had lost all meaning to him. The boring but comforting routines of regular life seemed far away.

They all then convened in the kitchen to enjoy a simple yet tasty lunch of grilled chicken and macaroni salad. Besides the new sliding glass door and patio, this room had remained mostly unchanged. Samuel even took a peek in the closet and found the little tick marks for himself when Mom measured his height back in the day. As he dug into the food, he felt the feelings of peace and safety he always got when his mom made him meals in this place again. No revelations of a dark past could take that away. For much of the time while they feasted, Amanda had her chair almost pressing against her grandma's, talking nonstop about her life, school, friends (not Kyle), interests. It made Samuel feel a happiness he hadn't in months seeing his little girl so pleased talking to her beloved grandma. Shelley talked little of herself, just wanting to hear about her guests, or when she did speak, she was focused on telling about her other kids, their spouses, the grandkids, great-grandkids. Samuel realized that no matter what pain he faced in his life, he was truly blessed to have such a wonderful mom. Which made the next thing he had to say hard.

"Mom, I'm thinking about visiting Dad." Silence filled the room. He hadn't even told Amanda that he was planning on doing this. But the idea came to him right before they hit the road. The most significant part of this battle with the gorillas was mental. He needed to be strong and secure in himself before the final battle. And one lingering issue from that standpoint was the relationship with his father and his feelings of bitterness and abandonment towards the man. Even if it went badly, at least he could say he tried.

"Oh, Sammy, I don't think that's a good idea," Shelley said with all joy abandoning her face and leaving just concern as she took a short intake of breath. "He's just an old, lonely, hateful man. I don't know why you'd do that to yourself." As usual, she deferred or deflected her feelings to others, but he knew that the mention of the man she once loved affected her too. She never did get remarried. She had a few "men friends," but nothing ever developed very far. And it was all because of the specter of Claude.

Samuel started to open his mouth and then stopped, thinking for a second. He wanted to explain this without telling his mom all of what was going on. Shelley was a worrywart. Whenever one of her kids let her know something concerning, she would wake up thinking about it in the middle of the night and not get back to sleep. He learned this the hard way when Sandra was going through her chemo; his mother had to eventually turn to mental health meds just like him to help her sleep. After that, he vowed to either not tell her things or put them off until he could frame them in a positive light. In this case, there was a lot she should never know, definitely the gorillas but also Bennett. He knew she would somehow blame herself for all of it. The apple falling far from the tree might be trite, but it fit here in more ways than one. He didn't want to lie either, though. "I've been thinking a lot about my childhood lately," he said (*not a lie*). "I feel like the more I put off confronting him, the weaker I'm going to be in facing any challenges ahead." *Well done, man.*

She looked long and hard at him, and despite his best efforts, she still appeared worried, and now the sadness was creeping in too, her eyes a little downcast, her cheeks losing some color. She turned to Amanda. "What do you think about this, hon?" Peter and Carter were still in the room, but it was almost like they had disappeared and a spotlight had been put on the three family members.

Amanda was a trooper as always, and didn't miss a beat. She reached out and lay her hand on Shelley's and rubbed them. "Dad needs this, Grandma. It's kind of like when he put off getting help mentally years ago. I remember him talking about when he and mom broke up, and he had that mental break from that and work stress. That first counselor he saw said he had to mourn his childhood. Back then Dad, and I think Mom too, thought that was an overreaction, but maybe it wasn't. He has to grieve what a crappy father he had. And he has to face that demon."

Holy cow, she's smart. I totally forgot what that counselor said. And dear Lord, how right that was.

Shelley nodded her head. "I understand. But I still don't like it. I haven't heard from him in twenty years, but I'm sure he hasn't changed. He'll belittle you again."

Always worried about her baby. Samuel got up, went over to Shelley and hugged her tightly. "If he gets nasty, I'll say my peace and get out. I promise."

CHAPTER 2

Samuel knew he could easily touch base with his father since he heard a few months ago from his Uncle Matthew that Claude (Matt's brother) had been put in a retirement home in Derby, a town not far from Shelley's. The next day, Sunday morning, he made his way there, borrowing his mom's Kia while Peter showed Carter around his favorite spots in the tiny East Eden. Amanda stayed back and was helping Shelley with a Kinkade nature puzzle at the dining room desk when he left.

As Samuel pulled into the parking lot to his father's place, he felt a strong weariness in his bones. Part of it was seeing Claude again, but he also got little sleep the night before. He tried at first to stay in the old bedroom to face his fears, but he only made it an hour with wide-open eyes darting around at the shadows cast by the moon in the unlit country. Even with Amanda's night light plugged into the outlet near the door, he felt too jumpy. So he retired to the living room and got a few hours of restless slumber on the couch. Now he took a deep gulp of the Tim Horton's coffee he bought on the way over and shook himself into action. He stepped out of the car and looked around. The home was a small institution that promised extra focus and care due to its size. It was called Elder Love. As he opened the door to the building, he wondered how much love Claude Redden allowed them to share. It was a clean, immaculately white modern facility, its lobby decorated brightly with paintings of sunflowers, green pastures, and farmhouses (re-

THE GORILLAS ARE COMING

minding him a bit of the Kinkade puzzle and also Hector's office). As he walked the hall to his father's room, he saw smiles on the faces of most of the elderly, which was pleasant. He passed a meeting area, called Angela's Haven (named after the founder). There were several small round tables set up in the middle of it and cushy couches and recliners pushed up against the far wall near the big bay window, which looked out to the small garden outside. Shelves stood against the west corner of the space and had various games on them: chess, backgammon, checkers, Monopoly. On the opposite side to the right was a long leather couch and matching recliners. A large screen TV was secured to the wall on this side, currently set to *Meet the Press*, though none were watching. Two of the old men were engaged in a chess game at one of the tables, and it looked like a serious competition, both their faces intense and focused. A bigger group was clustered around the window just chatting, men and women. He also came upon a dining hall filled with much more of the silver-haired, and the conversation was louder here at the long tables while the residents pressed their forks into their eggs, bacon, and toast. He knew nursing homes were not always the most ideal environments, despite the caregivers' best efforts, but it seemed like here they received the necessary attention. It was not a depressing place. He took a right down a long hallway, the residential section, and finally reached room 23, his father's, and paused outside the room. *You'd think after facing off with my childhood nightmares in the flesh, I wouldn't be afraid of this man, but I am.*

He took a deep breath and knocked. An ancient-sounding voice said, "What?"

Samuel opened the door and stepped in. Seated near a window in the corner was his father. He was positioned so he could have been watching the outside world but only stared down at his hands. Unlike his mother, Claude had not aged well. His face was covered in wrinkles and cracked, with prominent crow's feet around the eyes and age spots spread over his forehead. He had little hair left on his head, but what remained was snow white (though he had a surplus sticking out of his nose and ears). His lips were bluish, chapped. He appeared frail, unhealthily thin, like he would break if he moved too much. Despite his past feelings, Samuel felt sympathy for the man.

The room was another pleasant sight, though. Again, it was so clean that it almost shimmered. The living area was small but attractive. Besides the chair Claude was currently lounging in, which was another one of the comfortable furniture choices (an armchair with soft linen in the seat and wooden legs), there was a bed in the middle of the room pushed up against the wall to the left, made up. A compact stand with a twenty inch television on top was across from it. A few feet past the TV, not far from his dad, there was a door, which Samuel assumed led into the bathroom. More cheery wall pictures lined each side of the living space: a beach and ocean at sunset, cornfields, a wintry shot of horse and carriage. A little desk was tucked in the corner near the entrance door, which had nothing on it, clearly not used. Samuel made a special note of no framed photos on either the desk or the two bedside end tables. "Who is it?" Claude asked.

Samuel wasn't sure if his dad was short of hearing like Shelley, so he spoke up, "Dad, it's Samuel. Your youngest."

"Huh? Youngest? Youngest what?"

"Child." *He's senile.*

"Oh, yes, Samuel." Claude looked up and squinted his eyes at the man just inside his door. "Come pull up a chair, young man."

Samuel grabbed the leather chair from the desk and pushed it over on its wheels, and sat across from Claude. "It's been a while. Are you okay, Dad?"

Claude grunted, glancing at his lap. "The food is garbage. And I'm old. I shit my pants regularly. How do you think I am?" Samuel was about to answer when his father added, "But what could I expect from the dreamer?"

Samuel was so taken aback that he accidentally pushed back on the chair, rolling a couple feet. He paddled his feet and moved it back in place. *So he does remember some of it. And he hasn't changed a bit.* "What did you call me?"

"The dreamer. The weak one. The one with the nightmares. If Shelley had her way, you would have been babied forever." Claude had stopped looking down and was now glaring at his son, the expression making Samuel flash back to the short-tempered man he lived with for those early years.

But he wasn't the only testy one in the room. *I'm not a little kid anymore, and he's not going to push me around.* It was progressing quickly past testiness; Samuel was getting pissed. It felt like a slow burn, a sensation of warmth that was spreading deep from his gut to his face. He knew his complexion was probably turning red, and he started to grind his teeth, another one of his nervous habits. He didn't care how old or weak this man was. They were going to have it out. "Well, she did have her way, didn't she? You left us. And I turned out fine."

"You don't look fine," Claude shot back. "You look stressed and angry, son."

"Don't call me son. Don't pretend to be a father now." Samuel hesitated for a moment before just going for it. "You know what, Dad? The dreams were real. The creatures were real. And if you would have shown one ounce of sympathy instead of being the tough guy, maybe I could have dealt with it better then."

Claude coughed out a nasty laugh. "Sure, they're real. Gorillas, were they? You're still the same baby you were then."

Samuel clenched his fists and closed his eyes. "And you're a horrible person. It was never my fault that you left. Or Mom's. Or the others'. I'm glad you were alone and miserable for the rest of your pitiful life."

Samuel then felt a hand on his pullover lapel and opened his eyes in shock. His father had reached over and grabbed him, just like when he was a kid. And shockingly, this seemingly fragile man was pulling him closer. Samuel took his right hand and put it on his father's gripping one. And not gently. "Don't. Just don't."

"And what are you going to do, baby? Hurt me? I'm going to teach you a lesson I never had the chance to before."

Samuel's earlier anger had transformed into a burning fury. He wanted to beat the shit out of this wretched excuse for a human. That was when he saw it. His right hand latched onto his Dad's left was glowing. He stared at it in awe. He never quite got a good look at this phenomenon before, and he noticed now that the yellow glow was slowly turning red. And that warmth he felt a few minutes earlier, which he initially took as just simple emotions, was now almost making him feel feverish. Then his father gasped and cried out. "It burns!"

He let go and looked at his hand. Its radiance was slowly dissipating again. *If I could only learn to control this.* In just a few seconds, his appendage was just regular flesh again. But he could have sworn that he saw an afterimage of crimson - similar to how the glare of the sun can affect your eyes - drifting towards the window. He looked back to his dad and saw the look of anguish there. Claude was shaking and appeared like death warmed over, as if he'd lost an additional few pounds and should just be put in his coffin. Samuel felt slightly sorry for him again. But not that sorry.

"GET OUT OF HERE, YOU DEMON SPAWN! GET OUT!" his father screamed. This hurt Samuel at first, bringing back the feeling the night of the zoo massacre, that maybe he was evil for creating the monsters. But that was momentary. And what happened next surprised him. He let out a mirthless laugh. Claude's mouth gaped open in astonishment.

A nurse came tearing into the room. She was middle-aged, with graying brown hair and significantly overweight. But she moved like a short distance runner. "What's wrong, Mr. Redden?"

"GET HIM OUT OF HERE. HE TRIED TO BURN ME!"

The nurse, bemused, stared at Samuel. "What?"

Samuel shook his head as he stood up. "I'm his son. And he's a scumbag. He lies and he's unpleasant. I'm sure you're used to that by now."

Samuel walked briskly past the woman and then half ran out of the room. *That went well.*

Later that day, after the three Reddens ate a scrumptious meatloaf dinner, Samuel was seated on the single bed in the small bedroom that Amanda always slept in when they stayed over. This was right next door to his old room, the one he moved into when he was a teenager. In his pre-adolescent days, Shelley used this space as a craft area after his sister Sabrina got married and moved out. But when he turned fourteen, he transitioned into this room facing the front yard since his nieces and nephews would often come to stay nights, and he wanted his own little getaway. He had just finished telling Amanda about her grandpa. He wouldn't say much of anything in front of Shelley, only stating she was right and he was a cranky old man. He didn't want to cause her any more sadness. But he told Amanda all. She was sitting on the window sill on the far side of the room next to the dresser bureau. "At least I confronted him," Samuel said after finishing his story. "And the hand thing igniting again was an added benefit. That was interesting."

"Geez, Dad. Glad I never met him," Amanda said, her heart more focused on her father's pain than the supernatural occurrence.

"Me too." He pushed himself up from the bed, went to the window, and hugged her. His eyes passed to the distant woods while they embraced. *Not long now.* Then as if in answer to this thought, he heard a knock. He went over and opened the old wooden framed door. Peter Darwin entered with Carter behind him.

"It's time, Reddy," Peter remarked. "It's an hour before sunset. We should reach Terrian before it gets dark. You know, in case they're around. This is their original stalking ground."

Samuel nodded. "Don't I know it."

Peter and Carter left. Amanda moved away from the window and joined Samuel in the archway leading to the hallway. She took both of his hands in hers. She felt a bit cold, and he knew it wasn't the house since Shelley had the heat cranked. "Honey, I don't know where this journey will take us from here or how long we'll be gone," he said. "If, for some reason, we're gone for more than one night, please cover with Grandma."

"Oh, Dad," she said, squeezing him so tightly it bordered on being a bear hug, as if she didn't plan on letting go this time.

He could see the two of them holding each other in the bureau mirror's reflection, and it made him so sad to be doing this to her. At that moment, he noticed the two sai resting on the dresser top, taken out of her travel bag, at the ready. "Keep her safe." Then he added, "I know you will."

She nodded, her face buried in his chest. "Absolutely. But I still hate this. I want to be looking out for you."

"I know. But Pete and Carter got my back. And I have a feeling it's all going to come down to me in the end. Alone. Like how it started. One way or another, this is the final stage. It's almost over."

CHAPTER 3

Samuel told his mom they were going for a nature hike and that they might camp out. She got scared, but he insisted that Carter knew how to safely do this. She asked where their tent was, and he did something he hated doing, lie, saying it was in Carter's jeep. He hoped Amanda could distract her if Shelley watched closely out the window as they left. But he asked Carter to rummage in his vehicle for show and figured that would help.

Even though it was only November 1st, winter's cold fingers were reaching out already, which was not unusual in the northeast. The thermostat on the porch said 40 degrees when they left, but with the bitter wind, it felt more like 25. So they were all bundled up. Samuel had on a Batman hoodie and beanie winter hat. Peter was wearing a heavy winter coat and gloves. Even the usually lightly garbed Carter had disposed of his summer wear, but he won in style as usual. His lower body looked ordinary enough with tan work pants on – though Samuel wondered what ridiculous size they were – but his jacket was a waterproof black duster. It was similar to what the show *Angel's* title character had worn, or maybe a better comparison was a wild west gunslinger. And his shotgun was somehow hitched on his belt inside the buttoned-up outerwear, furthering the image. Each of them also took a backpack with water and protein bars, and the other two carried their weapons as well. Carter helped Peter with his heavy metal projectiles, putting half in his sack. Again, if Shelley looked out, Samuel sure counted on Amanda to come up with a good story.

When Peter had told Samuel that Terrian lived in the sprawling woods past the field across the road, his first thought was of the gorillas. That was the direction they took off to. As the trio jumped over the ditch at the far side of the street and landed on the muddy earth that used to hold rows of corn in his childhood, Samuel had to pause a second to take it all in. He could see the swath of large trees in the distance, and his chest felt funny, tight. *I can't believe I'm doing this. Marching headlong into the dark forest of my nightmares. They could be lurking around any corner if they're still somehow bringing the darkness with them. Though, if I'm interpreting what King said correctly, they're not here; they're in some other dimension. But what is it about these woods that they made it their sanctuary? Can Terrian answer this question and all the others I have? Fill in the puzzle pieces? No matter how sure I am that they are no longer in this place, it still gives me the creeps.*

He stopped his ruminating and picked up the pace to catch up with his friends. The three of them did not speak while marching upon the mostly level country plain. It was generally smooth, but the sogginess combined with the occasional tangle of weeds made it a methodical, careful walk. And while they didn't talk about it beforehand, to Samuel it felt like a waste of energy to chit chat, and he guessed his companions felt the same. So each of them was left to their own thoughts about the newly approaching phase in this weird adventure. It wasn't long before the trees loomed above them, though, after only five minutes of slogging away. And it came faster than Samuel wanted. He swallowed, looking at the wide trunks of the natural behemoths. Many of the leaves had fallen and blew around their feet now, but there was enough left on the limbs to show their dazzling fall colors, striking yellow, burning red. There was also a hint of a pine scent wafting to his nostrils. This was the one type of tree he could recognize by sight. He also seemed to remember his mom saying there were birches and alders in there too, but he never had much interest in studying these specifics even when he took nature walks. Perhaps his childhood fears prevented him from ever looking too close, even in Delaware Park. And one might think the sights and smells in this place would come across as pretty, but he couldn't feel that. Samuel swore there was a deep shadow ringed around the forest, and more so than should be at this hour. It made him think again of the gorillas' new power. He finally spoke. "This still scares the hell out of me. Even after the gorillas were purged from my mind, these woods terrified me as a kid. They're foreboding, yes?"

Peter nodded, "Like that cool cat Tolkien's dark forest."

"I've seen a lot of woods and forests in my time," Carter added, "and you're not wrong. There's a blackness to these. And not the cool kind of black." He smiled as he said this, and it relieved the tension a bit. "But time's a wasting, so…" Carter barreled ahead, bending a large low hanging branch askew with his strength and girth, and he disappeared. As usual, Samuel was impressed with the big man's fearlessness, but he also knew there was a path back there. His brothers used to go down it when they went sledding on a nearby hill in the winter. He rarely went.

"Reddy, hold that branch for me, dear," Peter said. "It's still in eyeball poking range." Samuel did as he asked, agreeing with the necessity of that since Carter's incursion didn't break the limb. And it was right at face level for the tall hippie. *Carter might be able to barrel through things with his power, but we simple humans need to be careful.*

Peter sidestepped his way in and was now gone from sight as well. But he called back to his best friend, "Need me to reach out and hold it for you, Kemosabe?"

"No, with my Redden height, I can duck under it," Samuel replied. "Keep moving. I'll be right there." He looked back at his mother's home, now a small dollhouse reflected by the sun's last embers in the east. He said, "See you soon, Amanda. I love you so." He then turned, squatted a bit, forced back his anxiety, and dove in.

Once on the other side, it was as bad as Samuel had thought it would be. It was claustrophobic and stuffy being surrounded by the soaring trees. There was a path, though, (albeit overgrown by brush), and he noticed that Peter now took the lead. He knew where he was going. *Madame Takari took him here. How many times?* He felt the old bitterness of the secrets return but quickly pushed it back. There was no time for hurt.

Samuel confirmed this was indeed the old sledding path, though it seemed less constricting back then (the few times he went) and more of a straight forward track than this flora tangled mess they were walking carefully through now. After fifteen minutes, they reached a fork in the way forward. To the left was where his brothers would continue on for fun. But Peter stopped, facing right. There was a wall of green that blocked this way, more clustered together trees, man-sized weeds, crisscrossing vines. "We're going that direction?" Samuel asked dubiously. "I always assumed there was no way through here."

"There's a way," Peter said. "But we have to fight through. It's the magic in this part of the woods. Terrian and the spirits of the glorious glade continually fill in the passage with obstacles so the unbelievers won't make it through. It's not easy for us but a necessary defense. Our friend wouldn't even release the defenses for the Madame. He's quite protective of his secrecy, and you will see why shortly. But while my beloved psychic had magic to help her, we just have our sinews and bones." He glanced over to Carter. "Big man? You got this covered?"

Carter didn't say anything but reached into his bag and pulled out a gigantic machete that reminded Samuel of the line from the first *Crocodile Dundee* movie: "That's not a knife. This is a knife." He wondered how it fit in his pack. The primatologist took a deep breath and said, "Follow me." He began to hack away. It took a few strikes, but a small pinprick of dull light appeared. After several more swings and by reaching out with his large hands and pushing apart, there was enough of an opening to fit through. It still looked dark and unwelcoming, but there it was: the "way," as Peter put it. Carter grunted and ripped away some more at the remaining restricting pieces of nature. He began to progress through the torn wall, cutting as he went and exerting his full weight in ramming through. Samuel knew that despite his toughness, Carter was surely sporting his share of decent scratches from all of this. But there was room for him and Peter to come now.

To Samuel's amazement, though, it looked like the green was slowly starting to fill back in.

"Quickly, Sammy," Peter yelled, pushing him a bit. "It's quite alive here. Follow our friend's gap."

So Samuel did, not allowing himself time to think, or more importantly, fear.

They worked through this maze of flora for a good twenty-five minutes. A couple times, Samuel took out the asthma inhaler in the small pouch of his backpack and puffed away, which he rarely did living in the city. Despite the still present cold and wind, sweat was pouring down his face, and he also had his share of cuts and scratches now, especially on his arms. If he thought it was claustrophobic before, it was almost unbearable now. He could barely move his arms with the branches, stalks, and shrubbery that were fighting back, curling in upon him. It was the undergrowth from hell. But he had to keep pushing forward, or he would lose Carter's opening. He could even feel leaves brushing the top of his head, as if the tree sentinels were grasping down to stop him. And he had to keep his eyes on his feet, too: some huge stumps were jutting out of the ground, posing a real tripping danger. As he continued to struggle on, he noticed pecking sensations on his damp cheeks and observed bugs buzzing around his face. They kind of looked like mosquitos, but he couldn't figure out how they could still be active in this chilly weather. He was not a nature person, to the extent where he hated the family camping trips to Allegheny State Park when he was a kid. So this all felt like borderline torture. The terror of slowing down, losing Carter, and being stuck in this green tomb, was becoming too much. He finally rasped, "I can't. I can't do this anymore." Looking up, he couldn't even see the sky. The overhanging tree limbs were choking out even the hope of open space above him.

"I don't know if we can take a break," Carter said, a bit breathless as well. "Not with the way this place is acting. I've never seen anything like it in the wild."

"No need," Peter said behind them. "The cool dude Terrian is right through the next few feet."

"Oh, thank God," Samuel choked, catching his breath before taking a swig from his water bottle, having no idea how Peter was acclimating himself.

Carter hacked again, and this time, each side of the botanical wall seemed to part willingly. Samuel gasped. They were looking into a large clearing. After the preceding struggle, it was like an oasis to him. And in this glade, there was only one tree. But it was gigantic, the kind of tree he expected to see in California's redwood forests, not behind his mother's house in little East Eden, NY. While he didn't know his trees, he realized with its size this thing didn't belong here, as it towered above any other structure nearby. He thought if you were somehow brave enough to climb to the top, you would have no trouble seeing Canada clearly. He believed Peter was right about magic now; no way this mammoth wouldn't be spotted from the air. The tree wasn't what he would call beautiful, though. It was gnarled, decaying, not red but black, and its giant arms seemed to be reaching out at him like the gorillas' claws. Peter's Tolkien reference earlier was apt. It was like Old Man Willow come to kill him.

But Samuel felt drawn to it, so he brushed past Carter into the clearing. He took a contended deep breath, reveling in the fresh air and space and the sight of the slowly darkening sky. As Samuel approached the tree, his head suddenly hurt with revelation. He remembered a dream, a dream about this tree. It was back when he was a child, the night before Madame Takari purged the gorillas from his mind. He was feeling the greatest sense of déjà vu he ever experienced. He felt like he was existing outside of himself, somehow having leapt into his own brain from those many years ago. He approached the tree, just like in the dream, and circled it many times. He expected fear, but it did not come; he was just marveling at this alien creature that posed as an earth structure. Its knots protruded like tumors, its weathered gaps like mouths. Then he saw the eyes in one of the larger holes. He found himself saying something, but it was more like reciting it from memory, "Hello? I won't hurt you." But unlike in the dream, he knew he wasn't seeing the eyes of an animal, a raccoon or squirrel; he knew who was likely in there. The peepers disappeared, and he touched next to where they had appeared. The tree felt genuinely alive as if he were touching flesh and not bark, softer, malleable. Then he felt the tingling down his arm, and he wasn't surprised to see his right hand glowing as he touched the wood. "Ah, this," he heard himself say. He stared at his hand and made a fist, wondering once again what he might be able to do with it.

"The shiny hand! It's back again, Daddy-O!"

Samuel turned to his left to see Peter standing next to him, smiling and nodding with approval at this development. Samuel then looked down at both of his hands, moving them around and holding his palms up, thinking he even saw a slight shimmer in his left fingers too. He remembered this was when he woke up, after he realized he had older adult-sized hands. But just like at the house, the glow then began to slowly break up. It took a few seconds, but his skin became ordinary again. While disappointed at this, he still smiled widely as he turned to Peter.

"I dreamt this! The night before Madame Takari purged the bastards from my brain." Samuel suddenly felt good, really good. A sense of peace. He should have been scared of this monster tree, but it somehow felt like home.

"Groovy!" Peter didn't seem surprised at all.

Carter had joined them at some point, standing a few feet behind. "This is it? The creature lives in this tree?"

"Yes," Samuel said even before Peter could. His friends both looked surprised. "In both the dream and now, I saw eyes. But..."

"How do we get in?" Carter verbalized what was on Samuel's mind. "With everything that's happened, I can accept a mythical figure living in this amazing tree. But I don't see big old me squeezing in one of the cracks even if skinny white boy Darwin can. Plus, I'd hate to damage this thing. It looks like it could fall over. And how do we move around even if we somehow enter it?"

Peter chuckled. "You've come a long way, buddy. But still a ways to go. Magic doesn't have limits. This here beauty exists in the real world but it also remains on a magical plane. If the wise Terrian wishes us to enter, we will enter. Excuse me, Reddy." Samuel moved over a couple feet, knowing well enough not to question his friend about these things, and Peter pressed his palm against the larger slit where Samuel had seen the eyes. He then closed his own. "Terrian, my friend. Please welcome us. I know you've waited a long time for this, my man."

Samuel felt a weird tingling, similar to what he sensed in his hand, but over his whole body now. He looked at his arms and expected to see some effect like in the science fiction stories. But no, everything looked normal with his body. That was when he realized it, though. His form looked fine, but he was not outside in the woods anymore. He was in a chamber. His eyes darted around, and he saw Peter and Carter standing on each side of him; only Carter looked as dumbfounded as he did. Peter was just grinning ear to ear. Samuel looked around more and noted it was a large room. There was a bench in the far corner and three objects that looked like chairs, but like the bench, were rustic, clearly carved out of wood. The middle of the room was wide open, but there was a table made of the same substance in an alcove behind them. It was of a bizarre shape, though. The four legs were unnaturally tall, like baby giraffe limbs, so the top of the table was at least six feet off the ground. There were several neat piles of paper on top of this desk, along with an assortment of pencils, all lined up in the top left corner of its surface. Underneath, around the sizable leg hole, he could see many books stacked up. Two he noticed in his quick glance were a Shakespeare collection and a large history of the United States volume. Looking up, Samuel noted the jagged form of the ceiling and walls and knew all at once he wasn't in some building. The roof towered above him, maybe twenty or thirty feet tall. The room's width was spacious, the size of his living and dining room at home combined. While his rational mind wanted to doubt it, he knew the truth. He was inside the tree! The walls were made of peeling bark, and he saw moss and weeds poking out of holes. It smelled like a pine air freshener. His eyes now went to the far corner where the bench and chairs were, and he was shocked to see a fireplace somehow embedded into the wall of the tree. There was a spit set up on it, and some furry animal was clearly being roasted. The flames were crackling, and its warmth permeated the whole living space and brought back memories of sitting in front of his Mom's hearth in the cold winter months. *This is the most fantastic thing I've ever seen.* He found he couldn't speak.

Then he saw it. And wondered how he ever missed it. Seemingly emerging from the far wall was a figure. And it was the most giant creature Samuel had ever seen, short of the elephant at the zoo. Even larger than King. It now turned to the threesome. He took a step back. Behind him, Carter swung his shotgun out quickly, but Samuel felt rooted to his spot. Like in his nightmares.

It was a horrific troll.

Peter gently pushed Carter's gun aside as he ran to the figure. "No! Pete!" Samuel yelled. His only thought was his mind had created another monster.

But Peter wasn't listening, and Carter didn't have time to aim again. It was too late. The flower child leapt into the troll's mammoth-sized arms, and now Samuel was pulling out the staff from his backpack, coming out of his daze. Peter's joyous laugh stopped him from extending it, though. "Terrian! Terrian! How I've missed you!"

Samuel thought he would finally just wake up when he saw the next part. No way this could be real. The troll swung Peter around in a circle like a parent might do to their child. Then a voice came. It was tender, feminine almost. "Peter, my boy. The feeling is mutual."

Terrian the Troll put Peter down and now looked over at Samuel. It moved towards him, the rough sylvan floor rumbling as it did. And now Redden got a better look at the thing. Every limb was huge, appropriately reminding Samuel of tree trunks. But they appeared to be made of pure rock. The creature was wearing dirty rags from its shoulder to its sizable bottom, like a toga. Nothing covered the scabby bare feet. The facial features were intimidating too. Its nose was bulbous and long, the eyes sea green and hungry-looking. And jutting out of its large mouth were two long fangs, like tusks. Samuel backed up a couple more steps, not caring how happily Peter was reacting.

But then everything changed. The "monster" smiled widely, a slightly humourous but at the same time joyful expression. And raindrop tears poured down its face. Deep wells of caring could be found in the recesses of its eyes, looking similar to one of Henson's Muppets or even E.T. Samuel suddenly felt the peace he had experienced outside. *He's gentle, harmless. Not something to be scared of. This being is love incarnate.* Samuel Redden had just discovered the dichotomy that existed in Terrian. Monstrous appearance but the heart of an angel. He could even sense Carter relaxing behind him. The gorilla expert put his gun back in his belt and let out a deep happy guffaw.

Terrian halted his seismic pace a few feet from Samuel and then did another thing that perplexed the man. He got to one knee and bowed. Samuel had to steady himself with the whole tree quaking. Wiping away his tears with long, muddy fingernailed hands, Terrian said, "Samuel. My life's joy. My Golden Child. Welcome." He reached his hand out to Samuel and massaged his head. It was rough, uncomfortable but at the same time made Redden feel safer than he had in years.

Samuel had no idea why he did this, but it just felt right. He took the being's hand and kissed its sandpaper surface. "Terrian," he whispered.

CHAPTER 4

Terrian guided the men to the three chairs. Before he sat, Samuel asked a question that popped in his head as he continued to look around. It seemed mundane, but he had to know. "Where will you sit? And where do you sleep?"

Samuel and Carter watched in amazement (Peter just nodded approvingly) as this massive individual squatted and sat on the floor Indian style. Once again, there was a tremor in the tree. He then gestured with his hands in circling motions. "My bed is everywhere and anywhere in this room. My body is made for comfort in my nature home." He pointed to the trio of seats. "These are made for human comfort, my guests, not for me." He then tapped the bench with his humongous knuckles. "This was made for my guests to recline, but I don't imagine we'll have time for that."

"Fair enough," Samuel said, knowing he was smiling like a child discovering motion pictures for the first time. *I shouldn't focus on how tickled I am at this fantastic being; serious things are going on. But I feel like I've been dropped in some fairy tale. It's comforting. One more question and then I can move on.* "And the fireplace? How is that possible in here?"

Terrian straightened up a bit as if in pride and glanced back proudly at the fire. "It's a bit of your world's natural wonder and my world's version of what you call magic. The wood that burns inside that pocket is the actual tree you're sitting in. It doesn't spread to my living area, though, and overnight, my humble powers allow it to be re-born anew. So you're standing in a place of death and rebirth, the beautiful life cycle."

"Holy cow," Samuel said. He shook his head and looked at his friends. Carter let out a little sigh, like he was wondering how he ever managed to find himself here. Peter only grinned like a jackal. The three of them proceeded to sit down in the odd chairs. With a closer look, Samuel could see that they were basically natural recreations of plastic Adirondack patio chairs, with the armrests and sloping back. The earthy and twisted look of them, like they were carved right out of the tree, made Samuel think that Tim Burton would love to have these in his home. But upon easing himself into the seat, he was amazed how comfortable it was, and by the reaction on the others' faces, he was sure they felt the same. It was contoured to his body somehow, though they each looked identical earlier at first glance. He knew this sensation wasn't wrong or imagined: Peter's long legs rested cozily at the bottom of his chair, and even Carter's girth looked snug and relaxed in his. And the furniture was situated in front of the fireplace, which made everything feel warm, welcoming, and calming. It was obvious Terrian constructed them, and Samuel wondered how much was craftsmanship and how much was magic. It finally registered to him that the number of chairs matched the number of his group. He figured Terrian knew they were coming, but he wondered how he knew Amanda would stay back. Or that Kyle wouldn't make it. *Maybe I just need to let go and trust that he's supernatural and isn't held back by human limitations. You'd think I would be there by now. But this is even more unbelievable than the gorillas.*

Terrian now put his hands in his lap and said, "I'm sure you have a million questions. And I need to answer a lot of them. But time is short. You must take your final step before the gorillas lose patience and return to our world."

Samuel nodded. He removed his hoodie and hat and tucked them behind his back. It felt like it was 70 degrees in the tree. He noticed that Carter had already shed his duster, hanging it on the back of his chair. He had his shotgun resting at his shoulder, and Samuel wasn't sure if it was habit or a comfort thing. *I'm excited. I'm finally going to get the answers I need.* "Thank you. Do I start with my questions, or do you want to tell your story? I'm sure that's a big part of all this."

Terrian smiled, and with his toothy maw, it looked ridiculous, like a WB cartoon mixed with Dante. But the feeling it created in all those sitting there was one of serenity. "So gracious. I think if I tell my story, many of the answers you seek will be provided. Fair enough?"

Samuel said, "Yes. Sounds great." He looked to his left and right to his companions. "Okay with you guys?"

Peter was shifting around excitedly. He, too, now stripped down, removing his gloves and shedding his coat. He even kicked off his leather boots. "Preach on, brother Terrian."

Carter chuckled. "I still think I'll be waking up at Darwin's cousin's house soon, so by all means, go on."

Terrian kept grinning. "You have the most valuable allies, Samuel. I knew Peter's importance, but Michael Carter here is such a pleasant surprise."

Samuel turned immediately to Carter when it clicked that Terrian had just said his first name. Peter had his hand over his mouth, stifling a laugh like a six-year old being naughty in class. *Again, I guess I need to stop being surprised.* Carter looked flummoxed and just shook his head. Samuel then said, "Proceed, Terrian."

◆ ◆ ◆

The troll began. His melodic voice washed over the trio like a soothing dip in the ocean on a humid day. "My origins are a long story. And one for another time. As I mentioned, time is of the essence. But I will relate how our stories intersect." After saying this, Terrian paused. Samuel could tell a lot was working through the brain of this fantastic creature. It was as if he'd thought about this day for a long time, wanting deeply to say the next part perfectly, hoping to get it exactly right. And then he said it, and Samuel knew why the pause was so important. "I was sent here. Sent to watch over you, Samuel Redden." He looked sheepish now, like a child seeking approval.

All Samuel could say was, "What? By whom?"

"I cannot answer the second part of that question specifically. One day you will know this, but it's not important to help you defeat the gorillas, to complete the first steps of your journey. But just know that you are important. That there were powers from my land that deemed you oh so vital and deserving of a guide and protector."

This is starting to hurt my head. "I still don't understand. How am I important? And what have you done in this role?"

"By now, you've heard the term golden child from my dear friend Madame Takari." As he mentioned the Madame, Terrian's face changed as if broken from the inside. He took a moment, looking down briefly, and then continued, clearing his throat. "I'm sure you've wondered the meaning."

"Of course," Samuel said. He now looked to his friends and realized they were just observing intently at this point, not daring to interrupt to ask their own questions. *They know this is my moment. My time to be the focus. I hate it. I always hated being the center of attention. But even Peter is deferring. Maybe he knows some of this, but perhaps not.* "What does it mean?"

"Its meaning comes from the role you will play. Another question first. You know the unfortunate beginning of the gorillas. The brutal attack that tested my non-interference mandate to an unbearable level. That's the why of them being released. But what about the how?"

Oh, my God. He really is like a colossal version of Yoda. More riddles. "The how?"

"You underwent a traumatic event that led to the creation of the monsters. It opened a door that should have remained closed to you until you were older. But how did this horrible attack break the veil of the supernatural? Many children are abused, unfortunately." Terrian looked even more downcast, as if the horrors of this world affected him physically.

"True," Samuel replied. "So I have powers? Is that related to my hand glowing?"

"Very much, Samuel, my boy. Let me now tell you something no other human knows. The world of dreams and nightmares are real. They exist in a physical plane populated by beings just like this dimension is. When people dream, they tap into these creatures and the ideas behind them, while at the same time providing fuel and uniqueness with their own doubts, fears, and wishes. All here on earth have these sleep-induced creations. But only you can affect them. You can manipulate them. So in a moment of terrible pain, the darkness overcame you, and you brought the horrors into reality. Luckily restricted by rules you also instituted."

"The light and my brother?"

"Yes. Dreams are many things, but imagination is a big part. That's where the rules come in. And dreams are also guided by our emotions. And your intense feelings after being attacked broke a seal. Allowed the creatures from Sambala to escape." Terrian pronounced this unusual word as SOM-BAHL-UH.

"Sambala?" Carter spoke up for the first time since their host had begun.

"Sambala is the land of nightmares. There is also a flip side, the realm of good dreams. This polar dimension is called Luminescence. Because it is a world of light." Terrian stopped again and cast his blazing green eyes hard onto Samuel. "This is where you were created, Samuel. You are of Luminescence."

"No!" Samuel said, raising his voice. This burned him, made him feel testy towards the storyteller. "I'm human. I'm from here."

Terrian shook his head back and forth and sighed deeply. "I'm sorry to put this burden on you, precious Samuel, but no. Yes, you were born here. But you were created in Luminescence. And your embryo transferred to your mother through the magicks of that holy place. Do you remember how you were called 'the surprise' by your family? And how you've often felt a bit separated from this world? Like you slipped through somehow?"

"Oh my God," Samuel muttered. When facing various struggles in his life, Samuel had often thought he was a mistake, that he hadn't been meant to be born. That he had indeed slipped through, a cosmic accident. It reminded him of that *Twilight Zone* episode, "And When the Sky was Opened." Three astronauts were, one by one, eliminated from reality after an experimental space trip. They didn't belong anymore; they had slipped through, and the universe was course-correcting. Samuel always especially liked that one, related to the idea. The information was so overwhelming, he didn't even take the time to wonder how Terrian could know his thoughts.

"Yes, this is a feeling that came from somewhere real," Terrian explained. "But you are far from worthless. You may have felt you didn't belong here, but it was because you were better than all this pain and suffering. And another fact, one that may seem invasive and too personal, but I must state it. Your mother was on birth control and had no intercourse with your father for at least a year before your birth. When you were transferred into her, this fact was erased from your parents' brains. You truly were a miracle."

"Lordy," Peter said, "holy divine birth." He put his hand on Samuel's arm, and as if he read his friend's mind earlier about how much he knew, added, "I was never told this, brother."

Samuel glanced at Darwin quickly and just patted his hand. Turning back to Terrian, he asked, "So what does this all mean? And what about the hand?" *I really can't handle this. So might as well push my feelings down inside and get what I need.*

"Your gleaming fist and the accompanying feeling of warmth is the hidden power that was given to you from your true home, the land of light, the resting place of blessed dreams. It is there for you as a weapon to burn impurities. And also to bring hope. To destroy the land of Sambala. Bad dreams came into existence the same as original sin. As an aberration. Goodness and hope are meant to be the natural state of things. You are destined to eradicate the darkness with your blazing light. There is an age-olds prophecy in Luminesence about you, The Golden Child, and how one day you would destroy the evil."

Oh, man. It just keeps getting crazier. "But that makes no sense. I've noticed this power when mad, angry, borderline hateful. Nothing positive."

"You are mistaken, my boy. It comes out with any strong emotion, be it love, passion, anger, hatred."

"And this is how I'll win this battle?"

"Yes, but I am getting ahead of myself a bit. Now you must hear more of my personal story. I am from Luminescence. It is my home as well. I was transported here, similar to how I pulled the three of you into my tree, an instant process. In your stories, you would call it teleportation. It occurred on the day of your birth." Terrian stopped for a moment and gave an uneasy smile. "By the way, in my world, this form," he grabbed the side of his cheeks, "is not one of ugliness but of beauty." Samuel thought of the *Twilight Zone* again, "The Eye of the Beholder," that classic episode where the pig doctors and nurses were considered beautiful, and blond patient, gorgeous by our world's standards, was thought of as deformed, ugly. It seemed quite apt that this show was prominent in his thoughts now: he truly felt lost in "the zone". The troll continued, "I set up this living area in your woods. Fashioning the tree and also setting its magic in place. Its location was perfect, a bit off the beaten path, and my spells also influenced the active under and overgrowth that keeps others away. I was given knowledge of your language and customs via an implant before I arrived. And so I waited for your parents to bring you home from the hospital. That night I transported to your room. I looked down at you in your crib with such love and pity. And you started to glow. Your proximity to someone of your homeland brought out the power more easily. I knew at that point, I couldn't visit you anymore. You had to find your path slowly. Even if it was painful not to be close to you, not to actively protect you. But I was sent as an observer at first. Until this day came when I could guide you. I couldn't rush it."

"So you've been watching me ever since?" *I'm not sure I like that. I feel like my life was never private.*

"Yes. Usually at night, I could venture to the edge of the woods so as not to be seen. I can also feel your thoughts and emotions in a symbiotic way in moments of extreme stress and joy." He now smiled. "I was relieved when the gorillas disappeared. I didn't yet know how this happened, but knew it was so necessary. You weren't ready yet." His face then changed to one of disgust, and it made him look like his earth equivalent, a hideous angry monster. "I often saw the abominations running through these woods from your house, but I was not permitted to act yet, which frustrated me to no ends. They had a portal, so to speak, not far from here, where they returned to Sambala. But thanks to my lovely Madame, they were banished, and you experienced some joy in having your family. That made me feel content. I wished to follow you, but I'm safer here in the country. I missed seeing your face, even though I could still sense your feelings. And the beautiful lady and precious Peter here kept me updated on your specific life events." He held his hands out pleadingly and deep empathy again radiated in his soulful eyes. "I wept when your wife died and lived in contant fear of the creatures' return. But also looked eagerly forward to meeting you face-to-face. And now that blessed day has come."

"I understand, but how were they released again? And why have they completely crossed over now?" *Every piece of the puzzle just makes me more confused.*

"Each of your challenges in life made the barrier made by Lady Takari weaker. When your wife died, they almost broke through. But you went to see your therapist and changed your earth potions, I mean medications, once again. The spell was now holding on by a thread. The night before their return, you watched a documentary on gorillas on your television. Remember?"

Oh yeah. Now I do. It was on Animal Planet. Samuel nodded.

"It's not that you never saw a gorilla after Madame's spell. But this program covered battles between different gorilla tribes and showed male silverbacks protecting their families. That broke down the last line of defense, and unaware, you dreamt of them again. And this time, you created the new leader, the unholy King. The protection was shattered. For a long time, all of Sambala were putting their energies into breaking through. The combination of all these things let them re-enter this world easily. It was a confluence of all these factors that led to this moment. You obviously dreamt and had nightmares like an average human in the intervening years after the Madame's spell, but the gorillas were the gateway, your connection to the dream world, to your destiny."

Terrian paused, clearly to let Samuel digest all this, before adding, "But you were wrong to say that they have completely crossed over. They have not. They have one goal, and that is to kill you. Only you hold them back from total domination and subjugation of the earth realm. It is their goal to enslave the human race, so every waking moment will be a nightmare. They lust for the day when they can use people as simple batteries, gorging themselves on their fears and terrors. Bur since they come from you, they must eliminate their maker to be completely free. The monstrosities don't even care about leaving more traces now, hence your injuries remaining and the damage in your house not being rectified. They are more present in this plane now. You'll remember that Hector's murder was more of a scare tactic, jumping out like phantoms and causing his accident. Their physical disturbances early on were temporary or limited, including that one time they locked your bedroom door. But now they are physically murdering their poor victims. And moving like I do, teleporting around the all-important light. But remember, even as a child, you limited them with the almighty rules. You may have also noticed that all the gorillas are male, a feature only a young boy would put in effect. These elements are mostly still active, as shown by their need to carry the darkness with them to counteract the first rule. And as a sidenote, I am sure that power was assistance provided by the evil in Sambala. But I digress. Even a shred of rule number two remains, which is not what Madame told you: it now exhibits itself in the brotherly bond you've formed with these two special men. It helped you stand up to the monsters in your home. But if they destroy you, they will be able to kill unchecked in the daytime, no matter what strength is allied against them. You might not have realized, but they were so close to crossing over when you were a child, but thanks to your brother's involvement, you barely escaped several times and they were foiled. And so the Madame's action was also a world saver." *And Kyle's sacrifice too. I'll have to tell Amanda*, Samuel thought, that sadness returning.

Terrian was struggling too. One of those oversized tears now dropped from the watcher's right eye as he clearly ruminated about his friend. "I loved her." He sniffled and then said, "I sought her out after she helped you. I searched the ether for answers of the gorillas' defeat. Our two souls latched onto each other. She was overjoyed in discovering someone like me and I no longer felt like an outsider. She never let much time pass without us taking counsel together in this tree or on the few times I ventured to the alley behind her store. She provided me with writing supplies and the wonderful tomes, literature of your culture. She was actually with me here an hour before she was attacked. That was why she couldn't meet you earlier in the day. We were planning the next steps when she would bring you to me. The friendship we formed was the kind of special bond I never knew I could have when I was sent here alone. She filled an emotional need, and I can never repay her."

He snuffled even louder, sounding oddly like a boar. But Samuel's heart felt for him, any ill will about being spied on lost. He thought for a moment before asking. "Why was it necessary to bring Pete into all this? If you could watch me, sense me?"

"My range was limited after you moved from the country. I

could transport but had to be careful. As you can imagine. " Terrian gestured to his body. "And the Madame couldn't do it herself. It was vitally important you didn't remember her."

Samuel now turned to Peter. "How much did you know?"

Peter had a deadly serious look on his face, quite unlike him, "Not much, Daddy-O. I visited Terrian on a few occasions with the Madame when she shared your updates. And I was told that you were special, powerful. That's all. Again, I'm sorry."

Samuel waved this away. "I'm over it." He brought his attention back to Terrian. "Who are my real parents? Do I even have parents?"

"Not even I know that, my son. I'm a servant. I was given a job to do and was told of your power, your specialness, your origin, but not your makers. Not even I am allowed to approach the powers that be in Luminescence. I was assigned this role through a proxy."

Samuel now stared down at his hands and tried to control his thoughts, emotions. All was silent for about two minutes. He got ready to speak again and noticed his right hand begin to do its Luminescence thing. It was flickering. "Oh boy, there it is." Without looking up, unable to take his eyes off the glow, and trying not to get lulled by the tingling and warmth radiating throughout his body from the limb, he said, "Why Terrian? Why can't I control it? And how can I win this fight if I can't? Not only is King invulnerable to us, but his minions are a multitude."

Terrian sighed. "This is the one drawback of the Madame's decision. It had to be done, but you have had this power suppressed inside you for too many years. But I believe when the moment of truth comes, you will wield it." He paused a second and then added, "This is so important to remember. When at your greatest need, think of your great love, your great hope, the goodness and light in all. And your power will not let you down."

Samuel again just sat there thinking. He now looked around the wacky room and tried to allow the unreality of all he had learned soak in. Another couple of minutes passed. "All right. Questions, boys?" he asked, not bothering to glance at his companions. His eyes were glazed over, not seeing anything that was in the tree. He was viewing beyond, visualizing the gorillas.

Peter only shook his head, keeping silent and clasping his hands, tipping them towards Terrian prayer-like. He was looking his most meditative, mindful.

Carter said, "Well, sorry for being the real world guy here and the practical one. But how do we beat the monsters? How do we win?"

Terrian grinned, continuing to be pleased with the primatologist. "Before we get to that all-important part of our discussion, would any of you like to eat? The squirrel roasting over the fire here should be done."

They all replied in the negative, and Samuel hoped none of them made a funny face; he wanted to show as much respect as possible. He said, "Much appreciated, Terrian. But we brought our own food. And if time is of the essence, we should move on."

"As you wish, and you are quite right." Terrian said. "I won't beat around the bush, my friends. You must travel to Sambala. As I'm sure you know, that is where they have retreated to. They think they have you at a disadvantage fighting in that world of horrors, but they are wrong. You are the dream warrior, Samuel. You may not be of their world, but you have power in both the good and bad sides of that coin."

"But how?" Peter asked, coming out of his meditative state.

"This tree is imbued with the magic of my elders. And combining that with Samuel's burgeoning abilities, we can transport the three of you physically to Sambala from right here."

"The magic is strong enough for all of us?" Samuel asked.

"Yes. And it's vitally important too. Your group is a tri-power. Your union has a bit of its own magic. You must go together."

I'm so glad. I can't do this alone. I know that now. Samuel nodded as he looked at his compatriots. "I would have it no other way."

"Amen, brother," Peter added.

"Well, what are we waiting for?" Carter asked. "Let's go kill those motherfuckers."

Yes, let's.

A few minutes passed. Samuel had retreated to the other corner of the room. He pulled over the bench that was originally near the fire and was now sitting on it. Carter was looking through his bag, organizing what was inside. Peter was still near the hearth, chatting with Terrian; they were close together, their hands clasped. It looked like they were saying a prayer. Samuel understood the urgency of the situation. But he needed a moment to himself. He was amazed to learn that the cracks in the bark "wall" worked as windows, as he could see outside to the twilight-hued clearing. *This must have been where I saw his eyes.* Despite all the revelations, he still found himself marveling at his environment.

But his thoughts quickly returned to all the craziness he'd just learned. *Did he seriously tell me that I'm not from the Earth? That Mom isn't my biological mother? And this stuff about being some kind of dream savior is just too much. I don't know how I'm supposed to take all this in and then go fight these monsters to the death. I'm not that strong. Well, I wanted answers, and fuck, I sure got them.*

Just then, he had a mental flash, a visual picture of something that could have been a recollection. He was walking in the park. He guessed it was Hoyt, and he was with Sandra, holding hands. It looked like they had just come to the end of the walk, though, as the path came to a stop just outside a woodsy area. Sandra now turned to say something to him, smiling beautifully...

Then it ended almost as fast as it started. *Is my subconscious trying to tell me something? Is Sandra trying to reach out to me? After all I've seen, it's not like I can doubt those kinds of spiritual things anymore. Or is it as simple as my mind retreating again to happy memories to deal with the stress?*

But there was no time to explore this. Peter Darwin's voice reached over to him. "Reddy. Time to begin."

Terrian had drawn a large circle in the middle of the floor. Drawn wasn't the right word - he had actually carved this circle with his tusk-like teeth. It was quite a sight. He now gestured for the three of them to get inside of it. They all stepped in and stood there, holding their backpacks with their weapons inside. They left their winter garb. While Terrian indicated they could encounter any kind of nightmare there, including extreme cold, he said if they stayed on track, they wouldn't need the coats, gloves, and other wear. It would just serve as an encumbrance, most likely.

After a second, Terrian chuckled. "You must lie down, my brothers. To reach the dream world, you must be prone and asleep."

"Like we knew that," Carter grumbled under his breath. Samuel stifled a laugh. Peter had already dropped to the floor and was holding his arms above him like Superman taking flight. Carter and Samuel slowly joined him, easing themselves to the arboreal surface. Redden instinctively went in the middle.

This pleased Terrian. He nodded and smiled broadly. "Yes, the center is correct, Samuel. You must be in between your companions, so the magic we share spreads out to them. When it's time, you will grasp hands, but make sure your other hand is on your bags, or your weapons will not go with you."

Terrian now walked to the far end of the room where Samuel had vacated the bench. He dug into one of the wall crevices and returned with a small glass vial that contained what looked like parsley or some other herb. He then went to the opposite corner, to the left of the fireplace and a few feet from the wall, kneeled and peeled back the floor's bark. It came up like a loose floorboard. Samuel could hear running water! "This is my brook, which was on the ground where I erected my tree," Terrian said proudly. "I re-directed its flow so I could have drinking water." He then stood up, moved to the fireplace, and grabbed an object from what would be considered the mantle, in actuality several large branches laid upon each other in a row. The item looked to be a ceramic bowl of some kind. "Anything in here not made of the tree was brought to me by the Madame. This is one of them. She often used this in her rites." He then sprinkled the herb into the bowl, crushed it up with one of his considerable thumbs with a shockingly delicate dexterity, and dipped it in the water. A sweet aroma not that dissimilar from incense filled the air. Samuel knew it was stronger, more potent, though. "Drink," Terrian said to him, coming back to the circle and holding the concoction out to him. He sat up and gulped it down. It was horrible tasting, pungent, nothing like its smell, but he managed to swallow it with a shudder. Peter and Carter then took their turns. "Now put your heads back down, close your eyes, and join hands."

After they did this, Terrian reached out his gargantuan hand and very precisely laid his pointy fingers on Samuel's temple. "All three of you will now feel sleep coming upon you. But Samuel, focus all your thoughts on me." Despite indeed feeling that extreme drowsiness overtaking him, Samuel kept his mind fixated on the troll. After a moment, he could visualize some part of himself leaving his body, mixing with his new friend, and then coming back inside of him. If asked to describe it, he would have called it a mist or breath. And this was combined with a bodily sensation, which felt inside like a tingling, comfortable feeling, not unlike the glow hand surge. He could feel this power split into portions within himself, with two parts of the cloud substance continuing to flow in a cycle, pushing outwards into Peter and Carter. "The others are asleep and ready for you to take them to Sambala, Samuel. Transfer your thoughts away from me and zero in on the idea of the nightmare realm," Terrian continued. With effort, Samuel peeked out of his drooping eyelids, glanced rapidly but foggily to his left and right, and confirmed his companions were out: he could tell by the slow movement in their chests and their absolutely still forms. He visualized a nightmarish place, full of darkness and fear. "Now, you," Terrian added. "The magicks are working. Just drift away and let the power more fully flow."

Samuel closed his eyes again and felt something he often did when nodding off to sleep. Fear. Fear of death. Of never waking up. And of the gorillas. But it was so brief. The darkness overwhelmed him, and he passed into the realm of slumber while thinking of his life's love, his family, Sandra and Amanda. He would take them with him into the battle, his true armor. With the magic coursing through him like a flood now, he and his partners disappeared and Terrian was left alone.

"Godspeed, my brave warriors," the troll said, touching his fist to his wide forehead.

CHAPTER 5

Carter opened his eyes. He felt utterly disoriented. It took him several seconds to figure out where he was. Then it became obvious. He was lying down and could see the deep blue sky above him, peeking out of the towering branches of a banana tree. And it was warm, humid. Not an unusual place for him to be found in – it was the African tropical forest. *I feel weird, though. Like I was somewhere else and have forgotten something important. But it's elusive. Was I daydreaming?* He shook his bald head slowly. *Well, forget it. I'm in the one place that makes me the happiest, so just enjoy it. I must be on one of my research trips to observe the gorgeous gorillas.*

Carter placed his hands on the lush grass beneath him and pushed himself up. He picked up his backpack from the ground, the tip of the shotgun protruding out. He stretched. *I do feel every ache in my bones, though. Mike, old boy, might as well face it, you're aging.* He stepped out from under the cluster of trees onto a strikingly green plain that seemed to go on forever, flowing out towards the breathtaking horizon. Something about the thought of trees caused a sensation of déjà vu. *I don't know what's wrong with me.* But he pushed these thoughts aside. It was time to find the love of his life, a family of gorillas. He began to walk, taking a second to notice his long pants and wondering why in the world he would be wearing these in the extreme heat. But again, he found it not worth his attention. The gorillas were what mattered.

He didn't have to go far to find them. He took about fifteen steps on this open range and could see gathered under another group of trees to the east a congregation of highland gorillas. He wasn't sure, but he guessed he was in Uganda. Here were six of them, the male silverback and female along with four children. Two of the little ones were wrestling on the ground, a male and female. A slightly older male youth was sitting with his back to a tree, chomping down on a banana. The smallest, a female baby, was cradled in Mom's arms a few feet away near a large bush. The silverback was pacing around on all fours close to his family. *He smells me.* Carter slowly approached them, moving as silently as a ghost. He had learned from years of working with primates that you needed to avoid sudden movements, especially when meeting a family for the 1st time. When he got about five feet away, he dropped to his haunches, just as the apes often do, and held his hand out in an open palm. The first one to see him was the mother, and she looked over with wary curiosity. The male adult pivoted from his crawling around, leveled his steely gaze on the intruder, and proceeded to huff his unique, challenging noises, but Carter continued to look down with his hands held in a non-threatening way. *He's doing his job but must know I'm not a threat to his loved ones. He's not being overly demonstrative, beating his chest or growling.* The silverback then approached speedily and slammed his fist down in front of him when he got within a foot of the human. *Okay, maybe I'm wrong.* Carter then thought quickly, made himself prone on his side, and held his hand up to the leader of this unit. The silverback took a moment looking at this limb. But then he relaxed and patted Carter's hand. This signaled the rest of the group to be at ease. And the female now approached as well. She put her left hand, the one not holding the baby, on Carter's chest, and he knew it was safe to sit upright. He did so, but still with no sudden movement.

The two juveniles that were tussling decided they had a

377

new sparring partner. Without warning and in unison, they rumbled over to the man and pounced! The male jumped on Carter's back, wrapping his arms harmlessly around his neck. The female grabbed at his thick legs, and he let himself tip over. Then they were hopping all over him. He burst out laughing and grinned the biggest smile, his extremely white teeth on full display. This was his nirvana. He couldn't imagine heaven being any better. Eventually, the older kid came over, sat down, and just watched, picking at bugs on his skin. Carter wasn't sure how long he spent playing with the young ones while their momma and poppa reclined against a tree, but he wished it could go on forever.

It didn't.

All of a sudden, the male reared back on his feet and beat his chest. Carter immediately tensed into a battle stance, gently nudging the apes off him, standing up and looking sharply around. He couldn't see anything but noticed the silverback staring out to the distance to a hill beyond. The father then immediately grabbed his smaller young ones and put them behind him with his mate, grunting at the adolescent to move too. Carter started to feel a rumbling sensation under his feet. Then he saw it cresting the hill. Jeeps and trucks, too many to count. *Big game hunters. The scum of the earth.*

"Run!" he screamed. But the gorillas seemed shocked in place. He quickly yanked his rifle out of his pack that he left a few feet away, checked to make sure it was loaded and cocked it. He took three steps forward and started firing. He managed to hit a tire on the first jeep, and it overturned. This gave him great pride. He started firing again and destroyed the windshield of the next, disabling it as well. But then he felt the bullets whizzing around him. Men were standing in the beds of the trucks shooting at him. He was a fighter and had altercations with these types of people before, but never had he been surrounded by so many slugs ripping around him. Luckily these shots were not accurate at first, hitting the ground nearby and embedding into some of the trees. And the apes were enough under cover to be safe for now. He held his position for as long as he could but then began to retreat to the woods finally, knowing his luck couldn't hold out forever. This thought was prophetic as he felt a searing pain in the back of his left leg before he reached the forest canopy, and he dropped. He put his hand there and felt the blood. He was hit square, and the bullet was still in there. Clearly, the attackers were using some long-range military-grade weapons, not a shotgun like he was. He tried to drag himself further, wanting to get to the gorillas and try to scare them into action. But then he felt another projectile embed itself in his neck right next to his Adam's apple. He could feel the flow of blood there and put his free hand to it. When he pulled it away, his whole palm was covered in crimson. He crumpled further to the ground. "Go!" he screamed, shaking with pain and anger. But the gorillas still didn't budge, and Carter couldn't understand why their survival instinct wasn't kicking in. The vehicles - he guessed there were ten of them now left - skidded to a stop mere feet away. He could smell gasoline and hear the excited shouting of the scumbags.

Then the barrage occurred. The family of gorillas was mowed down. First fell the silverback, even though he finally made a courageous attempt to charge. He was hit in his groin and chest and plummeted back into the bush. Mom tried to shield her kids, rearing up in front of the older three and trying to place her baby on the ground, but she was leveled by a barrage of bullets. The infant was flung out of her arms in mid-motion with the explosive force. The baby girl smashed into a tree with a sickening thud. Its cry of shock and surprise was heart-rending. Mom collapsed as her body freely flowed its lifeblood, the ammunition causing huge craters in her body. The remaining children then huddled together, with the adolescent trying to push the others away into the jungle, but were killed in quick succession. The older brother had his head nearly taken off with a shot. The last two – who mere moments ago were roughhousing with such vibrant energy - just sat there transfixed, unmoving to the end. The girl was hit in the chest and the boy in the neck. They fell into each other, hugging and whimpering as their breath left them.

Then Carter screamed. No, more like a howl, the sound of a wounded animal. Any question that these assholes were big game hunters evaporated away like the gunsmoke in the breeze that carried along with it the stench of death. Poachers wouldn't have butchered them so. Then he heard the screeching of brakes and saw mud flying past his face as the vehicles stopped inches from him. And the last thing he glimpsed was the hunters, their faces in shadows as they jumped from the back of the pickup trucks. The final words heard in his full and vivacious life before the pain and darkness took him away was one of the assailants saying, "Goodbye, nigger. Just one more ape to die today."

Peter Darwin woke. He was also lying in a verdant environment, a field of sunflowers. It was a country locale, something out of Midwest America. He looked around and could see a picturesque white farmhouse in the distance and closer by, rows and rows of corn. The air smelled clean, and the skies were filled with the puffiest clouds he'd ever seen. And the sunlight was shining down with a magnificent warmth. He had no idea how he ended up here but didn't give it much thought. *I'm on some kind of mind trip. Groovy.* He didn't take the time to wonder how he was experiencing this since he had stopped taking the hard drugs many years ago and hadn't had a "trip" in what seemed like forever. He sure still liked to light a joint now and again, but no more psychedelic mind journeys for this man nearing 45.

But he didn't care now. He was in some kind of Serenityville, and he was going to enjoy it. *Time to explore and see what the beautiful world can unfold for me.* He leapt clumsily to his feet and noticed a backpack nearby. He figured he had some water and nature bars in there, so he latched it onto his back, a little surprised by its weight but not wanting to delay any longer. So he headed right over to the row of corn that was about ten feet away. When he was a kid, his dad and mom used to take him to fall festivals in Eden, and he loved to go through the corn mazes. He figured even if this one was more natural than a constructed labyrinth, he could find his way around. *I'm a cool dude of nature. This is my place, after all.*

So he plunged into the nearest maize aisle. For many people, this would have been claustrophobic and stuffy, but not for Peter Darwin. He took it all in with joy. He ran his hands along the corn stalks feeling their rough surface. His nostrils breathed in the earthy aroma of the ground, and there suddenly was such a lovely cool breeze. He strode with his long legs and began to sing *Purple Haze*, his heart filled with such peace and perfection. And then he smelt it.

He knew that smell. It was marijuana. He laughed heartily and looked up in the sky to see the smoke swirling right above him like a tornado. He inhaled deeply as some of the cloudy substance descended into his mouth, and he immediately felt that relaxing high that he knew so well spread through his system. He continued to stride along, moving a little slower now, taking in the mental ride.

But then something changed. The spreading mist kept following Peter, but it somehow smelled different. No longer the strong but natural herbal scent of weed, it now reeked, more pungent, almost like a sewer. He scowled up at the sky formation, and the wispy gray cloud changed into a deep black spiral. It caused an intensely personal connection for him, making Peter think of the cigarette smoke that had destroyed his daddy's lungs. But he focused more on the bigger picture, so not to re-live the pain of Robert no longer being with him. "Pollution!" he exclaimed. "You can't escape the bastards! Even out here in the bucolic country." Then the mini-tornado began filtering its pollution to the rest of the sky and it wasn't long before all Peter saw above him was blackness, as if night had suddenly appeared. He shook his fist at the air in dismay. Then he stopped in mid-thrust when he realized the sable twister had begun to move towards him as if the contaminants were chasing him. He ran.

Peter's impressive stride helped him move with urgency, but when he looked back and up, he could see the menacing dark wisp was still chasing him. He no longer felt cool, with sweat soaking his forehead and dripping into his eyes. His long hair was whipping into his face with the movement, also not help-ing with keeping his vision clear. He stumbled over a large root in the ground but somehow managed to keep his feet. But then he felt the pain in his lungs and a tightening in his throat. He gasped for air and continued to try to run, but after a couple minutes, found it useless. He fell to a knee. He gazed up to the skies again, begging silently to mother nature for mercy with tears in his eyes, but the darkened roof of the world had no reply as it descended to engulf him. He began to cough and hack roughly, and he hurled up part mucus, part blood. His greatest fear had come true: the world's degradation was in-vading his body, killing him. He thought again of Robert and sobbed. He collapsed, and now the darkness came to his eyes as well.

Samuel Redden was walking in a glade. It was ringed by a beautiful forest. He had no idea when he'd started this walk or how he got here. He wasn't sure of the location either, but it might have been one of the many paths of Delaware Park. But he realized he just didn't care. It was so gorgeous. The trees' leaves had their fall colors on them, a panorama of hues: sunshine yellow, pumpkin orange, chocolate brown. In the clearing, there were also blooming flowers clustered near some of the fallen leaves; Samuel was never a gardener and knew next to nothing about these things, but he was quite taken by the white and purple petals and yellow pistil of these growths. He didn't take a moment to wonder how these could be so alive with the autumn effects elsewhere. And if he was even minimally observant, he would have also noticed he wasn't wearing his trusty glasses even though he could see clearly. He touched the strap of a pack that hung over his right shoulder, now thinking this was a long hike. The more he looked around, the more he was sure this wasn't Hoyt Lake or any other part of Delaware Park. He had walked most of the trails there, and this was different. And while he didn't recognize it as a specific place, it seemed to Samuel that it was a composite of all the scenic areas surrounding his old country home in Eden. *This is just perfection. I could stay here forever. Something's weird, though. I have a funny feeling. I don't know about what, though.* But he forcibly ignored this, figuring it was his typical worries, the old doom and gloom trying to invade this wonderful time.

Then suddenly, at the tree line's border, a series of bushes rustled a bit. *A deer*, Samuel figured. But his heart fluttered, a sensation of fear rising up and gripping his throat, something primal, and it felt much more potent than the misgivings from a moment ago. He took a deep breath and backed up a step. He groped behind him for the knapsack on his shoulder, as if reaching for a weapon. Which was a weird thought since Samuel knew quite well how much a pacifist he was. But he reacted that way all the same. He turned his head behind him and debated running. But that didn't seem possible; he felt rooted to the spot.

Slowly the flora parted, a time that seemed like an eternity, and the figure squeezed its way into the clearing. *I hope it isn't one of the gorillas.* As soon as this thought occurred, Samuel almost found himself laughing despite the situation. *What nonsense is that?* He continued to stare at the movement being made near the forest. The shape was shrouded in the shadows, but he was pretty sure it was female based on its silhouette. It was thin and shapely, and there was an indication of long hair coming to the shoulders. Samuel felt like he knew that body, something instantly recognizable about it. Then it hit him. And the terror changed into joy.

"Sandy?"

She stepped more fully into the glade, the bright sunlight revealing her entirely. Standing before Samuel was his wife, Sandra Redden (formerly Crowell). Even though it had taken a moment, something he was now kicking himself for, the recognition of her form took full shape now. There was her shimmering red hair, her piercing green eyes, and on her curvaceous body, the simple beige top and blue jeans that she often wore on dates. His heart instantly ached, and his body got excited at the same time. Before him was the girl he became infatuated with in college and the woman who owned his heart in the ensuing years. But almost instantly, his thoughts blended from the happy to the sad, his unconscious mind unable to block out the conscious reality.

And that reality was that Sandra was dead. She died of pancreatic cancer about five years prior. But here she was, just as she was before her death, healthy-looking in her mid-thirties.

"This can't be," he muttered. *But please, God, let it be.*

"Don't do that, Sam," Sandra said, slowly approaching. The way the light wind gently blew her hair brought up memories of her running around the backyard with Amanda and Craw-ford, their old dog, good times when he reveled in her simple beauty. It made tears begin to well in his eyes. "We're here now. Stay in the moment."

Hearing her voice, that mix of gentle and husky, broke him. He ran to Sandra and took her into his arms. The emotions overwhelmed him like never before as tears just funneled out of his eyes. "It's been so hard. I've missed you so much."

She caressed his head, much like she had in times of stress and depression before. "I know. I'm sorry for leaving you."

That helped him regain some composure. He pulled back a bit and cupped Sandra's face in his hands. "No, it wasn't your fault. You can't blame yourself for getting sick. It's not like you smoked or took poor care of yourself, like Pete's dad. It's just that fucking disease. It can sneak up on you." When Samuel thought of his best friend, he had a glimpse of something in his mind's eye, of his deadhead friend shooting something blurry with a slingshot. But he immediately pushed this away, think-ing his feverish mind was just making shit up.

Sandra reached out and wiped away his tears, then took his hands. "You're not swearing all the time like that around Amanda, right?"

Samuel laughed heartily. He was always the one with the more filthy mouth. "Trying not to, babe." For a moment, he just gazed at his wife, again reveling at how much Amanda looked like her now. "She's great, by the way. Despite losing you and any mistakes I've made as a single dad, she pulls through. Her grades are great, and what a friend she is to Kyle. I wouldn't have made it without her." *Why did my heart suddenly hurt when I said, "Kyle"?*

"I'm sure she would say the same," Sandra said, and then

she kissed him deeply, passionately. Despite being in what he thought was a public setting, he wanted desperately to take her into the woods and fuck her right out here. He hadn't dated in the years since her death, choosing to focus his energies on raising Amanda, and his body almost ached with need now. He could feel his love's tongue curling around his, her breasts brushing gently against him, and he didn't know how he would keep it together. He could taste that old cherry lipstick she used in college and caught a whiff of lavender too, and the memory of their first date made him feel a bit off kilter in a wonderful way. Sandra smiled widely as they came apart, and this was another aspect that brought Samuel back to happy memories. She always had the most dazzling smile. She gave Jennifer Garner a run for the money with those dimples and how her whole face brightened up. "Walk with me, won't you, honey?" she asked him. "And then maybe we can do something else," she said with a knowing and naughty grin, seemingly reading his earlier carnal thoughts.

"That sounds perfect," he said excitedly. Beyond the sexual possibilities, he was pleased by the idea of a walk. They weren't hardcore hikers in their time on earth, but the two of them did really enjoy walking hand in hand at malls and parks. For many years, it was just he and she in these quiet moments, but then years later Amanda came along in the stroller or waddling right beside them. They both reached for each other's hand, naturally clasping fingers, and then began to move. Samuel noticed that Sandra was guiding them towards the woods' direction, and he thought that was as fine a way as he could think of. *There are probably some nice paths over there where we can see more of this beautiful locale. And like she said, maybe try those other things too.* He was feeling a little dirty. No, a lot dirty. He couldn't help it; she always did this to him.

For a couple minutes as they moved towards the lush looming foliage, they didn't speak. At this point, Samuel didn't feel talking was necessary. Relishing that wonderful comfortable silence again and being present was all that mattered. Any conscious thought of the impossibilities he was experiencing was gone; she was back, and they were together, and all was perfect. He could feel everything so clearly around him: the sweet smell of the nearby flowers, the sound of the warbling birds and the wind rustling the branches of the trees, the slightly moist feel of sweat between their skin. He didn't ever want to leave this ecstasy, this new and preferred reality.

They reached the trees, and Sandra started to put her foot through where she had exited a couple minutes before. But something struck Samuel. It was an abrupt physical sensation as if someone had punched him in the chest. From the inside. Like a defibrillator jolt. He let go of his wife and touched at his sore pectus, finding it hard to breathe. It took him a second or two to find air to inhale. Another few ticks of the clock passed while he tried to compose himself. He felt a little dizzy. "What the hell was that?" he mumbled.

Sandra pushed in closer and reached out to hold him again, but for some reason, he pulled away and took a couple steps backward. Sweat was beginning to build quickly on his brow, and even though the moment of physical pain and respiratory struggles had passed, that sense of terror had returned with a vengeance. It was all-enveloping, affecting every part of his body and mind. He looked hard into the woods beyond and could have sworn they had suddenly become dark, foreboding, a haunted fantasy world waiting to eat him up. "I can't go in there," he said.

"What do you mean?" Sandra asked confusedly. He just noticed something subtle about Sandra's voice. The husky had wholly replaced the sweet, and there was a tinge of sinister behind it, a hard edge. "Come with me into the beautiful forest, and we can be together forever."

"What about Amanda?'

"Fuck Amanda!" Sandra screamed.

He just about tripped over his own feet in hearing this, continuing to back away. *That's not Sandy. It's something else. Should have trusted my intuition.* "What did you say?" he snapped.

"Oh, don't worry about that, Sammy," the voice said, and now it actually sounded like a poor impression of Sandra. Samuel could have sworn he could hear a metallic creaking noise under each utterance, like gears were grinding behind the vocal cords. And another thing came evident to him. *She never called me Sammy.* "Come. Andi will be fine with the Greens. It's time we ended your pain."

"You're not my wife," he just about whispered. He continued to retreat, but she was moving in step with him. And yet another feature was lost – she was no longer walking smoothly, but stomping drunkenly, like the body was betraying her. "Get away from me." *Now would be a good time to wake up*, he thought. *Wait. Nightmares. I'm supposed to remember something about nightmares.*

"Of course I am, silly. Now get over here." The Sandra thing reached out both hands, resembling a zombie walk.

"No."

"Get your loser ass over here!" it bellowed. The voice was now deep and guttural, animalistic.

"Wake up, Samuel," he told himself.

"You're not waking up. You're coming with me. And then we'll get the teenaged bitch too. You're ours." At that moment, fake Sandra's face devolved. The skin began to bubble all over like it was burning. And a smell entered Samuel's nostrils, as if someone was mixing a concoction of skunk decay and flatulence somewhere nearby, a most unholy brew. The face continued to ooze and undulate, while the body did the same, the clothing dropping off, and the top of her finally took a new shape after a minute that felt interminable. It was horrific, grotesque. "Her" hair was gone, and lumps covered the chrome head. Its visage was colored pale red, and the character had a long witch's nose along with scabs of sores leaking a green fluid throughout the face. And the eyes were yellow with a pupil of red that was starting to grow. There was a cracking noise, and Samuel's eyes were torn from the ugly face to the legs. They were at first gooey versions of human limbs extending from the same blobby stomach, but that was changing now. Jagged protrusions burst out of the ooze, resembling spider shanks, a perfect two on each side. The being lurched forward on these while remaining upright like a biped, the grass beneath catching on fire from the acid dripping from the spindly legs. Oddly enough, no arms developed, which provided an even more perverse image, like a clean double amputation. Samuel felt bile rising in his throat. *I almost had sex with this thing.* Again, it seemed to read his mind. "Kiss me again, lover, and all your fears will leave you," it growled. At this, the creature opened its mouth, and a long lizard-like tongue began to protrude from its toothless maw and hurl itself at Samuel. He screamed as it wrapped around his head, the slimy tip moving towards his throat.

Then it all came back to him. The gorillas. Peter and Carter. Terrian. Sambala. *This is one of the realm's nightmares, tailor-made for me. This is why King wanted me here, to destroy me mentally before I get to him. And they sure got it right. It's the memory of my wife perverted. Well, fuck that. Terrian said I have power here.*

Samuel sneered, his fear and repulsion gone in an instant, and then reached out and grabbed the monstrosity of a tongue trying to invade him. "Nice try, King. Or whoever. But I'm no victim here." He managed to rip the tongue clean out of the mouth, and the creature howled in pain, sounding like a screeching banshee. Black-colored blood poured down his fingers, and pieces of the tongue stuck to his hands. The same discharge flowed freely down to the monster's arachnid bottom. "Bring it on, you ugly son of a bitch," he said calmly. "I'm not afraid of you."

The creature bellowed again, but instead of attacking, it simply disappeared, dissipating in a mist blown by the wind. Terrian had told Samuel that Sambala existed on a physical plane, but he got the sense that this whole scenario was a fabrication and that his body was elsewhere. And a second later, this intuition proved true.

The environment around Samuel drifted away as well. The woods, the glade, the flowers, the scorched grass all faded out and were replaced by new surroundings. He was now lying down in a dark area. He realized it was the opening of a dank, wet cavern. He appeared to be in a bigger cave system that branched into the next area. The rock walls were black as coal, giving off eerie jagged shadows into the dimness.

It was hard to see, so he dug in his backpack and lit a small flashlight Carter had put in there. His two friends were still prone on the ground on either side of him, just like at Terrian's. But they were no longer holding hands.

CHAPTER 6

Something felt off to Samuel. *Heh. Nice understatement, Redden.* But it wasn't just being in an alien environment; it was more about himself. Then he realized what: his glasses weren't on his face. Being nearsighted, he was able to look around the immediate vicinity with the light's help and spotted them a few inches to his left on the ground. He reached out and grabbed them, saw they were not broken in any way, not even cracked like his good pair, and put them back on his face. Now he sat up and kneeled, looking more closely at Peter and Carter. Even though the water dripping from the nearby cave was quite loud, he could tell his friends were alive by sound. They were both actually moaning and whining as if in pain. Otherwise, they showed no signs of lucidity; their eyes were fluttering, a telltale sign of dreaming, but they were motionless, their pack straps still around their wrists, same as his was when he awoke. *They're dreaming. Trapped in some personal horror too. And it makes sense. This is the land of nightmares. We're tapping into this place's power, and it captured us. But I broke free, and they appear stuck. Maybe I got away because of my power here. How do I wake them up?*

He gently laid a hand on their chests while holding the flashlight in his mouth, doing it gently as not to startle them. It didn't matter; they still didn't stir. He then took turns shaking them with a little more force. "Peter. Carter. Wake up, boys." This also didn't work, unfortunately, and he was a bit worried about jostling them harder. *I don't know how things work here exactly. Being too disruptive to them when they're in this state in the origin point of all nightmares could be disastrous. Not sure how I know that, but just another one of those feelings. And in this place, the intuition is stronger. I can just sense truths.*

Samuel leaned back against the hard wall for a moment and thought. *Since I was able to break the spell this place put on me and wake up, maybe I can do the same for them.* He wondered if being this golden child would allow him to enter their nightmares and pull them out. He knew this realm (dimension?) was constructed of the mental side of things, fueled by everyone's nightmares, but the three of them were also physically here, no longer in Terrian's tree. His companions were just ensnared in their own personal hell, nightmares made specifically for them. They were dreaming, no different than if they were laying in their beds at home, though he figured it was more concentrated, primal here, and tougher to escape. *Terrian probably thought we'd wake up together in a locale like this cave, which should lead to the gorillas, ready to move forward, but we let go of each other and were snared by the emotional power of this Sambala, subjugated to halt our journey.*

"But how do I get them out?" he muttered. "Terrian should have given me the dream world owner's manual." He chuckled darkly and then just remained still in his sitting position for several more minutes. Finally, he shut off the light and put it away, casting himself back in the dimness. He proceeded to cross his legs, close his eyes, and lost himself in a meditative state. Before he got here, he would have thought this would be more Peter's thing than his, but it felt natural, necessary. He remained in this state for several minutes, not paying heed to the fact that he was in a dangerous place and could be attacked at any moment. Not even taking any time to consider the surreal nature of his life now. He also stayed focused on combining a peaceful mental rhythm while still being on guard from being sucked into another one of his own nightmares. He could feel a force pushing against him a bit, and he knew it was the evil here. His only concern was helping his partners, and he used their faces as a guiding light. Then his eyes flashed open, seemingly not of his own will. He glanced down, and his right hand was glowing. It felt hot and kind of tingly, like when you warmed your hand at the fireplace after coming in from the cold. The limb's illumination wasn't a steady blaze but beat like a heart, blinking in and out, pulsating. Wasting no time, he placed this hand on Peter's chest.

The cave system morphed, changing shape. Samuel's eyes took in the slowly changing landscape, much as they did when he awoke from his dream. The gray dankness of the cave entranceway blurred away and was replaced by a foggy countryside. He was standing upright now and was existing entirely inside of Peter's nightmare. It looked to him like this might have been a beautiful pastoral locale at one time. Even with the black mist of pollution, he could make out the traces of a farmhouse in the distance and the corn stalks not far from the field of sunflowers that surrounded the lower part of his body. But he couldn't see his friend. Another instinct hit him, and he obeyed its command, waving his still shimmering, beating hand from left to right. The pollution scattered away like a receding cloud. *I have no time to revel in this. But, wow.*

Then he saw Peter. He was curled up in a ball a few feet into one of the rows of corn. He was mumbling something, but Samuel couldn't hear what. Redden wasted no time, quickly running to his pal. He knelt beside him and put his hand on his shoulder. He could now hear what he was saying, "We're destroying the world. We're destroying ourselves." Within the reality of the dream, Samuel was sure Peter hadn't been breathing just a minute before. But now, he was taking deep gulps of air, almost hyperventilating. Samuel knew being inside the nightmare that he could shake Peter a little harder this time, and he did, making sure he used his right hand. Peter cried out,

"Leave me alone, uncool toxins. Just let me die."

"Pete," Samuel said gently, "it's me, Samuel. You're safe, brother."

Peter grunted, rolled over on his back, and looked up into his long time friend's eyes. "Am I in heaven?"

Samuel laughed and said, "No, Iowa." Peter looked nonplussed, not registering the *Field of Dreams* joke, so Redden just continued, "Far from heaven. You're in the land of Sambala in your worst nightmare." Samuel spread his hands around. "And this nightmare demonstrated what a wonderful heart you have. Sure, the powers here succeeded in attacking you, but it was through your empathy, through your concern for the world, that they took advantage. Your fear of pollution and climate change was their gateway. "

Peter sat up, rubbing his temples and pushing away the sweat-soaked bangs hanging in his eyes. "Oh yeah, I recollect it all now." He smiled warmly at Samuel. "You truly are the Golden Child. You saved me."

"You can thank me later," Samuel said. "Carter is still stuck in his nightmare. And I fear the longer you remain, you can really die. Take my hand and make sure your backpack is secure. Not sure how the rules work here but don't want your weapon flipping out of existence."

Peter did this, his eyes getting wider when he saw the radiant body part reaching out to him. He beamed with admiration for his transcendent savior. Rays of light flashed outwards from Samuel's fingertips. When their fingers met, Darwin felt a gentle shock, similar to the sensation sometimes experienced when you touch metal screws on light switches. In the next second, Samuel was back to sitting cross-legged beside the horizontal Peter in the cave; this time, it seemed instantaneous, no more fading background, just like blinking in and out.Peter opened his eyes, dramatically rubbed at them, sat up, and looked around in wonder. "What is this, oh wise one?"

Samuel shook his head in mock dismay but couldn't help grinning. He found the flashlight again in his bag and passed it to the hippie. "I think this cave leads to the apes. This is their section of Sambala, the physical part of it. It doesn't make a lot of sense. Gorillas don't live in caves. But maybe mine do."

Peter nodded and, for another one of those rare times, was silent. He kept looking around, taking in the surroundings. "Stay here," Samuel said. "Don't move. We have to stay together." Samuel pointed at Carter a few feet away. "Let me get the big man."

Peter just now took notice of Carter. "He looks vulnerable. Hurry, buddy."

Samuel did just that, jumping over and grabbing Carter's hand. This time a brightness burned his retinas as he made the journey.

When Samuel emerged in the forests of Africa and his eyes cleared, he took a second to revel in the fantastic and complex nature of being in someone's dream. He'd never traveled to another country (well, except for Canada) and now felt like he was actually kneeling in the high grass of a strange continent. The sky was a dazzling sapphire hue, the quiet of the jungle serene, the gently rustling leaves of the ancient trees calming. But then he saw Carter, laying just outside the forest, his newest wound, a hole in his head, dripping blood. He couldn't help but let out a little cry. Pete had been lying down as if asleep, but this was more violent, brutal. And it made him mad. But he had nothing to direct his anger at. The big game hunters were gone. Samuel could see the gorilla family not far from Carter, and it made him queasy in the stomach, the charnel mosaic of it all. Seeing the male silverback gave him a second of pause, but in the next instant, he knew this was a wondrous, loving animal and nothing like King. And its lifeless body was pity inducing. The whole scene made him want to weep. He knew these apes weren't real, but they were to Carter, his friend. And how that must have destroyed him. And he also thought of Amy and her family, and his rage was redirected right to King.

But he pushed that all aside. *Forget it. That's in the past. Save the anger for later. Only then can I make them pay for Amy...and for Kyle.*

Samuel rushed over to Carter and dropped to the ground next to him. He looked at him with more pronounced sadness. *He really is dead here. But I don't think it's permanent. Yet. Just seeing him like this is terribly unnerving, though. He's usually so strong.* Samuel now saw that the headshot was simply the coup d'état and observed dried blood on both the neck and behind the leg. Still flowing with instinct, he touched where the bullet had gone in the forehead, since that was the killing blow, trying to ignore the sight of the thick congealing gore. He rotated his fingers in a massaging circle with his powerful, still burning hand and then shook the primatologist with his left. "Carter, wake. The adventurous life is not done with you yet. I need you. And so does the world. It needs your love of nature, of animals, of conservation. Wake, please." Samuel's voice was a little quivery: he wanted to believe his instincts, but his lifelong worry and fear of death, of losing loved ones took over.

But he had nothing to fear. Carter's dark eyes opened slowly, gazing at Samuel like he was a complete stranger. Samuel took his hand away and noticed no wound anymore. No blood, not even a scar. And the rest of his body was the same. Awareness now crossed Carter's face, and he whispered, "Redden." He put his fists into the soft ground and eased himself to a sitting position. He then looked right over to the dead gorilla family, and his face's skin rumpled up, the look of a lost boy. Samuel almost gasped seeing this expression in one he thought as unmovable.

"Don't look at that. Hold on," Samuel said. He couldn't let these images linger since it could make Carter regress. Samuel swiped his right hand in the same circular motion but towards the simian victims this time. The gorillas didn't get up and walk - he couldn't do that since it was Carter's dream - but he did make them vanish. The bush where the silverback had lain rustled a bit, but other than that, it was like they were never there. "They weren't really harmed," he said. "Not actually killed. They never existed, Carter. It was a nightmare, your greatest. And just like Pete, it was a selfless dream. You were protecting them."

"And failing. Again." Carter stood up urgently but had none of his regular confidence; his shoulders slumped a bit, his eyes were unfocused. Samuel saw clearly what was happening here. The nightmare had broken what semblance of strength the big man was maintaining after the losses they had suffered.

Samuel stepped up to Carter and laid his left hand on his shoulder – not sure what his powers would do if used unfocused, so he avoided using the still shiny one – and he had to reach up to do it. "You won't fail at the final test, Carter. We have the counterfeit gorillas to face, and we need the badass expert and warrior Peter called in. And *I* need my newest friend. Someone I know will have my back. You with me?"

Carter stared hard at Samuel, and it was like the metaphorical cobwebs were falling from his eyes, the thing of legend returning to reassert itself. He stood up straighter and nodded. He marched over to his shotgun lying on the ground and retrieved that and his pack. He came back to Samuel. "We're in Sambala," he said in a matter of fact fashion.

"Yep."

"And I can take out my frustration at being manipulated in this place on those ugly fake apes, right?"

Samuel smiled, feeling immensely relieved. "Affirmative."

Carter glanced over to the right side of Samuel's body. "So there it is - the aforementioned glow stick hand. You do have power here, eh?"

"Some at least," Samuel said modestly.

"Well, do your thing, and let's finish this."

Samuel placed his hand on top of Carter's much larger one, and then they faded away, giving the effects from *Star Trek* a run for the money.

Again, that instantaneous blinking into existence at the cave door occurred. Samuel returned in a kneeling stance, and the prostrate Carter slowly opened his eyes, looking around with a confused expression. Samuel figured it was partly the discombobulation of the trip, but maybe given his area of expertise, the primatologist was questioning the cave environment too. Carter lifted his upper body with his elbows and let out a relieved sigh, favoring this odd set up to his nightmare.

Peter was up and about, shining the light into the opening of the adjoining cavern but not going any deeper. "Carter!" he exclaimed, turning around after he sensed the movement behind him. He hurried over to them, giving his newly conscious friend a hand up, "You okay, Daddy-O?"

Carter shook his head. "Far from it. But at least I can do something about it now."

"I dig it," Peter said quite simply. The flower child now looked lovingly at Samuel. "You missed an amazing sight. Your body just locked into place, and you were motionless, like your soul levitated away. Statuesque. So groovy."

Samuel just nodded, still not ready to fixate on the wonders, got up from his kneeling position, and looked at the two men who had followed him into hell. He then glanced over to the ominously dark hole that led into the cavern. "Well, come on. The gorillas are waiting. And now we're coming *for them*. We're the predators."

He didn't wait for any reaction but simply stepped past the others and into the shadowed mouth.

CHAPTER 7

The cave cast impenetrable darkness, deeper than Samuel had ever experienced. He couldn't see a thing with Peter still behind him with the flashlight. He knew what this was intended to replicate instantly. The pitch-black night that allowed the gorillas to accost him all these years. He turned back in the direction of his friends. "Let's use my night light, shall we?" he said. He held up his hand and then realized why there was no illumination cast in front of him. His glow had gone out completely, not even a flickering left. "Son of a bitch," he cursed. "Why can't I maintain this, even here?" Samuel had a horrible thought. *If I can't figure this out, King will destroy me quickly.*

But he ignored these doubts, knowing they would do him no good now. But he still felt crestfallen, and the return of terror was chipping away at him. This wasn't just a regular absence of light. It seemed to have its own wall of blackness, thick but also alive somehow, like it had an intelligence. He felt like that little boy huddled under the covers again. But then he felt a firm hand on his shoulder. It was Carter. "No worries. Let's try mine," the big man said. He dug into his backpack and removed a much larger flashlight than he'd put in Samuel and Peter's bags. It was a large, lumen spotlight style light. He turned it on, and it cast vivid illumination several feet down the passageway. "Sometimes old school is the best way, brothers," he said, grinning.

Samuel smiled back, feeling more relieved than he cared to admit. Peter shut off his weaker beam, stowed the penlight away, and said, "Let there be light, cool dude."

Carter stepped in front and cast the light around more. Samuel thought, *this is what the Batcave would look like if Batman were a villain.* A small stream surrounded them, caused by the various cracks above, the drips of water he heard earlier. There were multiple ingresses for the water, causing flooding to be on each side, giving a sense of being closed in. Deep craters heaved up in many spots of the hard rocky floor in front of them, big enough for an elephant to step in. He could see stalactites on the roof that looked like they could fall at any time, and the way of them was unsettling. They appeared like they were from the mind of Salvador Dali. Some were pointy, misshapen spikes as expected, but others formed faces. These were shaped in the visages of hellhounds, demons, and, yes, his evil gorillas. They were leering at them. And Samuel could have sworn they were breathing, but he hoped that was just wind coming through the crevices. *I kind of doubt it, though.*

"Welcome to Dante's brain," Carter said with a slightly unsure voice. His confidence had returned since "Africa", but this scene would make anyone pause.

"No, welcome to the worst parts of my brain. My dark side created this," Samuel replied with a disgusted tone.

"And your light side will defeat it," Peter said confidently.

"Let's just go," Samuel said, pushing forward, trying his best not to regress, even though he could clearly hear his eight-year-old self crying out to him, begging him to stop. The threesome walked carefully through the cavern. Not much changed for twenty or thirty feet, but then they saw it, another opening about fifteen feet away. This gap was larger than the last one and somehow darker, more sinister looking. It seemed like an impossibility, but this was Sambala, not reality. Samuel would have a hard time describing the eerie feeling that spread out from that hole, but if you put a gun to his head, he'd say there was an emptiness there. But it wasn't a physical black darkness in this branch. It was a psychological darkness. In actuality, there was some illumination filtering out. But it didn't help alleviate this sensation. It was the green light that had penetrated his house when the gorillas attacked, the same sickly puke pallor. He received another remembrance from his childhood that hadn't come before: the gorillas would often be bathed in a similar light when entering his bedroom. In the chaos of everything that happened in his home in North Buffalo, he hadn't made the connection. He finally stepped through the gateway of the new cavern, suddenly realizing that when you became a player in a horror story, it wasn't as fun as sitting on the couch munching snacks and watching actors. He glanced at the shadows and expected a monster to jump out of them at any second. Carter followed behind him - not even needing to duck his large frame as he would have expected - and stowed his flashlight away. Peter brought up the rearguard, putting his hand out to the walls absentmindedly and then immediately pulling away, a slime-like substance sticking to them. He grunted in disgust and rubbed his hands against his worn-down jeans. The light seemed to be reaching out with its tendrils, and soon the three of them were bathed in it, again looking like refuges from Mars as they were a week ago. They stared at their hands and at each other with a horrible sense of déjà vu. This section had a slightly different setup than the last. While there were still the eerie stalactites (and this time Samuel discovered the faces were only in the form of his vampire simians), this floor had no creek, no gaping holes, no encumbrances at all. It was as if it was constructed as an arena, a gladiatorial place, where fighting and killing could easily occur. And it looked wider, the size of a small warehouse.

"This is where they'll come," Samuel said with surety. "It's the last stop. Before King."

"Then, as much as this is revolting, shall we go meet them?" Carter asked.

"No need," Samuel said. "They're on the way. I can actually sense them in this place. Prepare yourselves. On second thought, get behind me. Maybe I can use whatever these powers are to sweep them away, even without the glow. That way, we can get to King immediately without wasting much energy. But take out your weapons."

"One step ahead of you," Carter said, having already removed the shotgun from his pack fully and now cocking it.

"David reporting for duty to slay Goliath," Peter said, gripping his slingshot in one hand and removing several of the metal bearing balls from his bag with the other.

Then Samuel both heard and smelt it: the grunting, growling sound of his nightmare creatures and manure stench that often accompanied them. The clamor made the ground rumble, and stones and dust fell from the cave walls. He imagined it was what people in war heard when the opposition was marching towards them. Then towards the end of this chamber, permeating through the green glow, he could see pinpricks of many red eyes, peepers full of rage and hunger.

The gorillas started funneling into the passage from another cavity on the far side. Here they were again, with their jet black fur tinged with red, the unnatural fangs and long claws on their meat hooks. They came in crawling on all fours to fit through what was a smaller exit point, but when they made it out, each and every one of them stood erect on their legs. Many howled their inhuman shriek, some flexed their dagger hands, others snarled with their scissor champers grinding, bloody drool funneling down. Samuel felt the old fear trying to rear its ugly head unconsciously at the initial viewing of them. But that was quickly replaced with the self-assurance he'd gained in this place. And he stepped forward.

"Begone, you evil things!" he bellowed and then felt embarrassed by it. *Who do I think I am, Gandalf the Grey?* "I don't fear you anymore." He may have been making fun of himself internally, but if he had glanced back, he would have seen the look of surprise that passed between Peter and Carter. His voice was commanding, borderline intimidating now. Carter actually thought, "I'm not in charge anymore".

At hearing this forceful voice, a couple of the gorillas in the vanguard hesitated a bit, stopping their forward strides. But then they looked at each other, seemingly gaining confidence in their numbers, growled, and started to advance again. Since words weren't going to do it, Samuel looked down at his right hand. Still no glow, which he should have known since he felt none of the accompanying fire in his bones. But he hoped he could still utilize his gifts. So he waved his whole arm in a circle, a la Dr. Strange, expecting to plummet the gorillas into some bottomless pit of hell.

Nothing. Those Bigfoot sized steps were still progressing onward.

"Well, fuck," Samuel said. "He turned to his gorilla expert. "Carter, did you say something about old school before?"

"Yep."

"It looks like that's the only way now. So let's take these ugly sons of bitches apart." He took his bo staff out of his backpack, clicking the button immediately to extend it.

Carter flashed a sinister grin. Peter pumped his fist.

And the final battle began.

◆ ◆ ◆

The gorillas came on fast, showing agility that belied their size. But the trio was ready, working instantly to answer the threat. Carter and Peter stepped aside from Samuel a few feet to the left and right, innately using Carter's original strategy of spreading out without saying it this time. The cavern's wide dimensions allowed this, perfect for giving them each their own area to work in.

Carter's gun rang out with several loud explosions, echoing in the broad hollow, and he dropped four of the creatures in quick succession, the smoke filling the immediate area. The first two were headshots, one of them coming clean off and spinning above the blood spurt before plopping into the rock floor. The lifeless body then dropped like a ragdoll. The other's face made a ripping sound as it sagged from the side of its neck, its stunned eyes blinking before its body too fell, landing forwards with a loud crunch. Another he hit clear in the chest, the buckshot causing a hole the size of a cannonball and allowing a view of the apes behind it. An impossibility in the real world, but not here. This victim clawed at the air before whimpering like an animal caught in a trap and going to its knees. The last had its left arm blown off, its still clenching claws flying out and scoring the side of the rock wall. The beast looked shocked at the flow of blood pouring from his limb, which soaked the ground all around the cluster of monsters. It took another step forward, and Carter leveled two more shots to each leg, crumpling them. It collapsed backward, pushing against the feet of those behind them. Many of these screamed in rage.

Simultaneously, Peter was right in lockstep with Carter, firing the metal projectiles at some of the other gorillas. The satchel with his additional ammunition was strung on his shoulder. It was astonishing to Samuel how proficient his peace-loving friend had become with his weapon of choice in such a short time. Darwin killed three of his own to start. Two were drilled in the eyeballs. The initial mark was hit in the left socket, where it embedded so deeply in there it looked like the gorilla was wearing a metallic eye patch. He yelped and ran away into the wall, slamming its head into the rock and falling. The second didn't fare much better, receiving it in the other side, the bearing burrowing into his brain. His head instantly swelled, ballooning, and he sat down, holding its cranium, accidentally piercing it with its deep talons. The last one took a flurry of slingshot barrage, several balls in the neck and legs, before a finishing, killing blow to the brain. The ape actually beat its chest like its real-world equivalent before traipsing around like a drunk and too collapsing.

Samuel had moved forward, always watching where his comrades were shooting, and waded into a group far enough away. He was whipping his bo staff around like a master. He was pretty sure his powers were still working to some extent as his weapon was whizzing through the air with a speed he didn't know possible. The velocity and force of his swings knocked one gorilla ten feet into the air, where it buckled against the wall. The next two fell at his feet, squirming in pain, after taking shots to the neck and midsection. Having no compunction about killing what he knew as denizens of hell, he finished this pair up with several more blows all over their bodies. He could feel the blood lust entering him again and screamed as he whaled on them. He was sick of this, sick of being a victim. *DIE! DIE! DIE!* There were sounds of bones breaking and the squishing of skin being punctured. Blood began to well around these bodies. He finally stopped, breathing heavily.

Carter continued to drop gorillas to the point where a disturbing pile of them cluttered the floor. But a few wily enemies managed to take advantage of when he was re-loading to get right on top of him. He managed to not miss a beat, though, reaching into his pack at his feet and pulling out the fearsome machete from their journey through the East Eden woods. He dug this deep into an ape's neck, a thrust that went clear through to the attacker's collarbone, sending it reeling. And then he showed a heretofore unrevealed skill, landing a strong karate kick to another's belly. But a third had snuck in and dug its claws into his right arm. He howled and dropped his gun. Peter dashed over when hearing his friend's cry, but that was a mistake, putting him too close to shoot his slingshot. So he launched himself with abandon and fearlessness into the gorilla. He wrapped his long legs around the ape's midsection, grabbed the back of its head, and then dug his fingers into its eyes. The gorilla fell backward with Peter on top. Darwin then got up and began to stomp on him with an anger that Samuel now related to but never saw in his buddy. *Not sure where he's coming up with all this, but that nightmare probably affected him deeply. No one likes being toyed with.*

Samuel decided he was wasting time thinking and sprung into several more gorillas who were ready to converge on his friends. Six of the apes veered to meet him just as he heard Carter's shotgun start going off again along with the thud of Peter's slingshot blows. Redden figured he was on his own for this group. And they came on quicker than he expected. He used all that he had, both his feet and his staff, to try to clear them off. But they were crowding in on him, and he could feel searing pain as he was bitten in both the arms and legs. *Oh no.* Then a couple of his assailant's dropped away from him. Peter had broken free and hit them with the metal projectiles. *This is the second time my buddy has saved my bacon like that. I'm lucky to have him.* This reprieve allowed Samuel to push back, and he began swinging again with a fury, hitting one ape several times in the groin and then another on each side of its head. The last standing was rocketed away by a blast from Carter's shotgun.

Samuel ran over to his friends, who were immediately facing off with two more. "Back away," he yelled once he got a few feet from them. A thought had come to him. Putting all the focus he had into it, he threw his bo staff. It hurled through the air, twirling and turning, and it hit the first gorilla straight in the mouth, ricocheted off, and lodged itself right in the head of the second. He hurried over and yanked it out of this ape, not even recoiling from the sucking noise it made being removed.

"I didn't teach you that," Carter exclaimed, rubbing his arm where the ape had gored him. Samuel did a similar inspection and noticed the wound on his leg was freely bleeding. He ripped off a piece of his t-shirt sleeve and wrapped it around it. Carter did his own first aid but actually had a bandage in his bag for his wounded bicep. "I think it's the place and its effect on me," Samuel said. "I wouldn't have been able to go all Captain America like this at home. Doesn't make me invulnerable clearly, though." He then looked at Peter. "Seems like you're the only one not damaged," he said.

Peter glanced at himself and said, "It's early, dude." This proved quickly prophetic. Another pack came upon them, and Peter was slashed in the cheek. He grunted, stumbled back but regained his footing. "Thanks for that, blood brother," Peter said sarcastically. Then the three of them stood side by side and showed the teamwork that Terrian knew they would have. Carter and Peter continued to fell gorilla after gorilla with their long-range weaponry, and Samuel took care of any stragglers that made it past them. The fur was literally flying, and flailing simian limbs swung at the air as they fell.

There was a brief break in the action. Samuel looked around

and saw the twenty to thirty or so that they had killed on the ground. It made him proud. But then he glanced again to the crevice gateway. Just like at home, more apes were pouring through the cave wall, like insects. *How are we ever going to get through these guys? And if we do, will we have anything left for their leader? The all-powerful silverback?*

As if reading his thoughts, Peter said, "Time for you to go, my sweet prince."

"Huh?" was all Samuel could say. *What's he talking about?*

"Yes, he's right," Carter added. "We'll hold them off as best we can, but you need to find your way through them further into that green light. To King."

Oh, God, no. "I can't," Samuel said. "You won't make it. There are too many for even the three of us. That means death for you."

Peter put his hand on Samuel's shoulder, his face one of peace and acceptance. "It may. And it's something we're ready to do. Right, Carter?"

Carter placed his large paw on Samuel's other shoulder, his intense expression not wavering either. "Absolutely. And not just for you but for our world. I'm sure only you can beat that twisted silverback. And maybe once you do, these gorillas will lose their power."

"You don't know that!" Samuel said, his voice breaking. "I can't ask you to…"

"It's our decision, Reddy," Peter said.

"And don't count us out, Redden. We'll fight through this. We'll stay alive," Carter said, trying to sound confident, but Samuel was sure there was doubt in there.

Redden now peeked over at the encroaching gorillas, an uncountable swarm pouring through with more behind them. His friends didn't stand a chance. *We all know it. But they're right. Even if I stayed, they still might not live, and I would die too. And King would win. He's the key, not these ones from when I was little. Maybe because he represents that adult fear, all my terrors at being a grown up: paying bills, taking care of those I love, losing my sweet Sandy to disease, all of it rolled into one. All the insecurities I have to tackle.*

Samuel's eyes got misty. "This sucks, boys."

"Amen to that," Carter said, "but go. Win the day. And we'll keep these creatures here and away from you."

"Pete," was all Samuel could say to the man who had been at his side for thirty-five years.

His hippie friend was crying now but at the same time smiling broadly, his love for Samuel stretched out in every pore of his skin. "You're the best thing that ever happened to me, Reddy. You brought companionship, adventure, and most of all, true love into my existence. It's been my honor."

Samuel hugged him tightly and sniffed, his own tears pouring out now. "You'll live. I promise." Peter just nodded as he pulled away.

Samuel turned to Carter and shook his hand. "Thanks for all your help. I couldn't have done any of this without you."

"Go, you white pasted geek!" Carter yelled as the gorillas started to converge on them.

Taking a deep breath, Samuel closed his eyes, hoping he could use his gifts and simply transport himself to King like he did in the dreams. But when he opened them, he was still there in the cave. He muttered, "Motherfuck," and charged into the gorillas, swinging with his staff through the crowd, making a way through with a speed that would have seemed inhuman to an onlooker. He made a little hole and ducked through. *Ok, maybe I still have a little magic left. Fate just doesn't want to make it easy getting to the big boss.* Then he again heard the sound of Carter's gunshots and the softer thumps of Peter's projectiles striking the gorillas.

Samuel was now in a deluge of the smelly, clawing gorillas. Even with his little opening through the wall of hair, he felt like he couldn't breathe, his old fears of claustrophobia and asthma overwhelming him. He endured the shock of hot white pain as he was struck and bit several times, multiple more wounds opening up on his skin. But he kept pushing and swinging, and after a moment or two, he could feel a breeze, and he knew he was in the opening of King's domain. Samuel kept fighting, snapping his metal rod into his enemies' frames, knowing he was blasting them with a power he never knew he could have. The bodies kept dropping around him. Finally, he was free and looking back into the "doorway" towards his friends. It was hard to see as there had to be one hundred apes who entered the chamber. Several in the back turned and saw Samuel past them in the cave hole. They began to charge at him, shrieking, clearly not wanting him to be closer to their master. Just then Samuel somehow caught Carter's face through the crowd. He was smirking knowingly as he aimed his gun high. Whether that facial expression was directed in Samuel's direction or the gorillas', Redden wasn't sure. But he knew instantly what the gunslinger was doing and it panicked him further. An explosion rang out as the roof above him began to cave in. Samuel screamed, "No!", so wanting to run back and do something, anything. The last image he saw was some of the stalactites and stone ape visages falling down from the ceiling amongst his friends and their opponents before all was covered by cave debris.

Samuel had to step back to avoid the cascading stones from landing on him. After a moment, the avalanche ended, and he cried out, jumping up to the detritus. He put his hand to the makeshift wall. It was utterly collapsed in, not even a pinprick to look through. "No," he muttered again. He looked down at his hands, now completely saturated in this sickly, green glow, appearing fluorescent. His palms were all cut up as well as his face, neck, arms, legs, through his ripped shirt and jeans. Dripping blood from all these spots, enough to cause concern. But all he could think was how his friends were going to die.

But he didn't have much time to reflect on these morose thoughts as there were a few gorillas left on this side of the cave-in. He shrieked barbarically (sounding like the monsters themselves) and put all his frustration into killing them. They didn't stand a chance against him. Samuel didn't remember much of this as it was one big blur. But in a minute, he was looking down at corpses that didn't even resemble gorillas. They were just bloody husks. *I did that?* It frightened him a bit, but he knew he would need much of that berserker energy to beat the monster King.

Yes, King is the key! Stop wasting time, Redden. Your friends' lives can still be saved. And regardless, I have to finish this.

So he walked forward through the passageway. Its surface was the same as the last cavern, smooth as a baby's rump, no craters to stop him. But it was more compact. And while the ceiling was lower, his 5'8 form still easily fit, unlike the apes. The eerie stalactites from above were gone for whatever reason. He would have sworn the area was more like a hall-way in a house. It wasn't like being inside a cheerily human passageway, though, with the algae illumination covering him and becoming more intense with each step. About fifty feet up, he noticed the puke glare became almost too bright to look at, a spotlight of sorts. *That's it. He's in there. That's his lair.*

Samuel gripped his bo staff tight and strode the remaining distance to the gap. He wasted no time in stepping through. The light permeated into him as he shut his eyes against it, and he felt a coldness, a horrible chill. It went deep into his bones. He forced his eyes back open, but unfortunately, all was hazy now. He couldn't make out anything clearly. But slowly, shapes were given form, and he fully expected it to become some African veldt, like Carter's dream or a darker, more foreboding version of this cave.

Then Samuel could fully see, and yes, there was King, the Silverback. He was waiting for him, standing fully erect, ridiculously tall on his trunk-like legs, leering, his peepers yellow in rage, blood caked into his fangs and chin. He flexed his claws, growling under his breath.

And then Samuel realized where they were standing. It was his childhood bedroom.

CHAPTER 8

Amanda Redden was sitting on a plastic chair on her grandmother's porch at 12:30 in the morning. She had a wool sweater on and a blanket wrapped around her for the cold. And the sai were lying on her lap. Her eyes were active, continually searching the front yard in front of her and the woods beyond. She couldn't sleep a wink and at midnight finally had come out here. She had a bad feeling, a lot pressing in on her mind. First and foremost was the safety of her father, who still hadn't returned. But she also sensed that danger was imminent right here and now. She was right.

She heard low growling, like a dog protecting its master. And the shadows near some bushes at the road started to move. The furry shape of several gorillas emerged, a little stooped, giving them a hunchback appearance. The earlier growling then changed to a panting, excited sound. *They think they're just going to devour Grandma and me and further inflict emotional pain on my dad. Well, they're in for a bit of a surprise.*

Amanda gripped her two weapons tightly, shrugged off her cover, and walked calmly down the porch's three wooden steps to the ground. She could now see that green glow from the attack at her house, like a spotlight on these six approaching apes, who had already traversed half the lawn's distance. She knew she might be acting a little reckless. She could have turned on the porch light and hopefully kept them away from the house and herself. She had switched on the hall light outside Grandma's room before coming out, but honestly didn't care about her own protection. For one, she wasn't sure how much Dad's illumination rule would help her, and she also didn't want to make it easy on these fuckers. She actually wanted a fight. Before she stepped from the paved driveway onto the grass, Amanda closed her eyes and held her two sharp tools to her face, blessing them. Her mind flashed on a face. A kindly young countenance with a sarcastic crooked smile. Her heart swelled with love for her fallen friend, and this quickly turned to rage.

She put her feet onto the grass where she had spent many hours running around with her cousins. She held the sai out, pointing them towards the denizens of Sambala. "Come and get it, you pieces of shit!" She didn't have a moment of doubt, not even thinking how Madame Takari's slight protection was no longer with her. The gorillas accepted her offer. They straightened up their poses and loped towards the teenager. Amanda wasted no time, plunging her left sai into the first gorilla's brain, utilizing her flexing, muscular arms that she had been weight training on recently. It instantly dropped, collapsing backward. The rest of them roared and came onto her. She used her blades in a defensive pose now, crossing them out in front of her. This blocked the claw shots of numbers two and three. She turned to her Tai Bow skills, landing a kick across one of the assailants' chest and following that with an elbow to the cranium to the other. They both stumbled back, but she gave them no quarter, letting out her own primal scream, knowing her deaf grandma wouldn't hear, and stabbing both of them at the same time, in the chest and ear, respectively. The blood gushed from these wounds, and the two apes actually turned tail in fear, never having expected a warrior princess to oppose them, and stumbled towards the woods.

The remaining three showed no such reticence, however, leaping into action. But the Golden Child's daughter was ready, stepping forward to greet them.

One part of Samuel Redden's brain knew he was in mortal danger with his enemy standing across the room from him. But another aspect of it overruled, just held him standing there, mouth agape, disoriented. It was like he had stepped in a time machine and exited in his eight-year-old self's room somehow. There was his toy shelf with his Han Solo action figure (among others and vehicles). To his left below this display was his single bed jammed against the corner. Looking straight ahead, he could see Patrick's as well, pushed into the other wall. To the right was the desk they both shared next to the closet door. A few steps from his bed was their dresser near the window that looked out on the back lawn. Towards the foot of his bed was the other window, the one the gorillas entered from the side yard. There was the small area rug his mother had in the middle of the hardwood floor. His eyes worked their way diagonally to the closed door that led out into the hallway. He was pretty sure that is how he entered in here, even though he somehow ended up near his bed. And yes, just inside the entranceway was the one outlet where a Superman night light was plugged in. But instead of providing a warm, safe, comforting yellow illumination, it was flickering, cracked at its base, and projecting the gorillas' ugly green pale. The end table was there but no lamp. It felt like that was an echo of Claude. And glancing up, he saw there was no overhead light.

Pretty much an exact re-creation from 1985. This is too much.

Then that horrible deep, haunting voice was in his head again. **WELCOME TO OUR BATTLEGROUND, REDDEN. AN APPROPRIATE PLACE, WOULDN'T YOU SAY?** King remarked mentally. The creature was right in the halfway point between Patrick's bed and the door, standing in front of Samuel's toy box where less important playthings resided. Redden again was taken aback by the leader's size; standing at its full height, the hair on the top of its blood-streaked head rubbed against the ceiling. Its chest was puffed out, its talon hands resting on its side, a most arrogant stance. Its wide nostrils were puffing in and out, and the yellowish-red drool was welling at its jaws, the sharp teeth grinding a mechanical sound.

A month ago, Samuel would have been cowed by this terrifying image. But a lot had changed. He really didn't want to engage in conversation with this monster, but he felt compelled and couldn't help it, so he allowed his thoughts to flow. *Who made this, you or me?*

THIS IS ALL YOU, HUMAN. YOUR WEAKNESS. YOU'RE RETREATING TO YOUR CHILDHOOD.

Almost immediately, a thought came to Samuel, a revelation. It didn't originate in his brain, and he was sure it didn't start with King either. It was a message from the dream world. Whether it was from this place or from Luminescence, he didn't know. But it was clear and straightforward. *That was a lie.* This was an involuntary reflection, but of course, King heard it.

WHAT? King's thought was full of surprise and rage. It was a powerful projection, and Samuel again thought he would have folded if he wasn't in this realm. It still made him want to step back, but he held his ground.

It has nothing to do with my weakness. You lie. Samuel closed his eyes and tried to take more information in. *We're in this room, this place, because this is where it all started. There's many bedrooms like this in Sambala where innocence is changed to horror. But you're right that it is all mine; it's fueled by me, given character by me. But there's no retreat here. This is where your acolytes first came for me, and this is where it will end.* Samuel paused before adding, *You're just a big bully, King. That's all you are. That's all a lot of this place is. It's a twisted version of Luminescence. But one day, it will be gone.* He opened his eyes and grinned as he said this last part.

I SEE YOU'VE SPOKEN TO THE TROLL. King had regained his composure mentally. **ONCE I FINISH YOU, I WILL DRAG HIS GOOFY UGLY FACE HERE, TEAR IT OFF AND HANG HIM IN EFFIGY. ALONG WITH YOUR TWO OTHER DEAD FRIENDS.** King paused and then extended his own leering smirk at Samuel, a disturbing rictus display. **ALONG WITH YOUR MOTHER AND DAUGHTER. I'VE ALREADY SENT SOME OF MY FOLLOWERS TO FEAST ON YOUR TWO WHORES.**

No. Samuel felt one of his old panic attacks coming on. But again, something that seemed foreign to him welled up inside, something potent, a confidence he never knew. He refused to show his vulnerabilities to King. He let out a sardonic laugh. *More threats. I have a feeling your minions will have their hands full. I used to think you were so scary. But now that I'm in this place, you seem impotent to me. Let's stop this stupid bantering and fight.*

King once again seemed taken aback by this new Samuel Redden. The monster pursed his lips and glared, looking a bit unsure. But then he growled and beat his chest, reverting to the alpha male characteristics he was based on. Then he moved to his right, passing Patrick's bed and stalking Samuel. *This is happening. This is really happening now.* Samuel began to move in the same counter-clockwise circle as King, walking in reverse to not be caught flat-footed. He was still holding his staff, and he now gripped that tighter. Moving around the perimeter of the room made him want to glance more at the detail of his childhood sanctuary, the sense of nostalgia extra strong now.

But he was firmly focused on survival, so he never let his eyes leave King's. He tried to calm his breathing, knowing that this place of the mind probably had different rules than the real world. *So much of this is mental strength; my body may be here, but the mind is more powerful when it comes to dreams, I think.*

This little dance continued for a couple minutes, and then they both stopped, again across from each other at their original spots. A moment of silence passed, and Samuel knew what the characters in westerns felt like. All he could hear was his own breathing and King's snorts. Then it started. King charged at Samuel, shaking the ground and causing Han Solo to take a header off the shelf, and the human had to remind himself not to stare helplessly and in awe at the fantastic sight of an ape running at him like a human. Especially one of this girth and stature with its nightmare enhancements. This hesitation had happened before at many times in Samuel's life, but his new calmness in Sambala allowed him to think more clearly and unemotionally; the sight of King moving like this just reminded him of those drawings of apes evolving into man all at once. But he quickly reverted to defense mode, and he pulled his staff forward. King lunged, clawed hands flexing out in front of him, and Samuel managed to flash his weapon out quickly, landing a shot squarely in the face of the simian. There was a loud pop as one of King's vampire teeth shattered and landed on the floor. The creature stumbled rearward, and Samuel relished the look of shock and dismay on his furry, blood matted mug. *He still harbored the belief that he was invulnerable to me, even here. Well, take that, you fucking killer. There's a lot more of that to come. I owe Kyle that much.*

Samuel smiled again broadly and stepped forward, taking advantage of this momentary opportunity of confusion with his opponent. He swung his staff around with pinpoint speed and accuracy, landing another blow to the face, causing King's left eye to swell closed. Then he followed this with one to the chest, and the gorilla sucked in a pained breath. The third part of this attack was a low upwards arc into the groin, making King lurch unsteadily on his heels. Samuel felt a fury rising in him as his mind latched onto the memory of his abuse at the hands of Bennett. He whacked multiple more times at the head of King, all the while screaming. The blood began to flow from the wounds he inflicted in the gorilla's eyes, ears, and mouth. The ape finally lost its footing, landing hard on the back of its head, and the ground shuddered like an earthquake this time, toppling more toys and cracking the mirror on the closet door.

Clumsy Samuel was gone. Even with the shaking of the room, he remained still and calm. He then stood over his foe and took the end of the bo staff, and stuck it right into the mouth of the creature. He slowly pushed it deep into King's throat, which caused a very human coughing sound. Then suddenly, he paused. There was a fear and sadness in King's face, which stopped him. Samuel had come a long way from his days of never even wanting to kill a spider. But he still was a kind soul, and this allowed mercy to come into his mind. It was a huge mistake. This was not a comic book where the hero showed how much better he was than his enemy by letting them live and everything worked out; this was life and death and had consequences. His next act showed how much he still had to learn about this world he'd stumbled into.

Samuel pulled the staff out of the evil one's maw, the metal making a slurping noise as he did. For the first time, he noticed how the silver sheen was gone from his weapon; it was now slimy and covered in crimson. He then projected this thought: *I'll allow you to live, and you can slink off to some corner of this place as long as you promise to never enter my world again.* Then he heard a sound that put much fear back into him. King laughed, that unnerving maniacal cackle. Then Samuel felt a searing pain in his right arm. The creature had lashed out and landed his deep claws in him. Samuel did his best not to drop his staff, but the gush of lifeblood was like a downward spout. It distracted him. King got to all fours and charged towards him, pushing the unsteady Samuel back towards his old childhood bed.

King now opened his mouth and caught Samuel's left leg like a soup bone. He cried out in agony, the piercing, throbbing pain like nothing he'd ever experienced. But he did not lose all faculties yet. He swung with his staff and cracked the ape yet again in the head, making an indentation in the forehead and causing a hollow thudding noise. This forced the teeth off his calf. He stumbled back to the point where he was pushing up against his bed. He looked down at his leg and was aghast at how much blood was pouring from this limb now too. *If it translates to earth blood loss, I'm done for.* He looked over to King and was horrified to see that the cranial shot had not finished the monster. King was back on his feet, fully erect again. He sprung again at Samuel, knocking him entirely onto his little bed. Samuel tried to move, but the blood loss was definitely affecting him, and he felt lightheaded. He managed a weak swing of the staff and hit King in the chest, but it did nothing. The gorilla was on top of him now, the weak springs in the bed snapping and dropping them closer to the floor. He could smell that old stink now, the manure and blood reek that haunted his childhood.

King swatted out, and his staff went flying to the other side of the room. *Oh, God, no.*

King grinned madly. **THERE'S NO GOD HERE, BOY. NOW YOU'RE MINE.** King straddled him, a remarkably human and dominating pose, and with his size and Samuel's weakness, the man found he couldn't move an inch. His lungs felt restricted and his mind instantly reverted to childhood moments of reaching for his inhaler. And that wasn't the only ugly callback to years ago. He found himself returned to that revolted, helpless feeling when Bennett molested him. *But that's when it all started, isn't it?* Samuel looked into King's eyes, the yellowish urine-colored hue almost mesmerizing in its wideness, and then the gorilla's face changed, from its natural state to Bennett's thin sneering countenance. He didn't know if it was his imagination or the power of this place. But he wanted to puke.

Samuel didn't have much time to lose himself in this sense of the past coming to get him, though, as King then pushed his stinking mouth to his neck. He was disgusted by what came next when the creature's fur nuzzled at him in a tickling, almost caressing gesture. The sense of wanting to vomit was overwhelming now when he realized this was genuinely feeling like a rape. Again, he felt transported back in time to the church hall while a cold sweat prickled his forehead. Then King struck hard. The monster opened his fanged filled mouth wide and bit deeply into Samuel's jugular. It was like being attacked by a real vampire this time. King began to suck, and Samuel could feel the blood flowing out of him and into his assailant. The initial indescribable burst of pain as his throat ripped was too much for his whole being. He tried to flail out at King's back, but he had next to nothing left. He quickly felt his body get weaker, more helpless, and then it became absolutely frozen, locked in place. But the suffering was not abated, and worse, he could hear King's sucking noises like he was drinking from a stream.

The old terror of dying returned, and Samuel actually whimpered, now knowing how the characters in Ann Rice's novels felt when attacked by Lestat. Then all conscious thought left Samuel, and his eyes got fuzzy. But he could hear King's taunts: **YOUR LIFE IS EBBING INTO ME NOW. YOU WON'T LAST LONG. THEN I SHALL DO THE SAME TO YOUR PRECIOUS DARWIN AND CARTER. BUT THE BEST PART WILL BE WHEN I RETURN TO YOUR WORLD AND TORTURE YOUR DAUGHTER SLOWLY, KEEPING HER ALIVE AS MY SLAVE.**

This managed to awaken him from his coma-like state. He pushed his body up in a fury at King. But he only moved him an inch. And King continued to suck. *Amanda, I'm so sorry.* Within a moment, the darkness came to Samuel.

CHAPTER 9

T he light came to Samuel Redden, and he looked around. He was sitting in a hospital room. Across from him, he could see the closed door in the far wall leading to the lobby. A nurse walked by the window in the frame. There was another open door to his left that was clearly the room's bathroom. In this area close to the ceiling was a TV screwed into the wall, and it was currently on low volume tuned to AMC showing the original *Karate Kid*. He could smell that slightly unpleasant scent of antiseptic spray and sickliness, an undercurrent of pee and crap that couldn't be wiped out. And right in front of him was a bed. Its back was propped up a bit, and sitting up there looking towards him was an emaciated form. This individual was hooked up to all kinds of monitors and had nose filters inserted, which he figured was providing oxygen. *What is this? Am I in some sort of purgatory? Do I have to help this person to move on?*

Then he got a closer look at the frail patient on the bed, and realization struck him hard, like a punch to the throat. The person in the bed was female. It was Sandy. He understood now that he must have retreated once again to his past, that his mind on the verge of death had fixated on this memory. It was not a good one. This Sandra was not the woman of his earlier recollections, full of life and vigor. She was on her deathbed; the cancer had ravaged her body. Her face was pale, sucked in, skeletal. Her eyes dull. Her head bald from chemotherapy.

Not this, please. Send me to my end with a good memory.

But this had to play out just how it had years ago. So it did.

"That was hard," Sandra rasped. Her voice had changed from that sexy, breathy tone to a now short-winded rattle. Samuel now remembered that she had just said her goodbyes to ten-year-old Amanda. Hard was an understatement. How do you tell your little girl, who is about to go into fifth grade, that she will never see her mom again? It was brutal. Amanda wept horribly and kept clinging to her frail mother, who was also crying, but since she was so weak, she only had the strength for a few teardrops. Samuel had stood nearby and done his best to say all the right things to Amanda, but he felt like a liar, telling her they would get through it together, that mom was going to a better place, all the clichés. Eventually, Samuel's mom came in to take Amanda away, dragging the piteously crying sweety out gently. So here the two of them were, left alone. In a few hours, Sandra Crowell Redden would take her last breath and Samuel would be left with a gaping hole in his life. Amanda would be without a mother, and he would be a single dad. This moment was her last cogent one, and they all knew the end was so close; it was truly their goodbye. He remembered obsessing about that then. And the heartache was a feeling he never knew could go so deep. It was devastating. But he did his best to be "Mr. Positive".

"I know, hon," he took her cadaver-like hand in his, being oh so careful not to hurt her. "But we raised her right. She's tougher for me, that's for sure."

Sandra smiled, which helped her face immensely, hearkening back to who she had been most of her life. But it only made his heart hurt all the more. "You underestimate yourself, Sam. Just because you've struggled with mental health doesn't make you weak. It makes you strong."

Even in the end, she still worked on building me up. Samuel gazed at his beloved wife, and a lot of memories came flashing back to him: meeting her in the college book store, their first date, their wedding, Amanda being born, vacations at the beach. And not just these significant life events, but also the small, sweet moments, the times of routine family life that sometimes mean more with the deepest of loves. Binging TV shows together, bringing Amanda to the park, having dinner out at their favorite restaurants. And many more. He wanted to be stoic for her, to help her not be afraid. But he couldn't hold his emotions inside anymore. He started to cry harder than he ever had. He managed to blubber, "Sorry."

Sandra massaged his hand feebly, the tears welling in her eyes again. "For what?"

"You must be dealing with so many emotions and fears, and here I am being selfish." He tried to hold the floodgates in, but like most people know, that made it worse, causing him to gasp in between breaths.

"Nonsense," she muttered, "we share our emotions as a family. We're a team. And for some reason, that team is being broken up." She sighed in a labored way. "All our hearts are shattered. I don't want you to hide your emotions. We've never done that."

He smiled through his tears. "I've loved you ever since that day in the book store. Thank God I was an English major even if I've never really used the degree."

She managed a small laugh before breaking out in a coughing fit. Samuel's heart jumped, thinking now was the end. But she managed to get it under control, and he handed her the water bottle on the food tray. She took a sip with shaky hands. "I won't lie and say I'm not angry for not even making it to 40, my love. But I've lived many of those years with two people I adore. Some never get that."

He nodded, pushed his chair closer, and took her upper body in his arms gently. She laid her head on his chest. They sat like that for fifteen minutes.

Then Sandra pulled away slowly. "I have something to say to you, and it's really important." Her voice was just a barely audible wheeze now, so he had to bring his head closer to her face. "You've always been hard on yourself, Samuel Redden. And I know you've had a hard time finding your calling in life, always wanting to prove yourself and do more to help people. Let me tell you this: that day is coming when you will find your true path."

She paused and looked up intently at him, latching onto his eyes, blinking away her own tears, her cheeks damp. "Now listen closely. You're such a good man. No, that's minimizing it. You're so wonderful. You're going to be Amanda's everything, and she will be a better person for it. I think you've always feared the darkness. Don't let my death destroy you. You have something inside of you, Sam. I can't put my finger on it, but it's more than simple goodness. How do I say it? It's a light— a burning light of hope and love. You've held it in so long. But there's going to be a time when you'll need to release it to the world. And..."

She began to cough hard again, hacking with thick congestion, which alarmed Samuel. He brought her into his arms again. "Don't talk anymore. Just rest, baby."

"No," she whispered, "too important." She continued her last thought, "And in your greatest need, when you must finally unleash this beautiful shine to the world, you'll require a focal point. Let me be that. Remember our connection, our love, our shared heart. Then you will bathe this world in your golden light."

The Samuel who was remembering this and somehow standing outside of it all, thought, *did she really say that? Or am I imagining it?* He watched himself continue to hold his wife as she fell asleep, the last time he ever saw her eyes open again. He felt the sadness return but also a swell of love, this powerful love that burned in his life for such a short time but filled him with so much joy.

He stilled his thoughts. He let this power enter him. And burn within him. It shook him up a bit, the strength of it. It wanted to escape. It wanted to blaze forth.

CHAPTER 10

S amuel's eyes flashed open again. He was back in Sambala. Back in his room at the end of the hallway. He could hear a slurping noise and looked down to see King still suckling from his neck. He could feel the fur on his skin, smell the foulness, hear that horrible noise, but he was beyond it now, beyond all fear and pain. He knew how to unleash the power. It had already happened. Sandy made it possible.

No more flickering. No more brief surges of power only to disappear. It wants to come out, and I haven't been letting it. I haven't been allowing it because it's composed of love, hope, and charity. And this world had weighed me down. I let the darkness drown it out. No more. I owe her that much.

Hey, King.

The gorilla did not stop drinking but raised an evil eye at him. Samuel did not allow any more thoughts to flow. He simply grinned wide.

Then Samuel looked down to his neck and saw it. There was a golden sheen underneath the massive gaping wound in his neck. King just kept on sucking, unaware of what was happening. But then an instant later, he gagged, let go, and jumped back off the bed in a panic. The broken frame shook slightly under Samuel like a person experiencing the chills. The gorilla started coughing, retching, as if he was trying to purge a lung, another one of those human reactions, and quite a counterpoint to Samuel's recent memory. It brought its hairy hand up to its mouth. King never used that mouth for anything but attack, not communication, not mutual care. And now, he would not be using it for anything ever again. His jaw sloughed off and fell to the floor. His skin re-knit where it was, so there was just a blank space. The monster's eyes opened wide in utter terror.

WHAT IS HAPPENING?

Samuel looked down at the blood flowing from his neck wound, and then it just stopped. The blood that was currently leaking out reversed its flow. Then a light brighter than any sun poured out of the gaping hole, bathing the wound, healing it. In mere seconds it was like it was never there. This light then wrapped itself around Samuel's whole body, not only healing the rest of his wounds but forming around him like a shield. His facial features and bodily shape could still be made out, but he looked like a human star, blazing forth in its luminescence, a new kind of life form. And he felt like his body was on fire. It was an electric, jolting rush. But it didn't hurt and wasn't exactly the same warmth he'd felt before. He'd never experienced any sensation quite like it. The only way he could describe it was as if everything good and pure had been injected into his skin. What he didn't know was this was his true form, the way he would look in his home world. He stood up from his bed, surprisingly steady on his feet.

You want to know what's happening? He projected this thought at the wide-eyed, shuddering King. *It's simple. You've lost.* Samuel held his right hand outwards, fingers splayed. The dazzling light funneled out from him and wrapped around King. The gorilla's screams were something Samuel would never forget. He had no idea how the monster howled without the use of the mouth, but it came out of him all the same. It was the most ghastly, bestial utterance of torment he ever heard. But he did not feel pity for the creature. He thought only of Kyle, Madame Takari, Amy and her family, Hector, and the others these horrible creations of his had murdered or hurt. He knew this was a righteous kill, a necessary act for the world. But it was gruesome all the same. King didn't just disappear in the light. The rest of his body followed the way his mouth did. Each limb fell off in turn, the destruction moving upwards. He lost his feet first, then his legs, and finally, without anything to balance on, the form collapsed on the floor. The torso landed on its back. Then its arms cracked free and the fearsome taloned hands dropped away, scraping against the hardwood. From there, his stomach area split from the chest with a crack. At last, his head popped off the neck, landing upright.The terrified eyes scowled up at Samuel one last time before they closed.

Samuel walked up to the various body parts and looked down at them as he felt the illumination return to his innermost being. Then he immediately realized that he made that happen with just a thought. *I'm entirely in control now.* He inspected his body, now back to its human flesh, and saw all his earlier wounds on his arms and legs now healed up, the blood dried and clotted. He guessed he could use the light to remove any trace of them, but he didn't want to do that. He needed the scars, the reminder of when he finally found himself. He again glanced down at what remained of King. And then there was a gust of wind, and the pieces of the evil silverback vanished as if into nothing, like a vampire dusting, which he felt was appropriate.

Samuel then felt a presence. An evil that made King seem like a minor hoodlum with a knife. He reached his feelings out, and even with his utter confidence now discovered, stumbled back a bit when he experienced the darkness of the soul that connected with him. And he knew instantly that this was the ruler of the nightmare realm and that one day he would need to face him, her or it. But he knew that was not now. The battle was won, but the war had just begun.

But one day at a time. He closed his eyes and vanished from that room of his childhood, which had given him so much terror. But it also had provided him a lot of joy, and that was all he felt now.

Back in the cave, Peter Darwin and Carter were making their final stand. They were covered from head to toe with blood. They both looked like the title character in *Carrie*. They were on their knees holding each other up, their weapons broken and discarded next to them. There was a cluster of about ten gorillas left circling them. The ground was soaked with gore and ape corpses, in the ballpark of 50-70 apes. They had fought valiantly. But they were spent. It was over.

Even Peter was too hurt to say anything groovy or hip. He looked up to the heavens, wondering what the afterlife really was like and when that peace everyone talks about would come. All he felt was regret, the regret in letting down his best friend. Then he felt a shaking underneath him, another one of those earthquake sensations. His tired eyes searched for the source, and he pinpointed the exit where Samuel had left, the location of the cave in. He wondered if he was already passing to the great beyond, as what he saw was ridiculous. Rocks were rising in the air, dust was flying up. All this debris created the loudest noise he'd ever heard. Then standing in the opening was a golden man.

Peter found his voice. "Carter, my brother, look!"

Carter, ever the warrior, had been busy trying to figure out a way to rejuvenate himself and finish this fight. Now he stared dumbfounded where the weary Darwin was pointing at. "Holy fuck," was all he said.

The golden figure approached. The gorillas turned and seemed to be as transfixed as the humans by the sight. Slowly the blinding light left the face, revealing Samuel.

He looked angry. But his friends were beaming. "You are a vestige of the originals," Samuel said. "So King's destruction did not finish you off. I'm glad. You ruined a part of my childhood and have caused so much pain. It's over now, though. You deserve this." He waved his hand in a cutting left to right motion, and the gorillas screamed in fear, pain, and agony as they crumbled into dust. And Samuel felt the others die. The ones who were either not sent for this part of the battle or were on their way.

As he again pulled the golden power back into himself, he breathed out deeply. *It's over. It's finally over. Thanks, Sandy. I'll always honor your final words to me.* He looked at his friends and now realized what bad shape they were in. He ran to them. They were both sitting up, and he kneeled between them. "You did it," Peter said.

"*We* did it," Samuel replied. He helped the two of them up. They were a bit unsteady but able to stay standing with Samuel's arms still around them. As one, they all tilted and rested their heads on each other in a tired, warm embrace. They held that for a good minute. A bond of brotherhood had been formed that would only end in their deaths. Samuel knew how lucky he was.

"You're transcendent," Peter said.

"Yeah, I gotta give it to you, Redden," Carter added, "you're one crazy impressive white man."

They all laughed long and hard at this. But Samuel could feel them wobbling on their feet. And he also realized how tired he felt now, his bones had deep aches in them and he felt like he could sleep for a year. It had been a long night. *Another nice understatement, Redden.* "Well, let's get you healed up and return home," he said. As if in answer to this last part, the three of them felt a more powerful rumbling sensation under their feet. "And I guess we should hurry," Redden added with a sly grin. "This part of Sambala might not be here much longer. I get the feeling this place isn't used to defeat." And then he sensed something deep inside, feelings that had been lacking in his life for a long time. Confidence, pride.

"But how can you do that? Get us back?" Carter asked.

"With these powers," Samuel said, lifting his pointer finger and causing a bright spark to spread down his hand again. "Terrian knew I'd figure it out. He believed I would discover my true self and powers here. I just needed a push." His mind flashed on his wife once again, picturing her face as she turned to him in the college bookstore line all those years ago. He looked to the heavens and smiled joyfully, with a gleam in his eyes. "Let me take care of all of it," he remarked with great protectiveness for these special friends, his voice cracking a bit. "Take care of you guys. Just like you have done for me the last couple of months. Then I'll tell you my newest story."

EPILOGUE

S amuel was indeed able to transport them home using his powers after providing the healing to his companions with the light (they too wanted to keep the scars, though - Peter to show the deep recuperative power of the human body and Carter to add to his collection of wounds). When Samuel put his hands on their shoulders and zapped them back to Terrian's tree by just thinking of the destination, he realized he never asked how they would get back. Terrian indeed knew. And when they re-appeared in front of the troll, Terrian and Samuel just smiled lovingly at each other but said no words at first. Even though all three of them felt spent, they stayed awhile for the storytelling. Samuel encouraged the others to keep to the reader's digest version of the tale, though. He was desperate to get back to Amanda. Speaking of fathers, Terrian beamed at Redden like a proud daddy for most of it.

They returned to the homestead. It was early morning. Luckily, Amanda had left the door unlocked, and they snuck in before Shelley awoke. Samuel noticed the ground on the front lawn deeply trampled on, but true to form, there were no other signs of Amanda's battle with the apes. And when he peeked in the small bedroom, he found her with a couple cuts on her cheeks but no more worse for wear. The sense of relief was not small. Peter and Carter collapsed asleep in the living room while Samuel happily returned to his old room, marvelling at how the sense of evil had been purged from it and thinking it felt like a sanctuary again. He felt a triumphant rush when he removed the *Aladdin* night light from the outlet. He didn't sleep as much as he thought he would, though; he didn't feel tired at all and figured it was just the adrenaline from the whole experience.

Later that day, Peter and Carter drove back to the city. Peter was ready to resume his life's work as an educator, inspiring young coolio minds, and Carter decided to take a flight to Africa. He said he needed to be with loving gorillas again. Samuel and Amanda remained at Shelley's, saying they could get a ride home from her.

After the two of them ate lunch with Shelley – Samuel wearing long sleeves and an extra pair of jeans from his overnight bag to cover his injuries and explaining that Amanda had scratched herself in her sleep – father and daughter headed out to the deck to talk. They sat down on the porch glider, rocking back and forth and enjoying the country serenity. The unpredictable Western New York fall had taken another turn, brightening and warming up slightly. While the sun caressed their heads gently, he told her the whole story. She blanched when Samuel noted that he wasn't technically human. And there were moments of tears when he spoke about his vision of her mother. They held each other tight. This personal information he only shared with Amanda; he felt it belonged to them. When he told Terrian, Peter, and Carter the details a few hours prior, he had simply said he had a vision that taught him how to unlock the power and left it at that. Amanda then took her turn and explained how the six gorillas attacked out front, how she killed the first one, the retreat of the fleeing pair, and that she murdered the rest. She then waited on the porch for more, and indeed about twenty additional creatures came running towards the house around 5:00 A.M. But to her surprise, they crumbled into dust. That was when she knew they had won. Amanda held his hand and smiled. "You're a superhero, Dad."

She's something. Not fixating on the fact that her father is from another dimension or whatever. As optimistic and positive as usual. He adjusted his glasses (and was kind of tickled that he still needed them after discovering his power), glanced dubiously at her, and sighed. "I guess. It all seems like a dream, ironically enough. And there's so much I still don't know."

"I know what you're saying," she replied, "I lost Kyle, and I don't think I've even processed it yet with everything that's happened. I'm afraid how I'll be when that hits.

"I understand, sweetheart," he said sadly, squeezing her hand, "and I'll probably be the same way. We had already lost so much, and it's really not fair. But life's never been easy, you know?"

"I know," she said quietly.

"And..." he paused before continuing. He was staring down at his left hand now. No, he wasn't willing the glow to come but looking at something else golden. His wedding band. He'd never removed it, even years after Sandra passed.

"What?" Amanda said, touching his chin and making him gaze into her eyes, eyes that were glistening, but whether that came more from the remembrances of her mom or Kyle, Samuel couldn't say.

"All these reflections about your mom. It had been a while since I've done that. And it came just as this crisis began. I know I've struggled with ideas of faith and God over the years, but what if your mom was sending these memories to guide me. Maybe it wasn't just me remembering her last words, you know?"

Amanda flashed her beautiful smile, and again Samuel saw Sandy in it, but it didn't make him sad this time; it filled him with pride. "I have no doubt about that. She's looking out for us."

They just sat there for another few minutes, at peace, holding hands and looking out over his mother's large lawn, seeing the giant weeping willow trees bending in the breeze and beyond them, the woods in the distance. Amanda then mentioned something that took Samuel by complete surprise. "Did you realize tomorrow is election day?"

Wow, how the real world got pushed away by all of this. But it's appropriate. I regained my hope in Sambala, and now we can vote to bring some light back to this country. After the last four years of crap, and especially the tire fire that's been 2020, I can't wait for it to happen here too. "What do you say about taking another day off from work and school," he said, "and we'll do our democratic duty. We probably should have voted by mail, but we'll make it a nice father/daughter outing."

"I'd love it," Amanda said, smiling again. Then she quickly added, "Oh, I almost forgot! Uncle Patrick stopped by last night when you were gone. Grandma told him you were in town, and he wanted to see you."

This pleased Samuel. His brother had remained in Eden, married, had three children, and many grandchildren now. They stayed in touch, but sometimes life got in the way, and it'd been over a year since they'd seen each other. *I've been lucky to stay close with Pat and all my other brothers and sisters.* Some of his siblings had moved out of state, but several remained close to their mom and to each other. The holiday gatherings were always fun. "I wonder how much he remembered when the veil was lifted?" Samuel questioned, thinking he should have thought of this when he saw Mom the other day too. "Probably that I had a problem with dreams and then nothing else. He likely just pushed it aside. Maybe like a déjà vu feeling?"

"Could be," Amanda said, "ignorance is probably bliss for him and anyone else, right?"

"Yeah, I would say so," Samuel said. "Now that the immediate danger has passed, it's better to keep what we know to ourselves. It's too much. Not just how the average person would handle it, but what if the government got wind of this?"

"Oh, shit, especially our militaristic country" she said. "They would love to experiment on you to get to Sambala. There'd be no hesitation in releasing some dark nightmare to beat down on people they view as our enemies. Middle-Eastern Muslims, Mexican immigrants, whoever the bad guy of the month happens to be. Or they'd just try to siphon off your golden magic." She paused before adding, "Even if we get the change we want in the election, I wouldn't trust any politician with this power."

"Uh huh," Samuel said, nodding. Then a thought occurred to him. "Do you wonder…"

"If I inherited anything from you?"

Just like Sandy, she read my mind. "Exactly. I need to ask Terrian. He did say he would begin training and mentoring me. Have no idea what that's going to be all about."

"Maybe he can ride on your shoulders like Yoda did with Luke."

Samuel laughed heartily. "With his size, it might be a scenic view for him but kind of painful for me!" Amanda joined him in giggling away.

They sat again in silence for another ten minutes. Samuel then said, "Well, if you end up having powers, we'll handle it like we have everything else since you were my tiny little baby."

"Together."

"Exactly."

Samuel pulled at her hand as he stood, bringing her up with him. "Come with me," he said.

"Where?" his daughter asked.

"For a walk in the woods."

THE END

ABOUT THE AUTHOR

Mark Bermingham

 Mark Bermingham, author of The Gorillas Are Coming, cannot remember a time when writing was not part of his life, going back to his days in college at Buffalo State as an English major. Mark first saw publication as a fan, having many letters to the editor published in DC Comics' letter columns in the 90's. Years later, he contributed to blogs, mainly centering around his beloved city of Buffalo. He's penned several short stories while always going back to that world of nightmares and The Golden Child. Mark lives just outside of Buffalo with his caring school librarian wife, Heather, his crazy Saint Bernard mix, Grayson, and their newest addition, Apollo, the bearded lizard. He sincerely believes that his Bills are going to finally win that Super Bowl soon.

Follow Mark and The Gorillas Are Coming at these links:
The Gorillas Are Coming website: sites.google.com/view/thegorillasarecomingnovel
Mark's Twitter page: twitter.com/backissuecomics